Backstabber

Also by Tim Cockey
in Large Print:

Murder in the Hearse Degree

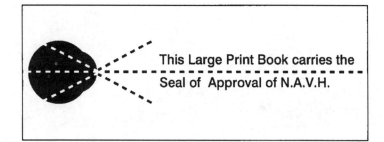

This Large Print Book carries the
Seal of Approval of N.A.V.H.

Backstabber

Tim Cockey

WHEELER
PUBLISHING

If anyone out there sees a speck of anything resembling real life in this book . . . shoot it. It's not supposed to be there.

Published in 2004 by arrangement with Hyperion, an imprint of Buena Vista Books, Inc.

Wheeler Large Print Compass.

The text of this Large Print edition is unabridged.
Other aspects of the book may vary from the original edition.

Set in 16 pt. Plantin by Minnie B. Raven.

Printed in the United States on permanent paper.

Library of Congress Cataloging-in-Publication Data

Cockey, Tim, 1955–
    Backstabber / Tim Cockey.
       p. cm.
    ISBN 1-58724-836-0 (lg. print : hc : alk. paper)
    1. Sewell, Hitchcock (Fictitious character) — Fiction.
2. Funeral rites and ceremonies — Fiction.   3. Undertakers and undertaking — Fiction.   4. Baltimore (Md.) —
Fiction.   5. Large type books.   I. Title.
PS3553.O277B33 2004b
   813'.54—dc22   2004057204

THIS ONE'S FOR ANDY.
HE DONE IT.

As the Founder/CEO of NAVH, the only national health agency solely devoted to those who, although not totally blind, have an eye disease which could lead to serious visual impairment, I am pleased to recognize Thorndike Press★ as one of the leading publishers in the large print field.

Founded in 1954 in San Francisco to prepare large print textbooks for partially seeing children, NAVH became the pioneer and standard setting agency in the preparation of large type.

Today, those publishers who meet our standards carry the prestigious "Seal of Approval" indicating high quality large print. We are delighted that Thorndike Press is one of the publishers whose titles meet these standards. We are also pleased to recognize the significant contribution Thorndike Press is making in this important and growing field.

Lorraine H. Marchi, L.H.D.
Founder/CEO
NAVH

★ Thorndike Press encompasses the following imprints: Thorndike, Wheeler, Walker and Large Print Press.

Acknowledgments

While slugging my way through this one I was given poignant proddings and pointers by Tim Aitken of Eight Branches Healing Arts, grave information by John (Digger) Ansberg of the Ansberg-West Funeral Home in Toledo, Ohio, and wholly unedited support from my editor to kill for, Peternelle van Arsdale. I also want to give a nod of thanks (a *nod* of thanks?) for the spirited enthusiasm of Chris Bumcrot and for the far-ranging resources of Applied Research and Consulting (ARC). Particular gratitude also goes to my agent provocateur, Richard Pine (thanks for the hooch, Richard), as well to Hyperion's Karin Maake and Natalie Kaire. An especially big acknowledgment hug has to go to Durham's best, Katy Munger (to the rescue!).

But if you really want to know who ultimately to thank for this book's ever actually seeing the light of day . . . don't look at me, look at Julia Strohm. She's the one.

Chapter One

Sisco Fontaine had a problem. He also had that ridiculous name, but that wasn't the problem at hand. The problem at hand was that the husband of the woman Sisco was sleeping with was lying on a kitchen floor with a knife in his back. The knife wasn't moving and neither was the husband. Blood had puddled out on either side of the body and there was a vivid fingerpaint swirl of red on the white tiles under the man's out-stretched right hand. Less than a foot away was a gun. A pistol. Ugly little bluish thing.

It was five in the morning. Not ten hours previous, I had been happily ensconced in my ugly armchair reading the exploits of the thoroughly insane Theodore Roosevelt. A quiet evening at home. Dog underfoot. Soft strings on the stereo. An imaginary fire in my imaginary fireplace. The first of my two mistakes had been the decision — around ten o'clock — to go for a stroll. The stroll took me by the Cat's Eye, where pretty Maria happened to be singing. One thing led swiftly to another and I'd found myself sitting on the windowsill behind pretty Maria slurping down pints of Guinness and humming along with Maria's sweet voice. Along came one o'clock in the morning, and during a heaving chorus of "Black Velvet Band" an errant tambourine slapped against my face. Not too bad a cut. Nothing that a tissue and a wee more Guinness couldn't staunch. By two-thirty I was negotiating a peace with my bed. The second mistake came a few hours later, some time after four, when the phone rang. Well . . . the mistake was in my answering it.

It was Sisco. And he was insistent.

The dead man was barefoot. He was dressed in a pair of gray sweatpants and a dusty rose T-shirt advertising a restaurant in Ocean City called Moby Dick's. The knife had gone in between the angled uprights of the y. As the Fates would have it — and one way or another the Fates *always* have it — I happen to have eaten at Moby Dick's in Ocean City myself just that past summer. I had the fish stew, which had come highly recommended, but which tasted metallic after the fourth slurp and had wound up giving me twenty-four-hour food poisoning. Food poisoning does a real number on your back muscles — among other things — and the creepy thing is that I had spent a large portion of the following day stretched out on the cool tiles of the kitchen floor in the beach house where I was staying. The uncreepy thing is that eventually I was able to get back up and continue on with my vibrant and ever-changing life. Not so Mr. Sweatpants. His ticket was punched.

I'm an undertaker, I can tell these things.

I closed my eyes and put my fingers to the bridge of my nose and squeezed.

"For Christ's sake, Hitch, what are you doing? Praying?" Sisco's voice was rough and whining.

I cocked one eyebrow, letting it drag the eye open. "It's called a headache, Sisco."

"Rough night?"

"Rough morning!"

"You want an aspirin or something?"

I released my nose. "I'll live."

Sisco pulled his hands from his pockets and bounced down to a squat. Sisco was a fairly lithe character, a wiry, lightweight kind of guy with dirty blond hair and a pretty face that any mother worth the title could see right through. He was wearing baggy gray pants with pockets all over the place and a nauseating Hawaiian print shirt. Rayon. The flowers shimmered when he moved.

"This is a real goddamn mess," Sisco announced, more to the corpse, it seemed, than to me. "Big-time fucking mess."

"What's his name, Sisco?"

"Jake Weisheit." He pronounced it *wise height*. I repeated the name to make sure I'd gotten it right. Sisco bobbed his head. "Uh-

11

huh. It's German. You spell it *we-is-he-it*. Pretty cool, huh?"

"Very cool, Sisco. And do we know what Mr. Weisheit is doing lying here with a knife in his back so earl-eye in the morning?"

"I've got no answer for that, Hitch. I swear I don't know."

"But I take it you two were acquainted."

That's when Sisco told me about Jake Weisheit's wife. He wasn't coy about it. I'll give him points for directness.

"I'm sleeping with his wife."

"Okay. And did Mr. Weisheit know this?"

"Yeah. I guess you could say the information came his way." Sisco craned his neck and considered the corpse. "Jake wasn't real happy about it. We kind of had a fight about it the other night."

My headache was making a renewed play on my temples. "How about some coffee, Sisco? I think it's time for you to start playing host."

Sisco rose and moved over to the counter where he pulled open a pair of overhead cabinets. About a hundred brightly colored brand-name products shouted out for attention.

"Jesus, look at all this shit. You see any coffee filters here?"

I was moving around to get a look at Jake Weisheit's face. I ignored Sisco's question. I squatted down, careful to keep clear of the blood. The face was resting on its left cheek. The nose was prominent, the forehead high, the eye fixated on my ankle. For no good reason I reached out and snapped my fingers about an inch from the man's face.

"He's dead," Sisco said from behind me. "Don't worry about that."

The watch face on Jake Weisheit's watch was cracked, presumably from hitting hard against the tiled floor when the man fell. I squinted through the cracks in the glass.

"Time of death, three-ten," I said, telescoping my weary body back up to its full height. Sisco was flipping the cabinets closed.

"Hey, you're good." Sisco reached down and picked up a red plastic bowl from the floor. He came over and stood next to me, looking down sadly at the corpse. "It's kind of creepy, isn't it."

"Why did you have me park in the garage?" I asked.

"Well, you know. I mean, a hearse. It draws attention."

"Sisco, have you called the police?"

Sisco's innocent act was thoroughly sub-Oscar. "The police?"

"The men in blue suits? With those colored lights on top of their cars? Did you at least call an ambulance?"

"But he's dead."

"That wasn't my question."

"Don't bust my nut, Hitch, okay? This is a

13

fucking mess here. I'm having a hard time trying to think straight. Check this out."

He handed me the red plastic bowl. It was the kind you'd use to feed a pet. There was a hole in the bottom of the bowl, less than an inch in diameter.

"What's this?" I asked.

"It's the cat's bowl."

"There's a hole in it."

"It's a bullet hole."

"Jake Weisheit shot the cat bowl?"

Sisco shrugged. "That's what it looks like. You can see over there where the bullet went into the floor." Sisco pulled a pack of cigarettes from his shirt pocket and flicked a cigarette neatly between his lips.

"They don't like that," I said as he produced a pack of matches.

"Like what?"

"Smoking at a crime scene." I held up the plastic bowl. "Or messing with evidence, for that matter."

"Who don't like it?"

"The men in the blue suits."

Sisco made a deliberate act of ripping a match from the pack, lighting the cigarette and blowing the smoke coolly from the side of his mouth. I didn't quite care for the look on his face. It was the look of someone who is about to honor you with information that you'd just as soon not be honored with.

"But that's just it, Hitch. We don't have a crime scene."

I ran a hand through my hair and took a grip. This wasn't going to be good. "Why don't you tell me what we *do* have here, Sisco? Why don't you tell me why I'm here?"

Then he told me. He told me the favor he wanted from me. I plucked the cigarette from his mouth and tossed it into the sink. I ran my hand up and down in front of my face, then in front of his.

Sisco frowned. "What's that for?"

"It's because one of us is dreaming," I said. "I'm just trying to figure out which one."

Polly Weisheit was sitting on a stone wall in a white bathrobe tossing golf balls from a wire bucket into a swimming pool. It was a kidney-shaped swimming pool and maybe one day I'll meet someone who can explain to me how it was someone hit on the idea of designing swimming pools to be this shape. For reasons that should be so obvious I refuse to air them, she threw like a girl. Leading with the elbow. Something spastic in the pivot. Like her husband, she was barefoot, but unlike him she was still on the O_2-CO_2 circuit. She was a dirty blond with terrier hair, a mass of hard curls with a mind of their own. So thick you could stick small items in there and lose them altogether. She was probably around forty, but could get away with less. Good bones can do that. Her eyes gave away nothing, but they were pretty nonetheless. Her complexion was pale, but then you've got to consider the circumstances, not to mention the hour.

A morning nip was still in the air. It was late October. Maryland had finally had a wet summer and the leaves were turning early. Polly and Jake Weisheit's house was located in a section north of Baltimore known as Ruxton, a heavily wooded area in a north/south-running valley between North Charles Street and the Jones Falls River. The Weisheit house was one of about a half dozen at the top of a rise. There was a generous backyard, the grass still minty and silver with dew. There was an orange lacrosse goal, along with a couple of unattended sticks. Trees separated the property from the neighbors', sporting full burstings of ruby and yellow. A half-dozen lounge chairs were scattered about on the stone patio. A gauze-like mist hovered just over the surface of the pool. Unseen, but near, a crow was clearing its throat.

Sisco made the introductions. "Polly, this is Hitch. Hitch, Polly."

"How do you do?" I said.

Polly was rummaging in the wire bucket for a ball.

"Hitch isn't real keen on our idea," Sisco

16

said. Polly Weisheit gave him one of those looks that I swear must be part of a woman's birthright. Sisco made the adjustment. "*My plan.*"

Polly Weisheit cocked her arm and sent the ball plunking into the fat end of the pool. The wire bucket was half empty, though of course I didn't know how full it had been to start with. I spotted a number of golf balls scattered on the stone patio. A barn door would not have been in terrific peril with Polly Weisheit aiming at it. She looked up at me with a sleepy, unfocused expression.

"What happened to your cheek?"

"I got hit with a tambourine," I said. "What happened to your husband?"

"Somebody killed him."

"That's the conclusion I reached as well. Do you know who?"

"No."

"Did you hear anything?"

"No."

"It looks like your husband shot his gun. There's a hole in the cat bowl. You didn't hear the gun go off?"

"No."

"Are you the one who found him?"

"Yes."

"Can you say anything besides yes and no?"

Polly Weisheit didn't look like the kind of person who falls for trick questions. She tugged the sash of her robe tight and fixed me with her weary look. "I came downstairs this morning to let the cat in. She's a smart cat. She stands under the bedroom window and yowls and she won't let up until you let her in. It'll drive you nuts."

"What's her name?"

"Priscilla. We call her Silly."

"Why do you let her out in the first place?"

"Same thing. She yowls to be let out. We're completely at her mercy. Jake calls her Rosemary's Cat." She corrected herself. "He *called* her Rosemary's Cat."

"What happened next?" I asked.

She didn't answer. She fished out another golf ball, but before she could toss it I caught her wrist. I don't know why I did it; my hand simply shot forward. Blame it on the hour. Polly Weisheit didn't seem especially happy about it. She flicked her wrist free. Sisco had pulled out another cigarette, but I backed him down.

"Your friend's kind of bossy," Polly Weisheit said.

"His friend is operating on two hours' sleep," I said. "He couldn't be nicer when he's had his full eight. Ask anyone."

Polly Weisheit started to respond, then thought better of it. She dropped the ball back into the basket and took a deep breath.

"Okay. So Silly was yowling and it woke

me up. At least I guess that's what it was. Jake wasn't in bed. I figured he'd gotten up and was letting her in. But she kept on making noise, so I finally got up and went downstairs. And there he was."

"On the floor."

"That's right."

"And you hadn't heard anything?"

"You mean besides Silly?"

"Besides Silly."

"No."

"You didn't hear his gun go off?"

"I told you that already. No."

"And you don't remember your husband getting out of bed?"

She shook her head. "I was having trouble getting to sleep last night and I took a couple of Tylenol PM. Those things really knock me out. I should really only take one of them."

"But you took two last night?"

"Yes."

"Any special reason?"

"For taking two? No. I just wanted to get to sleep. I could tell I was going to have a rough time dropping off so I popped the Tylenols. I'm still feeling a little dopey. Maybe you can tell."

"But you weren't knocked out enough not to hear the cat," I noted.

"Believe me, you could hear that cat yowling from the grave."

Three pair of eyes shifted momentarily to

the direction of the house, then back again.

"How was your husband before you went to sleep?" I asked.

She gave me a queer look. "How was he?"

"How did he seem? Was he anxious? Was his behavior at all unusual?"

"What are you, a psychiatrist? He was fine. He was normal. He was Jake." She made what I assumed was an attempt to roll her eyes, but I guess her heart wasn't in it. "He was Jake," she said again.

"What does that mean?"

"It means he got into bed and gave me a good long look at his back."

"I see."

"Are you married?"

"I'm not."

"Then maybe you're not familiar with this custom."

She gave me a heavy-lidded look. I sensed a smirk deeply embedded. I steered elsewhere, tipping my chin to indicate Sisco.

"So when does cutie-pie come into the picture?"

Sisco sniggered. "Funny guy."

"I called him," Polly said flatly. "He came out right away."

"The police are going to wonder why you didn't call them," I said. "The killer might have still been in the house. He might even still be there now."

"I called Sisco," Polly said again.

"And Sisco came right over, took one look at the situation and decided to call his friendly neighborhood undertaker to come out and do you a little favor."

Sisco muttered, "It was a dumb idea."

"No offense, Sisco," I said. "But I think you meant to say diabolically dumb."

"It's like I told you, Hitch, Jake and I had this huge fight a couple of nights ago. Out at the roadhouse. A ton of people saw it. I really lost it, man. A couple of guys had to grab hold of me."

"So then you came out here a couple nights later, got Jake down to the kitchen and stuck a knife in his back."

"Aw, listen to you. That's exactly what the cops will say. That's the whole *point*."

"So let's see if I've got this straight. To save you the hassle of explaining yourself to the police I'm supposed to whisk this body off in my hearse and figure out a way to quietly tuck it into a *grave?* Just make the damn thing disappear? When you hear it said out loud, is it stupid enough for you?"

"He left something out," Polly said.

"Why am I not surprised?"

"When he and Jake were going at it the other night, Sisco told Jake he was going to kill him. Everybody heard it."

Sisco rolled his eyes. "It's a figure of *speech*."

Polly made a pair of quotation marks in the air and pitched her voice lower. " 'You don't know who you're fucking with, Jake. I can have you killed like that.' " She snapped her fingers about an inch from my nose. It was a frighteningly good imitation. I told her so.

"That's good," I said.

Sisco was scowling. "Yeah, yeah, you ought to hear her Jimmy Stewart."

"I do a good Jimmy Stewart," I said. "Let's hear yours."

Sisco whined, "I'm *kidding*."

Polly and I shared a look. She turned to Sisco. "So is he," she said softly. She pulled another ball from the wire bucket and handed it to him. "Here you go, honey."

"Yeah, yeah." Sisco bounced the ball in his hand, then reared back and let it fly. No girlie toss here. Sisco wasn't aiming for the pool, he was going for distance. The ball sailed right through the mass of branches at the edge of the property and disappeared. A second later came the tinkling sound of breaking glass, followed by a loud, shrill alarm bell.

Sisco's face fell. "Shit. What's that?"

I answered, "I'd call that a Rube Goldberg way to call the police."

"What's that?"

"It's not a what, it's a who. Rube Goldberg."

"Well, who's that?"

"He's a guy who does easy things the hard way."

"Shit. Polly, go tell them it was an accident. Tell them they don't have to get the damn police out here."

But Polly was shaking her head. "Sorry, Rube. We should have called them in the first place." She corrected herself. "*I* should have just called them. I don't know what I was thinking." She turned to me. "Listen, why don't you go? I can't think of a good way to explain to the police what the hell you're doing here. It's going to be crazy enough. I shouldn't have let Sisco call you. I was just too fuzzy-headed."

"I should go too," Sisco said.

Polly fixed him with a look. "Uh-uh. You should stay put, lover."

"It's not going to look good."

"It's going to look a lot worse if they see *you* running from the scene." She slid off the wall. "I'm going inside to call the police." She clutched the robe tight at the neck then paused, her eyes traveling back and forth between Sisco and me. They traveled slowly, in a fashion that struck me as both slightly indifferent and slightly amused. She turned and headed off toward the house.

Sisco watched her until she disappeared into the house, then turned to me. "Hitch. That woman is an animal."

I gave him as insincere a smile as I could manage. "That's nice, Sisco. That's very nice."

23

Chapter Two

I sing praises to my water pressure. When I become an old man and my muscles start turning to jelly I might think differently. I might have to start bringing a stool into the shower and do the whole thing sitting down, else risk the piercing jets knocking me onto my poor old enfeebled can. But until such day, I sing praises to my water pressure, to its ceaseless symphonic blast. It is a small but significant glory and it goes down on my checklist of things that make me happy.

If anyone's keeping track, I also like coffee that tastes as if you could scoop it out of the cup in a solid mass, mold it into an orb and bounce it off the wall. And while I'm thinking of it, brainy women with inscrutable smiles. Those I can't get enough of.

So I was two for three as I sat there on my couch in my towel chewing happily on a cup of mud. I had clocked a few more hours of sleep since returning from the Weisheit residence and was feeling nearly human, all things considered. Sunday is Bach Day, as any overcivilized Anglo-Saxon knows. The Orchestra of St. Luke's was doing the honors — allegro, andante, adagio, all that stuff. I'm not so far gone into this that I can actually keep my Bach straight (Julia calls me opus hopeless), but then Bach's a guy you can pretty much count on no matter what you slap on the stereo. This particular one was heavy on the violins. With an occasional oboe moping around. Good Sunday stuff.

The appearance of the morning sun while I was out at the Weisheits' proved brief. By the time I returned home, a gray casing had moved in and the sky had lowered significantly. As I sat on the couch, humming along in approximate A minor, a light drizzle commenced and strengthened by increments — nearly in tempo to the Bach — until finally it qualified as a full-fledged steady downpour. I dragged the Theodore Roosevelt onto my lap and opened it to where I'd left off the night before. Teddy had just entered the New York legislature for the first time and was receiving catcalls for his dapper duds. He was flashing his big chompers at his fellow assemblymen. Alcatraz came up onto the couch with a lazy yawn and folded himself up next to me. A little wheezing from the nose a few minutes later told me he was asleep. As the rain increased to a perfect sizzle, a syncopated drip-drip-drip set up just off center in one of the windows. I leaned my head back on the couch and placed my hand down on the pages of the book.

And the best part of it was, I had no one to bury today.

I thought it was a crack of thunder that woke me up. It woke Alcatraz too, and we looked dumbly into each other's eyes as our brains scrambled to catch up. Then it sounded again. It wasn't thunder, it was the phone. I got up and crossed to the kitchen.

"Nephew?" It was Billie.

"Good morning, Chief," I said.

"I trust I'm not interrupting anything."

"No, ma'am. A small bevy of dancing girls, but they're about to take their break. What's up? We got a live one?"

That's undertaker doublespeak. My aunt and I swim in a sea of euphemisms. I glanced out my back window. I share a tiny scratch of backyard with my downstairs neighbors, Spiro and Doodle. Spiro owns a restaurant a few miles away on Eastern Avenue. He and Doodle have been living in the ground-floor apartment for as long as I can remember. They're quiet neighbors. No loud fights. No loud TV. Doodle brings me food on occasion. She says it's not easy to cook for two. I'm happy to help her out. I often find it hard to cook for one.

Spiro was sitting at the picnic table up by the back fence, his large meaty face in his hands, staring off into space. The rain was still coming down steadily, but to a large ex-

26

tent Spiro had bypassed the issue of proper gear by virtue of the fact that he was not wearing a stitch of clothing. He looked like a big wet pale bear.

Thunder sounded and the phone crackled. I had to ask Billie to repeat what she had just said.

"I just received a phone call," Billie said. "From an old friend of yours. Were you out in the hearse earlier this morning, Hitchcock?"

"I cannot tell a lie."

"I'm not asking you to, dear. I'm wondering what you were up to."

Out in the backyard, Spiro stood up. His body was considerably more enormous than I'd have thought. From my vantage point, Spiro's belly shielded his privates from view, which was just fine by me.

"I'm not trying to change the subject," I said to Billie, stepping closer to the window. "But you might be interested in hearing that as we speak, Spiro is standing buck naked in the backyard."

"That sounds attractive. Is Doodle with him?"

"No, it's just Spiro."

Spiro had turned his face up into the rain. His hands dropped heavily to his sides and he let out a mighty bellow. I reported to Billie. "He's crying out to the sky."

"Is he crying out in anguish or ecstasy? Can you tell?"

Spiro broke off his yelling and reached down and took hold of the picnic table bench. Bracing himself, he lifted the bench and set the end on his ultra-white thighs while he reset his grip. Then holding the bench at something of a forty-five-degree angle, Spiro waddle-stepped a few feet over to the plaster birdbath, and with much more speed and certainly more strength than I would have imagined he had in him, straightened to his full height, raised the picnic bench over his head and brought it crashing down on the birdbath. A piece roughly the size of a third of the entire birdbath bowl cracked free and tumbled to the ground. Spiro released the picnic table bench, letting it also drop to the ground.

"Anguish," I said into the phone. "It would appear that Spiro is upset. He just smashed the birdbath."

"I hope Doodle is okay."

"Spiro wouldn't hurt Doodle. He's devoted to Doodle."

"Listen, Hitchcock. You're going to have to worry about Spiro later," Billie said. "You need to come over here."

"But, Billie, this is a singular sight."

"I'm sure it is, dear. So step away from the window. Leave Spiro alone for now. Lieutenant Kruk just called here. He wants to talk to you about what you were doing with the hearse this morning. And I quote, *at an*

unreported crime scene, unquote. The lieutenant said there had been a homicide."

"Yes, there was. There was a man with a
knife in his back."

I could hear my aunt's sigh over the line.
"I'm hanging up now, Hitchcock. Hurry over,
will you? Have you had your breakfast?"

"I haven't," I said. "I'm waking up in
phases. I'd kill for some of your beaten biscuits."

There was another crackle on the line.
"Let's rephrase that, shall we?"

Sewell and Sons Family Funeral Home is
all of thirty-five footsteps from my front
door. A dynamite commute. I skipped the
umbrella and simply pulled my Orioles cap
down tight on my head for the dash up the
street. The sidewalk was slicker than I'd realized, and my flat-bottomed Converses planed
along the final ten feet, my arms pinwheeling
to keep me from pitching to the ground. It
was a grand — if cartoonish — arrival.

Billie was upstairs in the kitchen, beating
up the biscuits. As promised.

"You're a sweet old lady," I said, pecking
the floured cheek. A rosemary air lifted from
her.

"And so much more. Any more news on
Spiro?"

"Nothing to report. Things were silent
when I left." I dropped into a chair at the

kitchen table. Red and white linoleum. When I was three quarters my current height and over for a visit, I used to drape a blanket over this very same table and crawl under it for trips to the moon, to Mars, any number of celestial destinations. It always pissed me off when ugly Uncle Stu came by and started kicking at the sides of my spacecraft.

Billie asked, "What happened to your cheek?"

"This?" I touched the offended cheek lightly. "A little mix-up with a tambourine. Not to worry."

"I want to hear about this corpse of yours, Hitchcock," Billie said. "Lieutenant Kruk sounded very stern on the phone."

"You remember Kruk, Billie. That's the only note he plays."

Billie poured a cup of coffee and brought it to me, then continued on with her biscuits while I synopsized my morning for her. At the mention of Sisco Fontaine she let out a soft groan, but she didn't interrupt. She pulled out two cookie sheets and set tiny fistfuls of dough onto them, two dozen in all, in equal rows of four. She slid the sheets into the oven, then remained standing, gripping the back of the chair and attempting to keep judgment out of her expression as I finished up my story.

"So then you simply left?"

"Yes."

"You don't feel you should have waited for the police?"

I shrugged. "I could have. But calling me in was a bonehead move in the first place. I thought a discreet retreat made the most sense."

"Keeping a hundred miles clear of Sisco Fontaine would make the most sense."

"Be fair, Billie. At the end of the day, Sisco's a pretty harmless guy."

"At the end of the day? Do you need me to point out to you that he called you at the crack of dawn to try to rope you into his foolishness? I just don't understand you sometimes, Hitchcock. Generally speaking, you are not the most ignorant rock to come rolling down the hill."

"Thank you."

"I just don't understand this penchant for letting yourself get roped into trouble."

"It's just a deeply seated psychological need to set the cockeyed world aright," I said. "There's just so much injustice. There's so much pain, so much suffering."

Billie started to respond but something through the window caught her eye. "Oh, look." She tugged the window open and thrust her head out into the rain. "Yoo-hoo, Lieutenant Kruk! Come right in, the door's open!"

She pulled her head back in and closed the window. The faint exertion had brought up her natural pink. The rain set a few diamonds in her hair. She broke out her wicked grin as she reached around back for her apron strings.

"You bring him up here, nephew. I'll go fetch the arsenic."

If Lieutenant Kruk was happy to see me again he managed to keep his enthusiasm supremely in check. He was standing just inside the front door — a short man in a rain-splotched overcoat — as I came down the stairs. A trio of miniature puddles were forming about his shoes. His yellow hair was matted against his skull, his deadpan scowl just as lovely as ever. He must have seen something in my face that he didn't care for, because I hadn't even spoken a word before he said, "No bullshit, Mr. Sewell. Not today. I'm not in the mood."

As if he ever was.

"And I'm happy to see you too, Lieutenant. Let me take your coat."

"I'll keep it." He thrust his hands deeper into his pockets, in case he had to wrestle me for it.

"I didn't know you worked on Sundays," I said.

"People get killed, I work. Doesn't matter what day it is."

"I guess we have that in common. Though in my case they don't have to get killed, of course. They only have to die. But the idea is pretty much the same."

"Can we sit down somewhere?" Kruk asked. "Your office?"

"Billie would slaughter me if I didn't bring you upstairs. She's just pulling biscuits out of the oven. Are you familiar with beaten biscuits?"

Kruk put his hard stare on me, then stepped past me and started up the stairs with a resigned heavy step. Willy Loman came to mind. Or a gallows walker.

Billie greeted the detective like a bee greets a flower. I don't even want to describe it. Kruk gutted it out with iron grace. And for Billie, he did remove his coat. I noted the frayed Stewart's label as I hung it on the wall hook for him. The man was wearing an artifact.

We moved into the kitchen, where Billie beckoned the two of us to take a seat at the table. A basket of steaming biscuits sat on the table.

Kruk came directly to the point "Mr. Sewell, there has been a murder. A dark red hearse bearing Maryland tags [he quoted our tag number] was seen leaving the scene at approximately six-fifteen this morning. A person matching your description was seen driving the hearse. Would you care to tell me where you were at six-fifteen this morning?"

Billie leaned forward. "Biscuit, Lieutenant?"

"At six-fifteen this morning I was behind the wheel of the company hearse leaving the site of a murder scene," I said. "And may I add that it feels good to get that off my chest."

Billie sniffed. "Don't be impertinent, Hitchcock."

Kruk had pulled out a small notebook. He flipped it open and took a quick look. "The deceased has been identified as Jake Weese . . . Wise . . ."

"Weisheit," I said, giving it the correct pronunciation. "We-is-he-it. That's the trick to spelling it."

"So then you were familiar with Mr. Weisheit."

"Only met the man this morning."

"How about Mrs. Weisheit? Do you know her?"

"I met her for the first time this morning too. Approximately five o'clock. She was a good deal livelier than her husband. She was out back throwing golf balls into the swimming pool. I think she was in shock. She was also a lousy shot."

"I'm not asking you what you thought, Mr. Sewell. I'm simply collecting facts."

Kruk consulted the notebook again. "And Jonathan Fontaine? Are you acquainted with him?"

Billie uttered, "Jonathan. That's such a nice name."

"Sisco Fontaine," I said. "That's what he goes by. Sure, I'm acquainted with Sisco. It's nothing I'm particularly proud of."

"How long have you known Mr. Fontaine?"

"Since high school."

"You went to school together?"

"Yes. I was also in Sisco's first band, the Metaphysicals. I mainly played the harmonica. May I say we stank?"

"So you've been acquainted for a long time," Kruk said. "Would we call Mr. Fontaine a close friend?"

"We would not. Nothing like back in the Metaphysicals days. We bump into each other. Our paths cross. We'll share a drink, shoot the breeze. Like that. We don't exactly debate the great issues of our time. I'm not sure Sisco could even identify the great issues of our time."

"Prior to this morning, when was the last time you saw Mr. Fontaine?"

"That's easy. Two weeks ago. It was at the Mount Vernon Festival. His band was playing there. I was there with Julia. You remember Julia, don't you?"

Of course he did. A person could sooner lose track of their own feet than forget my ex-wife.

"Miss Finney leaves an impression," Kruk said simply. He pulled a ballpoint pen from his shirt pocket and thumbed the detonator. He scribbled something into his notebook. "Did you and Mr. Fontaine have any discussion at that time?" He looked up from the notebook. "And I don't mean the great issues, Mr. Sewell. Did you shoot the breeze? Did he mention anything about what he was up to lately? If he was seeing anyone? That sort of thing?"

Kruk had yet to touch his biscuit. I grabbed one from the basket and slathered it up with butter. "Julia and I wandered over during their break. Sisco was hitting on Julia. He always hits on Julia. It's hopeless, but that's Sisco. I spent most of the time talking to a woman named Angela."

"Angela?"

"She's one of Sisco's backup singers. One of the Kids." Kruk waited patiently for an explanation. "Sisco and the Kids. That's the ever-so-clever name of his group." Kruk was scribbling in his notebook again. "Honey blond," I said. "About five seven. Green eyes. A very interesting tattoo of a giraffe on her right shoulder blade. I saw only the neck and the head. There's a faint scar runs through her —"

Kruk looked up at me. "That's enough."

"I think she's a Pisces," I said, and I popped the biscuit into my mouth.

Kruk gave a heavy sigh. "Let me tell you the situation, Mr. Sewell. I have a pair of

36

stories here. Two statements taken at the crime scene this morning. One from Mr. Fontaine, one from Mrs. Weisheit. The statements were taken separately and the statements don't jibe. By your own admission you were out there. I want to hear why. I want to hear your story. It would be good if your story lined up with either of the two I already have."

"Are you going to tell me your two stories first?"

"No, I am not. And I want no embellishments, Mr. Sewell. It might surprise you to hear that I don't have all day to sit here and listen to you. Just give me simple clean facts."

Which is what I gave him. Simple. Clean. Short sentences, no difficult words. Kruk buttered his biscuit and nibbled it as I talked. We both finished at about the same time.

"So it's your story that Mr. Fontaine was attempting to conceal the homicide."

"It's not a story. It's what Sisco told me."

"And Mr. Fontaine told you that he was trying to conceal the homicide not because he was responsible, but because of the argument he and the deceased had had a few nights ago."

"And the threats that Sisco had allegedly made."

"Allegedly?"

"I wasn't there."

"Of course."

"If it means anything, Sisco agrees that it was a stupid thing to ask. Sisco tends to think of himself first and himself second."

Kruk flipped his notebook closed.

"How did his story do?" Billie asked as Kruk rose from his chair. She made a pair of quotation marks in the air. "Did it jibe?"

"Your nephew and Mrs. Weisheit told the same story," Kruk said. "It's Mr. Fontaine's version that is different."

"How did Sisco's go?" I asked.

"Different."

"Different how?"

"I can't discuss that with you. I will tell you that it sounded weak when he told it. It's only sounding weaker now."

"What about a good old-fashioned breaking and entering?" I asked. "A burglary gone wrong."

"It's on the list of possibilities," Kruk said. "It's not at the top of the list."

"What about Jake Weisheit's shooting the cat's bowl?"

Kruk shrugged. "Errant shot, most likely. I'm not so masochistic that I'd ask you for your theory about that."

"For what it's worth, I know it looks sort of bad for Sisco, but I don't think he killed the guy."

"Thank you, Mr. Sewell. But as I told you,

I collect facts, not opinions."

"I realize that. It's your job to keep an open mind."

Kruk fetched his coat and shrugged into it. For just an instant his hands didn't reappear when it seemed they should. It was as if they had mistakenly slipped into a limbo. Kruk patted down his yellow hair, which is always dead flat on his head and never needs patting down. He regarded me a moment.

"Let me give you a little look at my open mind, Mr. Sewell. Here's what I have. I have a murdered man and I have an undertaker and his hearse on the scene well in advance of the police being notified. I have a couple of conflicting explanations in my notebook as to why he is there in the first place. I have the undertaker's departure moments after the police are called. I have no record of the undertaker's calling in the body, as it seems to me he would know is his legal duty. And I have you now sitting here acting awfully damned unconcerned."

"Should I be concerned, Lieutenant?"

"What I'm telling you is that for the time being, I have plenty to keep an open mind about. And that's something you'd be smart to remember."

Billie rotated the basket clockwise.

"Another biscuit for the road, Lieutenant?"

Chapter Three

Spiro's mother was dead. This was the explanation for why Spiro had been naked in the rain in the backyard smashing the birdbath with the picnic bench. I'm not saying this is how *everyone* might react to the news of a mother's passing (in my case, I punched a hole in the wall), but it proved to be Spiro's way, and I'm not going to pass judgment. Doodle came upstairs and rapped on my door soon after my return from Billie's and told me the news. Spiro's mother had been living at a nursing home in Lutherville. Briarcliff Manor. Sometime during the night she had managed to lower the safety bars on her bed, slip past the night nurses and make her way outside, where she had been discovered at daybreak (about the same time I had been standing in the Weisheits' kitchen), sitting on a bench at the Lutherville Lite-Rail station still in her bedclothes. She was dead. She was clutching a copy of *Jane*, which of course is a magazine skewed to on-the-go young women, not fragile crones. Doodle told me that Spiro was horribly upset — don't tell *me,* tell the birdbath — and that he wanted his mother fetched from Lutherville and brought to Fells Point as soon as possible. Doodle said that he had attempted to call a cab to take him out there himself to get his mother's body, but that she had dissuaded him.

"He wants her here," Doodle said sullenly. "In the house. Spiro is rearranging the living room as we speak. I'm supposed to go out and buy a hundred white candles. In this weather."

"He wants the wake held in your living room? He doesn't want it up at the funeral home?"

"Is that sanitary? Holding it here?"

I assured her that it was. "We'll have to embalm her first, of course."

"Well, do a good job. He wants her here for two days."

"Please pass my condolences on to Spiro."

"Did you hear me? Two full days."

After phoning Briarcliff to arrange for the pickup, I pulled on a pair of Wellingtons and an old Army jacket, found my Gloucester fisherman's hat and took Alcatraz out for his morning rounds. We headed down to the harbor, me in a straight line, Alcatraz doing his pinball routine. Moran's tug was secured to the pier, dipping and bobbing, bumping up against the wall of old tires. Alcatraz looped across Thames Street and I followed, holding on to my hat against a sudden wet blast. The light from inside Stoney's Bakery looked warm and buttery. The shop's window glass steamed a quarter of the way up, making dappled silhouettes of Stoney's customers. As I stood looking out at the meteors of rain pocking the black water, my mind's eye opened up a small area roughly in the middle of the harbor, and there on an oval of white lay Jake Weisheit, facedown, with that large knife in his back. I wondered what sort of unconvincing story Sisco had tried to pass off on Kruk for why I was out there. It was a loaded scene, to be sure, the lover of the dead man's wife standing there twiddling his thumbs when the police show up. Sisco had done his cause little good by lying to the police about why he had called me to the house. But then again, the truth of the matter was so blatantly incriminating on the face of it that I suppose Sisco had felt he had no choice. The hole was already dug. No matter which way you looked at it, Sisco had proved piss poor on damage control.

Of course the question was, did he do it?

My mirage faltered and a swell of choppy black water washed it from sight. I whistled for Alcatraz, then saw him across the street at Stoney's door. Stoney was rubbing the dog's knuckley head and feeding him a pastry. She waved to me, then ducked back inside.

A message was waiting for me on my machine when I got back home. I tugged off the

Wellies and hit the Play button. It was Polly Weisheit She wanted me to bury her husband.

Interesting.

I traveled to Lutherville at half the normal speed limit; the rain wouldn't have it any other way. An accident just north of the Cold Spring Lane exit forced me off the Jones Falls and I took Cold Spring to Charles Street and then north on Charles. There was a second accident, this one near the Cathedral of St. Mary, so I slowed down even more. With my windshield wipers slapping time I kicked out a few verses of "Me and Bobbie McGee," which I followed up with a quick run-through of what I could fetch from the Kristofferson songbook. I arrived at the nursing home feeling somewhat maudlin about love, liquor and the human condition. Nothing new, really.

Briarcliff Manor is a large stucco building situated on a five-acre lot smack-dab in the middle of a moderate-income residential neighborhood of one- and two-story homes built mostly in the fifties. Neither briars nor cliffs are in any way a part of the landscape — nor are they especially the friend of the infirm and elderly — so I'm not sure where the name came from. The word *manor*, however, was appropriate. The building itself dwarfed the houses all around it, it being four stories tall and built at the top of a sloping piece of property. It used to be the home of Mathers Tuck, a man who had made his fortune in Vermont granite. How it was that Vermont granite translated into a large stucco home in Lutherville, Maryland, was a matter that I cannot report. Tuck had been one of those wealthy and apparently germ-conscious eccentrics, and when his wife took ill, Tuck refused to send her to a hospital but had instead hired a nursing staff for around-the-clock maintenance, as well as putting a pair of physicians on retainer to look after his beloved. His beloved toughed it out for several more years, but eventually succumbed to the inevitable systems failure. Tuck himself began to lose his color soon after, but remained sentient enough to arrange for his home's transformation into a nursing home facility after his death. Mr. Tuck bade the planet farewell, and within months after the settling of the estate, architects and contractors descended on the house, carving the floors up into bed-sized rooms, bathing facilities and common areas. The kitchen had been renovated to allow for the preparation of dozens of bland, easily chewable meals, and Mathers Tuck's study was gutted and transformed into the facility's dining area. The problem of moving leg-weary patients from floor to floor was solved by the installation of a freight elevator, complete with padded benches running along the rear wall.

I learned all of this from a brochure that I picked up inside the front door. I suppose I shouldn't say I learned *all* of this. The brochure did not specifically use the word *eccentric* in describing Mathers Tuck. I extrapolated that part myself both from the description of the man and the oil portrait of him hanging on the wall just inside the front door. An extremely bony head and the eyes of a crazed Civil War general. Not only did the eyes follow me as I moved past the portrait, but I could feel them on the back of my neck when I turned my back on the portrait.

There was a plastic sign on the wall instructing visitors to buzz the buzzer, so I did. It sounded somewhere down the black-and-white-checkered hallway, a noise like a goose being strangled. A minute later, a woman stepped down the hallway like a little soldier, arms swinging tightly, head erect, slicing the air as she went. She was trim, with thin sharp legs and a narrow waist. Fortyish. She was wearing a moss green skirt, tightly pleated, and an Oxford-style shirt, open at the neck to show me a string of small gray pearls. The lipstick was blood red. The eyes were blue, small and neutral. I held out my paw and she placed a small mackerel in it.

"Hitchcock Sewell," I said. "Sewell and Sons."

"Marilyn Tuck."

I indicated the portrait over my shoulder. "Your father?"

She retrieved her hand and hid it behind her back along with her other one. She stole a glance at the portrait. "Yes."

The resemblance was nonexistent. A fine thing too. Perhaps Marilyn Tuck wasn't likely to inspire a flotilla of ancient Greeks to cross vast stretches of water; even so, it wasn't an altogether unattractive face.

I held up the pamphlet. "I was just reading your brochure. So, I guess you grew up here."

"I did. In fact I was born in this house. My father was mistrustful of hospitals."

"Andy Warhol was mistrustful of hospitals," I noted.

She tilted her head back a smidge, sighting me along her narrow nose.

"Piece of trivia. Andy Warhol had a horrible fear of hospitals. He was admitted to one for something fairly routine. And he died."

"I wasn't aware of that."

"It was in an article I was reading. About karma. Andy's experience of course being an example of not such good karma. The article said that Andy still has some things he has to work out. Next time."

"Next time?"

"When he comes back."

She looked confused "Andy Warhol is coming back?"

"If you go in for that sort of thing. He won't be Andy Warhol next time. But whoever he is, he'll still have the whole fear of hospitals thing to deal with."

"That's very interesting," the woman said. Unconvincingly, I might add. "I guess I don't know much about that sort of thing." She pointed at my dripping umbrella. "Why don't you leave that?"

I dropped the umbrella into a chrome can and fell in next to the commissar. We headed down the hallway, passing a room in which a group of seniors were watching a game show on a large television set. Marilyn Tuck floated a hand. "That's the television room."

I hadn't exactly mistaken it for a jai alai stadium, but I kept silent. The hallway was outfitted with metal handrails, and as we rounded the corner we encountered an elderly man making his way slowly along the wall, hand over hand. He was ghostly thin, and he was wearing only one slipper. We stopped.

Marilyn Tuck addressed him loudly. "Mr. Coleman! Where is your slipper!" The man's response was painfully hoarse and unintelligible. She touched him lightly on the arm. "Stay where you are! I'll have an aide come help you!"

We continued on. One of the fluorescent

47

tubes overhead was blinking as we reached a pair of French doors. "That was supposed to be fixed," Marilyn Tuck muttered. Beyond the French doors was a large glassed-in room. This had been mentioned in the brochure. It was the atrium. Formerly the wraparound front porch of Mathers Tuck's home, it had been glassed in during the renovation, creating something akin to a greenhouse. A dozen or so residents were seated there, some playing cards, several playing checkers, others dozing in cushioned bamboo chairs. One old fellow was standing with his nose nearly touching the glass. Next to him was a young woman in a pink pin-striped uniform and white shoes. Moon-shaped face. Asian features. Filipino, perhaps.

Marilyn Tuck spoke to her. "Louise, Mr. Coleman is in the hallway. He's missing a slipper. Please see that he has two slippers."

Louise bobbed her head. "Yes, ma'am."

We continued on. At the end of the hallway we paused before a partially open door. Partially closed door. It can go either way. "I understand Mrs. Papadaki wandered off into the night," I said.

"We're looking into that," Marilyn Tuck responded somewhat grimly. "We have a little problem here, Mr. Sewell. I'm not happy about any of this."

She showed me into a room sufficient in size for a dedicated monk and maybe one or

48

two of his thoughts. The room held a straight-back metal chair and a bed. On the bed, under a sheet, was Spiro's mother. She was lying on her side, her tiny head resting on the pillow, the suggestion from the lay of the sheet being that her knees were drawn up. Marilyn Tuck pulled back the sheet.

I could see the problem immediately. Spiro's mother was lying on her side, her tiny head resting on the pillow, the suggestion from the lay of the sheet being that her knees were drawn up. *That* was the problem. Your classic corpse is naturally stretched out on its back in a simple straight line.

"You see?"

I saw. Spiro's mother was apparently locked in the position in which she had died. Her legs were bent, her shoulders were slightly hunched, her hands were situated in her lap. The fingers of the left hand were curled into an open circle. This, I deduced, must have been where the copy of *Jane* had been tucked.

Her shape was a result of rigor mortis, of course, though in this case an astonishingly swift onset. I leaned over the bed, placing one hand on the woman's hip and the other on her left knee. Even with a fair amount of pressure, the leg didn't budge.

"We tried that already," Marilyn Tuck said. "She's as hard as a rock."

"How did she manage to slip away in the

first place?" I asked.

"I'm afraid I can't give you an answer to that yet. I've received unsatisfactory answers myself. We had what in my opinion was an unacceptable number of agency girls on duty last night."

"Agency girls?"

"Nonregular staff. Temps. You must know this about nursing home facilities. We are chronically short-staffed. We rely on an agency to send us backup. Of course the agency staff is often not familiar with our facility and procedures, and certainly not with the needs of particular patients."

"I see."

"It's a problem shared by all nursing homes. Not just Briarcliff."

"Was one of the agency girls responsible for Mrs. Papadaki?" I asked.

The woman fiddled with her tiny pearls. "*I* am responsible for all of the residents at Briarcliff. I do not shift that responsibility."

I pulled the sheet back up to the corpse's chin. The expression on the face was peaceful. No rictus of pain, a factoid that I'd be happy to pass on to Spiro.

"I'll have the staff clear the hallway for you," Marilyn Tuck said. "We don't like bodies being rolled past the residents. Life is difficult enough for them at this stage." Word on the street is that life is difficult at every stage. But I saw her point. "I'll get Thomas to help you. Did you bring a van or a hearse?"

"Hearse."

"Pull it around to the back. By the kitchen." She gave me her hand along with a surprisingly warm smile. "It was nice to meet you, Mr. Sewell."

"Just call me Hitch if it's all the same."

"Fine. Hitch. And I'm Marilyn."

She turned and retreated down the hallway. Up the hallway. Like the door, it can go either way.

I went outside and pulled the hearse around to the rear of the building. I was met there by Thomas, a sinewy black man in his late fifties. Wild eyes and nicotine-stained teeth. Thomas was wearing a muscle shirt and a cranberry beret. He was also wearing a large leather support belt, which he slapped with both his hands.

"Fucked up my back at BG&E, you know what I'm saying? Thirty years and they bust my ass about disability. I'll tell you something, they don't *know* who they're fucking with." He jabbed a finger into my chest. "I'll take 'em to court. Don't mess with me, I know what I'm doing. I know my rights. I seen shit, you've got no idea. They don't scare me. I can look them right in the eye just like this, just like I'm doing with you, and tell them what they can do with themselves. You hear me? You hear what I'm saying?" He broke into a crazed grin.

I heard. What I heard was that Thomas was a lunatic. With an attitude. He asked me my name, and when I told him he broke into laughter.

"You're all right. Slap it here." His grip was rock hard. "I'm in shape. Don't matter if I'm an old man. BG&E screwed up my back, but I'm in shape. Somebody's got to keep this damn place going, you know what I mean? Bunch of old people here. We got to take care of them."

I pulled the gurney out of the hearse. Thomas held open the back door for me. Lunch was being prepared; the kitchen staff was all wearing paper hats. They could have been surgeons. Surgeons making soup. Thomas and I rolled the gurney down to Mrs. Papadaki's room and loaded her on it. After we got her into the hearse, I remembered my umbrella and popped back inside. On my way down the hallway I paused outside the atrium. I could see Mr. Coleman inside, sitting in one of the wicker chairs. He was wearing both slippers. I was about to continue on when I spotted a small elderly woman seated on a metal glider.

I knew her. I remained in the doorway until I was positive. It had been nearly fifteen years . . . but yes. It was her. Mrs. Mc-Namara. From Cumberland, which is the town in western Maryland where I had attended college. Mrs. McNamara and her husband — everyone knew him simply as Mac — had run the diner directly across from the bus station. Max Diner. The name of the diner pretty much represented the beginning and the end of anything approaching playfulness on the part of old Mac, one of the crankiest and most ill-tempered creatures you'd ever want to meet. Old Mac manned the grill like he was one of the hellslaves in Dante's Inferno, a spatula in one hand, an oversize fork in the other, griping and fuming in his thick canvas apron as he stood all day taking spatters of grease like shrapnel. In all my time at Max Diner, I saw Mac crack a hell of a lot of eggs, but never a single smile.

By contrast, Mrs. McNamara was like something straight out of a Frank Capra movie, all blushing smiles and harmless gossip. A petite woman with bobbed hair and an elfin face, she treated the Frostburg students with a sort of den mother's affection, readily lending her ear to our high melodramas and our tortured romances, our earnest ventures into our rapidly expanding universes. The McNamaras were childless (a rumor of a baby girl frozen to death under freak circumstances) and never once — in my presence at any rate — presented any outward displays of anything approaching affection toward each other. Mac snatched the food orders from his wife as if she were handing him tax bills, and although Mrs. McNamara affected a pose that was designed to make it seem that Mac's gruff exterior was simply the public face of what was really a lovable old alley cat, nobody bought it.

I had occasion once to witness the lovable old alley cat taking a swipe at his wife when he thought nobody was around to see. It was in the greeting card section of the drugstore on Cumberland's main drag. I was just rounding the corner into the aisle; the McNamaras were down at the far end. I recall the oddity of seeing old Mac in his entirety, which is to say he was pretty much burned into my brain as a creature without legs, a large aproned torso hovering behind the kitchen window at the Max Diner grill. Seeing him standing on a pair of legs next to his wife in a drugstore was peculiar enough. Then I realized a good second or two after the fact that what I had just seen him do was cuff Mrs. McNamara on the chin as she was holding a greeting card up for him to see. I turned away. I grabbed the first thing in front of me, which turned out to be a cheap plastic five-inch trophy to the World's Greatest Dad, and gave it the scrutiny deserving of an ancient rune, so shocked was I by what I had just seen. And so embarrassed for the both of them, but mainly for Mrs. McNamara. I would have preferred to disappear altogether, for Mrs. McNamara's sake.

Only later, back in my dorm room, had I replayed the scene in my head and replaced my desire to disappear with a determination to stride down the aisle and demand that Mac apologize to his wife and swear on the spot that he would never do such a thing to her again. I even pictured a confrontation, a scuffle in which I handily put old Mac in his place with a forceful yet jujitsu-like precision, never once really laying a damaging hand on the man. After-the-fact heroics. The simple truth of the matter was that I glanced up from the plastic trophy and made eye contact with Mrs. McNamara, who was putting the greeting card back on the rack. We both looked away immediately, which of course served as an acknowledgment of not only her husband's little act of barbarism but of a failure on either my or Mrs. McNamara's part to hold the man immediately to account.

And now here she was in a nursing home in Lutherville, a hundred and forty miles and two-plus hours from Cumberland. I stepped into the atrium and approached the glider. Of course she had aged. The rose was well gone from her cheeks, which were powder-colored and cracked with spidery lines, almost as if she had pressed her palms against her cheeks and left an impression there. Her hair was thinner, though still cut in a similar bob, and she still had what I would describe as her elfin features, a face that suggests a degree of mirth even when in repose. She had a pillow on her lap, and atop the pillow was an open hardback book. She was hunched slightly forward, aiming a large magnifying glass at the book.

"Mrs. McNamara?"

The woman raised her head to see who was addressing her and the hand holding the magnifying glass moved with it. A gigantic eye blinked at me. "I'm sorry to disturb you," I said. "But it's you, isn't it? Mrs. McNamara?"

She lowered the magnifying glass. Her face was drawn down slightly on the left side. Her eyes were clear, a rich iris blue.

"It's Hitchcock Sewell, Mrs. McNamara. From Frostburg. You probably don't remember me. It was a long time ago."

Her jaw softened and she came up with a petite smile. "Hitchcock . . . Sewell. Of course. I . . . remember you."

Her voice was small, with the faint trace of a flat Appalachian twang. I pulled up an empty wicker chair and sat down. "You're the last person I would have expected to see here, Mrs. McNamara. How in the world are you doing? Small world we've got here, ain't it?"

She set her magnifying glass aside and placed her hand on my knee. "I am not in . . . tip-top shape, Hitchcock. I had . . . a stroke in the . . . spring."

"I'm sorry to hear that."

"I'm sharp as a . . . pin. I just can't . . . talk so well, that's all."

"Well, it's great to see you. This is such a surprise. I didn't know you were in Baltimore. How's old Mac doing?"

"Old Mac is dead."

"He is? I'm sorry to hear that, Mrs. McNamara."

"Don't be." She patted my knee, then moved her hand and placed it atop her book. "Mac . . . died at the diner. Heart . . . attack." She gave a slow, catlike smile. "With a spatula in . . . his hand."

"I'm sorry," I said again. The image flashed again in my head, Mac striking his wife in the drugstore. This time he clutches his heart immediately, falls heavily to his knees and tumbles onto his side.

Mrs. McNamara cocked her head slightly. "Are you . . . visiting someone, Hitchcock?"

I blinked away my fantasy. "I'm not. In fact I'm working. I'm a mortician. I'm afraid I'm here making a pickup."

Mrs. McNamara asked, "Is it Anna?"

"Mrs. Papadaki? Yes, it is."

A low rumble of thunder sounded from beyond the glass. At nearly the same instant, a low rumble of thunder issued from the direction of two men who were playing cards in the corner.

Mrs. McNamara shook her head. "That's

Malcolm . . . Cohen. He does that . . . all day long." She raised her voice in the direction of the card players. "Malcolm? If you could go . . . an hour without farting . . . we would all be very . . . appreciative."

The offending player looked up from his cards. "That was thunder."

Mrs. McNamara threw me a mischievous look. "Malcolm, the sun can be out . . . and the birds can be . . . singing. And if you're in the room . . . there is thunder."

In a rocking chair behind me, a man in a pin-striped suit woke suddenly, with a snort and a bark. "Butter! Who's got fish? Paris!" He rocked, forward but failed in his first attempt to stand up. He gave it another shot, this time making it. He stood tottering. Off in the corner, Malcolm Cohen farted again.

Mrs. McNamara tilted her head to look up at me. "Am I in . . . a loony bin?"

A loud bell sounded suddenly. It sounded like a fire alarm.

No one in the atrium stirred. The bell sounded for fifteen seconds or so then stopped. A pair of aides appeared, clapping their hands like a pair of seals. One of them was the young moonfaced woman. Louise.

"Let's go. Lunchtime!"

Mrs. McNamara edged her way forward on the glider. "Oh . . . joy." I helped her rise. Her head came to just above my elbow. "You had better go . . . Hitchcock. Before they

. . . make you eat the food."

Louise came over to the two of us. "Do you need any help, Peggy?"

"No, dear. Thank you." Mrs. McNamara patted the aide on the arm. "Louise . . . this young . . . gentleman is Hitchcock Sewell. Hitchcock is . . . an old friend of mine."

Louise bounced her smile off me. "Nice to meet you."

"I knew Hitchcock in his . . . youth, Louise. You . . . want to watch out for him."

Louise blushed. "Okay, Peggy. I'll make a note of it."

Before I left I asked Mrs. McNamara if she had any family in town. She said that she didn't.

"I have a sister. She's still in Cumberland. She's not . . . well."

"If there's anything you need, you should give me a call. Let me give you my card."

I pulled out my wallet and placed a card in her hand.

She took a look at it, then gave me a crooked smile. "Don't . . . call me, I'll call you."

I left her. As I passed by the kitchen on my way out the back I spotted Thomas standing next to the sinks. He had one of the cooks cornered. ". . . they don't *know* who they're *messing* with."

I slid in behind the wheel. "All set, Mrs. Papadaki?"

No answer.

There never is.

Damn good thing.

Billie told me when I got back that the medical examiner's office had called to say that the earthly remains of Jake Weisheit wouldn't be ready for pickup until late in the afternoon. You'd think that it would be pretty cut-and-dried. A man with a knife in his back. How much is there to examine? But give that crowd at the ME's office the slightest excuse to weigh organs and go rummaging through stomach contents and they'll leap on the opportunity. In this case, to be fair, they had a number of other homicide victims they were working on. Sundays are no day of rest for coroners in cities like Baltimore. Too many Saturday-night shenanigans bring on a heavy Sunday workload.

Spiro had regained his composure. He had also dressed, which was a nice touch. He was waiting in Billie's apartment when I arrived. He wanted to see his mother immediately. I told him I didn't think that was such a good idea and Billie backed me up. But Spiro insisted.

"At least let me get her inside first," I said.

I went down to the basement and pulled open the garage door. We have a steep driveway ramp down off the street. I backed the hearse down the ramp and into the garage area. Mrs. Papadaki was light enough that I didn't need any assistance getting her onto a gurney and into the embalming room. I set her on the table and just out of curiosity pulled her up into the sitting position. Sure enough, she remained upright.

And that's when Spiro came into the room. He stopped just inside the doorway, his eyes the size of doughnut holes.

"Mama?" The word came out in a tiny voice, like the plaintive bleating of a lamb. An expression of joy trembled on his face.

"No, Spiro, she's not —"

Spiro galloped forward. "Mama!" I made a move to head him off, but a chicken might as well raise its wing against a barreling train. I bounced right off him.

"MAMA!" Spiro threw his arms around the stiff little body on the table. Unfortunately, he wasn't alert to the precariousness of his mother's balance and his knee rammed into one of her legs even as his arms were sweeping around the little woman. Mrs. Papadaki's body pitched off the table and tumbled to the floor.

Spiro turned white. His face contorted into childlike confusion. Again came the bleat. "Mama?"

Billie appeared in the doorway. She immediately took in the situation.

"Spiro!" Her tone was firm. *"Spiro!"* She raised an arm, pointing her finger back in the

61

direction from which she had just come. "Spiro, leave this room immediately!"

Spiro's eyes were wet "B-but —"

"Out. Now!"

He obeyed. Head low, he marched past Billie and out of the room. Billie remained in the doorway as Spiro's heavy steps sounded on the stairs. I fetched Mrs. Papadaki off the floor and returned her to the table. Upright, in the seated position.

Billie was impressed. "Well, look at that."

I headed home and noodled around with the Sunday crossword puzzle awhile (a seven-letter word for "loblolly"?), spent an hour on the couch with Theodore Roosevelt, then fell asleep. When I woke up I took the day's second shower, girded myself once more for the foul weather and headed out to the medical examiner's to fetch the body of Jake Weisheit. I stashed him in the basement, then went over to the Oyster for some darts and dinner. It was a Sunday night. All quiet on the eastern front. I gave Sally behind the bar a rundown on my exciting day, then got into an argument with a man named Snead about the death penalty. I'm against it, as I think all undertakers and other civilized human beings ought to be. Snead was for it. He made all the usual arguments, including the good-sounding ones, but he failed to win me over. Snead got a little hot on the subject, but I remained cool. Best way to win an argument.

Snead finally gave up on me. Before I left, Sally lined up three tall glasses of water on the bar. She made me drink them before I left. Sloshing, I headed home early to have a very serious talk with my pillow. It seemed glad to see me.

Chapter Four

God knows why I had such a restful sleep, but I did. I had three fantastic dreams in a row and woke up with the answer to a trivia question that had been nagging me for a week. I pulled the phone onto the bed and dialed Julia's number. She didn't answer, but her machine did.

"Tim Considine," I said into the phone, then hung up.

I fell back on the pillows. Like an insanely misshapen sun, Alcatraz's head rose into sight at the edge of the mattress and hovered there. I can never tell what sort of sleep my dog has had, there's simply too much sadness built into his face. I reached over and tugged the loose skin around his mouth into what passes for a smile in a human, but the results on the hound were pretty grisly.

I got up and pulled on a pair of jeans and a sweatshirt, then double-knotted a pair of ragged sneakers. Alcatraz and I hit the street.

The rain had passed some time during the night and left my corner of the world freshly scrubbed. The slightest nip in the air felt damn close to bracing and I broke into a light trot. I took a left on Thames and went as far as Durham Street, making a large loop to come back around to Eastern Avenue, then zigzagged the narrow streets back toward my place. Alcatraz was thrilled with the distance covered. He's a bachelor, after all, and it gave him the opportunity to leave his card at some less accustomed sites. He had a brief engagement with a Sheltie at Choptank Court, but I could see he was being toyed with, even if he couldn't. Scotty and Nance, the antiques lesbians who run their shop catty-corner from ours, were just opening as Alcatraz and I came around the final corner. Scotty waved; Nance pumped her fist in the air. Sunlight glinted off the stained glass of Saint Teresa's as we passed and hit me in the eyes with a sharp stab. I slowed, as did the dog, and pulled up at my front door, bent forward, hands on thighs, greedily gulping air.

There was a green Volvo parked at the curb. From the corner of my eye I saw a person getting out from behind the wheel. It took me a moment to register. Polly Weisheit. Her unruly hair was tied back with a red silk scarf. A pair of large silver hoops dangled from her ears. One of them caught the sun as she flipped the car door closed.

"There's been a problem," she said. "I'm afraid I can't let you bury Jake."

She handed the newspaper to me across the table. Stoney had just delivered my coffee and I welcomed it with a splash of milk. At the counter, someone was trying to pay for a pastry with a hundred-dollar bill. They were meeting stiff resistance. Polly Weisheit and I were seated at a small round table next to the window. Smoke from the plants across the harbor was curling into the sky in a van Gogh kind of way.

"I just want you to know that I didn't give them your name," Polly said. "I didn't talk to anyone but the police."

Jake Weisheit's murder had made the front page of the *Sun*, below the fold, alongside a story about a painted elephant being used as part of a protest at the Purdue chicken farms in Delaware. There was a photograph of the elephant being led by the trunk by a person in a rubber chicken suit. I had to figure the story would siphon plenty of readers from the article about the murder in Baltimore County. It would have siphoned me, were it not for my vested interest.

The article about Jake Weisheit's murder made a jump to the local section. I'm not sure where the painted elephant story jumped to. My name didn't appear in the story until after the jump.

Police have questioned Hitchcock Sewell, 34, coproprietor of Sewell and Sons Funeral Home, located in Fells Point. Neighbors reported seeing a hearse departing the Weisheit residence shortly before the police arrived. License plate identification, along with eyewitness descriptions of the driver of the hearse, led police investigating the murder to Mr. Sewell. Although no clear explanation has been provided for the Fells Point undertaker's presence at the Weisheit residence, a police spokesman says that Mr. Sewell is cooperating fully. The spokesman denies that Mr. Sewell is currently under investigation in the matter of Mr. Weisheit's death.

I folded the paper in half and set it on the table. "It says that I'm not currently under investigation."

"I saw that."

" 'Not currently.' Funny how that sounds."

"I'm sorry."

"It's not your fault. It's your boyfriend's fault."

"I wish you wouldn't call him that."

"But that's what he is, isn't he?"

"I suppose. Technically speaking."

"That's all I'm doing. Speaking technically."

"Are you trying to rub it in? I've got a murdered husband here, but I'm not exactly getting much in the way of sympathy." She scooted her chair closer to the table and jabbed her finger at the newspaper. "You see how they're playing this. Wicked wife and her little boyfriend."

"That's what I just said. Boyfriend."

"Well, I don't like it." She jabbed the paper again. The jump section included a picture of Jake Weisheit. It was taken at the beach. He was standing in the surf, holding a surf rod, posing with a fish.

Polly Weisheit jabbed her finger against Weisheit's thorax. "I didn't murder my husband. I want to tell you that right now. Obviously things weren't going all that well with Jake and me, but I didn't kill him. That's absurd."

"You can't blame the police for looking into it."

"Because I was having an affair? Let me tell you, there would be a hell of a lot of dead spouses in this world if every one of them that was being cheated on was murdered."

"But it happens."

"Of course it happens. I know that. It didn't happen here. Jake and I had a lousy marriage. That's just a fact of life. Take a look around. It's not that rare. I admit it. I stepped out. I cheated on him. We had grown apart. Plus Jake was withdrawn. He just didn't have any interest in me. I'm sorry, but I'm a person who likes a little affection."

"This is really none of my business, Mrs. Weisheit."

"For God's sake, it's Polly. We're wrapped

up in a murder together. I think we can go on a first-name basis."

"I'm not wrapped up in a murder," I said.

She smiled at me across the table. "Don't you read the paper?"

I picked up the paper and frowned at it. "Nice picture. Where is this? Rehoboth?"

"Bethany Beach. That was taken last year. Jake's parents have a place down there. Well, his mother does. Jake's father died last Christmas. Every single summer we make the trek. Family tradition."

"You make it sound like a chore. You don't like the beach?"

"Sure. The beach is fine. I just don't like being a guest when I'm on vacation."

"Did you give the paper this picture?"

"Me? No. They didn't even ask me. Jake's mother gave it to them. Evelyn loves that picture. Her prince at play. It's Evelyn, by the way, who doesn't want you handling Jake's funeral."

I set the paper down. "Appearances?"

"Exactly. With your name in the paper like that . . . Evelyn was appalled when I told her I had asked you and your aunt to handle the arrangements. You don't know Evelyn Weisheit. *There's* a woman who knows what being appalled is all about. She was furious with me."

"I understand the decision. Don't worry about it."

"Evelyn tried to yank the entire funeral from me. It's so typical of her. But I'll be damned. It's bad enough everyone knowing I was cheating on Jake. Now I'm supposed to step aside like I don't really care at all?" It seemed to me she had just told me that she didn't really care at all, but I said nothing. "It's just Evelyn's way of trying to squeeze me out of the picture," she went on, picking up her coffee cup. "I don't squeeze easy."

The widow Weisheit and I headed over to the funeral home to make arrangements to have Jake's body passed on to a less tainted funeral home, of which our choices in the greater Baltimore metropolitan area were nearly boundless. I introduced Polly to Billie, who smothered her with her special brand of nonunctuous sympathy. To my surprise, Polly broke into a mild crying jag under Billie's ministrations. Billie sent me off to get a glass of water, and when I returned, the two had moved into our small chapel and were seated in the rear pew. Polly's faucets were still running and her makeup was running along with them. Her eyes glistened with tears as she took the glass of water from me and proceeded to gulp it.

"Slowly," Billie cooed, and the tear-dappled face beamed appreciatively.

"This is . . . this is the first time I've cried," Polly said. "I'm a horrible person."

Billie patted her hand. "It can take time to

70

sink in, dear. It's natural."

Polly asked if she could see her husband.

"He's gruesome," I said bluntly. "He's had his autopsy. We haven't done any work on him."

The edge came back into her voice. "He's my husband. I'd like to see him."

Keep the customer happy; that's the rule. The three of us went down to the basement. Polly let out a cry when she entered the embalming room. It wasn't because of her husband.

"Shit." I hurried to find a sheet to drape over Mrs. Papadaki, who was seated upright in a metal chair against the wall.

Polly was hugging herself "Who's *that?*"

Billie answered. "That's Mrs. Papadaki." She turned to me. "Hitchcock, we have to dress and deliver ASAP. Doodle brought over a nice dress this morning."

Polly crossed the room and slowly approached the table where her husband was laid out. Thankfully he was covered with a plastic sheet. I looked at Polly.

"Are you sure?"

She set a hand on my arm and nodded. I pulled the sheet down no farther than the chin and tucked it there. Polly gasped and turned away. Billie led her from the room.

George Fink was more than happy to inherit the Weisheit funeral. Billie had run into

71

George and his wife recently and she suggested I give them a call.

"I read about you in the paper this morning," George said. "I said to Happy, 'Look here, Happy, old Hitch Sewell is picking them up while they're still warm.' What are you doing these days, Hitch, running around with a police radio? You're always up to something, aren't you?"

"That's me," I said blandly. "Always up to something."

George wanted to know if I'd be able to run Jake's body out to him. "Happy's got the hearse up at Druid Ridge. I could come pick up the body later in the afternoon, but I imagine the widow wants to get her husband settled as soon as possible."

I looked out my office door. The widow was seated on a padded bench in the front hallway, talking softly into a cell phone.

"I can bring him out to you, George," I said. "It'll be in about an hour or so."

"Good man, good man. I'll be here. I've got something I want to show you when you get here. You're going to love it."

"Can't wait."

I hung up. Polly Weisheit was too far away and was speaking too softly for me to make out the details of her conversation, which some would have me believe was none of my business anyway. I came out of my office and stepped into Parlor One. We have two parlors separated by a hard plastic accordion curtain on runners. We're able to handle two events at once. For the overflow crowd events, we pull back the curtain. In the corner I saw something you never want to see in a funeral home. It's not great in a regular home, either. It was a rat. Baltimore is the unofficial national headquarters for the Norway rat. They got here by stowing away on ships and then running down the guylines when the ships were tied up at port. At least that's what I read somewhere. This particular rat was over near the organ. I took a few menacing steps toward it. The rat could not have been less impressed. I raised my arms like a scarecrow and ran forward. This got its attention. The rat darted toward the altar, then took a sharp left and scampered up the aisle.

Polly appeared in the doorway. She stood unfazed as the rat scampered right past her feet. She indicated her cell phone.

"That was the headmaster at Martin's school. Martin's my son. He insisted on going to school today. He's trying to pretend that everything's normal."

"Is he all right?"

"If you consider breaking someone's nose with a lacrosse stick all right, I suppose so." Polly was carrying a large black leather bag. She dropped the phone back into her bag. "The mood I'm in right now, I could break *his* nose."

"I'll put in a vote that you don't do that."

"Yeah." She hoisted the bag higher on to her shoulder. "Look, would you do me a favor? I really don't want to deal with this Mr. Fink right now. Could you work out the details with him and then let me know? We've got insurance. It'll cover most of this. I've never arranged a funeral before. Just a simple casket. The basics. No frills. We'll hold the service at Roland Park Presbyterian. I'll handle that part. But I really can't deal with the rest of it. Could you do that? I'll pay you, of course. Here."

She pulled a checkbook from her purse, ripped a check from it, then tore the check in half. She handed one of the halves to me. "There's my phone number. Call me to-night." A muffled electronic tune began play-ing in her bag. "Yellow Submarine." She gave me a beleaguered look. "I'm ignoring that. Good-bye."

The big bundle of tied-back hair flounced left and right like a pom-pom. The front door shut behind it. I turned to see Billie coming down the stairs.

"I just got a call from Doodle. You're not going to believe this."

Chapter Five

Fink's Funeral Home is located on Joppa Road, between a Burger King and a sad-looking A-frame called the Chinese Pagoda. The Chinese Pagoda sells porcelain knick-knacks, shiny satin clothes, twenty-pound bags of rice, and wicker furniture of questionable virility. In fact as I pulled into Fink's parking lot I watched a wicker chaise collapse while being loaded into the trunk of a car.

I pulled around the side. A part of the parking area had been chewed up, presumably by the miniature backhoe that was parked nearby. George came out to meet me. George Fink has a long thin face and a stubborn insistence on a comb-over. He's in his early fifties. He is active on the board of the Maryland State Funeral Directors Association, an organization that has never really captured my imagination.

"Nice to see you, Hitch." George handed me a dead hand and showed me how well he'd been looking after his teeth. "What happened to your cheek?"

"Nothing. I got hit by a tambourine."

He gave me his best sly look. It wasn't all that great. "Chasing after those Gypsy girls again, Hitchcock?"

"Right. The Gypsy girls. So what's going on here, George? You putting in speed bumps?"

"That's what I want to show you. But why don't we take care of business first?"

Jake Weisheit was packed in a cardboard casket, the kind we use for cremations. As we moved the box onto George's gurney, George asked me about the upcoming funeral directors' convention. "So, are we going to see you in Spokane?"

"You'll have to look real hard, George," I said.

"Doggone it, Hitchcock, I know we're going to get you to a national convention one of these days. There's nothing wrong with mixing business with a little pleasure." He gave me a conspiratorial wink. "These things are a lot racier than you might imagine."

"What does that mean, George? Have you got pretty women popping out of caskets?"

His face fell. "Somebody told you." As fast as it fell, he broke into a huge grin. "Gotcha, didn't I?"

We rolled Jake Weisheit inside and directly to George's embalming room. It was neat as a pin. Maybe neater. As modern funeral homes go, Billie and I are a little frayed. But we're also inexpensive. Add to which, I vow never to resort to a comb-over. George and I lifted Jake Weisheit from the box and set him on the metal table.

"He was knifed. Am I right?" George asked.

"You are right."

George assessed the corpse. "I had a gun-shot to the face a few weeks ago. Young fellow. In his twenties. Happy and I really had our hands full. I have to say, I was real proud of the results. We took before-and-afters. You take before-and-afters, don't you?"

I told him I didn't.

"You should start. We've been taking them for almost twenty years. That's a lot of photo albums. Happy bought a scanner a couple of months ago. That's our next project, to scan them all."

I didn't want to ask why. George took hold of Jake Weisheit's chin and turned the head slightly.

"Do you mind my asking you, Hitch, what *were* you doing there? The story in the *Sun* was vague."

"Just call it bad timing."

"You don't want to talk about it, do you?"

"Not really."

"Are you in any kind of trouble, Hitch-cock?"

"I don't think so, George. I could have managed without seeing my name in the paper, but I suspect I'll live."

"Good philosophy. You're a smart cookie, Hitchcock."

The smart cookie followed George to his office. The carpeting was a seaweedy green. The walls were mint. I explained to George that Polly Weisheit had asked me to speak for her on the matter of the arrangements. George was disappointed. He loves the sales pitch. George has a video he likes to start off with. I've seen it. It's a horribly dated organ-drenched piece featuring three actors posing as a bereaved family (father, son, and daughter), along with a real live Omaha funeral director named Edward Fleming. In my view it is dreadful. Show me that video and I'll stow my loved one below my backyard rosebushes on a moonless night. I've heard good things about Edward Fleming personally, but on camera he is as stiff as the unseen corpse. And it doesn't help that anyone with even a passing familiarity with supermarket tabloids will recognize the actor portraying the son as the same actor who several years hence would blow his seemingly rock-solid sitcom career with a series of scandals involving Filipino housekeepers. It's a cheesy video, but George sticks by it nonetheless. Obviously, with me acting as Polly Weisheit's agent, George couldn't even approach the VCR, let alone launch into his spiel. It was clear I had ruined his fun.

He perked up though when he took me outside to show me his latest project. On the far side of the building, a large hole had been punched in the side of the building. A carpenter wearing a Walkman was framing the hole. I had read about this in one of my trade publications, but hadn't been aware that Fink's was in the vanguard.

"Drive-by viewing," George announced with so much pride he had to take his glasses off and wipe them with a handkerchief. "Too uncomfortable to meet with the family? On a tight schedule? Have a plane to catch? Or maybe you're not even acquainted with the deceased but you're just one of the curious. Now you can swing by, pay your respects, and if you want, sign the electronic guest book. That's going to be right there." He pointed to a stick stuck in the dirt. "Every home that's installed one so far has reported increased traffic. Happy and I are very excited. We should be up and running by Thanksgiving."

George walked me back to the hearse and let me squeeze his dead hand again. "Think about Spokane, Hitchcock. It's not too late."

I got behind the wheel, took a U-turn out of George's lot and drove up to the Drive-Thru window at the Burger King. I ordered a shake. The girl at the window had a couple of nose rings and a bad case of acne. Bad case of indifference, too.

But she was *alive!*

Sam showed up just after Billie and I had gotten Mrs. Papadaki dressed. Billie had given the old gal's hair a rinse and a blow-dry and had played with the face a little bit. The shoes Doodle had brought over seemed awfully boxy and in fact were too big. We wrapped Mrs. Papadaki's feet in adhesive gauze and the shoes went on snugly. Nobody would know the difference.

Ever.

"She looks like she's waiting for a train," Sam remarked astutely when he came down to the basement.

The three of us debated the best way to transport Mrs. Papadaki down the street to her son's place. Normally our corpse would be in a casket and there would be no question. But Spiro didn't want his mother in a casket. He had other plans. Putting Mrs. Papadaki sideways on a gurney, now that she was all gussied up and blown-dry, seemed a bit awkward. The obvious answer remained unspoken for several minutes.

It was Billie who found the right way to put it. "Oh, let's make a memory."

Sam is the size of a wall. Strong like bull. He had no problem positioning himself behind the chair holding Mrs. Papadaki and lifting it up to his chest. As a precaution, we strapped the corpse to the chair, one strap around the thighs, the other across the rib cage.

Decorum demanded that we cover Mrs. Papadaki in some fashion. We weren't going to waltz her down the street like she was a parade float. Billie fetched a plaid flannel sheet from upstairs.

"The hair," she worried. "The hair will flatten."

Not a problem. I positioned myself to the side of Mrs. Papadaki and lowered the sheet over her, holding it up slightly to keep it from actually touching the bouffant.

Sam and I made our way cautiously up the driveway ramp. With Billie on point, the three of us proceeded down the street. Nance and Scotty came out of their shop and watched as we passed along. Sam's view was impeded by the tent-like sheet, so his steps were slow and cautious, not unlike a bride's stuttering progress down the aisle.

"We should have gotten you a kazoo," I said to Billie.

"Hush."

Father Ted was sitting on the front steps of St. Teresa's, clipping a cigar. He rose solemnly as we passed and lazily made the sign of the cross with the cigar, then sat back down.

Spiro and Doodle were waiting at the front door. Spiro stepped forward as we approached. He was dressed in a black suit and a black tie and had on a too-small fedora. He was one pair of sunglasses shy of looking like a Blues Brother. We stopped at the curb and Spiro took hold of Billie's hand and leaned down, touching his forehead to it.

"Spiro?" Billie said gently after ten or so seconds had elapsed. "Let's get your mother inside where it's comfortable."

Spiro released her hand and stood aside. He covered his heart with both his hands and looked on forlornly as Sam and I stepped up on the curb.

Inside, Sam set the chair down gently in the middle of the floor. Spiro had prepared an armchair for his mother and outfitted it like a shrine, with candles burning and several vases of flowers. With an unintentional flourish — but necessary in order to clear the fragile hairdo — I whipped off the sheet like a magician revealing the vanished assistant.

Spiro wailed.

Chapter Six

I had dinner that evening with an extraordinary love bucket.

"Did you do something to your breasts?" I asked.

"No."

"Your hair?"

"No."

"Your mouth?"

"I treated a cold sore a week ago." Julia placed a finger on her lower lip, then twisted it like a key and gave me a Kewpie smile.

"It must be your buckskins," I said. "You look good enough to drag across the plains in a covered wagon. What did you do, just have a tryout for *Annie Get Your Gun*?"

Julia fingered the suede tassels at her breasts. "Do you like it or do you think it's silly?"

"Both."

We were at Tio Pepe's. Center Stage was running a production of *Hamlet*, and Julia had a date after the show with Mr. Hamlet himself. His name is Hans. Hans was actually Danish — considered one of the country's top actors — which is where my lovely ex-wife fit in. Julia is a painter. Her standing in the art world is way up there, but nowhere more so than in Scandinavia. No one can really say why. Julia and Hans were naturals for a high-profile fling, at least as long as the production was in Baltimore.

Our waitress came over and recited the specials. There were quite a few of them and the young woman made it through with only a couple of glitches. I took the herb-encrusted Spanish mackerel "that comes with a bombardment of flaming olive brandy." Julia went for a super succulent veal. No surprise there. I ordered an old-fashioned. Julia smacked her lips and the word *Sancerre* appeared.

"I think it's funny that you drink old-fashioneds," Julia said after the waitress had gone off to fetch our drinks.

"Because it's so old-fashioned?"

"Exactly."

A young boy came by with a basket of bread and Julia put her eyes all over him.

"They can cure this disease, you know," I said.

"They wouldn't dare."

While we waited for our drinks, Julia chattered a bit about Hans and his Hamlet. She said he was very dark in the role, which of course is as it should be. Hamlet lite is no Hamlet at all. I asked her about the Ophelia, and she told me that Ophelia was very dark as well.

"Gertrude?"

"Dark."

"The uncle?"

"Yes. Quite dark too."

"That's a hell of a family, those Hamlets," I remarked. I promised her I would catch the show before it closed.

Our drinks arrived and Julia proposed a toast. "To my dear friend and his old-fashioned ways."

"I'm not going to drink to that," I said. "That sounds like something you'd say at a seventieth birthday party."

"All right. May you live to an old-fashioned age."

"That's a little better. And may you dazzle till you drop."

We clinked glasses. My drink went directly to my brain and loosened a few knots up there. Roses bloomed on Julia's cheeks and she broke out a fresh smile.

I knew that Julia never keeps up on the news (her long running gag is to dash into a room and cry out, "They've shot Mr. Lincoln!"), so I told her that had she read the paper that morning she would have seen my name there.

"Did you start a war?"

I gave her the rundown on the Jake Weisheit fiasco. For me, it was a fiasco. For Jake Weisheit, it was obviously something altogether deeper. Julia rested her chin on a bridge of talented fingers and listened without comment. Some men crumble under this gaze, but I've had a lifetime under my belt. So to speak.

"The moment I heard Sisco's voice on the phone I should have hung right up and gone back to sleep," I said. "I shouldn't have let him drag me into it."

Julia agreed. "Sisco has always struck me as the type who thinks danger is fun. Until he's in it, of course. I suppose he has something of an outlaw complex, don't you think?"

"Sounds about right."

"But you don't think he actually killed Weisheit, do you? I can see Sisco waving a big knife around, but I can't actually see him planting it."

" 'Planting it.' That's good. No, I don't see it either. But then I guess you could say that about most of the people who end up killing people. You could say it about me."

"You're not a killer, honey. You're a lover."

"That's a sweet cliché, Jules, for which I thank you. If you'd read the paper this morning you wouldn't have gotten quite the same sentiment."

"They're not accusing *you*, are they?"

"The story doesn't outright accuse me. But it dangles the possibility."

"Why in the world would you want to murder Jake Weisheit?" Julia said. "Did you even know Jake Weisheit?"

"No."

"So that's ridiculous."

"Tell it to the judge."

Julia's eyes flashed. "Send him my way. I'll tell him."

Our salads arrived. Mesclun salad. Hopping with mandarin orange slices, walnut chunks and curls of red onion. The vinaigrette disagreed with my tongue, but there wasn't a whole lot I could do about it.

Julia asked, "So is she pretty?"

I had a mouthful of greens and disagreeable vinaigrette. I waved my fork in the air as I chewed and swallowed. "Is *who* pretty?"

"Who else? The widow. She must be attractive. Sisco only hits on attractive women." Julia batted her big browns.

I shrugged. "She's attractive."

Julia set her fork down. "Uh-oh."

"Uh-oh what?"

"Uh-oh, you simply said, 'She's attractive.' Like that's all you're going to say on the subject. Which means there's more to say on the subject, but you don't want to say it."

"And you received your doctorate in psychology from . . ."

"From Hitchcock U. I know you too well. Less is always more. What aren't you telling me?"

"Nothing. She's a moderately attractive forty-year-old mother and housewife —"

"*Ex*-housewife."

"Ex-housewife."

"Tall? Short? Just right?"

"Who are you, Goldilocks?"

"Sisco certainly didn't see her as a dried-up old housewife."

"I didn't say she was old or dried up. She's an attractive woman. She's got that frizzy hair that doesn't do a lot for me, but generally speaking she's not the Elephant Man."

Julia dipped a finger into her Sancerre, then into her mouth. "Do you think she had something to do with her husband's murder?"

"I don't know. She's got a hard shell. Billie was able to squeeze some tears from her, but for the most part she sounds more irritated with the whole thing than anything else. Not a lot of remorse going on. At least not on the surface. Of course she freely admits that she and her husband weren't exactly sailing on the Love Boat."

"So when you went out to the house and her husband was lying on the kitchen floor, she wasn't crying crocodile tears?"

"She was pretty blasé. Certainly no tears. She claimed she was still sort of dopey on sleeping pills, but who knows? That could have just been a story."

"You mean, to cover the fact that she wasn't freaking out about her husband's murder? Why not just freak out? Put on the appropriate act."

"Maybe she's not a very good actor." I stabbed at my salad. "Or maybe her heart is really as cold as ice."

"You sure know how to pick them."

"I haven't picked a damn thing."

"You're right. Trouble simply knows how to find you."

"And I know how to send it packing. I'm not getting involved in this thing. I took Jake Weisheit's body over to Fink's this afternoon and that's that. I'm done with it."

Julia picked up her wineglass and gave me a smile. "And I'm going to die a virgin."

Our meals arrived and we shelved the subject. My bombarded mackerel was superb. So was Julia's small talk. By the end of dessert Julia still had an hour to kill before going off to be a stage-door Johnny. We strolled over to Charles Street and to the Peabody Bookstore Café. Mr. Wow had just started his act and Julia and I took a table off to the side of the small stage and ordered some cappuccinos. While the younger Mr. Wow maybe deserved the name, the late-model version . . . well, he wasn't even pulling rabbits out of his hat. His animal was a little hamster, which was so clearly tucked into a narrow tube in the magician's sleeve as to render the moment almost laughable. That said, Mr. Wow had a warm and comfortable stage presence. His jokes were old, but he didn't pretend that they weren't. I've known Mr. Wow since I was a kid. He used to make regular appearances on my father's Saturday-morning kids' show on WBAL and irregular appearances at our house for dinner. There was a series of Mrs. Wows, but they never seemed to stick around very long. My father said Mr. Wow simply chose poorly. My mother's perspective was more shrewd. "He makes them disappear."

Mr. Wow had just finished pulling a bouquet of paper flowers from a seemingly transparent fish bowl. He plucked a wriggling fish from the petals — it was clearly rubber — and pretended to swallow it. The rubber fish ran down his coat sleeve and dropped to the floor.

Mr. Wow raised a snowy eyebrow. "For my next trick I'm going to make the Taj Mahal turn purple."

He raised his arms in the air and stood motionless for about twenty seconds, glanced to his left and right with an impish look on his face, then dropped his arms. "There, I did it. You'll have to go see for yourselves."

"Mr. Wow is one sexy beast," Julia said, joining in the applause. Up on stage, Mr. Wow had started pulling a multicolored scarf out of his coat pocket. This would take all night.

I dropped Julia off at Center Stage just as the crowd was pouring out onto Calvert

Street. " 'The potent poison quite o'er-crows my spirit,' " I said.

Julia shouldered open the door. "I love it when you talk that way."

I drove back to Fells Point and found a parking spot down the block from my building. I peeked into the first floor window. Mrs. Papadaki was still seated in the armchair, aglow from the nearby candles. The rest of the lights in the house were off. Even to someone who does what I do for a living, it was creepy. No question.

As I turned from the window I was aware of a man standing on the sidewalk, about ten feet away. I hadn't noticed him as I'd approached the building. The man was wearing some sort of brimmed hat; I wasn't able to make out much of a face as he approached. For a moment I thought it might be Father Ted. The build was about right. Plus Father Ted owns a fairly dilapidated fisherman's hat to which he is tenaciously loyal.

It wasn't Father Ted. I would have much preferred it to have been Father Ted. Father Ted might have asked me if I wanted to pop down to the Oyster for a nightcap. Or he might have simply leaned up against a parked car and fired up a stogie and launched into one of his obtuse rants about determinism.

What he wouldn't have done was come forward in a sudden rush. He wouldn't have muttered, "Keep the hell away from Polly

Weisheit," nor would he have followed this with two extremely hard fists to my ribs and some sort of bogus karate-style chop to the side of my neck.

I dropped to my knees and doubled over. My lungs felt contracted to the size of a squeeze toy. My attacker moved on and I looked up to see him stepping swiftly down the sidewalk. No telltale limp. No squeaky shoe. No wallet stuffed with ID falling unnoticed from his pocket. He reached the corner, passing in and out of the cone of light from the streetlamp. The coat he was wearing was green. The pants were beige.

Or off-white.

Cream.

Stone.

Bone.

Oyster.

You tell me.

He was gone. A couple passed into the cone of light. They stopped smack in the middle and wrapped themselves in a long and apparently satisfying smooch.

As if someone had flipped a switch, my breath rushed back to me. I gasped and took a greedy lungful of air. A searing pain sliced through my chest.

Chapter Seven

They were lined up in the street. I spotted Big Sally, chatting animatedly with Joan Sandusky and Mitzi Weingarten. Tony Marino was there, looking, as always, on the verge of tears. I saw Scotty but I didn't see Nance. Probably holding down the shop. Katrina Pelopannos, the best belly dancer the Acropolis has had in a long, long time, was there, wearing a coat that went down to her ankles. Her oil-black hair tumbled in lavish waves down her back. Johnny Pepper, Katrina's morose boyfriend, was with her, fidgeting from foot to foot, still failing to grasp that he was one of the luckiest people on earth. A few people behind Johnny and Katrina stood Carol Shipley, formerly of Heyhauge, Maine, packed into a tight black dress and smoking like a one-woman factory. The line stretched halfway down the block, all waiting to get into Spiro and Doodle's.

I was sleepy and cranky from a lousy night in the rack. That's two of the dwarves right there, isn't it? Maybe not. I can never quite nail those guys down. I had banished Alcatraz from the bed, the better to thrash about. My entire chest felt like it was off its hinges and hanging poorly. I couldn't even enjoy my shower; the jets were too frantic. When I tried to raise the bar of soap above my waist I saw stars.

I dressed with geriatric speed, then chewed a couple of aspirin and called my doctor. His receptionist told me that he was with a patient. The receptionist's name is Donna. Life has not treated Donna kindly. Her first husband died in a fluke accident (he and Donna had been tug-of-warring a stubborn vacuum cleaner hose extension, and when it suddenly came loose, Donna's husband had back-pedaled right out the window, thirty-two flights above Cathedral Street), and her second husband ran off just after Donna's fiftieth birthday to marry a young slip of a thing and start a new family. Donna reminded me that I was to remain on the lookout for disoriented widowers, and I promised to steer any candidates in her direction.

I pocketed a few more aspirin and took Alcatraz downstairs, prevailing upon Tony Marino to take him on his rounds for me. I told Tony he could drop the dog off at Billie's. I moved up the line and asked Sally what was going on.

"It's Spiro's mother. The word's out."

"The word? It's a small dead woman seated in a chair." Mitzi Weingarten giggled at this. Mitzi Weingarten giggles at everything

94

that comes out of my mouth. I could recite the nutritional information off a box of Grape-Nuts to Mitzi Weingarten and the woman would be in stitches.

"Where's Darryl?" I asked Joan Sandusky. "I've never known him to pass up the chance to see a dead person."

"Darryl's in school. But he came by earlier."

"Of course."

I didn't have it in me to work the whole crowd. Luckily my car was in the opposite direction from the line. As I approached it, I discovered that I had forgotten to grab the keys. I continued on and circled the block and phoned Billie from the corner across from the funeral home.

"Long story," I said. "Could you throw me down the keys to the hearse?"

Billie appeared at the window and tossed the keys. The pain in my chest kept me fairly statue-like. The keys bounced off my shoulder and — some days we're lucky — dropped right into my hand.

The hearse was low on gas, so I filled the tank at the Crown station on Caroline Street. Two black girls around eleven or twelve came over while I was gassing the beast.

"There a dead person in there?"

"Not right now," I said.

"You bury people?"

"I do."

"You *like* it?"

"You have no idea."

Giggles. "You look like a movie star." More giggles.

"You think so?"

"Yeah, I do."

"What movie star do you think I look like?"

"I don't know . . . *Whoopi Goldberg!*" They threw their skinny arms together and gyrated with laughter. I got the nozzle back on the pump and screwed on the gas cap.

"You're cute, mister," one of the girls said. "You got a girlfriend?"

"Not at the moment."

"Maybe *I* can be your girlfriend."

"Maybe you can. What's your name?"

"Halo. And this is Bridget."

"Hello, Halo. Hello, Bridget."

"If you're going to be my boyfriend you can't bury people no more. I don't like that."

"That's my job," I said. "That's how I earn my money. You don't want a boyfriend who doesn't have any money, do you? How am I going to buy you nice things and take you off to Paris if I don't have any money?"

The girls went nose to nose and pulled long faces. Halo cried out, *"Paris?"* and the two screamed and ran off. They stopped at the curb and Halo called out, "Hey!" She puckered her lips and made a loud kissing sound. The two shrieked again and continued running down the block.

It was bruised ribs, two of them possibly fractured.

"Does it hurt when I do this?" The doctor did *that* and I saw more stars. "How about this?"

"Yes, that hurts too."

"No sex," the doctor said.

"No, not even a suggestion. The guy just punched me and walked off."

"I meant no sex for the short term. No strenuous activities. That includes heavy lifting, Hitchcock. As in dead weight, if you catch my meaning. I don't want you hoisting corpses around without someone assisting you."

We can land a man on the moon (a man and a little *car*) and we can split atoms practically with our eyes closed, but present the gurus of modern technology a fluff ball like a couple of fractured ribs and they're trumped. My doctor as much as admitted that it was all for show as he wrapped my chest several times in a large bandage. Since I was already in his office he thumped my back, rummaged in my ears, blinded me with a pin light and made me pee into a cup. I had an aspirin in my pocket and considered dissolving it into the pee cup, just out of malice, but then I remembered that I am not by nature malicious. I stopped to chat with Donna for a few minutes as I was leaving.

The doctor came out of his office with a folder. "Remember. No sex."

Donna delivered me a Cheshire grin. "Join the club."

Yes, I was curious as to who had attacked me. I had plenty of clues. Green jacket, colorless pants, a hat, and he knew Polly Weisheit. One approach would be to visit all the clothing stores in and around Baltimore and see if the salespeople could recall a male customer purchasing any of the various items of clothing any time in the past — oh, I don't know — five, ten years?

I took another approach. I'm sure that Julia would call it old-fashioned of me to describe a person as comely, but that was the first word that came to my mind when Polly Weisheit's door opened and I found myself confronted with a young woman of about eighteen or nineteen (if I were truly old-fashioned I'd simply call her a girl). She was blond and brown-eyed, with perfect skin and a wary look on her pretty face. There was a tortoiseshell clip in her hair. She was in jeans and a brushed denim Ponderosa jacket, with the sleeves pulled back to the elbows. She was wearing no makeup and in my opinion didn't need any. Did I mention that she was comely?

"Can I help you?" Her eyes flicked past

98

me and locked on the hearse parked in the driveway. She darkened. "Is that my father?"

I glanced over my shoulder. "Oh. That? No, it's . . . my car was unavailable. I'm sorry, I wasn't even thinking. My name is Hitchcock Sewell."

"I'm Jennifer."

"You're Polly's daughter?"

"Yes, I am. Can I help you with something?"

The eyes were a soft caramel. She was barefoot. Narrow at the waist.

My ribs ached.

"I was hoping to see your mother. Is she in?"

"She's taking a bath right now. She's got a terrible headache."

"This isn't a good time, then," I said.

"Well, it's not really a good time in general. I mean, right now isn't." She squinted past me at the hearse again. "You're the undertaker."

"I'm not Mr. Fink."

"No, I mean you're the undertaker they mentioned in the paper. You were here the morning my father was killed."

"That's right." She studied me a moment. I felt a tiny flush in my cheeks. A little buzzing around the rib cage.

"Why don't you come in?"

She pulled the door open and I entered the house. Morning shadows had crisscrossed the front hallway during my only other visit to the Weisheit residence. In broad daylight the place took a nice even hit of sunshine.

"Why don't you wait in the living room?" Jenny said. "I'll go tell my mom that you're here."

"I really don't want to disturb her. Tell her it can wait."

"I'm sure it's fine. Besides, *I'd* like to talk to you."

She took the stairs in a prance, her bare feet falling silently. I veered into the kitchen, simply to have another look at the scene of the crime. It was all so blandly normal now — Any Kitchen, USA. No knives, no guns, no blood. Though actually, there *were* knives. Of course there were knives. It was a kitchen. People in kitchens don't generally cut things with blunt instruments. On the wall next to the sink I spotted a plastic knife holder, the kind that hold knives from the itsy-bitsy up to the small meat cleaver range. The knives were held there with magnet strips. There were four knives holding to the magnets. Room for two more. None of the knives seemed large enough to have been the one plunged into Jake Weisheit's back. Of course the knife that killed Jake Weisheit wouldn't be parked on a magnetic strip. It would hardly have been wiped clean with a dish towel and replaced alongside the others. It would be in a plastic bag in a locked room somewhere in the bowels of police headquarters. On a shelf. Or in a box. Waiting for its day in court.

I noticed that there was a new cat bowl, this one blue. I wondered if the other cat bowl was also tagged as evidence.

There was an Andrew Wyeth calendar on the wall next to the refrigerator. October's image was *Christina's World*, with that poor girl stapled to the side of the hill. I looked to see if there were any engagements scribbled in for this past Saturday night. A green line had been drawn through both the Saturday and Sunday boxes. PARENTS' WEEKEND was printed above the line. I took a peek at November. Wyeth's lover Helga standing in front of a window. Browns and blonds. I ran myself a glass of water from the faucet and went back into the living room and sat in a colonial rocker. It had several pineapples stenciled on it. The living room was comfortable — pricey furniture, some antiquey pieces, some new stuff. I was looking at the couch across from me, wondering what seemed wrong about it, when the odd-shaped white pillow in the corner of the couch stood up and stretched exactly like the cat it was. That's what had been wrong. The cat came out of the stretch and gave me a who-are-you look, then jumped to the floor.

"Silly," Jenny said, coming back into the room.

"Excuse me?"

"That's Silly. The cat's name. Priscilla, actually."

"Oh, yes," I said. "The cat with the hellish cry."

"You've met?"

"Your mother told me."

"Mom said she'll be down in a minute. Would you like something to drink?"

I held my glass up. "I helped myself. I hope that's all right."

"Sure. I hope you got it from the pitcher. We have lousy tap water."

"I didn't. But it won't kill me."

Bad choice of words, but Jenny Weisheit didn't seem to register them. Her sleeves had slipped down over her elbows and she pushed them back up and dropped into a chair. Silly pounced up into her lap.

"This really stinks. I mean . . . my father. I still can't completely believe it. It's just not real. I keep expecting him to walk into the room any minute."

Not going to happen. She could sit here until the sun cracks open and dodo birds once again walk the earth. It wasn't going to happen.

"I had that same feeling when my parents died," I said. "I was twelve. I kept thinking that they weren't really permanently dead. Like they were hanging out somewhere in an interim space and they were both clever enough to figure out a way to come back."

"That'd be nice, wouldn't it?"

"Were you here when . . . were you here on Sunday?" I asked.

"You mean when Daddy was killed? It's okay, I can say it. No. I was in Ohio. I'm in college out there. My second year."

"I've never been to Ohio."

"Where I am is really nice. Central Ohio. It's farm country. And the school is a very pretty campus. It's in a small town. It's one of those places where you can really drop out of the world if you're not careful. We're in a bubble out there."

"I was in a bubble too when I went to college," I said. "Not quite as far away as Ohio. I was in Cumberland. There's nothing at all wrong with a bubble."

"Well, mine sure burst. I was just about to go to lunch with some friends. It was parents' weekend and —"

"I saw that on the calendar. In the kitchen."

"Yes. Mom and Daddy and Martin were supposed to come out, it was all set. The place is called Denison University. It's a big lacrosse school. Martin's thinking of going there next year. But Daddy called me on Thursday to tell me that they weren't coming out. He didn't say why, only that things had come up and it wasn't a good time and he was sorry. I was disappointed, but what can you do? So . . . Sunday. I was about to head off for lunch and my mother called and said Daddy's been killed, come right home. Then I went out with my friends and I didn't say anything about it all through lunch. It was too surreal. I guess I just hadn't processed it. We had lunch and then the waitress came around to see if we wanted dessert and someone suggested we split a thing called Murder by Chocolate. Suddenly I just said it out loud, like I was mentioning something funny that had happened back in the dorm. *Somebody murdered my father this morning.* The next thing I knew, I was nothing but tears."

For a moment I thought she was going to give a replay. She caught her breath and gazed in the direction of the window. "I just can't believe someone would hate him enough to kill him. I just don't understand that. Did you know my father?"

"No, I didn't."

"But you're a friend of Mom's?"

"I only met your mother on Sunday. I know Sisco Fontaine."

"Oh, him."

"Yes, him."

"Can I tell you how creepy it is to find out your own mother is running around with a guy like that? I mean, I've seen his band play a couple times. I've actually gone out dancing where he was playing. It sort of freaks me out."

"Makes you want to stay out there in your bubble, doesn't it?"

"So he's a friend of yours?"

"I've known Sisco on and off since high school."

"Do you think he killed my father?"

"It just doesn't fit for me, Jenny. It's not how I see Sisco. But I honestly don't know."

"If you did know — if he told you, for example — you'd tell the police, wouldn't you?"

"Absolutely."

"Even though he's a friend of yours?"

"Your father was killed. I wouldn't protect whoever did that."

"I'm kind of creeped out just being in this house." Jenny pulled the tortoiseshell clip from her hair and shook her hair loose, deftly setting it back into place with a sweep of her arm. Silly jumped out of her lap.

Just then, Polly Weisheit came into the room. She was also in jeans. She was wearing a brown V-neck sweater. Like her daughter, she had pulled the sleeves up to her elbows. Funny thing, genetics. She gave a hard glance at her daughter, then looked over at me.

"Sorry to keep you waiting. Did Jenny get you anything?"

"Jenny offered," Jenny said. "He already had some water."

If the daughter's tone was curt, it was neatly masked. Of course family members pick up on nuances much better than strangers can. Polly gave her daughter another hard look but said nothing in response.

Jenny stood up from her chair. "It was nice to meet you. Thank you for listening to me." She turned to her mother. "Now *he's* a nice man."

Polly waited until her daughter had left the room. "She knows about Sisco," she said flatly.

"So she said."

Polly gave me a sarcastic smile. "We don't keep any secrets in this family. How can we, with the newspapers spelling it out."

She took the seat her daughter had just vacated. "So what brings you back to the scene of the crime?"

"A couple of fractured ribs and a couple of questions."

"Oh? Who has got the fractured ribs?" she asked.

"I do. I've also got the questions."

And I got the answers.

A longtime acquaintance of Polly Weisheit's was the person who had played the bad tune on my ribs. Chip Cooperman. It seemed to me that a guy named Bruno or even Sal would have been the better candidate for the well-placed sucker punches. Couldn't a strapper like me handle the likes of a fellow named Chip? But then Chip is sometimes short for Charles — at least I think it is — and Charles can also morph into Chuck. I can more readily accept a guy named Chuck playing paddy-whack on my ribs.

Polly Weisheit poured herself a glass of white wine and asked me if I'd like to join her. The water I was drinking surely had no hold on me, so I accepted the offer. The little hand had slipped past twelve, so a glass of wine wasn't completely decadent. Besides, this was a house of mourning. All rules are suspended in a house of mourning. The wine was a pinot grigio. From a region north and east of Rome. The artwork on the label was bland, but the wine was pretty good. I couldn't help but envision it dripping off the ragged ends of my splintered ribs, though I knew I was being overly dramatic. I made sure to set the glass down after each sip. This lessens the chance of guzzling. I was my own designated driver. One glass would have to be my limit.

I described for Polly the encounter on the sidewalk outside my building the night before. The man, the hat, "Keep the hell away from Polly Weisheit," the punches, the cheesy karate chop. I told her that two ribs were fractured. I didn't tell her that I wasn't supposed to have sex. Two good-looking people sitting in a nice room sipping white wine, the topic of not having sex doesn't seem completely appropriate.

Polly picked up the big clue that the attack hadn't been random. "Keep the hell away from Polly Weisheit." Gargantuan clue. I suppose it's conceivable that I could have misheard and the warning had actually been "Keep the hell away from polyunsaturates," but then this would have come from a person inordinately interested in the betterment of my health, and pokes to the ribs followed by a chop to the neck just doesn't square with the notion of a roving health Samaritan.

"That was definitely Chip," Polly said. "I'm sorry. Chip Cooperman has a lot of problems. I'm afraid extreme possessiveness is one of them."

"He's possessive of you? Why?"

"It's a long story." She took a sip of her wine. "Actually, it's not. Chip Cooperman has been in love with me for nearly twenty years. If you want to call it love. I never did anything to encourage him, believe me. It's one of those things. He just locked onto me."

"Twenty years is a long time," I noted.

"Chip and I worked together my first job out of college. An advertising agency. Robertson, Mann, Donatello. It's called something else now. I'm still friends with one of the guys who runs it. Nice guy. He's one of those birding freaks. In fact he took his wife to Iceland last month to look at birds. Who knew? I figured they had nothing but penguins in Iceland."

"I'd think puffins," I said. "But I'm lousy about birds. One yellow breast flying by pretty much looks the same to me as another. So you and this Chip character worked together?"

"Right. At the ad agency. We were copywriters. You know how that works? You write something up, you throw it back and forth with the other copywriters. It's not Faulkner, but it was fun. I was an English major with a minor in archaeology."

"Interesting combo."

"If I had gotten out of college and someone had handed me a shovel and offered to send me to Thessalonica, I guess everything would have been different."

"That's how life works."

"I don't know exactly when it was that Chip got his fixation on me," Polly said. "A group of us would go out sometimes after work. The Owl Bar had these great happy-hour freebies. Chicken wings, little quiches, you could basically call it dinner. One night when a few of us broke off and decided to go down to South Baltimore after the Owl Bar, that was the first time I realized something was up with Chip."

"How so?"

"We were in a bar. A guy offered to buy me a drink and Chip shoved him right off the bar stool. I couldn't believe it. The guy wasn't being rude or anything like that. He

109

just asked if he could buy me a lousy drink and suddenly Chip turned into the Incredible Hulk. The guy was very good about it. It could have been a huge fight, but he could tell that Chip was blotto. We hustled Chip out of there. He didn't want a ride home. He insisted on taking a taxi."

"He was embarrassed."

"He damn well should've been. I just chalked it up to liquor and weirdness. No one said anything about it at work the next day. At least not to Chip directly. I wasn't even sure that he remembered anything had happened. I pretty much forgot it myself after a while. Chip and I got to be decent friends. He was a big history junkie. American history. He knew details about all these historical characters the way you'd know gossip about your set of friends. He liked to sit and talk about them like they were still alive. Like he'd just gotten off the phone with Paul Revere or just had drinks with Betsy Ross. It was weird but fun.

"Anyway, I won't bore you with all of this. The point is, I never saw Chip in a romantic way. It just wasn't there for me. And then one day out of the blue he told me he was in love with me and I was the girl of his dreams and all this other crap. I was dating a couple of guys at the time and Chip said none of them was good enough for me. Said they were all jerks. He was probably right about that. A lot of jerks out there. But the kick is, Chip said that *he* wasn't good enough for me either. He said he was better for me than the others, because he understood me better, whatever the hell that meant. But he said he wasn't holding any illusions that I could love him as much as he . . . oh, God, it was one of those horrible conversations."

"He put you up on a pedestal."

"Exactly. Then he elected himself for life to the job of dusting and polishing the stupid thing."

"Were there other incidents?"

"Oh, God, yes. He was Jekyll and Hyde. Along with whatever other screws are loose, Chip has a drinking problem. He just goes blind. Completely irrational. He'd call guys I was seeing and get abusive with them over the phone. He'd start calling my apartment when I was out on dates and leaving these long, rambling messages."

"But you say he wasn't really trying to win you over for his very own."

"No, he just wanted me to know that I could do better than these guys I was seeing. I can't explain it. My love life became his prime concern. It was like having your very own guardian angel, like it or not. There was this one guy I started seeing pretty seriously. More than seeing, actually. We were engaged. I told Chip this is the one, now just back off. He wouldn't hear it. He went over to this guy's apartment and confronted him. Big mistake. The guy ended up breaking Chip's nose."

"A lot of that going around."

"What do you mean?"

"Your son."

"Oh. Right. *That.* Another testosterone monster. Anyway, after that incident I really had to start backing away from Chip. I mean, as a friend. What the hell else could I do? In fact it wasn't too long after this that I started seeing Jake."

"Wait. What happened to your engagement?"

"Oh, I broke that off. It was an intense relationship. Very intense. But not the kind of thing you should try to turn into a marriage. We both ended up agreeing on that. And Chip was actually okay about Jake, as it turned out. They already knew each other. You know how Baltimore is. It's a pretty small town in a lot of ways. Plus, Jake happened to be a history buff himself. The two of them could yak away about, I don't know, Eli Whitney's cotton gin or whether or not Benjamin Franklin was actually gay —"

"Was Benjamin Franklin gay?"

"I couldn't tell you. The next time you see Chip, you can talk to him about it."

"The next time I see Chip, I'm going to drop a refrigerator on his head."

"Look, I'm so sorry he did that to you. It's

totally ridiculous. It's been ages since he flared up like that. Chip's been married twice. But both of those went belly-up. His second wife killed herself. She got into the bathtub with a razor blade. That was a little over a year ago. I went to the funeral. Which was the biggest mistake I could have made. He must have thanked me a hundred times for coming. He called up Jake about a month later and invited us to an Orioles game. Jake accepted. Jake loved going to the Os' games. We were in the seventh inning stretch. We're standing up. You know, 'Take me out to the ball game' and all that, and Chip leans over and whispers into my ear that he still loves me."

"How sweet."

"Right. How totally psycho. I didn't tell Jake. I probably should have, but . . . well, Jake and I were already having our problems by then."

"Sisco?"

"Not exactly. Not yet anyway. Just . . . problems." She was nearly finished with her second glass of wine and she realized it. She set the glass down. "Christ, look at me. I've got to host a wake tonight."

"I should be going." I stood up. Shooting pains ran about my torso.

"I'm sorry about . . . you know. What happened," Polly said again.

"Do the police know about your friend?"

"About Chip? Why should they?"

"You're joking with me, right?"

"Chip didn't have anything to do with Jake's murder. Is that what you're thinking?"

"Call me crazy."

"You're wrong."

"Please don't say he wouldn't hurt a fly. My ribs couldn't take it."

"I know Chip. He wouldn't kill Jake. It makes no sense."

"Jumping me makes sense?"

"He saw your name in the paper. Who knows what he was thinking?"

"Sisco's name is in the paper."

"Then maybe he'd better keep an eye out. Have you contacted the police?"

"No."

"I can't tell you not to, but I wish you wouldn't. I'm telling you, Chip could not have killed Jake. I just know it." She stood up and I followed her to the door.

I asked, "So are you all set for the funeral?"

"Your Mr. Fink is kind of creepy."

"He'll run a good show."

"I wish you and your aunt were handling things. I shouldn't have let Evelyn bully me."

"It'll be fine."

We reached the door. She paused. "I wonder if I could ask you another favor? For God's sake, feel free to say no."

"What is it?"

"This whole funeral thing is freaking me

114

out. No one is coming right out and saying it, but I know I'm getting the blame for Jake's death. I'm not feeling terribly supported. My one good friend is out of the country. The rest of them are all Jake's friends, really. I just — I guess I was wondering if there's any way I could convince you to come to the funeral tomorrow."

"Me?"

"It doesn't make sense, I know. I'm just feeling real isolated now. I'm sure it's the last thing you want to do. It's not like you don't go to enough funerals."

She was certainly correct on that count. I couldn't see any good reason to attend Jake Weisheit's funeral. So far my involvement with the Weisheit family had already earned me a visit from the police and a couple of unhappy ribs.

"Sure." It was a voice sounding very much like my own. "Why not? It'll give me a chance to see George Fink in action. Maybe I can pick up a few pointers."

As Polly reached for the door it burst open and a large teenage boy lumbered into the house. Big kid. Buzz cut. Sixteen, seventeen. He was out of breath, his cheeks pink with sweat. He was wearing a St. Paul's sweatshirt, baggy blue gym shorts, and a glazed expression. He stopped just inside the doorway and ran his arm across his face, wiping off the perspiration.

It was Martin Weisheit, Polly's son. She introduced us. Martin managed a mumbled "Hello."

"Were you out running?" Polly asked.

The boy ignored the question. "I should have gone to school." He made certain that it sounded like an accusation.

"I'm sorry, Martin. Your father doesn't die every day. I think a few days at home with your family is appropriate." Martin looked at me as if to ask, *Isn't she a bitch?* "Your grandmother is due soon," Polly said. "Why don't you go take a shower?"

"Is that your hearse?" Martin asked me, ignoring his mother.

"Yes, it is."

"Nice of you to park it right fucking out front."

"Martin!"

He gave me a smirk. "Nice to meet you." He moved past us, taking the stairs two at a time.

"Asshole," Polly hissed, glaring in the direction of the stairs.

"Don't worry about it. He's right. I should have brought my own car."

"There is a polite way to say it."

I shrugged. "Someone murdered his father. Being polite to a total stranger isn't the first thing on his mind. Don't worry about it."

"He's just pissed at his mother. I'm public enemy number one these days. Maybe you noticed Jenny's not so keen on the old lady either."

A piercing shriek sounded from the second floor. Polly started, but I recognized it immediately.

"Who," I said.

Polly was perplexed. "What?"

The shriek was cut off by a pair of slamming power chords from an electric guitar.

"The Who," I said. "They rock, they roll."

Polly aimed a peeved look up the stairs. "It's loud enough to raise the dead."

On that note, I took my leave. Polly remained in the doorway as I headed out to the hearse. She was leaning against the doorjamb with her arms crossed. One of them untucked itself and she gave a small wave. There were two large windows above the front door. Sort of an odd design. Jenny Weisheit was standing in one of them. Her wave was bigger, looser. If only Martin Weisheit had appeared in the other window to give me the finger, we'd have had a trifecta.

I smiled at the house — where in the world would I have aimed my wave? — and gingerly got in behind the wheel. Inspiration struck. I flashed my headlights.

In tandem, the two women turned and disappeared.

Chapter Eight

Polly Weisheit's story kept looping through my head as I sat at my desk doing some work. Mrs. Papadaki was to be buried just up the street a piece, at Greenmount Cemetery. Pops and his crew were scooping out the earth. I got on the phone to Pat Tyler of Tyler Monuments to discuss the inscription for the stone. Doodle had dropped it off.

"How's your Greek, Pat?"

"Better than my Russian. Gads, Hitch, I cut a stone last week looked like a message from outer space. That's one hell of a funny-looking language."

"Fire up the fax, Pat, and I'll send this over. See what you can do with it."

I had a brief business meeting in my office with Billie to discuss the new line of kicky colors that one of Batesville's intrepid small competitors was trying to peddle.

"What do you think?"

"They're eye-popping."

"Uh-huh."

"I think they're supposed to be hip."

"Uh-huh."

"Kids might go for them."

"The orange one is kind of nice."

"They remind me of a box of Crayolas."

"That's probably the idea."

"It might catch on."

"Might."

"So what do you think?"

"I don't like 'em."

"Okay. That's it then."

Meeting over.

I opted not to inform Billie that her nephew was sitting behind his desk with a couple of fractured ribs. Billie worries. She thinks I have a reckless streak. Plug her in and turn the dial to the proper setting and she'll effuse like Spinoza on the reasons she feels I have a reckless streak. It's Billie's sense that I lead with my jaw sometimes simply to see if something interesting might happen to it. She's wrong, of course. But I keep my protests mild.

If I were the litigious type I might have phoned my lawyer to see what kind of soup we could lower Chip Cooperman into. There was an argument to be made that Sewell and Sons might be forced to turn away bodies as a result of my ginger condition. But I didn't feel like making the argument. It's not only that I'm not the litigious type, but more that Polly's portrait of Chip Cooperman had inspired my sympathy more than my bile. I wasn't happy about being jumped, of course, but I think that a situation like this one required my remembering not to take the mugging too personally. It wasn't about me. It didn't matter to Chip Cooperman if I was Gandhi or Pol Pot, I was pretty much just a six-foot-three carbon unit, species male, that Cooperman perceived to be a threat to his fantasy. And it doesn't take a terribly bright bulb to understand the fragilities and dangers involved when you start messing with a person's fantasies. Chip Cooperman was going mano a mano with his own little demons. I just happened to have been standing in the wrong spot when it happened.

There was a larger question, of course. Given Chip Cooperman's helium-based grasp on reality, what were the chances, despite Polly's assurances to the contrary, that Mr. Obsession had made his way to the Weisheits' kitchen on Sunday morning and pulled his guardian angel act on Jake Weisheit?

I took the question with me to Jimmy's Restaurant, where I chewed on it a while. I also chewed on a sourdough roll stuffed with tuna fish. I was able to reach conclusions about the tuna sandwich a lot quicker than I could Chip Cooperman. Too much mayo. Inferior onion. Could've used some pepper. I left Jimmy's filled, but not with satisfaction.

Marilyn Tuck was waiting in my office when I returned. She was sitting in one of my two guest chairs, perfectly erect as if drawn up by a string from the top of her head.

"Well, hello," I said. "Have you been waiting here long?"

"Not long. Your aunt said she expected you back soon." Her arms were crossed tightly on her chest and she didn't seem inclined to release them. Her eyes followed me coldly as I swung behind my desk. She looked a little wan. A little peaky. A little pissed.

I dropped into my chair. "How can I help you?"

"I have just come from the Papadakis'. Let me ask you something. Am I supposed to take Mrs. Papadaki's condition as some sort of joke?"

Her condition? Her condition was that she was dead. Any punch line there was well beneath me.

"I'm sorry. What do you mean?"

"She is sitting upright in a *chair.*"

"Oh, that condition. Of course. Yes. Well, it's a little unusual for a wake. You're right about that."

"I had assumed you were going to take care of that."

"Fair assumption."

"Was that your suggestion, then?"

"It was the family's wishes."

"It's horrible. Why didn't you talk them out of it?"

"It was the family's wishes," I said again. "I offered to hold the wake here, but Spiro

121

really had his heart set on having his mother at his place. He says it's what she would have wanted. You see fewer and fewer at-home wakes anymore. As for the rest of it, I don't know what to tell you. Spiro got it into his head. He didn't want her supine."

"It's a freak show." She crossed her legs with an almost military briskness. It was impressive how much animosity she was able to pack into the act.

"Don't you think that's an overreaction? The corpse is lying down, the corpse is sitting up. It's logistics, really."

She looked disappointed in me. "I don't think that Mr. Papadaki is in an emotional condition to make that sort of decision. You're the professional here. I'd think you would have counseled against something so . . . well, so perverse."

"I could show you books on funeral traditions around the world. This is child's play if you really look at it."

"Apparently there was a photographer."

"A photographer?"

"From the *Sun*. He was at the house earlier today taking pictures of Mrs. Papadaki."

"That's peculiar."

"It's more than peculiar. It's upsetting. I hardly think it does the situation any good if Mrs. Papadaki becomes a funny little photograph in the newspapers, do you?"

"The situation?"

"It's not easy running a private nursing home, Mr. Sewell —"

"Hitch."

"Yes. Right. Hitch." She recrossed her legs and gave a tug to her skirt. Worked her small fanny into the back of the chair. Unconsciously I squirmed along with her. You'd have thought Billie had sprinkled the joint with itching powder. "Briarcliff is my father's legacy. You read our brochure, you know all about that there's a perception among some that my father's estate was more substantial than it really was. The fact is, much more of it went into the setting up of Briarcliff than I think most people realize. I'm not sitting on any sort of pretty endowment. Briarcliff is like any other private nursing home facility. We run close to the margin. I work hard to realize my father's dream. What happened to Mrs. Papadaki, her wandering off the way she did, it was unfortunate, and it was an embarrassment to Briarcliff. It is not the sort of thing that happens. Mr. Papadaki has been very gracious concerning the conditions surrounding his mother's passing. Still, I don't think it's going to help matters if Mrs. Papadaki becomes a public laughingstock."

I finally got it. The cottony section of my brain parted and light flowed in. "You're worried about a lawsuit."

Marilyn Tuck did not move a muscle. But her voice dropped an octave. "I am not worried about a lawsuit."

"I think you are."

"You are misunderstanding me."

"That's not why you came down here? Not why you went to Spiro's?"

"I came to pay my respects."

"Don't get me wrong," I said. "I'm not a litigious person myself. Bad things happen. It's part of life. I don't see why an entire profession should exist for the sole purpose of profiting because of it."

"You mean litigation lawyers?"

"Yes. So believe me, I'm not suggesting that Spiro should sue you."

"That's good to hear. I would as soon steer clear of lawyers myself, thank you very much. I'm a firm believer that situations can be handled between parties without having to resort to the courts. People can come to an agreement among themselves. It simply requires a dialogue."

"A dialogue."

"Yes."

"Did you and Spiro have a dialogue just now?"

"As I said, Mr. Papadaki is an understanding man. But I'm distressed about this photographer. I just don't want —"

She was interrupted by my phone ringing.

"Excuse me." I picked up the phone. "Sewell and Sons." The first thing I heard — the only thing — was the sound of seagulls.

My neighborhood is lousy with seagulls, I'd recognize that sound anywhere. "Hello? This is Sewell and Sons Family Funeral Home."

Nothing. Just more seagull sounds. Okay, so there's a seagull out there who has figured out how to put a quarter in a slot and push small buttons. But why me? Then someone spoke. I recognized the voice immediately. Even if I hadn't, the message was a dead giveaway.

"I told you to stay away from Polly Weisheit."

I palmed the mouthpiece. "I have to take this." I swiveled my chair and spoke back into the phone. "Chip? This is Hitchcock Sewell. But you know that. Look, I don't —"

"Leave Polly alone."

"Listen, I don't know what you've gotten into your head, but I didn't really appreciate our little meeting the other night. I have no —"

"Leave her alone."

"Fine, I heard that. My rib cage heard that loud and clear too. Next time why don't you just drop me a line?"

There was a pause. "Leave her alone."

The man certainly wasn't straining his vocabulary to deliver his message. I opened my mouth to press my point, then stopped myself. Reason? Logic? Common sense? Chip Cooperman had been on this kick for nearly twenty years. A few choice words from me weren't going to change anything.

"Okay," I said. "Whatever you say. I'll leave her alone. No problem."

But the line had gone dead. I had no way of knowing if he had heard me. Somehow I doubted it. I returned the phone to the receiver.

I swiveled my chair back forward. "I'm sorry. That was just —"

Seagulls.

I jumped up from my desk so fast the woman gave a start. I hurried over to the window and pressed my nose against the glass. I couldn't see well enough, so I pulled the window open and leaned out. There was no one at the pay phone on the corner. Of course it takes only two seconds to walk away from a pay phone. Across the street, Darryl Sandusky was sitting on the front steps of St. Teresa's, practicing his sneer.

I called out to him. "Hey, Darryl, did you notice a man just now over there at the corner making a phone call?"

"Nah."

"Is it possible there was a man there and you just didn't see him?"

"Could be. How would I know?"

"What are you doing over there anyway?" I asked. "Are you waiting for Jesus?"

"Very funny."

"Jesus loves the little children, you know," I

said. "That means you."

"You're nuts."

I pulled my head in and shut the window. Marilyn Tuck had gotten to her feet.

"I should be going. I apologize if I sounded testy. Things are a little exhausting for me just now. Seeing Mrs. Papadaki like that, it took me by surprise."

I walked her to the front door and stood watching as she headed down the block. She took tiny steps, but took them swiftly. Her heels beat a fading staccato against the sidewalk. From across the street Darryl called out, "Who's your new girlfriend?"

I tilted up against the doorjamb, crossing my arms. "Darryl, how much would it cost me to get you to go out and play in traffic?"

Darryl mimicked me, crossing his arms over his pudgy chest. "A million bucks."

"Would you accept a check?"

"Very funny."

Chapter Nine

Jake Weisheit's funeral service was held at the Roland Park Presbyterian Church on Roland Avenue. If you saw the movie *Diner*, you've seen the church. They filmed a scene here, one in which one of the characters passes out in his underwear in a crèche in the middle of a frosty night. The church is across Roland Avenue from one of the country's first official shopping centers (if you believe the plaque), a collection of Tudor-style buildings that now includes a restaurant, an ice cream place and a travel agency. There used to be a drugstore there called Morgan & Millard, the Morgue for short. For several decades it was a popular weekend-evening gathering place for neighborhood teens. *I'll meet you at the Morgue.* I'm sure parents just loved hearing their kids throwing that one around on the phone.

Jake pulled a decent crowd. A steady stream was flowing into the church as I arrived. My Valiant was having a recurrence of its little backfiring problem, so I parked several blocks away. The air was crisp. The large lawns were already under their first blanket of leaves. Catty-corner from the church was a large stucco house with green awnings. At the edge of the property, near the sidewalk, stood the large bleached-out husk of a dead tree. It stood maybe thirty feet; the top had been lopped off, along with all of the branches. A colossal old bone jutting out of the earth. According to the carving on the side facing the sidewalk, Susie loves Roger. I guess it pays to advertise.

I was confronted by Happy Fink as soon as I entered the church. When they say *fireplug*, they mean Happy Fink. I have no idea where the name came from, for she's a truly sour little thing. She squared off in front of me.

"What are *you* doing here?"

I ignored the question. "Hello, Happy. It's good to see you."

Happy handed me a program. "Go see the corpse. George is very pleased. And take a look at the flowers. They're spectacular."

Jake Weisheit looked just fine. Handsome in repose. He was in a simple blue suit and striped tie. I questioned the choice of a buttonhole, but this wasn't my funeral. Hair. Makeup. All fine. The flowers. Sure, they looked fine too. A fine job all around. Nothing to hyperventilate over. I noted that the arrangement from Sewell and Sons had been relegated to a rear position, slightly obstructed by a fussy tangle of lilacs. I aimed a thumbs-up at George Fink, who was standing discreetly off by the lectern. George was in stone-faced mode. He was tugging on his gray gloves, like a professional killer. He acknowledged me with a stiff nod.

As I retreated up the aisle I spotted the Weisheit family. Polly, Jenny and Martin were seated in the front pew, along with an older woman whom I took to be Jake Weisheit's mother. Jenny's cheeks were touched with tears and she was staring off into space. Her brother was fidgety. Polly Weisheit looked tired. She was seated next to the elderly woman, who was talking to her — insistently, it seemed — under her breath. Polly caught my eye as I headed up the aisle. It was a grim look.

I stationed myself on the aisle near the rear, so that I could watch as George made a minor production number out of closing the lid of the casket. His every gesture was snail's pace; gravitas in deceleration. True, you don't want to simply step over and flip the lid closed like it's the end of piano practice. But still.

Just before the service got under way a woman slipped into the empty pew directly across the aisle from where I was seated. She was tall, slender as a willow, dressed in a smart maroon suit and cream-colored blouse and wearing a pair of cat-eye sunglasses. On her head was a greenish silk scarf, wrapped turban-like. As she eased into the pew with an almost liquid grace, she carefully removed the sunglasses and slipped them into her purse. There was a translucent quality to her skin, but by that I don't mean to imply a healthy glow. Quite the opposite in fact. Her cheekbones were a bit too pronounced. So, too, the chin and the eye sockets. I placed her somewhere in her fifties. She made the sign of the cross, then lowered herself onto the prayer bench, where she remained a full minute before easing herself back onto the pew. One hand lifted reflexively to the turban, giving it a poke and a little tug. I didn't intend to stare and only realized I was when she turned her head and caught me. Her eyes were pale and they considered me a moment in a sort of dull stare-down before breaking off and turning her attention to the program.

The service was a blur, as it would tend to be for someone who has attended eight million of them. There were several hymns, which the congregation delivered in a unified murmur, and a somber pep talk from the pastor. The fact of our guest of honor's having been felled by an ugly act of violence did not go unreflected in the overall energy within the church. It especially did not go unreflected in the first eulogy, the first of two. It was delivered by one of Jake's long-time friends, a trimly bearded man whose name appeared in the program as Tuby Schultz. I assumed a typo and later found out I was correct. He was Toby Schultz. Schultz's eulogy was a general recitation of barbecues and camping trips, touch football games, the old school days . . . a thumbnail sketch of the deceased in his finest moments of bonhomie. It was a nice enough little portrait. It made you think maybe it would have been nice to share a beer with the guy. It didn't make you feel like plunging a knife between his shoulder blades, that's for sure.

Schultz spoke comfortably. He seemed at ease in front of a crowd. His left hand chopped the air as a means of punctuation; he was in full command of the dramatic pause. As eulogies go, I found this one a trifle blowhardy. But the man did stay on point. He projected well. He made eye contact throughout the room. Schultz concluded with a sappy salute to the closed casket and a "So long, buddy," then quit the pulpit.

The second eulogizer was Jake's uncle, Gregory Weisheit. If the elder man lacked the vigor of Toby Schultz's effort — delivering his memorial in a thin nasal monotone — he nonetheless seemed a bit more sincere. Gregory Weisheit covered the angle of Jake's parents, one of whom was indeed — as I had surmised — the woman I had seen chewing softly on Polly Weisheit's ear in the front pew. Evelyn Weisheit received warm kudos from her brother-in-law for her skills as a wife and a mother. "She surrounded herself with great men," was one of the ways he put it. "And by her presence she made them greater.

"We are all aware of the legacy of my brother James," Gregory Weisheit continued. The fact was, I was clueless on the matter, though I was not about to raise my hand to admit to my ignorance. "James was a visionary, and he could not have achieved his extraordinary levels of success without the partnership of his loving and devoted wife. Likewise my nephew, Jake, benefited immeasurably under Evelyn's guiding hand. James and Evelyn Weisheit were a class act, and together they created and nurtured another class act in my nephew Jake. And Jake in turn . . . along with his wife, Polly, has given the next generation a class act in their two children, Jennifer and Martin. We grieve a life so inexplicably and brutally cut short. But I take some measure of solace in knowing that my brother is looking down and is anxious to greet his son. For them at least, this is an occasion of happiness."

He stepped down and took a seat. Jenny Weisheit came up to the pulpit, read a passage from the Scriptures and collapsed into tears. Faucets burst throughout the church. As we rose to take a crack at one more hymn, the woman in the green turban gathered herself and made a whispery exit.

I felt as if a ghost had passed by.

★ ★ ★

As I headed past the dead tree stump on my way to my car, a person stepped from behind it. He was wearing armadillo boots, a cowboy hat and a tiresome smirk. My favorite little outlaw.

"Hello, Sisco."

Sisco glanced across the street at the church. "Did I miss anything?"

"It was loads of fun," I said. "Some games, a few songs. They handed out party hats, though I see you brought your own."

"Funny. Did you see where they mentioned you in the paper?"

"Yes, I noticed that. It made my day. So what are you doing here?" I asked. "Besides keeping that dead tree company."

"What are *you* doing here?" Sisco asked. "That's the question. You're not handling the funeral, are you?"

"I'm here strictly on a civilian basis."

Sisco's eyes narrowed. "So how's Polly? Is she torn up? Is she a cold widow? What? I haven't heard from her since Sunday. That's four days." He showed me on his fingers how many four was.

"If you include Sunday it's four," I said. "But you did see her on Sunday. So technically it's been three days."

Sisco ignored my advanced mathematics. "She hasn't called."

"Do you think maybe she has other things

on her mind, Sisco?"

"One lousy phone call? It's not like I can pick up the phone and call her. I tried once. The boy answered. I just hung up."

"Calling would not be good."

"Do you know the police pulled me in on Monday to question me some more?"

"They're only doing their job, Sisco. They questioned me too."

"A man plays around with a frisky house-wife and look where it gets him. Hell, I was making a woman happy. That's more than *he* was doing." Sisco jerked his thumb in the direction of the church. Jake Weisheit's casket was being rolled out the front of the church and taken to the waiting hearse. Polly emerged from the church, along with her children.

"You get a load of the daughter?" Sisco asked.

"She broke into tears at the pulpit just now," I said. "Why don't you muzzle the wolf, Sisco?"

"Huh?"

"Show some respect. Her father is dead."

"All I said was she's hot."

Some of the guests from the church were walking by. Sisco was leaning up against the dead tree as if he was Peter Pan loitering at the mouth of the secret headquarters. Maybe cowboy hats escape notice on the streets of Austin, but in Baltimore wearing such a hat will earn you a second look.

"Let me teach you a nifty word, Sisco," I said. "Incognito."

"What the hell have I got to hide from? These people? Funerals are public events. I could have gone into that church if I'd wanted to."

"I think it's better that you didn't."

Across the street, George Fink was escorting Gregory Weisheit and Jake's mother to their limo.

"Is that Jake's mother?" Sisco asked. "I heard she's a Grade A bitch."

"So, the word *respect*. It just doesn't cut it for you?"

Sisco gave me a peeved look. "Come on, Hitch, what's wrong with you? Polly told me Jake's mother rode her ass all the time. I'm just repeating what I've heard."

The hearse pulled slowly to the corner, then stopped. Other cars began to position themselves behind it.

Sisco hooked his thumbs into his belt loops. "Maybe I'll go to the cemetery."

"Sisco, listen to me. Today is not your day, okay? It's Jake Weisheit's day. I don't care what you thought of him or even *if* you thought of him. This is his day. It's the last one he's ever going to have. I'm sorry if your nose is out of joint. But be a man and see things for what they are."

"I don't need you to lecture me."

"You shouldn't be here, Sisco. You

shouldn't be at the cemetery. Just take the day off. Let the Weisheit family bury this guy without your lurking around on the sidelines. What's between you and Polly Weisheit from this point on is something you can deal with later, okay? My suggestion? Give her some space. I don't think your popping up on the widow's arm right now is terribly smart."

"The police already think I did it," Sisco said sullenly. "They think I killed Jake."

"Sisco, if the police thought you killed Jake you'd be in jail right now, not standing here next to a dead tree passing quality time with me."

"But they don't have any evidence. You can't arrest someone on suspicion."

"Actually, you can. It's called suspicion of murder."

"I didn't do it."

"So who did, Sisco? The police don't seem to think it was a burglary. What does Polly think? What did Polly say when you first got to the house?"

"You saw her."

"Cool as a cucumber."

"Cold as a fish," Sisco said.

"Let me ask you something. When Polly called you up on Sunday morning, did she tell you that her husband was lying dead on the floor?"

"No way. She just said I had to come over right away. I asked what about, and she said not to worry about that, just to get over there."

Across the street the procession began its move down Roland Avenue. A blue banner snapped smartly from the antenna of the hearse.

"Let me ask you something else, Sisco. What did you tell the police on Sunday? When they asked you why I had been out there at the Weisheits', what did you tell them?"

He shrugged. "I told the cops I knew Jake had to go to a funeral home and that you were a friend and everything, so I called you. I said I was just trying to help."

"*That* was the story you told them? That you dragged me out there at five in the morning to fetch the body?"

"It was all I could think of. The truth wasn't so hot. When they called me back in on Monday, I went ahead and told them the truth."

"Polly told them the truth on Sunday," I said. "Right off the bat."

Sisco looked at me blankly for a few seconds. "She did?"

"It's what they ask for, Sisco. It's what helps them with their investigation."

"Shit." He stuck his thumbs into his belt loops and stared off at the line of cars.

"Do you think Polly brought you to the house so the police could peg you as their best suspect?"

"Why the hell would she do that?"

"Sisco, did Polly ever say anything about a Chip Cooperman to you?"

"Who's that?"

"I'm just asking. Did Polly ever mention someone named Cooperman? It's an old friend of hers."

Sisco's eyes narrowed. "How come you know so much?"

"I don't know so much. I'm just asking questions."

"You think she's throwing me to the wolves to protect someone else? That's low, man. She wouldn't do that to me. That woman's all over me. You're pissing in the wrong direction, Hitch." Sisco removed his cowboy hat and gave it a couple of swats. Maybe he was hoping for some trail dust. He dipped his head back into the hat. "I'm outta here. Screw this. I've got better things to do with my time."

Sisco stepped away from the tree and directly into the street without even looking. A police car had just rounded the corner from Roland Avenue and was cruising slowly down the street. If it had been traveling at a regular speed it might have clipped Sisco. As it was, the driver simply rolled the wheel to veer away.

The officer in the passenger seat gave a two-finger salute through the window. "Good morning, gentlemen."

All very pleasant. Officer Friendly.

But I know when I'm being scrutinized. Apparently so does Sisco.

Sisco snapped as the car floated past, "What are you looking at?"

I started toward him. "Sisco —"

He wheeled on me. "What! What's your problem? You saw him!"

Chapter Ten

The graveside service was brief. Jenny Weisheit had pulled herself together and it was her brother's turn to wrestle with tears. Polly, who was seated between the two, made an attempt to comfort her son, but the boy was clearly not interested in her help. Martin smeared his face with the sleeve of his jacket, his gaze locked on the casket in front of him. Martin's grandmother was seated next to him. Evelyn Weisheit was a matronly woman with white hair in a cotton-candy do and a rubbery pink face currently stuck in the locked position. A lot of bosom and an attractive black-and-silver shawl covering it. I've seen my share of mothers burying their sons, and Evelyn Weisheit was holding up admirably. She sat with her hands folded in her lap, regally erect, and stared straight ahead at her son's casket. Whatever emotions were ricocheting through her breast were not for public consumption. The woman was either terribly brave and stoic or medicated up to the eyeballs.

I found myself standing next to Toby Schultz and his wife, or someone I assumed to be his wife, a compact woman with a pageboy cut and a pair of boxy black glasses. Soft, barely audible sighs escaped from her lips at regular intervals, though from her expression she could not have seemed less interested in the goings-on. Schultz's eyes scanned the gathering nearly nonstop. He reminded me of a Secret Service agent.

I was scanning too. I was curious about Chip Cooperman. Would my assailant pass up the chance to fold the widow's hand into his and speak his soft nothings? I realized that even if he showed, I wouldn't know him to see him. I picked out seven men who could have been my late-night assailant, then dismissed four of them who seemed to be here with a lady on their arm. It was my inscrutable hunch that the Chipster would be flying solo. That left the three remaining candidates. One was thick and balding, one had a blueberry birthmark on his cheek and one had an extremely runny nose and could not stop sneezing. My ribs tingled as I considered each of them.

There wasn't a whole lot to be said at the graveside service that hadn't already been covered back at the church. The minister said it, and the crowd began to disperse. Only one of my candidates, the sneezer, spoke with Polly. His demeanor was decidedly un-psycho. I struck him off the list. I watched as Evelyn Weisheit bade her grandson to help her stand from her folding chair and then she guided him to the headstone a few feet from the open grave. She stood a moment with her head bowed while Martin stared sullenly at the marker, then made the sign of the cross and released the boy's arm.

One of my two remaining Chip Cooperman candidates — the one with the blueberry birthmark — was standing near my car. As I started over, someone touched me on the arm. It was Jenny Weisheit.

"Mom wants to make sure you're coming to the house." Her face was without affect.

"Actually, I was thinking about skipping out," I said. "I don't usually attend the post-funeral gatherings."

"I wouldn't blame you. I'm not exactly expecting a whole load of fun. But anyway she told me to come over and ask you."

I asked, "How are you holding up?"

"Okay, I guess. It's all pretty unreal. It's like I said to you at the house, I keep expecting to see my father show up any minute and tell us it was all a mistake. Even at the wake last night I was thinking he'd open his eyes. The whole thing will go away. But I guess it's not going to."

"Jenny?"

It was Polly Weisheit, calling from the limo. Jenny took herself in a hug and scuffed a step backward. "What'll I tell her? Will you

143

come to the house?"

"Sure."

"Good. I'll tell her. See you there."

The leaves in the yard behind Polly Weisheit's pool had been raked into no less than a dozen perfect little piles, small red and yellow pyramids scattered about on the lawn. Three decent sized piles would have been sufficient. I stood with a whiskey in my hand looking out at them.

"Look at those fucking leaves," Polly Weisheit said. Polly was standing next to me. The reason the whiskey was in my hand was because I had just lifted it from hers. She indicated the leaves. "That was Gregory. 'How can I help?' he asks. Then he comes out here and turns the backyard into fucking Hobbit land."

"I never read *The Hobbit*," I said.

"I never did, either. But this is what I picture."

I pictured dwarves with funny hats and a lot of connecting tunnels, sort of like an ant farm. But like I said, I never read it.

"Thank you for coming," Polly said.

It was the fifth time she had said this in the last hour or so, so I was pretty sure she meant it. The widow Weisheit was not sloppy drunk — so far she could hold her juice — but if she kept lapping down the whiskey at the pace she was going at it, things were liable to shift.

Polly took a few steps into the yard, kicking at one of the piles. She turned back to face me. "Did you hear how many fucking times my name was mentioned in the eulogies?"

"I wasn't counting."

"You wouldn't have to count too high. One. Gregory mentioned my name exactly once. Toby fucking Schultz didn't even do that."

"You're saying *fucking* a lot," I noted.

"Have you got a problem with that?"

"I'm just pointing it out."

She gave an unattractive cackle. "It's my party and I'll say *fucking* if I want to."

She stepped up to me and took her drink back, spilling some of it on her wrist. On the stone wall beyond the pool I spotted Martin Weisheit. He was sitting in nearly the exact same spot I had first seen Polly several days before. He was by himself, looking vaguely disgusted. Which is to say, he was looking considerably like his mother.

"Doesn't Martin have any friends here?" I asked.

Polly shook her head. "He told them not to come. God forbid he let anyone try to make him feel better."

"Isn't that a little harsh?"

"That's me, isn't it?" She took a sip of her drink. "I'm the hardhearted widow and all-around lousy mother. Plus whatever the hell else they're all saying."

"You wouldn't be feeling a little sorry for yourself here, would you?"

She raised her glass and pointed at me. "You think you're smart."

"I'm not stupid."

"Take a look. I'm a pariah. Everyone here is convinced I had something to do with Jake's murder. It's been no secret that Jake and I were having trouble. And with that stuff in the paper about Sisco being out here that morning." She tapped her glass against my chest "And you too, for that matter."

"Me?"

"You're the tall, dark and handsome stranger. The black widow's new friend."

Toby Schultz and his wife were coming out of the house. Polly spotted them. "Christ. Toby and his dykey wife in those stupid goddamn glasses."

Note to self: Polly doesn't much care for the Schultzes.

God has His plan, and it often includes setting several pieces onto the same square even when they'd rather not be there. Perhaps He finds it amusing. Or instructive. Toby Schultz and his wife came over to us.

"Hello, Polly," Schultz said, running his hand smoothly down his tie. He turned to me. "I don't believe we've met. I'm Toby Schultz."

"Hitchcock Sewell."

146

"Were you a friend of Jake's?"

"You know damn well he wasn't," Polly said.

Schultz placed a hand against his wife's back. "This is my wife, Betty."

The woman offered her hand. Okay, I was thinking. It's a wig. And the glasses are fake. This is really Neil Sedaka.

"Nice to meet you," I said.

Blink once for "Same here." Betty Schultz turned to Polly. "Mrs. Weisheit was asking for you."

"I'm Mrs. Weisheit," Polly snapped.

"You know what she means," Schultz said. "Evelyn's asking for you."

"What does she want?"

"She wants you," Betty Schultz said. The woman looked at Polly as if she was determining where to take the first bite.

Polly slid her arm through my elbow. "Are you ready to go meet the Duchess?"

Toby Schultz growled. "For Christ's sake, Polly, she just buried her son. Show some respect."

"*Her* son. *Your* friend. You let me know when I get a piece of this, Toby, all right? You'll be sure to do that?"

"Just behave."

Polly gave a salute. The reference to Schultz's little salute at the conclusion of his eulogy was clear. "Aye, aye."

As we crossed the patio, I detected something from the corner of my eye, something flying through the air. It landed in the water with nearly no splash. It was the wire bucket from which Polly had been lobbing golf balls the morning her husband was murdered. I looked across the pool in time to see the retreating back of Martin Weisheit. I opened my mouth to speak, but Polly cut me off.

"I'm dealing with it."

Polly insisted on walking me into the house with her arm affixed to my elbow. I took a hard look from Jenny Weisheit as we passed through the kitchen. Evelyn Weisheit was in the best chair in the room. Gregory Weisheit stood like a footman just behind her. A small alligator case was on Evelyn Weisheit's lap. It was filled with loose photographs and Mrs. Weisheit was going through them. There was a stack of photographs on the table next to her. As we approached, the woman handed a photograph from the case to Gregory, who glanced at it and placed it neatly on the pile.

Polly released my arm. I couldn't swear it, but I think she squared her stance. "What are you doing, Evelyn?"

The woman looked up from the box of photographs. She calmly took her daughter-in-law's measure. "I am taking some photographs of my son and my grandchildren, dear. That is, if you don't mind."

"And if I do?"

I wanted to snatch that glass out of Polly's

hand again. There were the makings here for the whiskey's being tossed into the older woman's face.

Evelyn Weisheit did not rise to the bait of her daughter-in-law's tone. "Of course I wouldn't steal anything from you, Polly. I would hope you wouldn't object to my having a few of these pictures."

"Looks to me like you're cleaning out the whole box."

"That's hardly the case, dear." Evelyn Weisheit made a gesture and Gregory picked up the stack of photographs and handed it to Polly.

Polly tucked her drink glass into her breast and started flipping through the pictures. "I see you've got everyone but me here."

Evelyn Weisheit looked at me as she spoke. "I believe you are in some of them, dear." A trace of a smile twitched on her lips.

Polly continued fanning through the photographs. "There's my ass . . . and that's my elbow."

"I believe there's a pretty one of you eating a corn on the cob," the older woman said. "I believe it is on Jenny's birthday."

"This? You can barely see me."

Jenny had just come into the room, carrying the platter of brownies. She headed over to us.

Evelyn Weisheit closed the alligator case and settled her hands lightly atop it. "Polly, what is your point?"

"I think you know what my point is, Evelyn. As far as you're concerned, the one good thing about Jake's dying is now you can finally erase me from your life."

"That's harsh, dear. And it's not true. You're upset."

"It's harsh and it is true and I *am* upset. And stop 'dearing' me, Evelyn. You're not fooling anyone. This whole fucking day has been about Jake and you and the kids and I'm sick of it."

Jenny started. "Mom —"

Polly wheeled on her daughter. "And don't you start, missy."

Evelyn Weisheit showed some voice. *"Polly! That is enough!"*

I readied myself to lunge for the glass, but there was no need. Polly dropped the stack of photographs to the floor and stormed off, taking the lion's share of the room's energy with her. Those of us remaining shared a communal silence. My eyes remained on Mrs. Weisheit, whose restraint under Polly's rude barrage struck me as something heroic, if not also a little chilling. Her natural pink had darkened slightly, but otherwise her composure was intact. Unlike her brother-in-law, who had gone nearly ashen.

I knelt down and gathered the photographs and handed them to Gregory Weisheit. As he busied himself squaring off the stack of photographs, Evelyn Weisheit leaned forward slightly in her chair. "I'm sorry. We haven't met. I'm Evelyn Weisheit. Jake's mother."

"I'm Hitchcock Sewell. Nice to meet you, Mrs. Weisheit."

"Mr. Sewell. I believe you are the undertaker, am I right about that?"

"You are."

"I was wondering who Polly's new friend was. She does surprise us with all her friends."

"I only met your daughter-in-law for the first time this past Sunday," I said.

"Yet here you are."

"Polly invited . . . she requested that I attend the funeral. She asked me out to the house. I'm very sorry about the loss of your son, Mrs. Weisheit. I have to tell you, you're showing remarkable courage."

"Jake was my only child."

"That's what I understand."

"He did not deserve what happened to him."

"Of course not."

She folded her hands on her lap and studied my face. It was a placid gaze but at the same time piercing. The edge came off when she offered a smile. "You have kind eyes," she remarked. "So did my son."

A body brushed past me. It was Jenny Weisheit. She placed a hand on her grandmother's shoulder. "Would you like a brownie, Gran?"

"Have you met my granddaughter, Mr. Sewell?"

"I have," I said.

"She has her father's eyes." She smiled again, laying her hand atop Jenny's. "Isn't she the most beautiful thing you have ever seen?"

Jenny looked up at me, blushing. "You don't have to answer that."

"No he doesn't," Evelyn Weisheit said. "I can see it in his face."

Chapter Eleven

Jonathan (Sisco) Fontaine was arrested and officially charged with the murder of Jake Weisheit. The arrest took place the evening of Weisheit's funeral, though I didn't hear about it until the next day. Julia phoned me at the office with the news, just as I was getting ready to go fetch Mrs. Papadaki from Spiro's. I had decided to take Mrs. Papadaki's casket down to Spiro's and load the little lady in directly from there.

"I was just watching Marty and Don, and guess what?"

Marty and Don are the two most popular wake-up guys on Baltimore television. Marty Bass and Don Scott. Think Dino and Jerry. Bob and Bing. Julia has a thing for Don Scott that just won't quit. She's also very good friends with Mrs. Don Scott, so there will be no developments on that front.

"Don says they arrested Sisco last night around six o'clock. Then Marty came on right after the news and said, 'Hey, I used to party with that guy. Check it out.' He ran a clip where he was onstage with Sisco's band. It was part of an interview he did with Sisco sometime last year. Marty was squeezed between two of the Kids. They were singing 'El Paso.' "

"Marty Bass sings like a cat on a fence."

"They're pushing this as a celebrity crime," Julia said.

"America loves its celebrity crimes."

"Yes, sir, we do."

"I saw Sisco yesterday outside the church service," I said. "He was pretty spooked."

"What church service? For Jake Weisheit? What were you doing there?"

"Polly Weisheit asked me if I'd go."

Julia spent the next three hours forming the word *I-n-t-e-r-e-s-t-i-n-g*. Sam poked his head into the office. He was wearing a porkpie hat. It looked stupid on him. That's just my opinion. I gave him the I'll-be-right-with-you signal.

"It wasn't interesting," I said into the phone. "Except to witness Polly Weisheit's isolation from the rest of the world. Though I've got to say, she makes it pretty difficult for people to cuddle up to her. Still, she was a widow hung out to dry."

"So do you think she and Sisco were in it together?"

"That's one of the obvious thoughts, of course."

"I hear a *but*."

"You do. I can't see Sisco being so stupid."

There was a pause. "Sisco?"

"I suggested to him the idea that Polly was

154

setting him up. She certainly seems to have gone cold on him since Sunday."

"And well she should. The smartest thing would be for the both of them to throw suspicion on each other. It takes the focus away from their being in cahoots."

"Cahoots."

"Defined by *Webster's* as two people acting together to murder one of the two's husband."

"Darling, you need a more liberal *Webster's*."

Julia said she had to go. "My Dane is stirring."

"Hans is there?"

"He is. Ask me what I'm having for breakfast."

"Do I want to hear this?"

"Hamlet and Eggs."

"You're pretty, but you're nuts."

"I feel the same way about you, pumpkin."

The *Sun* had run its photograph. I had the newspaper on my desk. The picture showed Spiro and Doodle sitting together on their couch, holding hands. In the foreground was the unmistakable silhouette of a woman's head and her shoulder. In boldface, the caption lead-in read: **Don't Take This Lying Down.**

Spiro and Dorothy Papadaki conduct the wake for Mr. Papadaki's mother,

Anna, in the foreground, at their home in Fells Point. Mrs. Papadaki died Sunday morning at the Briarcliff Manor in Lutherville. Sewell and Sons Family Funeral Home, also of Fells Point, arranged this unusual pose for the deceased. Mrs. Papadaki's funeral is to be held Thursday.

I showed the picture to Sam. "You seem to be getting a lot of publicity these days," he said.

"Lucky me."

"Maybe you'll start getting people asking for personalized poses, you know? Man playing a guitar. Woman reading a book. Like that. You can make it a whole new sideline."

"Designer poses."

"Right. That idea."

"You're a forward thinker, Sam."

The forward thinker and I got the casket down to Spiro's. Mrs. Papadaki was such a small woman she fit in sideways without any problem. Doodle made Spiro wait in the bedroom until the transfer was completed.

We rolled the casket up the street and into St. Teresa's, where a group of a dozen or so were gathered in the front several pews. I was surprised to see that one of them was Mrs. McNamara. She gave me a little wave as I came up the aisle. A young black woman in a starched white dress was sitting next to her looking bored out of her gourd. Billie was

156

coming down with something; she was feeling punky and was staying holed up across the street. As Father Ted pulled the levers and flipped the switches up at the altar, I stepped outside. A limo driver named Ellis was cooling his heels out in front of the church. I knew him. Ellis was working on a career as a rapper. He kept a notebook on him at all times, to scribble down his inspirations. Ellis was driving limos to support his stab at stardom. He nodded as I joined him on the sidewalk.

"Yo."

"Yo back at you."

Ellis proceeded to string together a couple of sentences that left me senseless. I recognized most of the words, but that didn't really do me any good.

I asked him. "What are we calling you these days, Ellis?"

"Dr. Puppy."

"Dr. Puppy. I like it."

Ellis told me that Mrs. McNamara had hired him to bring her down to Fells Point for Mrs. Papadaki's funeral. The gal sitting with Mrs. McNamara was from one of the temp services that supplies workers to Briarcliff. He said the temp's name was Teresa, just like the church.

"Ask me, she's a dope," Ellis said. "Don't ask me, she's still a dope. Whole way out here she's got a Walkman on and she's doing her Little Sissy like she don't care *how* stupid she looks. That old lady's too nice to slap her and I'm driving the car, so I can't." He held up his cell phone. "I got her number, though."

"So what you're telling me is you think she's cute."

"Shit. She want to Little Sissy on my face, I guess I got time for that."

A low-pressure system moving into the east from the Great Lakes region was bringing falling temperatures and gusty winds to the area, in advance of a storm system that was moving across the plains states. One of those gusts took Ellis's hat right off his head just as the small crowd was emerging from the church. The hat rolled neatly just out of Ellis's reach for about twenty zigzagging feet. Spiro seemed to be in good shape. Billie and I were springing for a limo for Spiro and Doodle. I ushered them into the car, then turned to see Mrs. McNamara standing in the door of the church. She must not have heard about the low-pressure system moving in from the Great Lakes, for she was wearing only a light jacket against the chill.

I took the steps two at a time (there are only four steps; this was not a major effort). "Hey, young lady, who let you go out dressed like that? Do you want to catch your death of cold?"

Mrs. McNamara looked down at her jacket,

then up at me. "I'll survive."

"Step back into the church for a minute." I looked to Teresa, who was slipping a pair of headphones over her ears. "Take her back inside," I said. I held up a finger. "One minute. I'll be right back." Teresa responded with a funky head bob.

I raced across the street to the funeral home and up the stairs. Billie was in her favorite chair, juggling tissues.

I asked, "What's the dope, antelope?"

"I'm fine," Billie said. "Truly. It's all in my head." She proceeded to cough like a coal miner.

"That's your chest," I told her. "Your head's that thing up there with the silvery stuff on it." Billie attempted to throw a tissue at me. It had to be most unsatisfying. I borrowed Billie's hunting jacket. "You weren't planning to go out and bag a moose, were you?"

Billie did not deign to respond.

Back at the church I wrapped the jacket around Mrs. McNamara's small shoulders. She winced a smile at me, clutching at the collar with her hamster hands. I thought she was looking a little pastier than when I'd run across her on Sunday. As I helped her to the car, I asked her how she was feeling.

"A little . . . woozy, Hitchcock. A . . . little weak."

In my estimation, Teresa the temp was a

complete waste of money. At the cemetery she stood next to Mrs. McNamara chewing gum and wagging her head to an internal tune. Maybe she would catch Mrs. McNamara if the wind blew her over, maybe she wouldn't.

Spiro came through like a champ. I think the several days spent with his mother had helped him out. He stood stoic and erect, and at the designated moment he stepped forward and sang a touching song in Greek. The wind swirled a little cyclone of red leaves around the small graveside gathering as Spiro sang his song. The leaves circled us. At the end of the service Mrs. McNamara toddled forward and set a hand on the casket. Her cheeks were wet with tears. Doodle came over to her and the two embraced.

I accompanied Spiro and Doodle back to the limo. There was to be no official post-funeral bash. I told Spiro and Doodle that they had the limo for another three hours. "Do the town. Better yet, go out into the country. Go see the leaves. Horse country looks great this time of year. I'll tell the driver to head you out Shawann Road."

Ellis was on a cell phone, cursing at someone on the other end. As I stepped over to see what was going on, he ended the call with a dissatisfied poke at the tiny Off button.

"Problem?" Ellis pointed his cell phone at the car. The car had two flat tires. One of them was the front left tire. The other was the spare.

"And no one to come get us. That problem enough?"

Mrs. McNamara looked as if she very much needed to get off her feet. I took her arm. "Come with me." I signaled Teresa to tag along and I led them to the hearse. Mrs. McNamara stumbled along the way. If not for my hold on her arm, she'd have tumbled to the ground.

"I . . . need to sit."

"Come along then."

As I pulled open the passenger door of the hearse, Teresa came to life. "I'm not getting in no hearse. No way."

"Don't be silly. Get in."

"Uh-uh. That's for dead people. I'm not getting in a dead people's car. No way."

I helped Mrs. McNamara into the car. Teresa made a series of faces but eventually got in next to Mrs. McNamara. Add Sam behind the wheel and I was odd man out, so I scrambled into the rear.

Sam twisted around in his seat. "Now you lie down and be quiet back there. That's how it's done."

Sam drove us back to Fells Point, where we transferred to my car. I put Teresa in the back and she retreated to her Walkman. By the time we hit Broadway she was funking and chunking.

Mrs. McNamara inclined toward me. "She thinks she's . . . Little Sissy."

It was still lunchtime when we arrived at Briarcliff. Mrs. McNamara asked me if I would like to stay for lunch. "Please, Hitchcock. My . . . treat."

I stayed. Lunch was meat loaf and cold carrots. Dessert was a brown gelatinous square. They served a tea that seemed to have been strained though high-grade cardboard.

Mrs. McNamara watched my face as I negotiated my meal. "You wonder why . . . people die here?"

Mrs. McNamara only picked at her food. It wasn't a culinary issue; she told me that she had been having digestive problems lately. "I think it's my blood . . . thinner. That's for my heart. I would . . . swear they've changed the dose, but they say they haven't."

"Well, you have to eat something, Mrs. McNamara."

"I'm . . . so dry all the time now. It's hard sometimes . . . to swallow." She chased a sliced carrot around the plate with her fork. "Hitchcock, do you remember . . . our egg creams?"

"You mean at the diner? Of course I do. There was a whole little egg cream cult going on among the students for a while.

We'd get to be like zombies. M-u-s-t h-a-v e e-g-g c-r-e-a-m."

"That . . . would be good."

"I don't suppose they could whip up one of those for you here, could they?"

Mrs. McNamara folded her hands together and set them on the table. "They . . . are very limited."

Besides Mrs. McNamara and me, our table included a woman in a wheelchair who barely spoke above a whisper, a bosomy, florid-faced woman called Babs with fairly unconvincing red hair and a bosomy Atlantic City sweatshirt, and a cagey fellow who introduced himself to me as Frank Sinatra.

"You, I've heard of," I said.

"Strangers in the night." He winked at Mrs. McNamara. "Two lonely people, we were strangers in the night."

Babs sniffed. "You're stranger, all right."

The old guy wasn't really loopy; he knew who he was. He was Leonard, a retired optometrist from Essex. Leonard looked to have been one of his own best customers, wearing a pair of glasses with lenses thick enough to stop a bullet.

"I once examined the eyes of Spiro Agnew himself," Leonard told me. Rather, he *declared* to me. Babs shook her head.

"The Spiro Agnew eyes. Lord help us."

The woman in the wheelchair whispered excitably and completely incomprehensibly.

"This was when he was running for governor," Leonard continued, unfazed. "Do you remember Spiro Agnew? Maybe you're too young. When were you born?" I told him. "Ach, you're a baby. Spiro Agnew was governor of Maryland and then he went on to become Richard Nixon's vice president. He resigned in disgrace. He didn't pay his taxes. Does it occur to the second most powerful man in the world that it might not be such a bad idea to pay your taxes? I could tell way back when he came in for his eye examination that he thought he was smarter than water. You can't —"

Babs interrupted. " 'Smarter than water.' Why do you always say that? It doesn't make any sense. What is 'smarter than water' supposed to mean?"

"It's an expression."

"It's not an expression. It's something you made up. An expression is something everybody has heard. Nobody knows this but you. An expression *expresses* something. What does 'smarter than water' express? How smart is water in the first place?"

Leonard's five pounds of glasses shifted in my direction. "You know what I'm saying, don't you?"

"About Spiro Agnew? I think I get the picture."

Leonard gave Babs a triumphant look. "*He* is smarter than water."

164

Mrs. McNamara was looking tired. She asked me if I would accompany her to the atrium. Babs tugged on my elbow as I stood up and mouthed largely, *"Take care of her."* Leonard appeared to be miffed that he hadn't been allowed to finish his Spiro Agnew story.

"I was talking," he muttered.

I walked Mrs. McNamara to the atrium. It was nearly full. Faded flowers seeking sun. Vines stretching out for a nap. A glumness had come over Mrs. McNamara. As she settled onto the glider, her energy seemed sliced in half.

I pulled a wicker chair up close to the glider. "Mrs. McNamara, is everything okay? You're not looking any too perky."

"I hate . . . funerals."

"They're not exactly the most thrilling way to spend a day."

She sat back and closed her eyes, and for a moment I thought she had drifted off. When she opened them again, they were filled with tears.

"What's wrong, Mrs. McNamara?"

"I don't know. Maybe . . . it's Anna. I'm going to miss Anna." She reached over and took a hold of my hand. Her fingers were ice. Her voice dropped to a whisper. "Hitchcock . . . I don't like it here. They . . . drop people."

"Drop people?"

"Sometimes when they . . . transfer people from bed. Or help us . . . to the bathroom. They . . ." She closed her eyes again. "I am . . . getting sick here."

"Have you ever been dropped, Mrs. Mc-Namara?" Her head shook. Almost imperceptibly.

"No."

"Did they drop Anna Papadaki?"

"I don't think so." She withdrew her hand and picked up a magazine. "I have . . . money. I am provided for. I want to . . . leave."

"What say I come back out some time when you're a little less tired and take you for a drive. The leaves are turning, we could head out into the country. We can go searching for an egg cream. That could be our mission. How does that sound?"

Mrs. McNamara took up her magnifying glass and aimed it at the cover of the magazine.

" 'Lose . . . thirty pounds in thirty . . . days.' " She lowered the magnifying glass, running the tip of her tongue along her lips. "In ninety days . . . I would . . . be gone."

I left her. As I headed down the hallway toward the front door, I could hear a buzzer sounding though from precisely which direction I couldn't determine. There was a man sleeping in a wheelchair in the middle of the hallway. Or maybe he was dead. I wheeled him over by the wall and parked him there.

"Excuse me. What are you doing?"

I turned around. The question had come from a woman who had just rounded the corner. She was fiftyish, short and stout (no handle, no spout), and wearing a nurse's uniform.

"Who are you?" she demanded. "What is your name?" She stood with her hands on her hips, emanating that certain je ne sais quoi of a commandant.

"The name is Sewell," I said. "Hitchcock Sewell."

The face remained stony. "You're the undertaker. What are you doing here? Is there something I don't know?"

I explained to her that what she didn't know was that the car that Mrs. McNamara had hired to take her to Anna Papadaki's funeral had suffered two flat tires and that I had driven Mrs. McNamara and Teresa the temp back to Briarcliff. The arms left the hips and crossed themselves over the woman's ample bosom. "I was not informed."

"Blame me. I wasn't aware that I was supposed to inform anybody."

"I am responsible for the movement of my staff and the well-being of the residents."

"I'm sorry," I said. "But you are . . . ?"

"Phyllis Fitch. I'm the nursing administrator at Briarcliff."

"It's nice to meet you, Mrs. Fitch."

"Miss."

I assured her that everything was fine. "I've just left Mrs. McNamara in the atrium. I think she's a little tired from her outing."

"I'll look in on her."

"Phyllis?"

We both looked up. Marilyn Tuck was coming toward us down the hallway. She gave me a sharp nod. "You saw the paper?"

I nodded back. "I did."

She turned to the nursing administrator. "Phyllis, you did see to it that no one received the paper today, didn't you?"

"I told you I would."

"I'm just checking."

"No one got the paper today." I couldn't be certain, but I seemed to detect a growl in the woman's voice.

"Well, we have another little problem now," Marilyn said. "I just got off the phone with Andy's wife. It seems Andy and his sons were playing with some sort of toy rocket. I didn't follow all the details, but apparently Andy fell off the roof of his house. He broke his arm. It's in a cast up to his elbow."

"Who's Andy?" I asked.

Marilyn answered. "Andy is our piano player. We have a cabaret every Saturday. We hold it in the dining room. It's terribly popular. For many of our residents the cabaret is the high point of their week. Andy is very

168

good with the residents. He knows all the standards."

"Ravel has a whole set of piano pieces to be played with one hand," I said. "I saw Leon Fleischer tear through them once down at the Meyerhoff."

"I don't believe the residents are going to sing along with Ravel."

"We can't cancel the cabaret," Phyllis declared.

"That's correct, Phyllis," Marilyn said. "We'd like not to. But what do you propose we do without Andy?"

"I can play the harmonica," I said. "But I guess that's good for about five minutes. So what you need is a new piano player."

"We need someone who can keep a crowd of geriatrics entertained," Marilyn said. "I don't care if it's a sword swallower. It'll be a shame if we have to cancel the cabaret."

"We can't cancel the cabaret," Phyllis said again.

Marilyn took a beat. "We're agreed on that," she said evenly. "It would be unfortunate. Why don't we put our heads together and see if we can come up with something?"

A slight blush came to Phyllis Fitch's cheeks. She moved in behind the old man's wheelchair and with a grunt started down the hallway.

"She's all business," I remarked.

Marilyn grimaced. "She is. Phyllis has been

here forever. She helped nurse my mother and then my father. She was devoted to my father. He stipulated her position at Briarcliff in his will. Phyllis isn't exactly easy to warm up to, but her dedication is unquestioned. She would fall on her sword." Down the hall, Phyllis and her charge rounded the corner and vanished. "Listen, you can find your way out, can't you? I have some matters I need to attend to."

As I passed by the room of one of the residents on my way out, I spotted Teresa standing in front of a window. Her headset was on and she was moving her outstretched arms like they were waves on the ocean.

Out front, Thomas was raking leaves. I greeted him, but he didn't respond. He wielded the rake with intent. As if the leaves were his enemy. And the enemy was all around him. He was chopping at them like a man possessed.

Chapter Twelve

Lieutenant Kruk wanted to see me. I had a message on my machine when I got back home. Alcatraz was practically performing a mime show of a dog wrapping his leash around his neck and holding up the loose end in a hung-from-the-rafters pose, so I took him out first for his frolic, then got back into the Valiant and pushed the D button.

Police headquarters is a large square gray building with city hall on one side and what remains of Baltimore's once-famed run of strip joints on the other. There was a time in Baltimore's history when the luminous Blaze Starr probably could have won a race for mayor. The bump and grind of city government. Ten-dollar beers for everyone. Her Two O'clock Club lives on, a lonely relic of bygone burlesque.

This was not my first visit to Kruk's office. I had had cause to visit his sanctum several times in the past. My world is alive with dead bodies, after all, and so is his. Kruk was seated at his desk, a large industrial-green thing that tended to dwarf the man. I accepted the offer of coffee from the woman who ushered me in.

"Black?" she asked.

"You've got to be joking."

Kruk waved away the offer. He was leaning back in his chair, holding a small stack of papers. His body language seemed designed to let me know that for the moment, at least, the papers were a lot more compelling to him than I was. Give me a chance to place a bet and I'd wager that Kruk already knew what was typed up on the papers. He was simply being cagey.

My coffee was brought to me in a paper cup. I leaned forward and placed it on the edge of Kruk's desk. A little puncturing of territory never hurts. Kruk tossed the papers onto the desk, stared at the cup for a few seconds, then turned his lovely gaze to me.

"If it's tickets to the policeman's ball you're hawking," I said, "a simple phone call would have done. Not to say I don't appreciate the personal attention."

It takes more than a lousy policeman's ball joke to crack the detective's nut. "You attended the Weisheit funeral yesterday," Kruk said. He seemed satisfied with his short declarative statement.

I beat his socks off with my response. "Yes."

"You were seen by one of my men coming out of the church."

"Okay."

"You were seen in discussion with Jonathan Fontaine."

"Right again. This is leading somewhere, I assume."

"You then attended the services at the cemetery."

"You left out the part where I stopped to tie my shoe."

Kruk looked disappointed. "Does it ever wind down, Mr. Sewell?"

"Of course it does."

"I'd like you to remember that this is a murder investigation. It's not the comedy hour."

"You weren't laughing," I noted.

"You weren't funny."

"So then I don't know what you're complaining about." I leaned forward and took up the coffee cup and hazarded a sip. I winced and placed it back on the exact spot. I knew Kruk was waiting for a crack about the lousy coffee. I kept him waiting.

After a few more seconds of silence Kruk said, "Jonathan Fontaine was arrested last night for the murder of Jake Weisheit."

"This is what I've heard. I hear Don and Marty were all over it this morning."

"Mr. Fontaine is an entertainer. The media enjoys exploiting this sort of thing. There's nothing we can do about that. Mr. Fontaine has maintained his innocence."

"I see. Does this mean you're going to set him free?"

"His hearing is —" Kruk checked his watch. "His hearing is any minute. Depending on the judge, bail might be set. If Mr. Fontaine could post it, he could be freed. I don't like the idea myself, but that's not the part of the law I deal with."

I said nothing. Despite how it might seem, I like Kruk. He suffers an essential personality deficiency, not to mention that inexplicable yellow hair, but he is a rock-solid public servant who probably works harder than his salary warrants. He *is* cagier than he appears and I happen to have an aversion to being peppered with questions, which happens to be John Kruk's stock-in-trade. So we'll never hug trees together. But in my way I respect him.

"I would like to know what you and Mr. Fontaine were discussing yesterday outside Roland Park Presbyterian," Kruk said. A pigeon landed on the window ledge just behind him. From my angle it looked like it was sitting on Kruk's shoulder.

"I was raising the possibility that Polly Weisheit set him up. That she could have killed her husband and then called Sisco over to be at the scene as a way to implicate him."

"I see. And what did Mr. Fontaine have to say about your theory?"

"Mr. Fontaine isn't too happy that Polly hasn't spoken with him since the murder."

Kruk's eyebrows traveled north. "Polly?"

"Polly Weisheit."

"I know who you're talking about. So you think the woman killed her husband."

I shrugged. "Beats me. It's a theory. Jake gets up to let the cat in. Pol . . . Mrs. Weisheit follows him downstairs and stabs him in the back. Did the killer use one of the kitchen knives?"

"It appears so."

"So it fits. Except the gun. Jake Weisheit was holding a gun. At least that's how it looked. And it had been fired. At least that's how it looked." Kruk raised an eyebrow. "I don't want to assume what I don't really know," I said.

"The gun had been fired."

"So maybe Jake took a shot at his wife."

"And she dodged the bullet, grabbed a knife and ran around behind him and stabbed him fatally in the back? That's a pretty speedy woman."

"I wasn't there. We're just talking theories. Maybe Jake just got fed up with Silly. And took a potshot."

"Silly?"

"The cat. Her name is Priscilla. They call her Silly." Kruk said nothing. "What about the gun? Did you trace it?"

Kruk picked up a pencil and pretended to

scribble on a piece of paper. "Trace . . . gun. Thank you, Mr. Sewell. That's a wonderful idea. I wish we had thought of it."

"This is not the comedy hour," I reminded him.

"The gun is registered to Jake Weisheit. He had a permit. Perfectly legal."

"So if he is not going to shoot the cat, why the gun? Maybe he thought he heard a burglar. Maybe he *did* hear a burglar."

"Or maybe the gun was planted on the kitchen floor after Mr. Weisheit was already dead," Kruk said.

"By whom?"

"That's a question, isn't it."

"By Sisco?"

"That's an answer."

"By the lady of the house?"

Kruk aimed his pencil at me. "By you?"

"There's one I certainly hadn't thought of. Me. Let's see. Me . . . Hmm, that's a tough one. Do we have any thoughts as to why I would do such a thing?"

"I was hoping maybe you could tell me that yourself, Mr. Sewell."

"I hate to dash your hopes, Detective. But since it didn't happen that way, I'd be hard put to explain why it happened that way, which it didn't do."

"I see."

"You're being coy with me, Detective. I'm sure you would know whether or not Jake

Weisheit fired that gun. There would be powder burns."

"And if someone were to have put the gun in Mr. Weisheit's hand after he had been murdered and fired it, there would've been powder burns on that person's hands as well. Except by the time we could have made those tests, that person might have driven home and taken a shower."

"I hope you don't take this the wrong way, but sometimes I wish you'd think about keeping a slightly less open mind."

"It's an occupational hazard, Mr. Sewell. But in this particular case it's difficult not to keep it wide open. Especially when I place you at the murder scene and then later at the funeral, where as best I can understand, you have no business. When you're seen outside the church talking with Sisco Fontaine."

"Mrs. Weisheit asked me to attend the funeral."

"Why? It was being handled by another funeral home."

"I know. I made most of the arrangements with Fink's myself."

"And why is that?"

"Mrs. Weisheit asked me to."

"Mrs. Weisheit is asking you to do an awful lot, isn't she? Is there anything else Mrs. Weisheit asked you to do that we should know about?"

"Like?"

"Like killing her husband for her?"

I picked up the coffee cup again and feigned a moment's thought. The pigeon outside the window took a step forward, cocking its head. "No, I don't recall that being on her to-do list."

"Or asking you to remove the body from the scene?"

"That was Sisco."

"That is the statement we have from you and from Mrs. Weisheit. You might recall that Mr. Fontaine offered a slightly different explanation for why you were allegedly called out there."

"And I recall you thought Sisco's explanation was a stupid one," I said.

"Which he later changed, to line up with the one made by you and Mrs. Weisheit."

"I know there's a point to all this."

Kruk placed his hands behind his head. "I've just made it, Mr. Sewell. You and Mrs. Weisheit gave the same statement. Mr. Fontaine gave a different one."

I waited. Kruk waited. It dawned on me where he was headed. "It's Polly and *me* who are ganging up on Sisco? Is that what you're saying. *We're* setting *him* up?"

"Polly."

"It's her name."

"Are you always so familiar with your customers?"

"She isn't a customer, remember?"

"You told me that until Sunday she was a perfect stranger."

"Perfect. That's correct."

"Are you always so familiar with perfect strangers that you call them by their first names and make funeral arrangements for them and attend their husband's funeral *and* go to their house afterward?"

"You should have been a cop," I said. "You're good at this."

"I have not heard one answer from you that I like, Mr. Sewell. Not one."

"I have to say, Lieutenant, you're awfully hard to please."

Kruk lowered his chair and came forward on his desk. I can't say as I cared for the look he was giving me. And I'm sure that's just how he wanted me to feel.

"You have embarrassed my office in some of our past dealings and I'm wondering if I haven't been bending over backward for you on this Weisheit affair so that I don't look like sour grapes." I prayed for the woman who had brought me the coffee to burst into the room and cry out, *Lieutenant Kruk, you don't look like sour grapes!* It didn't happen. Kruk went on. "After our talk on Sunday, I granted you the benefit of the doubt. I saw an extramarital affair, a murder and an ill-advised scheme that brought you to the scene."

"And what do you see now?"

"Now what I see is you continuing your involvement with Jonathan Fontaine as well as with Polly Weisheit. Now your presence at the Weisheit residence at five in the morning is beginning to bother me a little more. I'm keeping an eye on you, Mr. Sewell. Fair warning."

"Lieutenant, if I were involved in any way with the murder of Jake Weisheit, would I attend the funeral and go to the house and sit here and refer to Mrs. Weisheit as 'Polly'? You can check my grade point average at Frostburg. I'm an above-average cookie. Would I be so stupid?"

"We're through here, Mr. Sewell," Kruk said. He fell back in his chair.

"But I haven't finished my coffee," I said.

Kruk made a temple of his fingers and set his chin on it. Behind him, the pigeon took off.

"Would you be so stupid?"

Chapter Thirteen

It occurred to me only after I had left the building that I had forgotten to tell Kruk who the killer was. Granted, it was only a guess. But I thought the hunch was decent. I felt it in my bones. Specifically in my ribs.

The way Polly Weisheit told the story, Chip Cooperman would have beheaded a simple shoe salesman if he caught the guy so much as sneaking a glimpse at Polly Weisheit's gams while helping her try on a lousy pair of pumps. Polly had said to me that Cooperman was actually okay about Jake, that he liked him. But maybe she was lying. Maybe she was protecting Cooperman. Maybe Chip had caught wind of Polly and Jake's marital troubles and thought this was a perfect time to step in and confront his rival. Maybe it was time for the guardian angel to come swooping down. So he enters the house early Sunday morning and dispatches Jake. Polly comes downstairs and sees Chip standing there in a cold sweat, Jake on the floor, blood beginning to appear from underneath him.

Oh, Chip. You shouldn't have.

Or maybe Polly witnesses the whole thing. Maybe the three of them are there kicking up a huge scene, and when it is over, Jake is dead. Either way. Doesn't matter. Polly sees poor hopeless Chip standing there with blood on his hands. All for the love of her. A tiny compartment opens up in her heart.

Chip, this is horrible, but it's done. Go away. Leave. Work up an alibi. You're a troubled man, but there's no gain in your rotting in prison for this. Go.

He leaves. Polly composes herself. Weighs the options. Picks up the phone and calls Sisco. *Sisco, get over here right away. We have a sit-u-a-tion.*

I crossed Commerce Street. On a stool at an open door sat a guy you'd expect to see riding a Harley and waving a bat. He was murmuring, "Girls live, girls live, girls live." Or maybe it was "Live girls, live girls, live girls . . ." It depends on where you come in on it. He parted a black curtain to show me a woman on a small walkway bathed in purple and red lights. She wasn't wearing any shoes. Among other things. The smell of tobacco and beer wafted out the door. The guy on the stool dropped the curtain and leered at me.

I reached Calvert Street and crossed over. There is an island in the middle of Calvert Street. A statue. Some foliage. A homeless man was asleep on the island. A castaway. As

I reached the curb, another thought came to me. What if Polly's story to me about Chip Cooperman was itself a pack of lies? Or at the very least, a convenient rearrangement of the facts. Whose word did I have that Cooperman was an unstable oaf who trotted the streets of Baltimore as Polly Weisheit's self-appointed guard dog? I had Polly Weisheit's word. Who was to say that the relationship between Cooperman and Polly didn't have an entirely different angle? Who was to say she wasn't dancing the naughty tango with her old friend Chip Cooperman?

Chip. Go away. Leave. Work up an alibi. I don't want you rotting in prison for this. Go. But first, give old Polly a big wet kiss, eh, lover?

Several news vans were parked along the west side of Calvert Street. I went up the stairs to the courthouse and dumped all my change and my keys into a plastic tub and walked through the metal detector. I made like the letter T and was wanded. My belt buckle brought a burping from the wand, but I was deemed unlikely to gather a roomful of hostages with my big bad belt buckle. Certainly they didn't want me shuffling along the halls of the courthouse with my pants down around my ankles. They let me through.

Courtroom 4-B has a very high ceiling. A pair of elephants on piggyback would fit inside and still leave room for a juggler on top. There were no windows. The walls were a dark cherry. Anything and everything that could be polished had been polished. Up near the empty jury box, the Maryland state flag and Old Glory hung limply from their stands.

A number of cameramen were gathered in the rear. I recognized one of them. Big guy named Kenny Rogers. (Better than being a little guy named Kenny Rogers.) Kenny's father worked at WBAL with my own father in days of yore. Kenny's father was retired now and living in Essex making stained glass doodads as a hobby. My father got hit by a beer truck just twenty-eight years shy of retirement. The differences go on from there.

"Hey, Hitch. What brings you here?"

"Don't you read the papers? I'm a marginal suspect in the Weisheit murder."

"No kidding? Did you do it?" Kenny asked.

"Yeah, but I got away with it. I thought I'd come take a look at the patsy they're sending up for it."

"Sisco Fontaine. Sisco and the Kids. You ever see them play?"

"I have."

"They're not bad," Kenny said. "I like those Kids. Those little cowgirl outfits? I saw them at the Mount Vernon Festival a couple of weeks ago. We were covering the festival."

"I was there."

"There was this one," Kenny said. "This

blond. Good enough to eat."

"You're subtle, Kenny. Her name is Angela."

"You know her?"

"Sisco introduced us. She's very nice. We talked a little Plato. Then she had to get back onstage and shake, shake, shake. Which reminds me, we made a vague date. She was going out of town for a couple of weeks. She's probably back now. I have to give her a call."

Kenny shook his head. "You have to be reminded to call a girl like that?"

"I've had a lot on my mind," I said.

"Right. You killed this guy the other day. I forgot."

"Exactly."

I took a seat in the rear of the courtroom. The court bailiff and a policeman and a couple of those people you always see milling about in the front of a courtroom were yukking it up near the judge's bench. A few minutes later, as if by an invisible signal, they all went to their corners and the judge appeared. Kenny and his colleagues shouldered their cameras and Sisco was brought into the courtroom through a side door.

He looked nervous and confused, though when he spotted the cameras he straightened his shoulders and found one of his smirks. His lawyer looked like he had been lifted directly from a seedy used car lot. There was certainly no oil shortage on the top of his head. The judge seemed bored. He wore a pair of bifocals on the end of his nose. After hearing Sisco respond, "Not guilty, Your Honor," to the charge of planting a large knife in Jake Weisheit's back on the morning of such and such and so-and-so, he listened without comment to the assistant prosecutor argue the points of Sisco's arrest for the murder. The prosecutor averred that Sisco was a dangerous person and a flight risk and urged that bail be denied.

Sisco's lawyer then stepped forward and gave his side of things. Aside from mispronouncing *Weisheit*, he did okay. He stressed the complete lack of physical evidence and made certain to include the words *circumstantial* and *alleged* at least half a dozen times each. He also suggested that "Mr. Fontaine's status as a well-known popular entertainer" was being unfairly used against him, and he cited Sisco's celebrity as a factor that mitigated the notion of his being a flight risk. The judge wasn't buying. He ran the matter through his judicial mill and came up with a hundred and fifty thousand dollars bail. The show ended and Sisco was taken back out the way he came in.

Kenny was yawning as I headed out of the courtroom. "Wow. That was riveting."

I noticed a man leaning up against the wall next to the window. He was easy to notice, with frizzy Afro-style hair cleaved down the middle, the style famously preferred by Bozo the Clown and Larry of the Three Stooges. His shoulders were stooped, his head hanging vulture-style, and he was chewing on a tooth-pick. Gnawing. Practically masticating. He gave me a furtive glance — at least that's how it felt to me — and pushed himself off the wall as I headed for the elevator. He got on the elevator with me and moved immedi-ately to the rear. Call me paranoid, but I could feel his eyes crawling all over my back as we descended to the first floor. It oc-curred to me that maybe Kruk had whistled for one of his minions as I was leaving his office. *I'm keeping an eye on you. Fair warning.* Maybe I had just grown a tail.

The elevator arrived at the first floor. The door opened on a woman who was crying softly and being supported by a man who looked scared to death. They got onto the el-evator. I headed for the exit, still feeling Bozo's eyes on my back. I didn't want to turn around, but as I reached the door, I did. A man in an electric wheelchair whizzed silently past me. Bozo was nowhere to be seen.

I headed over to the Center Stage box of-fice and asked about ticket availability.

"What night?"

"What've you got that's good?"

"We just had a nice pair of orchestra seats turned back in for tonight."

I asked for the pay phone and was directed around the corner, next to the restrooms, where I made a call. Framed photographs of previous productions were up on the brick wall. I recognized one of the actors from the early years of *M*A*S*H*. He was seated in a Model T and wearing a boater and a three-mile-wide smile. I returned to the box office after my call, holding up two fingers.

The guy in the box office held up two fingers as well. "Peace."

"The tickets," I said. "I'll take them."

It was only a few blocks to the Walters Art Gallery, so I left my car where it was and hoofed it. They had a William Blake show; my God, what a turbulent genius *that* guy was. A nearsighted man was practically resting his nose against the glass of each drawing and was moving at a pace that was in irritating syncopation with mine, so I finally moved to the end of the exhibit and walked it backwards. The nearsighted man and I met up around Blake's middle period, where things were just starting to really bubble. I knew the madness that lay up ahead, but I didn't say anything to the guy. I reached the beginning of the show and left the gallery.

I ping-ponged around a few of the other galleries a bit, but Blake pretty much exhausts you. As I approached where I had parked my car, I saw it sitting on the flatbed of a tow truck, the flashing yellow lights bouncing off the bottle green. I ran over to the driver. "That's my car."

He removed the cigar stump from his mouth.

"It belongs to the city now."

"Come on. Put it back."

"No can do." He twisted in his seat to take a look out the rear window. "It's a nice car."

"It would be nicer if it were back on the street where I could get into it and putt-putt happily away from here."

"Can't do. The paperwork's all written up."

I pulled out my wallet. "How much?"

"Are you trying to bribe me?"

"A donation to your favorite charity?"

"That's illegal. I could lose my job."

"I know a way to avoid that," I said. "Don't tell anyone. I promise I won't either."

He gave me a long look. I saw very little happening in the look. And very little chance I could avoid the tow.

"You want a ride to the lot?"

"Sure."

"Get in."

The ticket was fifty dollars. The tow charge was a hundred. The city lot where my car was towed was located less than half a mile from the point of the infraction. If I had been parked all the way down in Sparrows Point I would have been charged the same

189

amount. I dedicated all of twenty seconds conducting a seminar on prorating to the Burgess Meredith type behind the caged window at the lot. He was a listless listener. He sharpened his fingertips against his stubbly cheek, and when I was finished he said, "Hundred dollars." Just like he had when I started.

"You want to sell that car?" the tow truck driver asked me as he was unshackling the chains that bound it. "I might be interested."

"Sure," I said. "Three hundred thousand dollars."

"You're crazy. It's not worth that much."

"Take it or leave it."

He left it. I checked to see if he had left any nicks, but he hadn't. As I drove out of the lot I thought about whether I should tell the police about Chip Cooperman. He was certainly worth their looking into.

"My ass," said a voice. I was the only one in the car, so it must have been mine.

Chapter Fourteen

The lights came up for intermission and Angela turned to me.

"Fudge brownie."

"Go for it," I said.

The aisles were filled with waddle-steppers and we joined in. Our seats were only three rows back from the stage, so our trip to the lobby took several minutes. Angela squeezed my hand, then zigzagged through the crowd to reach the café. She was paying for her fudge brownie by the time I caught up with her.

"You want a bite?" She aimed a corner of the brownie at my mouth. "I don't know what got into me. Halfway through the first act I just started to see a fudge brownie floating above the stage."

Angela held one hand just below the brownie, to catch crumbs. I was reminded of Billie, how she sometimes picks up both her saucer and her cup and holds them like this. The similarities ended there. Angela was a good head taller than Billie and of an altogether different body type. Broader shoulders, just to pick an example. Younger. Tauter. Her face was open and attractive, framed by a cascade of honey blond hair. She had told me while we were waiting for the play to start that she grew up in a ranch house in Bel Air, Maryland, across the street from her father's service station. Her mother died when she was young and she had no siblings, and she knew all about rotating tires, changing oil and resetting points. She bragged to me that by the time she was fourteen, she could replace an entire exhaust system twice as fast as her father could. I could well imagine teenage boys plunging screwdrivers into their mufflers simply for the excuse to watch Angela moving around under the lift. Not just teenage boys, come to think of it.

Angela offered me another bite of the brownie. I declined. She popped the rest of the brownie into her mouth. I grabbed a couple of coffees as chasers. We nabbed a pair of chairs at a small round table and I asked her if she was enjoying the play.

"Oh yes. Hamlet's a complete mess, though, isn't he? I mean, that poor guy is a real piece of work. Does he kill himself at the end? He sure seems headed there."

"All will be revealed," I said.

Angela saw that the line for the ladies' room was stretching out the door.

"I'd better get in line."

She squeezed past me, giving me a little peck on the top of my head. As she reached the restroom line, a woman whom I recognized emerged from the bathroom. The woman took a drink from the water fountain, then came into the café and sat down at the table next to mine. She hadn't noticed me, or if so my face hadn't registered. I leaned forward into her field of vision.

"Hello." A pair of hawk-like eyes blinked behind the glasses. "Hitchcock Sewell. We met yesterday, at the Weisheit funeral."

Toby Schultz's wife stared for another few seconds. "Yes, you're Polly's new friend." It sounded more like an accusation.

"I wouldn't exactly put it that way. I only met her a few days ago."

"I suppose in her way Polly can be *friendly* when she wants to be."

"Let me take a stab here. We would put you in the not-liking-Polly camp, am I right?"

Betty Schultz made a little clucking noise. "I don't pretend to understand Polly Weisheit," she declared. "I never have. I know I'm supposed to be speaking kindly of her at a time like this, but I'm sorry, Polly and I have never warmed up to each other. I've always been civil with her, but you saw her behavior yesterday. You saw how she treated her mother-in-law. It was disgraceful."

"People aren't always at their best at a time like this," I said. "She's under a lot of stress."

"You don't have to defend her. I've known

193

Polly Weisheit for years. She is a self-serving woman and that's really all there is to it. Everything always comes back to her. I honestly have no idea how Jake put up with her for all these years. The most patient man on earth. It's Toby's fault, really. He's the one who introduced them. Polly browbeat that poor man. Nothing Jake did was ever right as far as Polly was concerned. In my opinion, Jake was way too good for her. Plenty of better women would kill for a husband like that."

She sat back in her chair and blinked myopically. A touch of pink rose into her cheeks. The couple at the table behind her burst into laughter. Betty Schultz turned a sour eye onto them.

"Who do you think killed Jake?" I asked.

The woman's head pivoted slowly. She hesitated before giving an answer. And it wasn't much of an answer. "I prefer not to speculate."

"I assume you know that the police have made an arrest."

"I do."

"But you prefer not to speculate."

"I make my living as a judge, Mr. Sewell. I'm on the circuit court."

"I wasn't aware of that. A judge. That's impressive."

"I don't say it to impress. I say it as a means of explaining. I am trained to remain impartial."

"That doesn't preclude you from holding opinions, does it?"

"Everyone holds opinions. That's human nature. There is a difference, however, between holding and sharing."

"I can't argue with you on that."

"Of course not. There's no argument."

"So . . . are you here with your husband?" I asked, changing the subject. She had set her hands on the table. They were small, meaty hands. Boxy. As unattractive a collection of little sausages as you could hope to see.

"No. Toby had some business to attend to at the last minute. I turned in his ticket."

"He gave a nice eulogy yesterday," I said. "He speaks well in public."

"Toby gives a lot of seminars. He is in public relations."

"So he's comfortable at a dais."

"I suppose that's a way of putting it."

"He must be taking Jake's death hard. It sounds like Jake and your husband went way back."

"They did. To junior high. Yes, Toby is horribly torn up over what happened. Jake and he were like brothers. Toby is Martin's godfather, you know."

"I didn't know," I said. "There seems to be a lot of anger in our Martin."

"That would be an understandable emotion, considering."

"I guess you heard about his incident at school the other day."

"You're referring to Martin and his classmate? Toby had a talk with Martin about that. Apparently there had been some bad blood between Martin and the boy. Actually, between Jake and the boy's father, as well."

"Oh? How so?"

Betty Schultz sniffed. "The two had words recently at one of the school's football games. Personally I think it's ridiculous. If parents are going to behave badly on the sidelines, I think they should just cancel the sport altogether. What kind of message does that send?"

"So was that Martin's beef? That this kid's father had been in an argument with Jake?"

"So it seems."

"What's Martin doing with a lacrosse stick at school this time of year?"

Maybe it was my imagination, but a glimmer of animation seemed to flicker for just an instant behind the glasses.

"That would speak to the matter of premeditation."

I realized that Angela was standing next to me. I'd missed her approach. I made the introductions. The lights were being blinked for all of us to return to our seats.

"Back to Elsinore," I said.

As we made our way back to our seats Angela asked, "Who was that woman? She kind of creeped me out."

"She's a circuit court judge."

"How do you know her?"

"I met her at a funeral."

The lights were going down. Angela patted my hand. "You need to get out more."

The lights came up on the King, the Queen, Polonius, Ophelia, Rosencrantz, Guildenstern and a couple of Lords.

King: *And can you, by no drift of circumstance*
Get from him why he puts on this confusion,
Grating so harshly all of his days of quiet
With turbulent and dangerous lunacy?

Billie asks this same question about me sometimes. It's largely rhetorical. At least I think it is.

Angela's hand remained on mine through the next hour and a half of treachery and swords and poison. Eventually they started dropping like flies. When Hamlet finally keeled over, Angela's hand was still on mine, squeezing mightily.

Chapter Fifteen

"God, what a *fantastic* shower."

Angela was rolling the sleeves of my bathrobe back off her wrists. She put a finger in her ear and corkscrewed it around. "You could sell tickets to that thing."

I was already showered. Already dressed. Standing at the stove scrambling up some eggs. Angela watched as I sprinkled some dried basil onto the eggs, along with a little paprika, a little dill and a pinch of poppy seeds.

"Poppy seeds?"

"It's an experiment."

"I've heard somewhere that poppy seeds attach themselves to the insides of your stomach. They don't digest."

"Would you like me to remove them from the eggs?"

"Of course not," she said. "It's too late. How could you?"

I thought a moment. "Tweezers."

"I think we'll live. So how are those ribs this morning?"

"You know what they say. No pain, no gain."

Angela came over to me and made a mess

of my hair and I made a mess of hers and neither of us said anything about it because we were too busy kissing and it wasn't the kind of kiss where you talk. Angela smelled like Dial soap, but she felt like Ivory liquid. My bathrobe felt better on her than it does on me. She slapped my hand once . . . but only once. I didn't slap hers at all. She was my guest; free to go where she pleased. Though I nearly stepped on one of her feet as we caromed gracelessly into the next room.

"I can fix that backfiring in your car," Angela murmured, tugging at my sweatshirt.

"Mmmm."

"Carburetor. Simplest thing."

"Mmmm."

"Wouldn't hurt to flush your system either."

"No, I guess it wouldn't."

I had never known Dial to smell so good. Angela's wet hair was cold against my skin. She took a step back and handed me my bathrobe, bunched in a ball. "Here. Do something with this, will you?"

The backup singer slash mechanic crawled onto my bed on all fours. I simply let my experiment in the kitchen burn, burn, burn.

I'm irresponsible that way.

Angela told me about the fight Sisco had with Jake Weisheit a couple of nights before

Jake's murder. Sisco and the Kids were performing in a club in Glen Arm, a roadhouse kind of place called Penny's. It's a smallish club: a bar, a place to stand with your drinks, a place for the band to set up. The fire marshals would knock heads if more than about sixty people tried to occupy the place. I used to frequent the club a fair amount. Penny is the name of the owner. He is a large blubbery gumdrop of a man, an old hippie type with a thin gray ponytail, faded T-shirts and bowling shoes and a story about Janis Joplin, a jeep and a secluded pecan grove outside Oaxaca that he never tires of telling. Penny has told me a dozen times how he wants his ashes scattered on the site. I've told him a dozen times I'm not the man for the job.

According to Angela, it was at Penny's that Sisco and Polly first met.

"I remember this woman sitting at a table just drilling Sisco with her eyes. She was drinking like a fish, but holding it pretty well. At least as best as you could tell. For all I know, she would have fallen right over if she stood up. But let me tell you, she was putting out heat. I mean, *I* could feel it. Sisco made a beeline for her when we took our first break. The next week she was back. Same table. Same heat. I had a feeling about her."

"What was your feeling?"

"That she was married. Don't ask me why. You just got the sense that this woman was doing something she knew she shouldn't be doing, but that she didn't care."

After the tragic loss of our experimental eggs, Angela and I had popped over to Jimmy's for some breakfast and then headed to the National Aquarium. We were standing at the dolphin tank. I couldn't swear to it, but I believed that two of the bottlenoses were mimicking us. One of the dolphins was chattering away, its partner polite, attentive, debonair, hanging on every chirp.

"Sisco likes to think of himself as an outlaw," Angela continued. "He's one of those 'trouble is my middle name' kind of people. His ego is a lot bigger than he is. But you know what, I've got to say, you get past the bullshit and he's actually a pretty sweet guy."

"You don't think he's a narcissistic weasel?" I asked.

"Is that how you see him? I thought Sisco and you were friends."

"Oh I like Sisco all right. I just like saying *narcissistic weasel.*"

"He's fun to work with. He's been helping me work up a song that I wrote. He's a fair arranger."

"You rotate tires *and* you write songs?"

"It's basically a country-western song. It's called 'Midnight Morning.'"

"How does it go?"

"You want me to sing it for you? Here. I'll give you the opening." She tapped her foot lightly, locating the rhythm.

"Got nothing in my pocket,
My car's a rusty bucket,
And the man I love ain't worth a hill
of beans."

She stopped. "Sisco wants to change that line to 'And the life I lead ain't worth a hill of beans.' I've been teasing him that a real man will sing a girl song."

"Maybe you're expecting too much of our Sisco."

"Do you want to hear more?"

I did. And so I did. Angela placed her arms on the railing of the tank and leaned forward. The dolphins had quit their yapping.

"But the moon is sitting pretty,
And there's music in the city.
And tonight I'm feeling richer than the queen."

"Let me guess. Sisco's having trouble with that line too."

Angela smiled. "I'm trying to get him to push the envelope. We were going to try the song out at Penny's next time we played there. But of course our bad boy outlaw is in jail."

We moved down the winding ramp, where the lighting is a low, shadowy blue. The walls are continuous rows of tanks, floor to ceiling, so you get the sense that you are meandering toward the bottom of the ocean. Angela's hand meandered into mine. We stopped and watched several dozen sea horses as they floated in a loose formation, alternately lifting and sinking like some sort of aquatic calliope. A gentle drift of question marks.

"So what do you think happened?" Angela asked. "You don't think Sisco actually killed that man, do you?"

"It doesn't feel right to me. The stupidest thing in the world would have been his staying at the house. We've got to credit Sisco with having enough brain cells to understand that."

"Why didn't he leave when you did?" Angela asked.

"Polly wouldn't let him. She said he'd be in bigger trouble if he was spotted leaving the scene."

"I guess that's true. But if we believe the story, she's the one who called him to the scene in the first place."

"That's what I keep thinking," I said.

"That she was setting him up?"

"There has to be a reason why you don't immediately call the police."

"Time," Angela said. "Stalling for time. The thing is, she wouldn't have to tell the police the truth about when she discovered her husband, would she? If there's no one else in the house who is going to stumble onto him, she can pretend that she slept in as late as she chooses and then say she came downstairs and found him dead. There wasn't anybody else in the house, was there?"

"Not when I got there. Not that I saw anyway."

"No kids?"

One of the sea horses had drifted away from the pack. It rose steadily, helplessly weightless, rocking gently forward and backward.

"There's a daughter who was off in college in Ohio," I said. "And then there's Martin. That's the son. I met him when I went out to the house the day before the funeral."

"But on Sunday? Was he there?"

"I assume he wasn't there. I sure didn't see him. I can't imagine Polly coming across her husband on the kitchen floor and simply letting her son stay asleep in his room. And even if she did, with Sisco showing up and then me showing up . . . no, it makes no sense. He couldn't have been."

"Convenient for the killer," Angela said.

"Or maybe the killer knew that the son wouldn't be home."

"That would certainly argue for someone who knew the family."

We continued on down the ramp, passing a school group, fifth grade or thereabouts. They had clipboards and marking pens and were scribbling furiously.

"Tell me more about the scene at Penny's," I said to Angela after we had moved past the schoolkids.

"Well, I can tell you that Sisco made no real secret of the fact he was sleeping with the woman. We have . . . I guess I should say we *had* a regular Monday, Wednesday gig at Penny's. She always showed up on Wednesdays. Sisco introduced me to her. She didn't really have much to say to me. I could sense that she was sizing me up, like she thought maybe I was the competition. She's not warm and fuzzy, that one. For Sisco's sake, I hope the sex is good."

"Sisco told me she's an animal."

"What are those animals that have sex and then kill their mates? He wants to make sure she's not one of those." Angela laughed. "Who knows? Maybe that's what happened to her husband."

"Polly Weisheit made it pretty clear to me that she and her husband hadn't had a lot of intimacy going on for a while."

Angela shrugged. "Maybe that's why she killed him."

"Cold."

Angela squeezed my hand. "You might want to keep this conversation in mind."

205

We paused at a tank featuring a fish with a snout that looked like a chain saw. The fish looked terrifically unhappy.

Angela continued. "Shit hit the fan last Wednesday. We had just taken a break and Sisco was sitting off at a table with Polly. All of a sudden in comes this man. He goes right up to the table and you could just tell he was her husband. He was very out of place. Suit and tie. He and Polly started snapping at each other. He starts with 'Come home immediately' and she comes back with 'I'll do what I damn well please.' You can see this poor guy is very uptight. He was trying to keep the argument quiet. I felt sorry for him. Here's his wife lounging around a club with Sisco Fontaine. It's embarrassing. So then, of course, Sisco joined in. The husband says, 'I'll deal with you in a minute.' You can probably guess what Sisco says."

" 'You can deal with me right now.' "

She touched her finger to the tip of my nose. "You got it. And that's when the guy lunged at Sisco. He was a lot bigger, but Sisco was way too scrappy for him. Plus, you know Sisco. This was his big chance. An honest-to-God bar brawl. Of course it wasn't anything like the movies. It was more like a wrestling match. Like they were trying to yank each other's heads off. But Sisco did get in some punches. He went a little berserk. He was just starting to work over

Polly's husband for real when a couple of guys pulled him off. That's when Sisco started yelling, 'Get the hell out of here! The next time I'll kill you!' "

"That's what he said?"

"Quote. The next fucking time I'll fucking kill you. Unquote."

"And so today our Sisco sits in a prison cell."

"He didn't kill that guy," Angela said. "I know it looks bad, but I just don't believe it."

"After the fight, did Polly leave with Jake?"

"She did. I was kind of surprised."

"And the band played on?"

"Oh, yes. Job's a job. The second set royally stank. Sisco couldn't get into it at all. Penny jumped all over him when we were through. I thought *they* were going to start going at it. It was a lousy night."

I drove Angela back to her place and dropped her off. As she elbowed the door open, she thanked me for the eggs. I reminded her that I had let the eggs burn.

"I know. Thank you."

I had some business to discuss with the pastor of St. Barnabas. I found him in the parish house at the top of a ladder. He was painting the ceiling. Michelangelo, he was not. I picked up a roller and rolled half a wall as we talked. The subject was exhumation. Not one of my favorite subjects, but it was something we had to deal with. There was a family tug-of-war going on over a re-burial issue. It was moving inexorably toward the courts, and the pastor and I needed to map out our strategies. The paint was on the peach side, which I thought was all wrong for this room. But the subject was exhumation, not aesthetics, so I kept a zipper on it.

A Lincoln Town Car was parked out in front of the funeral home when I returned. The driver was seated behind the wheel reading *USA Today*. The president was visiting China. He was pictured at the Great Wall, where he was shown in a photograph playing with a yo-yo. The intricacies of diplomacy. The driver wore a thin blue tie, a blue jacket and a black mustache, neatly trimmed. He looked like a person who was accustomed to waiting. I was curious to a degree about the yo-yo, but not enough to interfere with his reading.

I found Billie seated on one of our benches just inside the door. Seated next to her was Evelyn Weisheit. They looked like they were posing for their portrait, except that Billie's expression was pinched up as if she were seated next to an excessively ripe wheel of cheese. It turned out she was on the verge of sneezing, which she did just as I closed the door behind me. She was doubly blessed, first by me, then by Evelyn Weisheit.

"Hitchcock, I was hoping you would be

back soon," Billie said, sniffling. "This is Mrs. Weisheit."

"We've met," I said and stepped forward. "How do you do, Mrs. Weisheit?"

She inclined her head. "Mr. Sewell."

A warning bell went off in my head. We're a funeral home, after all. It's not usually good news that brings people to us. I glanced at Billie for an indication, but she was sniffing cheese again.

"A-choo!" Billie produced a handkerchief and gave us her best Canadian goose imitation. Evelyn Weisheit leaned ever so slightly away from her. "Hitchcock, I have 'business' downstairs, dear. Unrelated to Mrs. Weisheit's visit."

"Business," when my aunt says it like that, means a corpse. She turned to our visitor. "You'll excuse me, won't you?"

Billie toddled off toward the basement, a muffled sneeze sounding as she made her way down the stairs. Evelyn Weisheit cast her gaze about the lobby.

"I believe I prefer your home to Fink's," she announced. "I believe I was in error in directing my daughter-in-law to take our business elsewhere. Generally I find such a suburban feeling to these establishments. You and your aunt have managed to avoid that."

Whether she was responding to our buttery sconces or our yesteryear wallpaper, I couldn't say. Billie and I have discussed remodeling now and again, but the idea never generates enough enthusiasm for us to actually pick up the phone and get things started. When Billie married ugly Uncle Stu back in the fifties she set the place up as much like a normal residence as she could manage, and that's pretty much how it has remained.

The woman continued. "I was just now visiting Jake's grave site. And my husband's, of course. I am considering installing a mausoleum. For the entire family. I had this thought after James died, but now that my son has . . . well, I think it would be an appropriate memorial. I recalled Polly mentioning that you were in Fells Point, so I had Richard bring me down to see you. Perhaps you could assist me in this."

I told her that I would be happy to help her out and she followed me into my office. She noted my Magritte print.

"A favorite of my husband's. James was an architect. I don't know if you were aware of that."

"I wasn't."

She took a seat, lighting on the edge of the chair. "James Weisheit is considered one of the ten most influential American architects of the last half century. I'm surprised you don't know of him. He was a brilliant man. Quite handsome as well. You men are so blessed, aren't you? Age becomes you. James passed away last Christmas."

"I picked up on that from the eulogies," I said. "I'm sorry." I pulled open one of my file drawers and began leafing through the folders.

"You have never met a more charming man. James had such charisma. You are familiar with the cliché of the person who lights up a room when he enters. My husband was the embodiment of that cliché." She opened her purse and produced a green leather wallet, from which she pulled a photograph. She leaned forward and placed it on the desk, tapping her finger against it. "Have a look. This was our twenty-fifth wedding anniversary."

I swung around from the files and picked up the snapshot. Sometimes I think undertakers spend half their careers looking at photographs of the once living. This one featured a somewhat younger Evelyn Weisheit, quite bangled and baubled, looking lovingly at a tall tanned gentleman who was holding a champagne glass aloft, apparently delivering a toast. Yes, he was quite a handsome man, a warm smile and lively eyes under a shock of silver hair.

"The both of you are very attractive," I said, sliding the photograph back to her.

"James was special," she said again. "Everyone who met him felt it. He has left behind quite a legacy." Her gaze drifted off in the direction of the window. "I'm afraid to say the fruit remained on the tree."

"Excuse me?"

"I'm sorry. I'm speaking about my son, Jake. I loved him, of course. He was my only child. And he was in every way a good man. Good morals. A good father to his children. But I'm sorry to say, he simply didn't have his father's spark."

I wasn't sure why the woman was telling me all this or if there was any wisdom in my putting the question to her. My profession accustoms me to lending an ear; often that is the most important service that Billie and I provide. I have a face that people will talk to.

Evelyn Weisheit gave it a good hard look. "You never met my son. Is that correct?"

I found the folder I was looking for and tossed it onto the desk. "That's correct."

"But you're a friend of Polly's."

"That's a misconception that seems to be taking hold," I said. "The fact is, I only met your daughter-in-law the morning your son was murdered."

"Polly seems to think highly of you." Her face was without affect, her tone too even for me to gauge.

"Your daughter-in-law doesn't seem to have many friends. Sometimes people latch onto a stranger."

The woman's eyebrows rose. "Latching onto strangers appears to be one of my daughter-in-law's hobbies. One that would

212

seem to have gotten my son killed."

"That would be assuming that Sisco is guilty."

"You're saying you think he is not guilty?"

"I can't see why in the world Sisco would want to murder your son."

"They had an altercation."

"Yes. I know about that. But that's just a fight. That's an entirely different thing from Sisco's going over to your son's house and putting a knife in his back. Personally, I just don't see why he'd do that. Sisco didn't actually think he was going to be running off with Polly. It wasn't that sort of passionate love affair, Mrs. Weisheit. It just doesn't make sense."

She took back the photograph and slipped it into her wallet "Of course you defend him. He is your friend."

"I defend him because the picture doesn't make sense to me. Sisco killing Jake doesn't add up."

"The authorities seem to feel that it adds up."

"Do you think, then, that your daughter-in-law was involved?" I asked. "I mean, directly? Do you think it was the two of them who killed your son?"

"As I understand it, the two of them called you in. Am I correct? You were asked to remove the body. It all seems very plain to me. They simply wanted Jake to disappear."

"Excuse me, Mrs. Weisheit, but why would *I* agree to do something like that?"

"Well, you didn't, did you?"

"But why would Sisco and Polly even think I would? I mean, if they were thinking straight. Which I admit, Sisco certainly wasn't."

Evelyn Weisheit gazed at me a moment before answering. "I suspect you have heard of money?"

"Money? I'm familiar with it. It comes, it goes. That stuff?"

"My husband's estate was not inconsiderable, Mr. Sewell. My son was due to receive a handsome inheritance. As well the children. You ask me why in the world your friend would murder my son, or how you might be persuaded to be of some assistance to the murderer? I'm sorry, but I think you are being either a little naive or a little disingenuous. Money moves mountains in this world, Mr. Sewell. It can prove very persuasive to some people. I understand your friend is the leader of some sort of band? I wouldn't imagine he realizes a terribly good income from that sort of work."

"He enjoys the work," I said. "And you're right, he's not likely to get rich doing it."

"Mr. Sewell, your friend was sleeping with the golden goose. I have absolutely no trouble in seeing why he would want to murder my son."

The matter-of-fact tone of her voice was a little chilling. Her gaze on me was steady and frank.

"You're assuming Polly was ready to leave your son and throw in with Sisco. If you don't mind my saying so, your daughter-in-law was having her cake and eating it too. A cushy life in a nice big house and her little escapade on the side. I don't know the woman very well, but I can't see that she'd be anxious to give up all that."

"My son spoke to me on a number of occasions about his marriage, Mr. Sewell. He was distraught with Polly's behavior. I don't think it will surprise you to learn that your friend Mr. Fontaine is not my daughter-in-law's first indiscretion. My son suffered through considerable heartache with that girl. For the sake of the children, he was determined to ride things out. Once Martin was out of the house and into college, however, and it was just the two of them together in that house, you can rest assured that things were going to change. I was insisting to Jake that they change. Polly knows all this full well. The clock was ticking on that marriage. You're correct about Polly and her cake. But trust me, she was on the last slice and she knew it. And if you think I was planning to sit back and watch that little tramp try to work a good settlement out of my son, then you don't know me. Miss Polly was getting out while the getting was good. *That* is why she murdered my son, Mr. Sewell. A wife has a much better claim than does an ex-wife. Or I should say, a widow does. The authorities are being cautious about this, as maybe you can understand. But I have spoken with them. I am convinced they will come around to the truth."

She snapped her purse shut. Accepting the finality of the gesture, I spun the folder around and slid it toward her.

"Mausoleums," I said. "All shapes, all sizes. Room for two, room for four, room for six. Marble. Granite. Prefab. Customized. Open air. Enclosed. Whatever you want, Mrs. Weisheit. I can steer you to some dependable suppliers."

She picked up the folder and gave it a cursory glance. "I can have these?"

"If you'd like."

"I'll look at them." She stood. "It was nice speaking with you, Mr. Sewell. I apologize if I was blunt. I would warn you about my daughter-in-law, but you appear to be a man who can look after himself."

"It's one of the things I do best," I said.

I'm not sure that this deserved a withering look. But that's exactly what I got.

Chapter Sixteen

"H-a-double r-i . . . g-a-n spells —"

Mr. Wow put his hand to his ear. Malcolm Cohen called out, "Flanagan!" then laughed so loud at his own humor that a pair of uncontrollable farts split the air. Mr. Wow shielded his eyes and scanned the room.

"Whoever that was, do that again and I'll make you disappear." His geriatric crowd tittered. "Better yet, do that again and *I'll* disappear." He produced a magic wand and held it in front of him. "Gentlemen, start your engines." The wand collapsed in a droop and Mr. Wow made a perplexed face. "Sorry, ladies. As if you need to see that one more time." Mr. Wow rubbed his hands together like a silent film villain. "I was planning to saw a woman in half today. But the last time I did that, the woman left me. Both of her."

Mr. Wow. The hardest-working man at Briarcliff.

I was seated near the rear of the dining room. I had arrived early with Mr. Wow in tow and helped Thomas shove the tables against the walls and set up the folding chairs. Thomas had cast a suspicious eye on the tuft-headed Mr. Wow as he puttered about readying his act. The residents began drifting in, walkers, wheelchairs, shuffling slippers. I had been surprised to see Mrs. McNamara being wheeled in. The nurse named Louise had guided her to the far side of the room. A plastic bag hung from a pole attached to the chair. A clear tube ran from the bag to a small patch on the back of Mrs. McNamara's right hand. She was wearing a thin white nightgown, with a red blanket folded over her lap. I wanted to check in with her, but Mr. Wow had just set me to work placing the mirrors into his magic fishbowl. Once the residents were all in place, Marilyn Tuck went to the front of the room and explained to the gathering that Andy, their regular entertainer, was unavailable today but that "through the good graces of a friend of Briarcliff" — and here she acknowledged yours truly — "the show will go on." I picked up a chair and moved it next to Mrs. McNamara. She gave me a wan smile just as Mr. Wow uncorked his act.

Jaded old me, I knew the routines. Mr. Wow donned his black cape and plastic fangs, and as he approached Mrs. McNamara, I skidded my chair out of the way.

"Good bite, madam. I mean . . . good night."

Mr. Wow leaned down and made as if he were biting Mrs. McNamara's neck. The other residents gasped at the appearance of red. Mr. Wow quickly drew back, brandishing a large red silk handkerchief. He settled the handkerchief on Mrs. McNamara's head, then yanked it back again, revealing a black rubber bat.

"Hey, lady, don't bat your eyes at me!"

Mrs. McNamara looked at me sadly as Mr. Wow returned to the front of the room. "He's . . . bad."

I was stunned by how sickly Mrs. McNamara looked. She explained to me in a whisper that she had become so dehydrated and nauseated over the past several days that the most expedient way for her to get her nutrition was from the IV drip. She complained again, of the dizziness. Partway through Mr. Wow's antic presentation Mrs. McNamara closed her eyes. Her hand found mine. It was ice cold. I couldn't tell if she had drifted off, and we remained that way for nearly ten minutes. When Mrs. McNamara finally opened her eyes, it was to ask that she be returned to her room. I signaled to Louise, who came over to us. Louise knelt down and adjusted the blanket on Mrs. McNamara's legs. "Is everything all right, Peggy?"

"Mrs. McNamara isn't feeling well," I said. "Could you take her back to her room?"

"Certainly."

I accompanied them as far as the hallway. Mrs. McNamara lifted her hand. I thought she was gong to wave to me, but instead she reached for the small bandage on her other hand and before she could be stopped, had ripped the bandage off her hand, freeing herself from the IV tubing.

Louise nearly pounced on her. "Peggy! For goodness sakes, what do you think you're doing?" Louise slid swiftly behind the wheelchair — "Excuse me" — and leaned into it. The loose IV tube whipped and snapped like a writhing snake as Louise and Mrs. Mc-Namara disappeared down the hallway.

Marilyn Tuck came hurrying out of the dining room.

"What just happened?"

As I was explaining it to her, a man joined us in the hallway. I had noticed him earlier in the dining room, seated next to one of the residents. He was roughly my height, roughly my weight, roughly my age. I happened to feel that my face has a little more character than his, but then I'm so highly biased I'm barely worth listening to. He sported the urban lumberjack look. Khakis. Flannel shirt. Sturdy brown shoes. Fresh from the pages of Eddie Bauer. He listened solemnly.

"I should go see her," he said as soon as I finished.

"No," said Marilyn. "I'll go."

The fellow looked at me. "You're a friend of Peggy's?"

Marilyn touched him lightly on the arm.

"Scott, this is Hitchcock Sewell."

"Pleased to meet you. Scott Monroe." I expected a hard grip and that's what I got.

"Scott's with the ElderHeart organization," Marilyn explained. "Are you familiar with them?"

"The name is familiar. I've seen your ads, I think."

"We're an advocacy group," Monroe said. "Locally based. We're a voice for the geriatric generation. We advocate for the interests of the elderly on any number of fronts." He ticked them off on his fingers. "Issues regarding pharmaceutical companies, HMOs, problems with landlords, illegal utility shutoffs, you name it. Trust me, there are no shortages of leaks in the system when it comes to the welfare of the elderly."

"So you're a watchdog," I said.

"Exactly. That's right. ElderHeart is a watchdog. We're not just restricted to that, however. Plenty of the elderly need help sometimes filling out Medicare forms, help with their taxes, things like that. And homebound elderly sometimes just need a person to check in with them once in a while. A friendly face. We run the gamut. If you'd like, I guess you could think of it as partly selfish. We're all going to be there one day, after all. Knock on wood." And he did. He rapped his knuckles against the doorjamb. "We want to see to it that the elderly do not end their days in neglect or abuse."

"It sounds very noble," I remarked. "I'm impressed."

"Scott is tireless," Marilyn said. "Just ask any of the nursing homes around town. He keeps us on our toes." She added quickly, "I don't mean to imply that it's an antagonistic relationship. We work together with Elder-Heart to see that our residents enjoy the best possible quality of life."

"Speaking of which," Monroe said. "I'd like to see the files on Mr. Harvey before I go. He tells me that he is still receiving one-person transfers. We've discussed this."

Marilyn shot him a look. "They're two-person transfers, Scott. I promise you. I told you we took care of all that."

"I'm just telling you what Mr. Harvey is saying."

"Mr. Harvey's memory is not to be trusted. I think we both know that."

"I'd still like to see the files, Marilyn. Just to verify." He turned to me. "You see? I can be a bona fide pain in the tail."

"I'm sorry," I said. "I'm still thinking about Mrs. McNamara."

"She'll be fine," Marilyn said. "We've been having some dehydration problems. Peggy's a little weak from not eating enough."

A small eruption of laughter sounded from the dining room. Mr. Wow was having fun with eggs.

"He's good, by the way," Monroe said to me. "I understand you're responsible for Mr. Wow."

I held up my hands in protest. "Blame Mama and Papa Wow. I'm only the facilitator here."

"Honestly, I think he's great," Monroe said. "A man like that is a real role model."

"You'd like your kids to grow up to be like Mr. Wow?"

He laughed. "I'm talking about for the seniors here. Look at him. He's active. He's still supporting himself. He's contributing to the community."

"He contributes cheap jokes and rubber bats. But okay, I see your point. At least he's up on his feet."

"Exactly."

Just then several cries sounded from the dining room. Mr. Wow's hamster had gotten loose.

"I'd better get in there and help out," I said.

Monroe gave my arm another hearty pump. "It was good to meet you, Mr. Sewell."

"Hitch will do."

"Of course. Next time I'll shut my trap and let you tell me about your work."

I shrugged. "People die and I bury them."

"I'm sure there's a little more to it than that." He turned to Marilyn. "Why don't we go have a look at those files?"

Back in the dining room I was able to corner Mr. Wow's hamster before we suffered any coronaries. The remainder of the show went on without incident. Phyllis Fitch appeared as things were wrapping up. I asked after Mrs. McNamara and Phyllis told me that she was sleeping. She thought it best if Mrs. McNamara were left alone. Mr. Wow turned to the nursing administrator and pulled a flower out of her ear. She thanked him tersely and set the flower aside. I helped the magician pack up.

"Was that fun?" I asked Mr. Wow on our way back into town. He was fussing with his thirty-foot scarf. He looked over at me and grinned.

"You didn't tell me about all the babes."

I had a message on my machine from Sisco when I got back home. He was calling from the Maryland State Penitentiary, not two miles north of Fells Point. From the tinny sound quality of the call he seemed a million miles away.

"I've got to talk to you. This is just no good. I've got to get out of this fucking place." He wanted to know if I could come over to see him. He told me the visiting hours. "You don't have to make an appointment or anything. It's not like they won't be able to find me."

I checked in with Billie at the funeral

home. She was putting the finishing touches on a dead dentist. "Look at these teeth, Hitchcock. They're splendid."

Billie's cold was still enjoying its visit. My aunt assured me that she was well stocked with teas and soups.

"I am awash with liquids, dear."

I went outside and got into my car.

A loud bang rocketed from my tailpipe as I turned the key. I went back upstairs and gave Angela a call. "What are you doing right now?" I asked.

"I'm watching the PGA Tour on television."

I couldn't tell if she was kidding. Pretty young woman like that? So full of life? "Ever seen the inside of a prison?" I asked.

She said she hadn't. I told her I was heading over to see Sisco and asked if she wanted to join me.

"You're a fun guy," she said. "I stick around long enough, will you take me to the morgue?"

"That could probably be arranged."

"Give me a half hour. I want to get dolled up."

When I arrived at her place, she met me at the door, wearing a simple white knee-length dress, several turquoise bracelets, and large hoop earrings, and with her hair pulled back and tied off with a paisley scarf.

"Is this too much?" she asked.

"What the hell. Spin a few eyeballs."

Sisco cut not so nearly as elegant a line as Angela. His prison issues were severely wrinkled and baggy, an infirmary green not too far off the shade of Sisco's skin. There were bags under the bags under his eyes, one of which — the eye, not the bag — was swollen slightly and provided Sisco's only unpallid color, a vivid red and blue.

"What happened to your eye?" I asked Sisco once he had settled in behind the thick glass.

"A guy asked me for a cigarette."

"Why didn't you just give it to him?"

"I did. This is how they say thank-you in here." He grinned through the glass at Angela. "Hey, Ange. Looking good."

"Whatta you say, Sisco?"

"I say I've got to get out of here. This place is full of criminals."

I asked, "You're not bonding with your fellow outlaws?"

"Quit that. I'm serious. These guys brush their teeth with someone like me. This isn't the place for me, man. I can't survive this. You've got to get me out."

He looked scared, no question. His jaw was peppered with stubble, his hair trying out new directions. I had noticed when he was led in that he was wearing only one shoe. I asked him where his other shoe was.

He leaned close to the glass. "Someone

made me piss in it."

"Why?" Angela asked.

He looked back and forth between Angela and me, as if determining whether or not we could be trusted with a secret. "Because," he said hoarsely. "That's all. Just . . . because."

We were allowed to visit with Sisco for only fifteen minutes.

"My lawyer's trying to get the bail reduced," he said. "He's got to. Like, I've got a hundred and fifty grand lying around? I make it, I spend it. That's how I live. How the hell am I supposed to think I'd better save up my money in case I want to bail myself out of jail one day? Who does that?"

I considered suggesting to him that there are other reasons besides bail for setting a little nest egg aside, but I could see Sisco wasn't in the reasoning mode.

"What about you, Hitch?" he said. "Have you got a hundred and fifty grand you can put up for me?"

"I don't," I said.

"If you had it, would you put it up for me?"

"What's the point of speculation, Sisco? I don't have it."

His face fell. "I've got to get out of here. Angie, talk to Penny. You know how he nickel-and-dimes us. That guy's loaded. Talk to Penny, Ange. Tell him we'll work free for a fucking year if he'll bail me out."

"Hey, speak for yourself."

"You mean you'd let me rot in here too? Some kind of loyalty."

"Sisco," I said, "don't start making enemies of friends. We'll talk to Penny."

"Talk to Polly too."

A guard came over to Sisco and tapped him on the shoulder. "Five minutes."

Sisco snapped at him. "Just back off, all right?" He turned back to the glass. "Polly. Talk to Polly. That family has got plenty of loot."

I thought about Evelyn Weisheit's visit, her talk of Sisco's and Polly's angling for Jake's money.

"But if it turns out that Polly killed Jake? That she was setting you up? In which case she probably wouldn't be so keen to bail you out. She'd have you right where she wants you."

"That's cruel, man."

"I'm just saying, Sisco. And even if she didn't kill her husband, how is it going to look if she bails out the man everyone thinks did it?"

"It would look like she's got the balls to stand up for her convictions. Look, Polly does have balls. Trust me on that. That's no everyday housewife sitting out there."

"It would've been a lot easier on you if you and Jake hadn't gotten into a fight out at Penny's," I said.

"Hey, he brought that on. I was minding my own business. That's my office, man. I was doing my work."

"Angela described the fight for me."

"So people fight. So what? Jesus Christ, you've got certified killers in this place, man. They're fighting all the time. Just because two people go at it doesn't mean they're going to kill each other. And Jake came after me first. You saw it, Ange. Is anybody thinking about *his* temper in all this?"

The guard moved forward and gave Sisco another signal. Sisco waved him off.

"Get Polly to spring me. Come on, Hitch. If you're not going to bail me out, that's the least you can do for me. Either that or figure out who the hell killed Jake. I'm serious, man. I'm innocent. Somebody's out there having a big laugh over this because they think they got away with it. That's just not right. Hitch, you know that's not right. You've got to help me. Promise me you'll talk to Polly."

"Sisco, I don't really think that —"

"Promise me. Come on, man. Put yourself in my shoes." Angela raised an eyebrow. Sisco sneered. "Fine. Have your ha-ha. Put yourself in my *shoe*. I'm serious, Hitch. Just talk to her. She knows I'm innocent. I shouldn't be in here."

"I'll talk to her," I said.

The guard put his hand on Sisco's

shoulder. This time he kept it there. Sisco made a face. "My girlfriend's calling." He jabbed a finger against the glass as he stood up. His voice was muffled. *"Whatever it takes. Get me the hell out of here."*

Out on the sidewalk Angela was shaking her head. "Penny's not going to put up a hundred and fifty thousand dollars for him. Sisco's crazy."

"He's scared. He's grasping at anything."

"What about Polly? Sisco's right, isn't he? She's loaded. If she didn't have anything to do with killing her husband, why not bail Sisco out?"

"I'll talk to her, but I can't get a handle on that woman." I did get a handle on Angela, though, and steered her to the car. She moved with superb fluidity.

Angela wanted to pick up a necklace at one of the Harborplace shops, a place that sold nothing but butterfly stuff. The necklace was an actual butterfly — dead, of course — a small electric blue butterfly about the size of a postage stamp, sealed in a thin Lucite casing and attached to a silver chain. She put the chain around her neck and I attached it for her.

"You're good with clasps," Angela said.

"I sit at home and practice."

As we headed outside to take a look at the water, a woman with a baby stroller was having some trouble negotiating the doors. I reached past Angela to hold one of the two doors open. As I did, I caught a reflection in the door and turned just in time to see a man shoulder his way past Angela. He bumped into her, skirting the baby stroller and moved swiftly out the door.

"Hey!"

The woman trundled the stroller through the door, smiling me a silent thank-you for holding the door. I stepped outside and scanned for the man. He should have been easy to spot. He was the man I had shared the elevator with in the courthouse the day before. Bozo hair. I looked off in the direction he had gone, but I couldn't locate him.

Angela came up next to me. "Did you see that jerk?"

"I saw him," I said. I'm tall enough that I can see over most people's heads. But the guy had vanished. I took Angela's arm. "And I've seen him before."

We headed over to the water and watched a busker. He was playing banjo and using a clever arrangement of wires attached to the heels of his shoes in order to pound a bass drum and clap a pair of cymbals mounted on his back. Every song he played sounded pretty much the same, but then the average hanging around time is probably all of thirty seconds; it's not as if he needed a wide and varied repertoire. I handed Angela a dollar and she went over to the busker and dropped it in the straw hat at the musician's feet. He banged his foot, boom-booming his drum in a thank-you. I drove Angela back to her place, where she invited me in for some boom-boom/thank-you of our own. Angela was having dinner with her father that evening and she invited me along, but I had promised Billie I would help her with her dead dentist.

"I would never get between you and a dead dentist," Angela said. I discarded a half-dozen comebacks and felt the better man for it. I whistled a very intricate Duke Ellington tune on the drive home.

The dead dentist turned out to be a Shriner. The wake was to be held that evening at the Shriners' temple, a place called the Boumi Temple on Charles and Wyndhurst. I helped Billie bring the dentist up from the basement and load him into the hearse. Since Billie was insisting on hostessing the wake, I insisted on running the customer out to the temple to set things up. Billie handed me a bag of bobby pins.

"What's this for?" I asked.

She went inside and returned a minute later with a hat box. She made a ceremony of handing it to me.

"Have fun."

The banquet hall at the Boumi Temple was huge. There was a platform stage with a dais and a row of chairs along the rear lip. The Shriners (I thought of them as Boumis) wanted their comrade's casket on a second platform just in front of the dais, so that it would be elevated for all to see but not so that it blocked the cryptic insignia on the front of the dais, an insignia replicated on a gigantic blue velvet banner that hung on the wall behind the platform stage.

Getting the gurney and the casket up onto the secondary platform was a task. A half-dozen big-bellied Boumis helped. I made everyone back away while I worked on the dentist. With a few pillows and a number of strategically placed bobby pins, I was able to fix the dentist's head such that his fez sat as naturally as possible. Boumis stood cross-armed in each of the banquet hall's six doorways as I did my work. It was a little unnerving.

I counted sixty tables. There was a small ugly flower arrangement on each table, along with a pair of black candles. It was to be a sit-down dinner followed by eulogies and God knows what sort of secret-handshake hocus-pocus in honor of the fallen dentist. I was told that at one point during the evening the Shriners-only policy would kick in, at which point the dentist's family members, related non-Shriner guests and the official representing Sewell and Sons — in this case, Billie — would have to vacate the banquet hall and wait out in the corridor.

"Just don't touch the body," I told the

Boumi who was explaining all this to me. "The fez is precarious."

He gave me a look. Not one I particularly cared for. "We may have to touch the body."

"Please. Don't say that."

Chapter Seventeen

Maybe you've seen them in parades. Maybe you haven't. They are ATVs, all-terrain vehicles: three extremely fat tires, an engine, handlebars and a saddle-type seat. As their name suggests, they were designed to take people off the road, over hills, through the woods, across small streams, that sort of thing. They are popular with sportsmen and recreation types. Teenagers are drawn to them too, largely for the noise, as well as their facilitating the natural teenage desire to travel in packs and generally irritate others.

And Shriners like to ride them in parades. As well, I now report, in the occasional funeral procession.

I counted thirty of them. They were all the same color. Candy green. They all had whip antennas attached to the rear of the seat, with the Boumi insignia on a blue pennant snapping back and forth. They rode in formation, three abreast, ten full rows. They fell in behind the hearse as we pulled out of the Boumi Temple parking lot. The drivers were all in their fezzes, all wearing blue blazers with white scarves against the brisk mid-morning temperature. There is a toy out there on the market, a replica of an antique metal windup toy. It is a duck pedaling a tricycle, and on its head is a fez-like cap with a set of propellers attached, three of them, that whirl as the tricycle toddles across the floor.

Enough said.

We got the dentist into the ground, fez and all. Wife was presented with a blue banner, folded into a triangle. I was bracing for a twenty-one-kazoo salute, but I needn't have worried. The Boumis behaved with businesslike solemnity. The fact that they essentially co-opted the funeral from the dentist's family was mine to observe but not mine to address. Perhaps being the wife or child of a Boumi inures one to this sort of thing. A chubby Boumi concluded the service with a reading from a magical text of some sort. This was followed by a mumbling chant from the assemblage, and then suddenly everyone was feverishly shaking everyone else's hand.

"White man strange," Sam said as we pulled out of the cemetery. The noise of thirty ATVs kicking to life behind us backed him up 100 percent.

After checking in with Billie, I drove out to the Weisheit residence. A familiar-looking Lincoln Town Car was parked in front of the garage. I pulled up next to it. Martin Weisheit was in the driveway. He had his lacrosse stick with him and was bouncing a ball against the garage door.

"How's it going there, Martin?" I asked him as I got out of my car. He answered with a shrug and fired the lacrosse ball against the door, nabbing it cleanly on the bounce. For a big guy he had a nice fluid move. I asked, "Is your mother home?"

"Everyone's home."

I stepped to the front door. Martin cradled the ball expertly, then snapped his wrists and sent it careening off the garage door again. He caught the ball and in one swift motion fired it again. This time the ball came off the top of the stick, not from the pocket. It hit the garage door low and caromed sharply off the pavement, rocketing back past Martin's outstretched stick. If it didn't hit my passenger side window dead center, it was damn near. The sound was small. A simple *pop*. The window exploded into a thousand bits and simply disappeared.

Martin lowered his stick.

He glared first at the car, then at me. "Shit."

"You missed," I said.

Martin pressed his shoe down on the glass that had fallen to the driveway and dragged it back and forth, grinding the glass against the pavement. "I'm sorry. It was an accident."

"That's a pretty lethal weapon you've got there," I said.

237

Martin considered the stick. Before he could respond, the front door opened and I was nearly stampeded. Evelyn Weisheit led the charge. She stormed out the door with her hands waving about near her ears, as if she was warding off bees.

"I will be *damned* if I am going to —" She came up short, her only real choice other than barreling right into me. She snapped me a look quite capable of severing my head from the rest of me. *"Excuse me."*

I stepped aside and she breezed past. Looking pained and helpless, Gregory Weisheit followed in her wake, and after him came Evelyn Weisheit's driver, who was doing a somewhat adequate job of containing his smirk.

Evelyn came up short in front of her grandson. "What is this?" she demanded.

The boy scuffed with his shoe again. "Glass."

"What is it doing here?"

Martin gave a shrug. "I broke a window, Gran."

Evelyn Weisheit looked to my car and back at her grandson. "You will pay for this to be repaired."

Martin mumbled. "Yes, ma'am."

The woman continued on to her car. Gregory Weisheit hopped forward like a frightened footman to pull open the door for his sister-in-law.

Polly appeared at the door. She called out mockingly. "Bye-bye, Evelyn. Come again anytime."

The doors slammed shut. Martin stepped away as the car reversed, crunching over the bits of glass from my broken window.

As the car pulled away, Polly turned to me. "How did that happen to your window?"

"It's nothing. It was just an accident."

Polly stepped past me and over to my car, where Martin averted his gaze. Polly crowded in on him.

"I have had just about enough of you and your accidents. You will clean this up and you will apologize to Mr. Sewell."

"I did."

"And you heard what your grandmother said. Whatever it costs to repair this comes out of your pocket, is that understood?"

Martin gave the grunt, the universal grunt that from a sullen teenage boy means yes. He offered no resistance as Polly snatched the lacrosse stick from his hand.

"Let's see how well you handle a broom, young man." She turned and marched back to where I was standing. The smile on her face was for me to see, not Martin. "Wouldn't you hate to have me as a mother?" she muttered, softly enough that Martin couldn't hear her.

She continued on into the house. I followed.

Jenny was standing at the foot of the stairs. "I guess you think that was funny," Jenny snapped.

Polly set the lacrosse stick down, leaning it against the wall next to the door. "What? Martin?"

"You know what I'm talking about. Gran. I can't believe how rude you were with her."

"I was no more rude to your grandmother than she was to me," Polly said calmly. "Coming out here acting like she owns the place. That's over now. She'd better just get used to that."

"That's not the point."

"Oh, I think it *is* the point. Maybe Miss Evelyn could roll right over your father, but the Duchess is going to need a much bigger steamroller if she wants to flatten me."

Jenny stomped her foot. "It's not about *you*. It's about Daddy. It's about Grandpa. I just can't *believe* you sometimes."

Polly took a step toward her daughter. "Listen to me. It happens to be about a whole lot of things that you couldn't possibly understand. The bottom line is, I don't have to listen to Evelyn trying to boss me around in my own house. That's just not going to happen."

Jenny slammed her hand down hard on the banister. "It's *her* business, too. God, you just love to piss people off, don't you? No wonder you don't have any friends!"

She spun on her heel and pounded up the stairs. Polly watched her daughter disappear, then turned to me.

"It's such a wonderful thing to be loved."

I asked, "What was that all about?"

"That was all about Jake's mother not getting her way in this house. For once."

"Meaning?"

"Meaning . . . meaning I need a drink."

I followed Polly into the living room, where she indicated the liquor cabinet in the corner. "I'd like a vodka, please. I'll go get some ice. Make yourself something too." I began to protest and she gave me a look. "Indulge me, okay?"

While Polly went off to the kitchen, I stepped over to the liquor cabinet and glanced out the window. Martin had pulled open my passenger side door and was sweeping the broken glass out of the car using a magazine. I poured a short glass of vodka and for myself chose a bottle of Stab and Kill. It's a bourbon. The label reads "Cabin Still," but that's just a technicality. Polly came back in from the kitchen with an ice bucket. It was nearly full.

"Are you expecting company?" I asked, dropping a pair of cubes into each of the glasses.

"You're company."

"I'm not *that* thirsty."

She took her glass from me and raised it.

"Is there anything you can think of worth toasting to?" She clinked my glass. "To another day we're not dead. What the hell."

I took a seat on the couch. Polly pulled the rocking chair up close to the coffee table. She was wearing a faded red tennis shirt, clam digger jeans and no shoes. She took a sip of her drink, then cradled the glass in her lap. "Have you ever heard of the James E. Weisheit Foundation?"

"Rings no bells."

"Evelyn's husband set it up a number of years ago. Do you know about James?"

I decided not to mention Evelyn Weisheit's visit of the other day. "I gathered from his brother's eulogy that he was a minor god of some sort."

Polly laughed. "That's the story. But it turns out we're all mortal. James was a wonderful man, that's very true. He was an architect. The majority of his stuff was commercial, though in his later years he did a number of residences. There's a library in St. Louis that really put James Weisheit on the map. And an opera house in Portland. But mostly it was the office buildings. I could show you some pictures. There was nothing cookie-cutter about his work. The man definitely had the touch. Anyway, he started the foundation originally to give money for architectural programs, but it expanded to a more general thing. Money to charities and hospitals and arts groups. Some nationally, but mainly in the area. When James died last year, the foundation did some restructuring. Evelyn became sole chairman and Jake was named president of the foundation."

"Was that what your husband did? I mean, full-time?"

"No. Jake was a lawyer. Corporate law. He and Evelyn and Gregory handled the foundation business out of James and Evelyn's house. It's out in Greenspring Valley. The foundation primarily gives to a lot of the same organizations every year. Five thousand, ten thousand dollars. It really didn't take up a lot of Jake's time. Jake had an office here as well. After his father died, Jake brought some of his files and papers over here. It wasn't really foundation stuff. There'd been talk of having a book written about James and his career. Evelyn was pushing the plan. Jake was in the process of sorting through some of his father's papers, trying to get them organized. They were going to be looking for a writer, nosing around for publishers, stuff like that, to see if he could get the project off the ground. It's a long story, but the point is, Evelyn thinks she can just waltz in here and clear out Jake's office."

"And you think she can't."

Polly grinned. "She forgot to say please."

"They're her husband's papers."

243

"It doesn't matter. This is my house. That was *my* husband's office. I've got a right to tell her to back off."

"Aren't you just being malicious? Do you really care about all that stuff?"

Polly rocked forward and set her glass down on the coffee table, then fell back in the chair, crossing her legs. "Maybe I'll tell you that in a minute. But first I want to know what you're doing here."

"Sisco," I said.

"Sisco."

"I saw him yesterday."

"How is he?"

"Prison doesn't suit him. He looked pretty miserable, in fact."

"I'm sorry to hear that."

"You haven't spoken with him."

"Sisco Fontaine and I have been incommunicado."

"Since Sunday," I said.

"That's right."

"He was upset that you hadn't called him."

"I've been a little preoccupied."

"That's what I told him."

Polly investigated a spot where the wall meets the ceiling for a long moment, then found my face. "I'm afraid Sisco was starting to get the wrong idea about me. I mean, about the two of us."

"What wrong idea is that?"

She picked up her glass and set it back in

her lap. "Look, Sisco was a fling. I'm not going to sit here and defend it to you, I already told you. Jake and I had a paper marriage. But that doesn't mean I saw Sisco Fontaine as my white knight."

"So you wouldn't kill your husband in order to go off with Sisco?"

I didn't consider it to be a funny question, but it raised a good laugh from the woman across the coffee table from me.

"You're going to have to come up with a better one than that."

"Well, what about Jake then? You're running around on him. Was he running around on you?"

She shook her head. "Didn't happen. Trust me. Not Jake."

"So you reject outright the idea that Jake might have been murdered over some sort of personal affair."

"Jake was way too much of a Boy Scout. Frankly, that's partly what attracted me to Sisco. Not that I really fell for that little outlaw act of his. But he's fun. He knows how to have a good time."

"And girls just want to have fun."

"Well, go ahead and shoot me. Yes, I do want to have fun. The problem with Sisco was that he said he was in love with me. I don't know whether I believed him, but he was putting pressure on me to see me more often. He was talking about my leaving Jake."

"Why not leave him? You said it yourself, it was a paper marriage."

"Leave here? For what? To go off with Sisco? I didn't say he was *that* much fun."

"Sisco wants to know if you would bail him out."

"Me?"

"You've got the money."

"A hundred and fifty thousand? Cash? Check my purse, mister. I'm a little low."

"The point is, you could pull it together."

"The point is, I'm the widow here. How the hell would that look?"

"That's what I told Sisco. But he's desperate."

"I'm sorry he's in jail. But they won't be able to keep him in there forever."

"Let me ask you something. Just suppose. Is it possible that Sisco could have come over here last Sunday morning and gotten into a fight with Jake while you were upstairs asleep? You said you had taken some medicine and were pretty zonked out. And I'm not saying it was his plan, but maybe things got out of hand, and the next thing Sisco knew, he had killed your husband. And then he took off. You come downstairs in the morning and find your husband on the kitchen floor and you call Sisco."

"Of course that's possible. It's what the police think happened."

"Do you?"

"Do I think Sisco killed Jake? I don't. Sisco can be a hothead, but I don't think he'd be so stupid he'd do something like that."

"Did you call him at his home?"

She shook her head. "I don't even know his home number. I always call his cell."

"So you don't really know where he was when you called him."

"The police asked me these same questions. No, I guess I don't know where he was."

"So if you wanted to cover up for someone else killing Jake — your friend Chip, for example — how convenient that you call up Sisco and get him to come over. He said to me that when you called him up you didn't tell him that Jake had been killed, only that you wanted him to come over right away."

Polly had started to take a sip of her drink. The glass froze halfway to her lips. "That's horseshit."

"It's just a theory."

"It's a horseshit theory. Chip didn't kill Jake."

"You don't seem to want to tell the police about him."

"It's pointless. He's innocent. He doesn't need the harassment."

"When you saw your husband lying on the kitchen floor with a knife in his back, why didn't you call the police?"

"Simple. Because I was stupid. I was half zonked on that stuff and I just wasn't thinking straight. Of course that's what I should have done, but I didn't. Jake was dead. I checked. I looked for a pulse for something like five minutes. He was dead. There was no real hurry. It was stupid not to call the police, but all I could think was that I didn't want to be alone. So I called Sisco."

"Even though it would look bad for him when the police got there?"

"I wasn't thinking about that."

"So if you're positive that he's innocent, why won't you help him get out of jail?"

Polly pushed herself out of the rocker and went over to the liquor cabinet. She topped off her drink and dropped another cube of ice in the glass. She stood looking out the window. After a moment she turned back around. "I want to show you something."

"What's that?"

"Here. Top off your drink."

I got up from the couch and took another splash of bourbon, then followed Polly out of the living room. I hesitated as she started up the stairs.

She turned around and gestured with her glass. "Come on."

A little stone splashed in my heart; I felt like I was climbing the gallows stairs. The last thing I needed was an ugly scene in Polly Weisheit's house.

"That's my room down there," Polly said casually as we reached the top of the stairs. She was indicating a door at the far end of the hallway, to our left. She took a right.

I followed her into what had most likely been designed as a bedroom but had been converted into an office. Metal file cabinets. A large desk. A fax machine. A shelf filled with as many books as file folders. Loose papers scattered about.

"This is Jake's office," Polly said.

I moved farther into the room and Polly closed the door. I detected a second click. "Did you just lock the door?" I asked.

Polly stepped forward. "I don't want us to be disturbed."

Chapter Eighteen

My drink was long gone. The last of the ice was little more than a chip, no larger than the size of a guitar pick. The early setting sun was shooting a faint orange wedge against the closed door of Jake Weisheit's office. The wedge had been growing longer and thinner. The tick-tick-tick of a small round black clock on the wall ebbed and flowed, sometimes disappearing altogether, other times a loud incessant metronome.

The office included a futon couch on the wall opposite the bookshelves. Polly was balled up on the small couch, hugging her legs to her chest. "So what do you think? It just goes to show you never really know a person."

The person she was referring to was James Weisheit, Jake's late father. I didn't bother reminding Polly that I never knew the man in the first place. I took her point.

"How many are there? Have you counted?"

Polly ticktocked her head. "No. But it must be near a hundred, don't you think?"

They were letters. Handwritten letters. No envelopes, only the letters. They were collected in a shoe box. They had been arranged in the box in chronological order. The earliest of the letters dated back fifteen years. I had only scratched the contents of the first box. The letters represented one side of a two-way correspondence. They were love letters, written — so Polly told me — by James Weisheit. He had signed his letters with the single letter J. They were addressed simply to "My Dearest M." From the sampling I had gone over sitting at Jake Weisheit's desk, several features of James Weisheit had become quite evident to me.

For one thing, he was a terrific writer. He crafted his thoughts and feelings with color and directness and a use of the English language that I would almost call arcane except for the fact that it brought the object of each sentence so vividly to life. It was clear from reading his letters that he was a man of considerable intelligence and knowledge — no slouch in the brains department — and one possessed of a passionate curiosity for the workings of the world, animal, mineral, vegetable, spiritual. He was witty, he could be barbed when he needed to be, and he was so thoroughly enthralled with the person receiving his missives that it was almost embarrassing. The man was smitten. He was poetic in his gushings. Mildly pornographic at times. And he held the woman — there was no doubt it was a woman — in such a fanciful esteem that it was almost schoolboyish. Just from the relatively small sampling I had gone through, it was achingly clear that the man was addressing his muse, or at the very least the woman he had appointed to be his muse. The letters were — to overstate it as much as I dare — an astounding display of affection.

One other thing about James Weisheit was clear from his letters. The man despised his wife. Loathed her. Thoroughly. Completely. With a passion equal in its darkness to the incandescent blast of delirium he professed for the object of his driven scribblings.

Do I make myself clear?

Polly told me that she had run across the box of letters the night after Jake was killed.

"I couldn't sleep. I didn't want to take any more pills. I was just roaming the house. God knows why I came in here. The box was in a larger one, in a file box that was sitting under that wooden bench."

"And Jake never mentioned these to you?"

"You must be kidding. Jake never breathed a word about this. How could he? You see what they say about his mother. You have to understand something, to the Weisheit family this is completely scandalous. James and Evelyn were . . . well, you heard Gregory's eulogy. 'A love of epic proportions.'" She pulled a letter from one of the boxes and waved it in my face. "How much bullshit is that?"

Polly was convinced that the letters were what Evelyn Weisheit was really after. "It has to be. Evelyn is usually a cool cucumber, but you saw how she was just now. She must know about these. It must be killing her wondering if I've seen them or not."

"You didn't say anything?"

"No. Not yet anyway."

"Who do you suppose the woman is?" I asked.

"The mysterious M? I don't know. I'd love to find out. I figure she must be dead, though. I don't know why James would have his letters back from her otherwise."

She unfolded the letter in her hand and skimmed it. As she did, her smile grew. Dark and devilish.

"He calls Evelyn *loathsome*. You have no idea how much that makes my day."

It was bracing as I started off toward home. Martin had managed to pick up most of the bits of glass, though a few of them still sparkled from the floor and from the crease in the seat as I pulled out of the Weisheit driveway. Polly had offered to have Martin affix a piece of cardboard over the missing window with duct tape, but I didn't want to risk damaging the paint. I was more concerned about the weather. A roll of purple clouds had appeared above the vanishing strip of the horizon, and even as my whiskers sensed a night of rain in store for the Baltimore metropolitan area, the first thick drops began to fall. As I reached the stop sign at the bottom of the lane the sky ripped open. Unless I wanted a seat full of water I would have to find my steed a friendly stable. I punched the R button on my transmission and a minute later was knocking on the Weisheits' front door. Jenny answered. She told me that her mother had taken off just seconds after I had. I explained the situation with my car window and Jenny offered to move her father's car out of the garage and let me tuck my Valiant into dry quarters. She refused to listen to my talk of calling a cab to run me home.

"I'll take you. I need to get out of the house. Besides, I want to know what you and Mom were doing in Daddy's office." She added, "With the door closed."

The rain was a full deluge by the time we hit the Jones Falls Expressway. Jenny gripped the wheel firmly, hunched over slightly for a better sighting of the road surface. The wipers could barely keep the windshield clear. I asked if she wanted me to drive.

"I want you to talk. My mother is up to something, I can tell."

"I'm not sure she'd want me telling you."

"Is it something to do with my father? I have a right to know."

"It's not about him."

254

I told her. Jenny Weisheit had more right to know than I did. She listened in silence as I described for her what her mother had shown me in her father's office. I summarized fairly, I thought. I pulled a few quotes from the letters. Caught the general drift. Following my directions, Jenny took the President's Street exit off the Jones Falls and took a left on Pratt. We skirted the edge of Little Italy and took a right half a mile later onto Broadway. The rain was still pounding as we pulled to a stop in front of my building. Jenny remained with her hands white-knuckling the wheel.

"I can't believe this. *My* grandfather? James Weisheit? A secret lover for fifteen years?

"That looks to be the case."

"What about *Gran?*"

"He hated Gran," I said simply. "The kindest word I saw about her was *imperious.*"

"You're wrong." She shook her head. "James and Evelyn Weisheit loved each other. Everyone knew that. They were the perfect couple. You didn't know them. They were glamorous. I used to think of them as something out of a Fitzgerald book."

It would be my guess she wasn't suggesting that her grandparents had been superficially enthralling but ultimately found to have feet of clay. That *is* Fitzgerald, isn't it?

Jenny finally released the wheel. "Can we get out of this car? If I tried to drive any-

255

where right now, I swear I would run this thing right into a wall."

"You can come up if you'd like. Let me go open the front door first. Then make a run for it."

We reached my apartment only slightly moist. Alcatraz met us at the door. Treated Jenny like an old, old friend . . . me like dust.

Jenny knelt down and took a handful of loose skin. "I *love* this dog."

Jenny quit the dog and took a look around the place. I realized that I was starving and asked her if she felt like sticking around for a bite. "You might as well wait until the rain lets up. I could whip up some faux Greek."

"What's that?"

"You cook whatever meat you've got handy, then you spice it like it's pastry. Nutmeg, cinnamon. Like that."

"Where'd you learn that?"

"Where do you think? From a faux Greek."

I had some ground beef in the freezer and I nuked it into submission. I dug up a red pepper, some olives, an onion. I started to bring up the subject of Jenny's grandfather again, but she stopped me.

"I need to sit with it."

She helped me carry the kitchen table into the front room, where we could enjoy the rain while we ate. I uncorked a bottle of Bull's Blood, a Hungarian wine of modest quality and price to match, and put some Bill Frisell on the stereo. I went back into the kitchen and ladled the ground beef concoction onto two plates. When I brought the plates to the table, Jenny was standing at my bookshelf, holding a framed photograph. I noticed that she had taken off her shoes.

"Are these your parents?"

"Yes."

"God, they're good-looking people. Your mother is beautiful."

"Was," I said.

"Oh. I'm sorry. Your father?"

"Both of them. They died when I was twelve. Car crash."

"Do you have any siblings?"

"No. There was a sister on the way, but . . . no."

She replaced the photograph and came over to the table. "I'm worried about my brother."

"This would be the brother with the world's most destructive lacrosse stick?"

"He's angry."

"Lady, it shows."

"And I can't get him to tell me about it. I've tried to talk to him about Daddy and he clams up. It's such a boy thing. Mom says just to give him his space. I'll tell you this, *she'd* better give him his space. He's furious with her. I wish he'd see someone."

"See someone?"

"Professionally. A psychiatrist. He needs a safe place to let it all out. I started seeing one at college this year and I think it's great. I feel kind of guilty, leaving Martin at home to deal with my mother all by himself."

"Were Martin and your father close?"

"Close? Sort of. Not really, I guess. They didn't argue with each other the way Martin and Mom do."

"I'm just wondering about this incident at his school. I understand from Betty Schultz that Martin was defending your father's honor. So to speak."

"Betty Schultz, huh?" Jenny laughed. "Now there's a pill and a liar."

"The word *dynamic* doesn't spring to mind."

"It sure doesn't." I poured two glasses of Bull's Blood and handed one to her. "To be honest, I don't know what Martin thought he was doing. Apparently Daddy had some sort of argument with the guy's father. Which surprises me. Daddy always had an even temper. Maybe he was under some stress at work. More likely at home, I guess. Being out in Ohio, I'm just so out of touch."

"What's the word on Toby Schultz?" I asked. "He seems to think highly of himself."

Jenny took a sip of her wine. She set the glass down on the table. "Mr. Schultz was Daddy's best friend. He's Martin's godfather. He told me at Daddy's funeral he was going to have a talk with Martin."

"Betty Schultz mentioned that too."

"Martin is just trying to proceed like nothing has happened. That's all he'll say to me, that he wants things to be the way they were. He's got a football game tomorrow. Home game. He's insisting on playing. Daddy isn't even dead a week. I don't know why, but I just feel like it's the wrong thing to do. Not to mention he could seriously hurt someone."

We ate. My God, what a fantastic meal. Jenny spoke awhile about her father, mainly stories from when she was younger, from when the fault lines in her parents' marriage hadn't yet become quite so evident. The portrait fit the ones I had already heard from both Polly and Evelyn Weisheit, and from the eulogies. Fine man. Straight arrow. Steady Eddie. At one point Jenny began to cry softly. I sat silently and let her go at it. After a time she looked up.

"I'll bet you see more tears in your job than most people do in a lifetime."

"Oh, it comes with the territory."

She set her napkin down on the table. "Do you mind if I ask you about what you do? I mean, about being an undertaker?"

I refilled our glasses and took a seat. "Go right ahead." I knew most of the questions she would ask, and she asked them. I tried to make my responses sound like I hadn't given them a hundred times before. I trotted out a couple of my best funeral stories and got the girl to laugh. Alcatraz always responds to a laughing woman, and he sauntered over to see what might be in it for him. Very self-absorbed. After we finished our food we cleared the dishes and took the table back into the kitchen. I ran a full sink and put the dishes in to soak. I poured myself some more wine and went back to the front room, where Jenny was looking over my music collection. I dropped onto the couch. Jenny's back was to me. Her fingers were tucked into the rear pockets of her jeans and she was bending from the waist, reading the titles. The rain had abated somewhat, giving over to a series of long, rumbling thunders. Jenny lifted a foot to rub the back of the opposite knee, which was when I realized I hadn't taken my eyes off her.

"Your music is making me feel stupid. I don't recognize half this stuff." She pulled one out "Bug Music?"

"Don Byron. He named that one after a Flintstones episode."

"How weird is that?" She put the Don Byron on and came over and sat down on the couch next to me. *Right* next to me. If she had had freckles I could have counted them. Even the small ones. She pulled her hair back, coiling it and tucking it in such a way that it remained suspended off her neck.

Nineteen years old, I thought.

Twenty tops.

She turned to me. "Do you find my mother attractive?"

"She's an attractive woman."

"She's had affairs before. I don't know if Daddy ever knew. I seriously doubt it."

"But you did?"

"When I was in high school, early on. Ninth grade. I came home early one day. I can't even remember now why. I know I wasn't expected. I heard her. Heard them."

"Them."

"My mother. And a man."

"Not your father."

She laughed. "In the middle of the day? You didn't know Daddy. No, it wasn't him. I heard them, and when I realized what it was, I left the house."

"So you didn't see who it was."

"No. It was so shocking to me. I had never . . . well, I'd never heard something like that before. I was still a kid, really. Of course I was upset. I was angry that she would do something like that to Daddy. But there was no way I was going to tell him. I just couldn't bring myself to."

"Did you ever say anything to your mother about it?"

"No. At least not directly. But I got the feeling that she sensed something from me. Sometimes she'd look at me and it would be this expression. Smug. Or defiant. Like she and I were sharing a confidence and she knew I wouldn't betray it. Even if I wanted to. It was weird. It was . . . intimate." She held her gaze on me as she took a sip of her wine. "How old are you?"

"Thirty-four."

"My mother is forty-two."

"How old are you?" I asked.

She paused. "I'm almost twenty."

"So you're nineteen."

"Technically, yes." Don Byron's clarinet was making rude noises. At least they suddenly sounded rude to me. Jenny asked, "Have you ever been married?"

"Once."

"I wondered. I can see you being married."

"You would have had to look quickly. It was less than a year."

"What happened? If you don't mind my asking."

"Nothing happened. We had a wonderful relationship and then we got married. Nothing happened, so we pulled the plug."

"What was supposed to happen?"

"We didn't know. We just knew it didn't. It was an instinct thing. Hard to explain. We're still good friends. No bruises."

Don Byron gave it over to strings. Nice and lush. Maybe a little too lush. Jenny twisted on the couch so that she was facing me dead-on. Her coiled hair fell down onto her neck.

"Are you seeing anyone right now?"

Her eyebrows lifted with her question and they remained aloft while she waited for me to answer. It made her eyes even larger. She brought the wineglass up to her mouth and tapped it lightly against her teeth. Nice teeth. Hollywood white. I've got good wineglasses. Razor thin. There was a little chime as she tapped the glass against her teeth.

"Well? Are you?"

Life is actually a lot simpler than it seems. What I mean is, you can lie when the occasion strikes you and see how you fare. See if you're lucky enough to escape the nearly guaranteed consequences of deceit. Or you can tell the truth and keep the whole raft of potential complications at bay. This is simple, isn't it?

She was probably leaving for Ohio in a few days. Back to the bubble. Gone for good.

Nineteen, for God's sake.

"I am," I said.

Down came the eyebrows. "You are."

"She's a singer," I said. "And a car mechanic."

She looked at me blankly. "You're going out with a singer and a car mechanic? All in one?"

"Is that so odd?"

She stood up. I thought maybe she was leaving, but instead she moved over to my ugly armchair, where she made something of an event of taking a seat.

"I'm sorry. I'm not normally like this."

"Forget it."

"I'll bet this happens to you a lot. Spaced-out women coming on to you."

"Why's that? You think I hold a certain appeal for the spaced-out woman?"

"You know what I mean. Confused and vulnerable."

"Oh. *That* spaced-out woman. There's a lecture in mortuary college about her."

"You're kidding."

I raised my glass to her. "I am."

Jenny brought her feet up onto the chair and tucked them underneath her. She rested her wineglass in her lap. For the first time I noted the faint similarity between Jenny and her mother. We spoke a few minutes longer.

"Martin says that Daddy seemed troubled the past couple of months. He was snapping at Martin a lot. That's something that hardly ever happened before."

"Sisco?"

"Maybe. I don't know."

Don Byron tooted his last toot and Jenny took that as her cue to leave. She fetched her shoes and put them back on. I took our wineglasses into the kitchen and rinsed them out. Alcatraz joined us at the door.

"Tell your mother I'll be by sometime tomorrow to pick up my car," I said, pulling open the door. "I'll have someone run me out."

Jenny had knelt down to give Alcatraz a farewell rub. She looked up at me. "I could run you out."

"That's silly," I said. "Run in. Run out. I'll have someone drive me out."

Jenny rose. It suddenly felt very cramped. A dark blush had come to her cheeks. "I mean . . . if I stayed. I could run you out."

"If you stayed."

She nodded slowly. "Is there really a car mechanic?"

"Would I make that up?"

"I don't know you that well. It seems to me maybe you might."

"Why would I do that?" I asked.

"I don't know. People do things like that sometimes."

"I didn't," I said. "She's real."

"And if she wasn't?"

I hesitated. "Jenny, are you spacing out on me?"

Her blush deepened. She backed away. "God, I feel like a complete fool."

"There's no need."

"I'm sorry. It's the wine."

"I thought maybe it was the dog."

"That too."

"Just so long as it wasn't me," I said.

She looked at me. "You know what? I'm going."

And she did. I waited at the top of the stairs until the downstairs door closed. Alcatraz was at the window when I came back into the apartment.

"Forget it, boy. It's just you and me."

The phone rang. It was Angela. "Hi there, cutie," she said. "What're you doing?"

I dropped onto the couch. "Nothing. Just sitting here thinking about you."

Alcatraz was padding across the floor. If bloodhounds could roll their eyes . . .

Chapter Nineteen

Angela picked me up in the afternoon and drove me to the Weisheits' house. She had phoned someone she knew who replaced car windows and windshields on-site. He was already there when we arrived, nearly finished with the job. He called my car "a beaut."

"I took a look under the hood. I couldn't resist. This baby must really cook."

I concurred. "She cooks."

"That tranny ever drop on you?"

"Tranny?"

"Transmission. Those push-button jobs."

"Nope. Never."

"That's the one drawback."

"Hasn't happened," I said.

"You're a lucky man."

I was hoping not to run into Jenny and I got my wish. I seemed to be suffering a slight non-morning-after morning-after, for which I know no cure. Nonsensical, but there it was. Polly made an appearance (looking a little morning-afterish herself, I thought). She and Angela spoke stiffly about Sisco while I stuck like glue to the window repair guy. Before we left, Polly cornered me by a horizontal freezer. Angela was in the driveway, talking carburetors.

"Jenny drove you home yesterday, I hear."

"That's right."

"Whose idea was that?"

"That was Jenny's. It was kind of her."

Polly screwed up her mouth, representative of any of a dozen possible thoughts, none of which the woman seemed inclined to share. She brought a finger to my chest and gave it a poke. "Watch it."

Angela followed in her car. We pulled out of Polly's driveway and started down the narrow lane toward the main road. A group of children were in a yard at the bottom of the lane piling leaves. I braked, glancing in the mirror at Angela behind me.

I didn't stop.

I pushed harder on the brake. The pedal wasn't compressing.

A Supremely Unwieldy Vehicle (SUV) had just that instant pulled into the lane at the bottom of the hill and come to a stop at a diagonal, effectively blocking the lane as a petite woman crawled halfway out of the driver's window to collect mail from a mailbox in the shape of a barn. I braked again, to no result. Simultaneously I hit my horn and punched the Lo-Drive button on my transmission, thinking *this* would be a fortuitous time for Miss Tranny to fall out. She didn't. Fortunately, I had not been accelerating down the hill, and the lower gear served to slow me even more. The woman in the Supremely Unwieldy Vehicle froze. Several envelopes slipped from her hand and fell to the road. I twisted the wheel to avoid the collision. My "beaut" bumped up over the dirt curb and drifted at a walker's pace some twenty feet across the grass, the renewed honking of my horn harmonizing with the squeals of the fleeing children. I traveled into the pile of yellow and red leaves, cleaved it and crushed it, and continued on over the bumpy grass, steering toward an imposing hedge at the border of the property. There I stopped. I punched the car into Park, pulling on the parking brake as the children surrounded the car like a litter of fairies. I reached down and felt under the brake pedal.

Angela appeared at the window. "Impressive. But you forgot to use your turn signal."

I held up the culprit for her to see. Martin's lacrosse ball.

The boys in blue were crushing the boys in white. St. Paul's creaming Boys Latin. It wasn't even a contest. By the second quarter they should have called the whole thing off and told everyone to go home and read a good book. The score was 31 to 0. St. Paul's was playing at home, which in this case meant they had a grandstand for their supporters. It was essentially a large cement block with several dozen tiers of bleachers, but an intimidating luxury compared to the muddy sidelines occupied by the poor souls who had to stand there watching Boys Latin take its whipping.

The ground was still wet from the previous day's storm. The field was one part grass, two parts mud, churned up now by twenty or so minutes of cleats. Angela and I were in the bleachers just off the fifty-yard line. There was a fair-sized crowd for a Monday. A wind was whipping from the north. Angela was underdressed — bless her — so I positioned myself as her windbreaker. Down on the near sidelines a half-dozen girls from nearby St. Paul's School for Girls roamed along with the action, acting as cheerleaders. Most of their efforts dissolved into hopeless giggles. But like I said, the boys in blue had things firmly in hand.

St. Paul's was kicking off. For the umpteenth time. The ball sailed end over end in a high arc as the bulls in blue thundered down the field. I wondered if maybe Boys Latin had decided just for a lark to field the astronomy club members instead of their usual gridiron grunts. Indeed, the players were spending a lot of their time on the field looking up at the sky. Perhaps they were praying for a blizzard. Or divine intervention.

Number 15 for Boys Latin caught the ball. He didn't take right off. He froze, scanning the field for the best opening. His mates had failed to secure one for him. White jerseys were already scattered all about the turf. The boy glanced behind him as if considering an extraordinarily unorthodox — but perhaps prudent — maneuver. Then he spun back forward and darted to his left and began galloping in a diagonal line directly toward his team's bench. He was no more than ten steps into his run back when Martin Weisheit threw himself full force against the boy's chest, grabbed hold of his face mask and with an interesting little corkscrew motion slammed the kid to the ground.

I turned to Angela. "That's our boy."

For all its ready accessibility, the face mask is not intended as a means of giving the opposing players easier purchase. Flags were thrown and St. Paul's was penalized. Martin trotted to the sidelines where one of his coaches bellowed at him. "Come on, boy! Think! You could break somebody's neck doing that!" Martin removed his helmet. His expression suggested that he was not only perfectly aware of this but perfectly okay with it.

"You're lucky you got away with something as simple as a broken window," Angela remarked.

Martin dropped his helmet to the ground and sat down on it, crossing his arms around his knees and staring off at the field. Some twenty or so feet from us a man leaped to

271

his feet, exhorting the St. Paul's coach to *"Put Clifford in!"* This was nothing new. The man had been popping up and down like a spastic jack-in-the-box since the opening kickoff. At the slightest provocation he was up on his feet, gnashing his teeth, haranguing the referees, the coaches, the boys on the field. The man was genetically incapable of keeping his mouth shut. I marveled he didn't lash out at the de facto cheerleaders.

"C'mon, Mitch! Give the boy some playing time, for Christ's sake!"

It was him, it had to be. The guy who had gotten into a fight with Jake Weisheit. As far as I was concerned, the question of why Jake Weisheit had mixed it up with this guy had already been answered. Not the full specifics, of course, but I was no longer sure how important they were. *I* was ready to go confront the maniac. And I'm a notoriously peaceful lamb. The man enjoyed plenty of space on the bleacher. A leper would have been more crowded. One could only imagine what the boy seated on the far end of the St. Paul's bench was thinking. The one whose face was half covered in bandaging.

Boys Latin fumbled the ball on the next play. There was a mad scramble to pick it up, but it kept squibbling away from the boys' hands. The marionette down the way was on his feet.

"Ball! Ball! Ball! Ball!"

"So what do you think?" Angela asked me. "Does he look like a killer?"

He didn't. He looked like a loser. Which isn't to say that losers can't be killers. In fact I'm sure it's a safe bet to say that in our ever-growing prison population you can find plenty of losers who are also killers.

"Let's go," I said as the halftime approached. "It was a stab in the dark anyway."

The St. Paul's players were gathering up to head for the goal area off by the scoreboard for the halftime exhortations. On one end of the bench, the sidelines maniac was still raising a fuss. His son stood at his side as the man lit into one of the St. Paul's coaches. Martin Weisheit was standing on the opposite end of the bench, his helmet in his arm. He was getting an earful himself.

I took Angela's arm as we came down from the bleachers. "Wait."

"I thought we were leaving."

"We are."

"Our feet aren't moving."

"Hold on."

After another minute, Martin took a friendly pounding to the shoulder pads and turned and jogged off toward the goal area.

"Come on," I said to Angela.

"In your way you're actually kind of bossy, aren't you?"

Angela and I made our way down the sidelines. The man who had been jawing with Martin was heading back into the stands. I took Angela's hand and we started up after him. It was Toby Schultz. He took a seat about eight rows from the top. He looked up at us as we approached. It took him several seconds to recognize me, partly I'd say because he was spending more of his gazing time on my friend.

I helped him out. "Hitchcock Sewell. Jake's funeral."

"Of course, of course." He rose and I steered Angela toward him to give him a better look. "This is Angela. Angela, Toby Schultz."

"You don't have a boy out there, do you?" Schultz asked as the three of us took a seat. "No, of course you don't. You're too young."

"I don't," I said. "You?"

"I have three girls." He laughed. "I'm a field hockey dad. No, I'm here to cheer on Martin. It's the boy's first home game since Jake died. I thought he could use a little support. I'm his godfather, it seemed like the right thing to do."

"He plays a mean game," I said.

Schultz made an exasperated face. "The boy is competitive. You don't want to squash that. I was a lot like that when I was his age."

Angela observed, "There's competitive and there's out of control."

274

"In fact that's exactly what I was just telling him. There's no gain in being straight-out reckless. Of course this is a difficult time for him. But he'll be fine. He just needs to blow off some more steam."

"Let's hope he doesn't blow it off on that Clifford kid anymore," I said.

We glanced down at the now-empty bench. The sidelines nutcase was lurking near the bench, hands in his pockets, pacing in small circles.

"Martin is under strict orders to leave Clifford Sparks alone," Schultz said.

"I take it that's Clifford's father."

"Ned Sparks."

"Someone should issue that guy a muzzle," I said.

Schultz shrugged. "I'm afraid Ned Sparks goes with the territory."

"So you know him?"

"Me? Oh, sure, I've known Ned since the sixth grade. I'll give him marks for consistency. He was just as obnoxious then as he is now."

"I understand Jake Weisheit had some kind of argument with Sparks a few weeks ago. I gather that's why Martin clocked him."

Schultz made a face. "I wouldn't go making too much of it. It was at the Gilman game. Ned was his usual obnoxious self and Jake, from what he told me, just got sick of it. He told Ned where to stow it. There was a little shoving. Amateur hour, I'm sure. Jake said it all came to nothing. He didn't know why he even bothered. Like I said, Ned Sparks has been like this since middle school. He's always had a chip on his shoulder about Jake anyway. You know how school can be. Jake was a popular guy. A good athlete. You see where Sparks is right now? On the sidelines? That's where he's always been."

Several minutes later, the teams reassembled on the field. Boys Latin kicked off to start the second half. The St. Paul's player who caught the ball zigzagged his way easily down the field on the way to yet another score. He could have stopped to pick daisies along the way. Down at the far end of the bleachers a familiar voice was already beseeching the St. Paul's coach. *"Come on, already. It's a blowout. Put Clifford in!"*

I turned to Schultz. "I heard your eulogy the other day. It was good."

"Coming from you, I guess that's a real compliment."

"I noticed, though, you didn't mention Polly Weisheit."

Schultz frowned. "What are you talking about? Of course I did."

"Actually, it was Polly who pointed it out to me. She was the one who noticed."

"She's wrong. Of course I mentioned her. You must not have been listening. I was the one who introduced Polly to Jake."

"That's what I hear. So the two of you go back."

"Polly and I used to work together."

"Was that the advertising agency?"

"We worked at a place called Grayson's."

"Is that the one with the guy who is into birds?"

"You're thinking of RM&D. No. That was where Polly worked before she came to Grayson's."

"Did you know a guy named Chip Cooperman? Polly worked with him at the bird-guy place."

"Chip? Absolutely. Now there's a sad case for you. Very unbalanced guy, Chip. You want to talk fights? Maybe Chip can relate to that poor Sparks kid down there. Chip Cooperman took a swing at me once. Totally out of the blue. He just showed up at my door and he was all over me. You've never seen such a temper. And no rhyme or reason. He just blew. I ended up breaking the damn guy's nose. I didn't mean to do it, but the guy just bulled after me. He could be like that. He would just go off."

"And why did he go after you?"

"That's what I'm saying, no reason at all. It was totally unprovoked."

A few minutes later the unimaginable happened. The quarterback for Boys Latin fell back for a pass. He got hit from his blind side and the ball popped out of his hands.

Another teammate — it was number 15 — scooped the ball up and began running madly down the field. Toby Schultz leaped to his feet. The kid was running like one of those bugs that skitter along the top of the water. His gyroscope didn't seem to understand how to move the setting to Forward. Above the yelling of the crowd, Ned Sparks could be heard howling, *"Kill him!"*

Number 15 easily traveled sixty yards to advance thirty. But he did it. He scored. Across the field the sparse crowd and the boys on the bench exploded as one. The team failed to make the conversion, but it hardly mattered. The players still leaped into one another's arms. They had been delivered.

Angela and I made our farewells and headed for our cars. I told Angela that there was a place nearby that made the perfect milk shake.

"How does that sound?"

It sounded good. Angela followed me to Windy Valley, a dilapidated diner-style place that looked like a battered shoe box.

"So what do you think now about your Ned Sparks?" Angela asked, working her twisty straw into her mouth.

"Well, according to Schultz, Sparks has never been a big fan of Jake Weisheit's."

"So twenty-some years after high school they have a fight at a stupid football game and then he goes off and kills him?"

I pinched off one end of the wrapper on my straw. "No, he doesn't. I think it's a different old buddy of Jake's who is worth another look."

"This guy Chip?"

I tilted my head back and blowgunned the wrapper into the air, nabbing it cleanly as it came back down. "Uh-uh. This guy Schultz."

I was only several miles from Lutherville, so I decided to swing by and look in on Mrs. McNamara. I hadn't had the chance to check in on her since the cabaret on Saturday and I wanted to make sure she was doing okay. Halfway there I remembered her talk of egg creams and I considered looping back to Windy Valley. But I didn't. Instead, I did stop off at a florist's on York Road and picked up a fistful of tulips. I was met at Briarcliff by Phyllis Fitch, who informed me that Mrs. McNamara was doing poorly. She didn't think my seeing her at present was such a good idea. But I pressed.

"She may not even be awake," Phyllis said.

"If that's the case I won't wake her. I'll just leave these flowers."

She relented and I followed her down the hallway and up a flight of stairs.

I was shocked. No simpler way to put it. Mrs. McNamara was lying in a bed, her face nearly the same color as the sheets. Her lips, which were also nearly white, were dry and cracked. I had to look closely to determine that she was in fact breathing.

"What the hell happened?" I whispered to Phyllis. "She wasn't like this a few days ago. She should be in a hospital."

"If her condition hasn't improved by morning, that's very likely. Dr. Little was here earlier. He's going to check back on her in the morning."

There was an IV bag hung on a pole next to the bed. The tube from the bag ran down to a small gray box on the table beside the bed. Another tube ran from the box and under the sheets. "What's this?"

"We're feeding liquid nutrition directly into her stomach," Phyllis said. "It's just a small incision. She's actually still on the drip at present. We're setting up the pump for overnight. That will regulate the feeding automatically."

"She looks wretched."

"You should keep your voice down. It's possible she can hear us."

I bounced down to a crouch, near the old woman's pillow. Her skin looked like parchment, like it would dissolve into dust if anyone were to touch it.

"It's Hitchcock Sewell, Mrs. McNamara," I said softly. "I brought you some flowers. I'm going to leave them right next to your bed. You get your rest now, okay? I'll check in with you later. We've got a date to go find you an egg cream. Don't forget that, all right? Keep some space open on your schedule."

On the way out of the room we bumped into Teresa. She recognized me from the other day, but she didn't say anything to me. Phyllis handed her the tulips and instructed her to locate a vase for them.

"And we'll be needing to set up the pump for this evening. You've worked with one of those before?"

"I'm leaving soon," Teresa said. "I'm off duty in an hour."

"You're *on* duty for the next hour," Phyllis said sharply. "Let's try looking at it that way, shall we?" Teresa didn't seem to find the distinction terribly exciting. Phyllis added, "You be sure to wait until the night staff comes on." She checked her watch. "And forget about the pump. We'll leave that for them."

As we headed for the stairs, Phyllis sniffed, "That one I could do without."

"I thought Teresa was just a day temp that Mrs. McNamara hired to go out to the funeral. Has Briarcliff hired her?"

"Not on your life. We're perpetually short-staffed. I specifically told Princeton I was not too thrilled with this one, but they sent her back anyway. I need to talk to someone there."

"Princeton?"

"That's the name of the primary agency we

use. Princeton Nursing Associates. I guess it is a little ironic. I can't say we always get the best and the brightest."

It was dark out by the time I left. Billie was up to her elbows in containers of Thai food when I dropped in to see how she was doing. Her nose was running riot, she was sneezing up a storm and she reported having trouble keeping her paws off her brandy bottle. You've never seen a happier little lady. I sat with her and watched some PBS and helped her finish off the Thai food. I joined her for a brandy, then found a bottle of beer in the fridge that looked lonely.

The PBS show was all about glaciers. It was an hour-long show and it moved about as slowly as its subject. By the time I left, that's about how I was moving. Glacially. I ran into Father Ted on my way home and he invited me out on his boat the next day. Father Ted did a stint as a naval chaplain back before landing his position at St. Teresa's. He likes, as he says, to keep his hand on the rudder. We agreed to meet at the pier at an ungodly hour . . . perhaps I should say a secular hour. Then I continued on, steering my own ship safely to its berth. Something akin to the gentle lapping of waves took me off to sleep.

Chapter Twenty

Mrs. McNamara was dead.

Billie got the call late the following morning. I was back from my sail about the harbor with Father Ted and was seated on a stool at the Oyster, my cap pushed back on my head, regaling Sally with tales of the tempestuous seas, when Darryl Sandusky came into the bar and gave me the news. Darryl had been hosing down the hearse — which is just something the kid likes to do — when the call came in to Billie. Billie thought maybe I'd be back from my sailing by then, so she sent Darryl off looking for me.

"Some old lady died," was how Darryl delivered the news. He must have run it over and over in his head on his way down the street, this measured and sensitive delivery.

Father Ted pulled his cigar from his mouth. "What lady?"

"Mrs. Something or other. From a nursing home."

He climbed up onto the stool next to Father Ted. I half expected him to take the cigar from the priest and stick it in his own mouth. I leaned forward on the bar so that I could see around Father Ted.

"Have you got a name on this lady, Darryl?"

"Mrs. Something. Mrs. Sewell said she's a friend of yours or something."

"McNamara?"

"That's it."

I lowered my heavy mug to the bar. The afternoon had been nice. Father Ted owns a thirty-foot Catalina Star and is remarkably adept at the helm, fluid and unflustered with the ropes and pulleys. The wind had cooperated, strong and gusty, and we'd clipped along the water at a fair pace. It's peculiar how being out on the water can make a person thirsty. Or maybe it's not peculiar; maybe it's obvious. Regardless, I was enjoying my stout and my small vacation from my vocation. In every sense, Darryl's news took the wind out of my sails. I paid up and headed up the street toward the funeral home. Maybe it was the stout, but I felt heavy. My legs felt like they were concluding a hundred-mile march.

Doodle was sweeping off her front steps as I passed. One look at me and she stopped sweeping. "Is everything okay, Hitchcock?"

I stopped. I must have had a hell of a look on my face, judging from Doodle's expression. "I was out sailing in the harbor this morning with Father Ted," I said. "It was nice. A little nippy, but pleasant. The Land of Pleasant Living. We were, just now down

284

at the Oyster having a beer."

Doodle gripped her broom handle with both hands and said nothing. I shrugged. Felt like twenty pounds of shoulder.

"Doodle, if I don't bury another person for the rest of my life, I'll be happy."

I pulled off my cap and flicked it angrily, with a flip of the wrist, like a Frisbee. It went about twenty feet and landed spinning on the pavement.

Thomas was bringing a pair of bulging garbage bags out of the rear door as I pulled up.

"You here for Mrs. McNamara?" I told him I was. He gave me an angry look as he pinwheeled both of the heavy bags into the Dumpster. "Well, she's sure dead, you can just get her out of here. It don't do any of the others any good." Thomas grabbed a bound bundle of magazines for recycling and held them to his chest. For a moment I thought he was going to foist them on me. "This place'd fall all the hell apart without me, you know what I'm saying? *I* know how to do things right. Put *me* on twenty-four hours a day, I could whip this place in some kind of shape. You won't get these old people dying every time you turn around. Not that shit. Not with me."

Thomas dropped the bundle of magazines right back where they had been, halting their bounce with his boot. "You hear what I'm saying?"

I went inside and found Phyllis in her office. She was on the phone and she signaled me to have a seat. Her end of the phone conversation was limited to a few terse responses. "Yes . . . no . . . no . . . of course not . . ." She looked exasperated. Her office was about the size of a large supply closet; the walls seemed to fold in on her as she sat at her desk. The room's lair-like quality was no doubt enhanced by the dim wattage of the office's only light source, a standing brass lamp located a few feet behind the desk. At length the nursing administrator hung up the phone. She glared across the desk at me as if I had arrived with a particularly feisty skunk riding on my shoulder. She slid a piece of paper across the desk. I glanced at it and dropped it back on the desk. It contained Mrs. McNamara's vital statistics, her date of birth, her social security number.

"Stroke," she said flatly, and she proceeded to clip off the points of Mrs. McNamara's final night. Around three in the morning Mrs. McNamara had been overwhelmed with a violent attack of vomiting and diarrhea. There was no indication that she had pushed her call button, and by the time anyone looked in on her, Mrs. McNamara had soiled her bed. The vomiting continued and she was taken off to the bathroom while her bed

286

was being cleaned up and refitted with new sheets. While matters were being taken care of in the bathroom, Mrs. McNamara apparently suffered her fatal stroke. It all happened quickly, Phyllis said, and according to the staff on duty, there had not been time to call for an ambulance. Mrs. McNamara fell, striking her head against the sink. She died on the bathroom floor. In her own mess.

Phyllis was not happy about it. "I was not here, of course. I was at home. But I should have been notified. That's procedure. I should not have arrived this morning to be told what happened. That's unprofessional."

She picked up a clipboard and stared at it with such fierceness I expected the thing to explode into flames in her hand. She shook her head slowly, then dropped the clipboard back onto the desk. The way she was looking at me I thought *I* might explode into flames.

"I contacted Peggy's family immediately. She has a sister in Cumberland. A Letitia Bodine. I recommended to Mrs. Bodine that we contact a local funeral home. She agreed. I told her you would be in touch with her." She handed me another piece of paper. "That's her number. I should warn you, she did not sound terribly coherent."

I looked at the paper. There were two numbers on it. "What's this other number?" I asked. "The Baltimore one."

"Oh. That's a Dorie Matthews. Mrs.

Matthews is the person who has been in charge of Peggy's finances. At least as concerns Briarcliff. I phoned her as well to let her know about Peg. I didn't get through to her directly, but I left her a message. I thought you might need to be in touch with Mrs. Matthews concerning your expenses."

I pocketed the piece of paper as Phyllis rose from her chair. She stood a moment, looking as if she had something more to say. Instead she clapped her hands together. "Shall we go get Peggy?"

I followed Phyllis down the hall to the infirmary, where the body of Mrs. McNamara lay on an examination table under a sheet. A man was seated next to her. Gray around the ears, but otherwise bald. Phyllis introduced him to me as Dr. Little. Little looked like he was on the verge of a sneeze. He also looked as if he needed a new prescription for his glasses.

He squinted at me as Phyllis made the introductions. "You here for her?" I told him I was. "Nice lady," he said. "You got the death certificate?"

"I do." I produced the document from my pocket. It's my job to fill out most of it. The essentials. Cause of death of course goes to the professionals. The doctor took the document from me and squinted at it as he filled it in and signed it.

"Nice lady," he said again, handing it back

to me. "I wish there was something that could've been done." He snapped his fingers. "Massive stroke. I'd say she was dead before she hit the ground."

I lowered the sheet for a look. Mrs. McNamara's hair had been sponged with water and slicked back on her skull. Her features were frozen in a wretched mask. She looked more like a little monkey than a human being. Had I not known, I can't even say for certain that I'd have recognized her. There was a large abrasion on her forehead.

"She apparently struck her head as she fell," the doctor said. He looked at Phyllis. "Since I'm here, I'll make my rounds." He nodded tersely at me. "Nice to meet you."

He was not out the door five seconds when a nurse entered. I recognized her from my first visit. The moonfaced young woman. Louise. She looked pale. She stopped short when she saw me.

Phyllis demanded, "What is it, Louise?"

"I . . . I wanted you to know that I've reshelved those boxes, Miss Fitch. Everything has been sorted and it's all back where it should be."

"Thank you, Louise."

"They're all back on the two shelves. On the right side. Labels all turned out. Like you said."

"Fine, Louise. We can discuss this later."

Louise's gaze traveled down to the table.

Her eyes grew wide. Phyllis was watching the young woman closely. Louise spoke in a whisper. "Oh, Peggy. It's so horrible."

Phyllis pulled the sheet back up over the dead woman's head. "It is. It's very sad. But it's something you have to get used to. Isn't that right, Mr. Sewell? You just have to learn to let it go."

Louise let it go, all right. She let it fly. Tears came to her eyes and she ran out of the room. I turned to Phyllis. "Is she new?"

"She's sensitive. She's very good at what she does, though. She takes orders. She's just . . . she'll be fine."

Phyllis said she would be in her office if I needed her. I returned to the hearse and fetched the gurney. Thomas was still adding additional stacks to his recycling.

"I'll help you with that," he said. He followed me back inside and we loaded Mrs. McNamara onto the gurney and brought her out to the hearse.

"Damn shame someone going so fast like that," Thomas announced. "I come in to work at six o'clock in the morning. On the nose, you hear what I'm saying? I'm always on time. Miss Tuck told me right away what happened. She said Mrs. McNamara has died overnight, Thomas, and she tells me to offer up a prayer for her soul. That's what she tells me. Miss Tuck is a good lady. She's got her daddy's heart. I tell her we're all going to die, that's how it is. You can't go getting upset. Miss Tuck's going to die. I'm going to die. You're going to die. The Lord's got it all set up. There's not room down here for all of us, you hear what I'm saying?"

"Miss Tuck was here at six this morning?"

"That's what I just said."

"Is she always here that early?"

Thomas tugged on his chin. "We got a sick lady who died. They called her. Miss Tuck cares what goes on here. What do you think? This place is her baby. Her daddy give her this whole damn place after *he* died and she's trying to take care of it like he'd want her to. She's trying to take care of a whole houseful of sick old people, what do you think?"

"I was just curious —"

But he was off. He jabbed a finger at my face. "You got what you came for now, didn't you? Didn't you? 'Cause *I* got work to do too. These old people are relying on Thomas to do his work. I *make* it look easy because I know what the hell I'm *doing,* but I'll tell you some shit . . ."

I left him to tell some shit to someone else. My patience for Thomas's mood swings was just too low. I realized I had forgotten the paper with Mrs. McNamara's vital stats. It was still on Phyllis's desk. On the way to her office I poked my head into the atrium. Leonard was there. The fellow I had lunched with the other day. Leonard was sitting on

291

the glider reading a paperback book. The cover showed an eagle with a clawful of feathers. The title was *Better Off Dead.* Not the kind of irony I was in the mood for.

He looked up as I entered. "You here for Peg?" I told him I was. "What the hell happened to her, that's what I want to know?"

"Apparently she suffered a stroke."

"You believe that?"

"Of course I do. I spoke with the doctor."

"Doctor." Leonard practically spit the word. "Retired pill pusher comes out here and says boo to everyone so he can collect from Medicare. *I* could make that kind of so-called rounds." He stuck a finger in the book to hold his place. "You've got eyes. This time last week Peggy was healthy enough to climb a tree. She was as healthy as you and me."

"I'm afraid I can't quite agree with you on that."

"You don't live here, you don't see it. She was healthy, I'm telling you. Then Peggy started complaining to me. They were putting all sorts of rot in her system and it wasn't doing her any damn good at all. She was getting all dried up. You saw her. She was constipated. She was getting dizzy all the time. That girl fell apart all at once, that's what I'm saying. The kind of money we pay at this place, that's not right. That's not good treatment. Woman like that lying in her own mess. There's no excuse for that. They fired

292

that damn little so-and-so who was supposed to be looking after her. That college girl. A little damned late if you ask me."

"What are you talking about? What college girl?"

"That's what I call them. College girls. College boys. These damn so-called helpers. They get them from a place called Princeton. Like the college. You get these underpaid, underskilled total strangers coming in and out of here like we're some kind of bus station, what kind of treatment can you expect? You know Lloyd Harvey? I saw that same college girl shoving spoonfuls of food into Lloyd that would've choked an elephant. You think she's paying attention? I can take one look in her eyes and see that she needs to find a new line of work."

"You're talking about Teresa?"

"Whatever her damn name is. Black girl. Plugged into her music all day long."

"But Teresa wasn't on duty last night," I said. "I was here when she told Miss Fitch she was finishing her shift."

"All I can say is, she's sure finished around here now. I saw her getting the boot first thing this morning. Nothing I'll be losing sleep over either. The patients around here with some money in the bank, they pay for their own people to come around and keep an eye on them. What does that tell you? Peg had some money. Lucky for her they didn't grab it away from her. They do that too, you know."

"Do what?"

"Steal. If you don't have someone looking out for you, they'll take it right out of your pocket."

"Do you mean the nurses?"

"I mean your damn bank account. They get you on their side, next thing you know they've got your checkbook and they're telling you how to spend your own money. Don't think it doesn't happen. The *Sun* had a reporter out here last spring looking into some of that monkey business." He shook his book at me. "They just cover it all up. Everybody's got a price. That's how it works. Who the hell cares about a bunch of half-dead people? I'm sleeping with my eyes open around this place, I'll tell you that."

"You're upset," I said. Immediately I wished I hadn't.

He looked at me like he thought I was a complete idiot. "I'm upset. Well, somebody hand the man a stuffed animal. Damn right I'm upset. Peg was a friend of mine. We sat right here on this seat just last week and laughed ourselves silly. She was as healthy as you are. Where is she now? Is she laughing now?"

I started. "I'm sorry —"

"Just go." He pawed the air with his book. "Get Peg the hell away from here. That's your job. You can make your nickel like everyone else. Sweet girl like that. It makes me sick."

I left him kicking at the air. I felt bad, but there was nothing I could say to him. I made my way to Phyllis's office. She wasn't there. The paper was where I'd left it on her desk. I took it. The door to Marilyn Tuck's office was closed as I passed by. I could hear voices coming from inside. One of them was that of Briarcliff's nursing administrator.

The very loud one. The very angry one.

Chapter Twenty-one

On the way back into town I took the North Avenue exit off the expressway, followed North to Greenmount and passed through the stone gates of Greenmount Cemetery. If I had a nickel for every time I've passed through these gates I'd be wearing some pretty fancy spats by now, I'll say that much. Five crows were lined up on the roadway as I entered the cemetery, big fat meaty boys showing no inclination to move out of my way. I slowed down and blew my horn. The crows hopped grudgingly aside, one of them answering my horn with a scratchy honk of his own. It's a cliché for crows to gather in cemeteries, but that's something that has never seemed to bother crows. We need clichés anyway, they're the world's most reliable truisms.

I steered my way up the hill, bearing to my left, then parked partly off the road and picked my way past the Hoffmans, the Tanners and the Kramers until I reached the Sewells — Mama, Papa and baby Joop. Ugly Uncle Stu was there as well, though his stone was set off from my immediate family's, leaving room for Billie. There was space for me too, oh joy, as well as room for a guest of my own should I one day locate someone I want to cuddle up to for all of eternity.

I did a little weeding and sprucing up around the graves. I don't usually mutter aloud to the dead. The exception is for my never-born sister, Jupiter. My parents died on their way to the hospital after my mother had gone into labor. They were flattened by a beer truck at the intersection of Broadway and Eastern Avenue. My sister survived the accident for several hours, but expired in the arms of a nurse just minutes before I came bursting through the doors of the emergency room. Later that evening Billie assigned me the task of naming her and I came up with Jupiter, based on my misreading of a flickering star that held my focus in the early evening sky.

"Joop. Silly little Joop."

I brushed at the grass around her stone, the way you'd brush the hair off a forehead. She would have been twenty-two now had the beer truck veered, a fact I'm aware is not worth reflecting on. But I seem to do it anyway. Of course I miss my parents terribly. A more suited pair of people I've yet to come across. But this little Jupiter pipsqueak, I'm pretty sure she's the real reason I make my regular pilgrimages to the Sewell stones. She's the one I miss the most. It would have been nice to see how she turned out, to see what parts of my parents were going to fold together and come out in new form. I would have liked to see her get a full turn, not just a few fraught-filled hours in an emergency room. My sister got the very short end and it does me no good to dwell on it, but I do. Julia says it's survivor's guilt. Until fifteen minutes before my father's car met the beer truck at Broadway and Eastern, I had been in the car with them. It was not just my hopping out at Billie's and ugly Uncle Stu's that spared me, but of course their swinging by to drop me off in the first place that ultimately timed their moment of crossing Eastern Avenue at the same moment as the damn beer truck. Three guesses how much good it does to bring *that* thought up.

Zero.

Zed.

Zilch.

I tugged at my trousers and straightened. I got back into the hearse and thanked Mrs. McNamara for waiting. I took the long way out of the cemetery, a drive that took me around the south end of the cemetery and past the Weisheit plot. A woman was standing at the foot of Jake Weisheit's fresh grave. The plot was a good fifty yards in from the road, so I couldn't see her clearly. But I could identify her. On her head was what looked like a turban. It was the woman from Jake's funeral, the one who had slipped into the rear pew just moments before the service began. I didn't stop but merely slowed. The woman was clutching flowers. She was standing tall and immobile, as still as the stones. The road veered softly to the right. I caught one more glimpse of her in my rearview mirror — she was taking a step forward — and then she disappeared.

Billie had a message for me when I got back. A representative from Spencer's Funeral Home in Cumberland had phoned as a courtesy to Letitia Bodine, Mrs. McNamara's sister. He was in possession of a document stating Mrs. McNamara's wishes that at the time of her death her body be cremated and the ashes scattered over her husband's grave, which was back in Cumberland. No burial. No service. She wanted simply to sift into the ground and join Mac.

"Spencer's has seen Mrs. Bodine and secured the release form and the cremation authorization," Billie said. "It's being sent to us overnight. Mrs. Bodine is coming in from Cumberland tomorrow afternoon to pick up her sister's cremains. What was the time of death, dear?" I handed her the death certificate. She gave it a glance. "Five o'clock. Perfect. Then you can run Mrs. McNamara out to Connolly's first thing tomorrow and have her taken care of."

She handed me back the death certificate. "Are you all right, Hitchcock? Is something wrong?"

"I'm fine. It just wasn't a very pretty scene out at the nursing home, that's all. One of the residents was practically ready to fire-bomb the place."

Billie reached up to smooth my forehead. "Frown lines, dear. A word to the wise."

I stowed Mrs. McNamara downstairs, then got on the phone with Connolly's Crematorium and made my reservations. Room for one. No amenities. No view. I phoned the number on the piece of paper Phyllis Fitch had handed to me. Dorie Matthews. After four rings, an answering machine picked up. I didn't bother leaving a message. Phyllis said that she had already left our number on the woman's machine.

I was still trying to shake off my visit to Briarcliff when I returned upstairs. Billie was standing at the kitchen window, holding the lace curtain aside so she could peer out.

"Hitchcock?"

"Yes, ma'am."

"There's a man outside. I noticed him just before you got here. I didn't think anything of it, but I was just trimming my chives and . . . he's still there. There's something peculiar about him."

I came up next to her and looked out the window. He was standing partly hidden in the shadows in the doorway of St. Teresa's.

"Yeah, I know him."

Billie asked, "Who is he?"

"I don't know."

"You just said you know him."

"I mean, I know him to see him. I've spotted him a couple of times before. I thought maybe I was being paranoid, but now I don't think so. He's been following me."

"Should we call the police?"

I let the curtain drop. "I think he *is* the police."

"You mean you're being watched? Nephew, is there something you're not telling me?"

"There's nothing to tell, Billie. Lieutenant Kruk had me into his office a few days ago, just to warn me to keep my nose clean about the Jake Weisheit murder. I noticed this guy about a half hour later. I saw him again at Harborplace the other day."

I looked out the window again. My own personal Bozo hadn't moved. If in fact this really was a police detective, he needed to have a good hard look at the how-to manual.

"I'll go have a talk with him." I moved away from the window and pulled open a drawer. I picked up a meat cleaver.

"Put that down."

"You don't think it raises my level of authority?"

"Down."

I put the cleaver back into the drawer. "Spoilsport."

"And don't get cocky with him," Billie

called out as I started down the stairs.

He was gone. He could have slipped around to the side of the church, so I stepped out into the middle of the street to be sure. As I stood there, I heard a loud tapping sound. It took me a moment to figure out what direction it was coming from. It was Billie. In her kitchen window. She stopped tapping, and when I looked up, she began pointing urgently in the direction of the harbor.

He was nearly at the corner. And moving fast.

"Hey!"

He took off. So did I. I ran down the middle of the street. The man hit the corner and disappeared. As I reached the end of the block he was already across Thames and was starting down Fell Street, which veers off Thames at a forty-five-degree angle. I started across the street without looking and nearly collided with a beige Stanza that was trundling along the cobbled street. The driver of the car hit the brakes. And the horn. I bounded around the stopped car and raced across the street. Fell dead-ends at a hotel and condo complex on the end of a pier. I knew this, but I suspected that the man I was chasing didn't. I saw him dart to his right onto a walkway that cuts through the complex. I ran down the street and cut in at a walkway about thirty feet before the spot

where the man had gone. Each of the walk-
ways leads toward the water and then splits
in a T intersection. To the left it was only a
short distance to the end of the pier. Unless
he wanted to dive into the harbor and swim
to Sparrows Point he would veer right and
try to double back. At least that was my
hunch. I didn't have the luxury of sitting
down and diagraming it. As I came to my T,
I veered left. And there he was. He was
maybe twenty feet away. He pulled up, spun
about and ran.

But I had him.

"Stop!"

He didn't. He pounded forward, closing in
on the end of the pier. Maybe he *was* going
to dive into the harbor. But about ten feet
before the end of the walkway he wheeled
around, and raising his arms, barreled into
me. Or I barreled into him. We barreled into
each other. I felt my ribs scream. The horizon tipped. It went sideways and disappeared.

Chapter Twenty-two

We were in the water.

I took a mouthful of the Baltimore Harbor and whipped my head clear of the surface, gagging on the brackish water. I started to cry out, but the next thing I knew I was back under the water, being pushed downward. I felt a hand on my head and a foot in the middle of my back, followed by a foot on my neck. He was trying to climb me! I beat at his legs and pushed away from him, allowing myself to sink further. I kicked at my shoes, but I couldn't work them off and in fact only succeeded in taking myself that much lower. The water was oily brown, with a whirl of foamy green bubbles above me where the man was kicking and thrashing.

I leveled off and made a coordinated kick and stroke upward. Something hard caught me on the jaw. I would call it a shoe. I was just about out of air. Nothing but exhale, which I did, joined with a cry that even for all the force I was giving it sounded horribly distant and muted. My parents' grave site flashed in my head.

No, thank you.

I kicked. I clawed. And I surfaced. Only a

few feet away the man was thrashing in the water, a look of sheer panic on his face. I took what passed for a breath and held it, doubling over into the water and successfully pulling off both of my shoes this time. When I surfaced again, the man's shoulders were under. His arms were barely breaking the surface. His eyes were wild. *"Grrpmlpm!"*

Whatever.

"Don't touch me!" I called out. "Okay? Don't grab me! Just relax!" I paddled forward and moved in behind him and got my arms around his neck. His arms started to flail harder. "Don't! Just go limp!"

He did. Or at least he did enough so that I could splash with my free arm and paddle the two of us to the pier. It wasn't even ten feet away. How ignominious it would have been to drown all of ten feet away from dry land. I dragged us to the pier and managed to get his hand onto a pole that ran vertically out from the water. At this point we had been spotted and several people had hurried over. They took hold of the both of us and helped us to clamber back up onto the walkway.

I flopped onto my back, gulping lungfuls of air, looking up at the clouds overhead. Beside me, the man with the frizzy hair was doing likewise. The only real difference between us was that I had a fistful of the man's jacket. A death grip. I wasn't letting go.

He hadn't shaved for what looked like several days, though he didn't exactly look like the type who was choosing to grow a beard. The skin on his face was slack and a little jowly. His eyes were sad. His lips were thick. Gravity seemed to have its hold on all of his features, including his gaze, which remained chiefly on his hands. His thick fingers were engaged in a gentle wrestling match with each other atop the bar. I looked into the mirror behind the bar, studying the man seated next to me. What I was trying to work out was this: Was he the type to plunge a knife into someone's back?

He was Chip Cooperman, the fellow responsible for my several cracked ribs and now my near drowning. Whatever fight had been in him was left behind in the water, and he had obediently followed me up to Thames and over to the Oyster, where he accepted a towel from Sally but refused her offer of a dry shirt or even a dry pair of socks. Sally sent Frank upstairs to fetch me a sweater and socks and I prevailed upon her to crank up the brass heater pipe that serves as the bar's footrest. These older waterfront bars have water-heated pipes running along at the base of the bar. They were originally designed to warm the tootsies of dockworkers on graveyard shifts during the frosty months. Sally slid a couple of mugs of black coffee onto the bar. She beefed mine up with a shot of Maker's. Cooperman set his thick fingers over his mug. It probably wasn't necessary. A man wringing his fingers like that, Sally's going to think twice before feeding him the poison.

Except for confirming his identity for me on the pier, Chip Cooperman had remained as mute as a number two pencil. From the looks of things he was pretty content to remain so for the rest of the afternoon. Sally started to say something to him, but I backed her off. I blew on my coffee and took a sip. The pipe at my feet was beginning to warm up. The heat rising up through my feet and the heat spreading down from my throat failed to meet by a long shot, but it was a start.

"I'm ready when you are," I said to him at last. "Do you want to explain to me exactly why I've become your new best friend?"

Cooperman brought the mug to his mug and sipped loudly. "Polly."

The name came out of his mouth like it was something tangible, as if the word itself were something solid and in fact not a little bitter-tasting. That was all he said. "Polly." As far as condensed answers go, I guess he had dislodged a pretty good one.

I picked up my mug and blew on it. "What about Polly? I told you on the phone, I'm not interested in Polly Weisheit. Not that it's really any of your business even if I were."

Cooperman looked as though his head was too heavy for his neck. He glared at the row of bottles lined up in front of the mirror. Or maybe he was glaring at his own reflection.

"She hates me." He set the mug down and ran a hand across his jaw. "She hates my guts. She thinks I'm pathetic."

"That's not at all what she said to me, Chip."

"I'll bet."

"It's not. She said you two used to be good friends and that you fell in love with her, but she just didn't feel the same way back. Look, that happens all the time."

"I can't explain it. You feel this connection, you know? It doesn't really matter, I mean, if she laughs in my face. It doesn't change anything. Polly's the one person who understands me."

I understood him. He was obsessed. Deluded. Grasping for the ungraspable. He was miserable. Self-loathing. Fixated on a dream. Suffering like a fish on desert sand. Derailed. A sad sack of flesh.

Cooperman consulted his fingers again. "She sleeps around. All the time. She's always been like that. I gave up trying to tell her to stop. It's degrading."

I wasn't certain which he meant was degrading, Polly's sleeping around or Cooperman's useless stabs at trying to get her to stop. Perhaps both.

He went on. "It's ugly. She chooses bad men. I thought when she married Jake, it would stop. But it didn't I told her she had to stop. She's *married.* She can't keep doing this. It's wrong. It's all wrong."

"Chip, it all sounds noble, I'm sure, but you can't be the one who is going to save Polly from herself."

He wasn't listening. "I'm sick of it. I'm sick of her sleeping around."

"I don't think she wants you as her protector."

His eyes narrowed. "What do you know about what Polly wants?"

"I'm just saying you're wasting your life trying to be Polly Weisheit's guardian —"

I wouldn't have expected him to show the speed, but suddenly he had a fistful of my sweater and he was rising off his bar stool. There was nothing slack about the face now. It was bright red.

"— angel," I squeaked.

"Fuck you!"

He jerked me backward and kicked at my stool, knocking it clean out from under me. If not for the grip on my sweater. I'd have fallen to the floor.

I gurgled, *"Chip —"*

"Fuck you! You think you —"

He didn't get the chance to finish his sentence. Sally had pulled her black-handled electric cattle prod from beneath the bar. Sally has a name for her black-handled electric cattle prod. She calls it Henry. Henry has two settings, which Sally has designated "hog" and "moose." Sally pressed her thumb on the rubber button and laid Henry gently against Chip Cooperman's neck. From Cooperman's response I'd say we were on "moose." Cooperman took out two bar stools, his and the one behind him, on his way to the floor. I barely missed getting clipped on the chin by one of his shoes. The man hit the floor with a thud and a twitch, his left leg kicking spastically a few times against the base of the bar. The few customers in the bar at that hour were all regulars. This scene, or some version of it, was nothing new. A low groan rose from the floor.

"Thank you, dear," I said to Sally, tugging my sweater back to order.

"What's his name?"

"Cooperman."

Sally leaned over the bar. "Mr. Cooperman? You've just met Henry. If you don't want to meet him again I'm going to ask you to behave more civilized in here. It's too early in the afternoon for this sort of nonsense. You can consider that a love tap. Next time you won't be so lucky."

She rapped Henry against her hand like a billy club as Cooperman slowly got to his feet. Cooperman righted his stool and sat back down. The nasty jolt seemed to have done him some good, all things considered. I detected a little more light in his eye. He murmured an apology as Sally topped off our coffees.

"That's a nice little violent streak you've got there, Chip," I said, settling back in. "Have you ever thought of having that looked into?" He said nothing. "Look, I didn't mean to provoke you, but you've got to see my side on this. A friend of mine is in jail for killing Jake Weisheit and I just don't think he did it. You come after me a couple of nights after the murder and rough me up quite nicely. Meanwhile Polly isn't mentioning your name to the police. *I* haven't mentioned it, for which I'll accept a thank you any time you're ready." Cooperman grunted his appreciation. "I'm just trying to get the picture here. You're the self-proclaimed big brother of Polly Weisheit. You're trolling around town in my wake . . . why? Because you think I'm sleeping with Polly? Change the channel, Chip. That's not what's happening. Polly was sleeping with Sisco."

"I know."

"But his ribs are safe in police custody. He probably isn't even aware how lucky he is."

"I'm sorry I hurt you."

"Well, thank you. I'm sorry you hurt me

too. So let me ask you something, Chip. About Jake."

"What about him?"

"You say you liked him. You think he was an okay guy."

Cooperman bobbed his head. "Yeah."

"But you weren't jealous of him? After all, he was married to . . . to the only woman who really understood you."

"Jake was okay."

"Did you kill him?"

Cooperman didn't answer immediately. He blinked several times at his coffee mug. "No."

I believed him. He seemed too defeated. He hadn't the energy for self-preservation. Down the bar, Sally was gnawing on a hangnail. Like an expert auctioneer she spotted my slightest motion and made her way over to respike my coffee. Cooperman slid his mug across the bar. Sally hesitated, then gave him a splash. He glanced at the both of us with guilty eyes as he took a sip. Sally brought a wooden bowl of peanuts onto the counter and moved down the bar.

"Let me ask you about someone else," I said. "Toby Schultz."

I saw something pass along Cooperman's eyes. It wasn't something friendly. "Toby Schultz is an asshole."

"What you're saying is, you don't much care for the man?"

"He's an asshole," Cooperman repeated. "Thinks he's a big shot."

"I ran into him the other day," I said. "He told me a story about the time he broke your nose."

"That was a hundred years ago."

"Polly told me the same story." I said. "Except she left Schultz's name out of it. She only said that some guy she was engaged to at the time broke your nose when you went storming after him."

"It wasn't exactly like that. I —"

"It doesn't matter how it was, Chip. The point is, Polly neglected to mention that it was Toby Schultz she had been engaged to. And Schultz went out of his way the other day to say that your attack on him came from nowhere. It seemed to me he was making an effort to keep me from knowing that he and Polly were once involved. And the same thing with Polly. Why do you suppose that is?" Cooperman shrugged. "Certainly it wasn't a secret Schultz was Jake's best friend. His wife told me that it was Schultz who introduced Jake to Polly."

"Betty Schultz knows what's going on."

"What does that mean? What's going on?"

"Schultz and Polly. They both think they're so smart."

"What do you mean?"

"They've been sleeping together for years. Off and on. It's like a big joke. They each got married, they have kids, and they still run around with each other."

"And Betty Schultz knows this?"

"She knows who she's married to."

"But how recently are we talking, Chip? Polly's been seeing Sisco the past several months."

Cooperman snorted a laugh. "You don't know Polly."

"So you're saying she and Toby Schultz have been sleeping together recently?"

"Yes."

"And you know this for a fact?" He turned to me. The look on his face was as clear as words on paper. "Did Jake know this?"

Cooperman smirked. "That's the biggest joke. No. He didn't know."

"How can you be sure of that?" I asked.

"Because when I told him, he hit the ceiling."

"You told him about Polly and Toby Schultz?"

"Yes."

"When?"

Cooperman took a sip from his mug. A distant light ignited in his eyes. "Two weeks ago."

Chapter Twenty-three

The release and authorization forms from Cumberland arrived first thing in the morning. God love the Pony Express. Letitia Bodine was due in some time midafternoon. That was still cutting it close. It takes several hours to complete a cremation, so I got Mrs. McNamara out to Connolly's Crematorium right after breakfast. My trip to Connolly's took me up North Charles Street, along the rim of Ruxton. I was still pondering the information I had received from Chip Cooperman the day before. Jake Weisheit's best friend, godfather to his son . . . lover of his wife. Toby Schultz was hiding in plain sight. And Jake had known. Chip Cooperman had seen to that no less than a week before Jake was murdered. I was tempted to swing to the left down Boyce Road and see if Polly was in. Maybe she'd be good enough to fill in a few of the blanks for me. But I had Mrs. McNamara to deal with. She was in what is undecorously called a cremation container, which is little more than a glorified cardboard box. It's the customer's call, of course, but I've never much held with the notion of parking a cadaver in an elaborate and expensive casket simply to turn around and burn lock, stock and barrel to a crisp. It's not my preferred method of turning a profit.

The folks at Connolly's were ready for me when I arrived. I waited until the jets were turned on and then left. In this business you learn to disassociate. Lord help you if you don't, else all you learn is to be miserable. Even so, as I pulled away from the crematorium I wasn't feeling too tip-top. Ever since picking up Mrs. McNamara the day before, my skin just wasn't fitting quite right. I recalled Mrs. McNamara's comment to me about residents being dropped. And I thought about Spiro's mother, her wandering off on her own the way she had. Not really good. Not good at all. As I waited for a traffic light to turn green I pictured Louise, the young nursing aide, bursting into tears and running off down the hall. I drummed my fingers on the steering wheel. My copy of Mrs. McNamara's cremation authorization form was on the passenger seat next to me. I picked it up. It's a standard form. It comes accompanied by a document spelling out in more detail than most people could possibly want to know exactly what is to be done to the recently departed. I doubted that Mrs. McNamara's sister had read the entire document. Few people do. For the faint of heart it is too disturbing, too clinical. Letitia Bodine's signature was barely legible. A couple of scratchy lines.

I dropped the form back onto the seat. A pair of teenagers crossed in front of me. They were wearing headsets, but even so they were prattling on to each other, making over-sized gestures, trying to outcool each other. I thought of Teresa. Teresa and her Walkman. I wondered if she'd have even been able to hear a call button when she was plugged into her music. The light turned green and I drove a few blocks and pulled into a dough-nut place on Joppa. I went inside and bought a couple of those twisty sugary things and a medium Coke. Time for a sugar high. The hearse was getting its requisite queer looks from the girls behind the counter. Eating es-tablishments would generally prefer not having a hearse decorating their parking lot. On occasion I am asked if I would please move it off premises. I took my Coke and twisty things to a table and mentally dared someone to come up to me. No one did, and after a minute I relaxed a little. I was uneasy, and I knew it wasn't about the social indeli-cacy of my hearse. I finished off one of the twisty things and was halfway through un-twisting the second one before I even realized it. I wiped my fingers clean on a napkin and went off toward the restrooms, where there was a pay phone on the wall. I called Infor-mation and got the number for Briarcliff Manor. I dialed the number and asked for

317

Phyllis Fitch. I had to wait a few minutes. I watched as a boy with a skateboard under his arm walked slowly around the hearse, nodding approvingly. Hearses are magnets for teenage boys. This one was sporting a backward baseball cap, an oversize Ravens jersey and denim pants with room for the whole family. He peered into the back, clearly hoping for gold and clearly disappointed that he didn't get it. He flipped the skateboard over his shoulder with a nifty move. It landed on the pavement, he hopped on, he was gone.

Phyllis Fitch came on the line. I identified myself. "I wanted to let you know that Mrs. McNamara is being cremated. We received a call from Cumberland. Her sister has a request for cremation. I just dropped the body off at the crematorium."

There was a pause. "Yes. Marilyn mentioned that to me. She spoke on the phone with Peggy's sister. This was after you had already picked up Peggy, of course."

"I tried phoning Dorie Matthews, but I didn't reach her. I didn't want to leave the message on her machine. If she gets in touch with you, you'll let her know?"

Phyllis said she would. "Is that all?" she asked.

I shifted the phone to the other ear. "As a matter of fact, no. It isn't. While I've got you, I've got a question."

"I'll try to help you."

"I'm curious. Something's been nagging me. It's about Teresa."

There was another pause. "Teresa?"

"The temp."

"I know who you mean. What about her?"

"What I'm wondering is, what was Teresa doing at Briarcliff yesterday morning? She wasn't supposed to be working past —"

"Yesterday morning?"

"That's right. I was talking with one of the residents when I was picking up Mrs. Mc-Namara and he told me that he saw Teresa out there first thing in the morning. He said he saw her getting canned."

"I'm not sure I understand what you're asking."

"She was about to knock off work the night I dropped in on Mrs. McNamara," I said. "I was there when she told you she was only on duty for another hour. You remember that. But it seems she was still out there in the morning. I assume she must have stayed on for another shift. I was just curious about it. You said yourself you didn't care for the quality of her work. I'm surprised she would be asked to do an extra shift."

"She wasn't," Phyllis said. "You're mistaken."

"But one of the residents —"

"One of the residents was mistaken then.

319

Of course I remember speaking with Teresa the other night. And she left after her shift. We have the paperwork that shows it."

"So she wasn't the person looking in on Mrs. McNamara the night she died?"

"She was not. That was Louise."

"Louise. I guess that would explain why she was so upset when I saw her the next day."

"I guess it would," Phyllis said curtly. She began to say more, but just then a large truck was passing the doughnut joint. From the corner of my eye I saw the zigzagging figure of the fellow with the skateboard, veering across Joppa. The driver of the truck yanked his air horn. *BWAAAAAA!* The skateboarder came cleanly up onto the sidewalk, the board flipping into his hand. He never looked back.

"I'm sorry," I said into the phone. "A truck just went by. What I was . . . hello? Are you still there?"

She wasn't. The line was dead. I jiggled the jiggywatsit. But dead is dead. You'd think I'd know that much.

When I got back to Connolly's, I was handed the aluminum urn containing Mrs. McNamara's ashes. The urn was still a tad warm. Several gold fillings had required additional pulverizing, but otherwise Mrs. McNamara had not given Connolly's any problems.

Letitia Bodine arrived soon after I returned. She had been driven in from Cumberland by a woman named Emily Spencer, a large, loud, red-faced woman who told me that she was doing a favor for her brother, who ran Spencer's Funeral Home. By contrast, Letitia Bodine was not much more than a string bean, a frail little thing in a powder blue dress and a set of pearls that I feared would drag her to the floor. The resemblance to her sister was more than passing. Same elfin face, though there didn't appear to be much spark in the old eyes. Emily Spencer guided the woman into a chair, then turned to me and let me try out her handshake. It was robust. Little bit of country flavor.

"Letitia doesn't trust the U.S. mail. She refused to let her sister's ashes be shipped. She insisted on coming down to Baltimore herself, though take one look at her, she doesn't even know where she is." She turned to the elderly woman and shouted. "Do you know where you are, Letitia!" The woman blinked a response. "See? I told Buddy we should just have the ashes shipped anyway, and what was she going to say about it? But did Buddy listen to me? You can bet he did not. He listened to this woman who doesn't even know who the dang president is. Sometimes I swear Buddy's a dope. This is a waste of my good time."

"It's my understanding that Mrs. McNamara

wants her ashes scattered over her husband's grave," I said.

The woman rolled her eyes. "That's what I hear, too. If you ask me, best thing could've happened to Peggy McNamara was old Mac keeling over when he did. But if that's what she wants done, we'll do it."

"So you knew Mr. McNamara?"

"Just enough not to care for him. I don't think anybody in all of Cumberland could find two good words to rub together over old Mac. He was just sour and ornery. That's my two words anyway. It never made sense to me someone with even half a brain getting married to him in the first place. Why in the world she'd want to go and spend eternity within spitting distance of someone like that, I couldn't tell you. But Buddy says that's what she wanted. Them's the orders, as they say. He had the paper in his hand. "Burn me up and scatter me on my husband's grave." She indicated Letitia Bodine. "And then this one wants to come all the way to Baltimore to pick up a silly box of ashes. I figure you've got the nuts running the nuthouse. Is this them?"

I had placed the urn containing Mrs. McNamara's ashes on the desk. Emily Spencer picked it up and placed it in Letitia Bodine's lap. The woman lifted it slowly to eye level and studied it, then brought it around to her ear and very gently gave it a shake. She looked as if she was trying to guess the contents of a birthday gift.

"Be careful," Emily Spencer snarled, and she lifted the urn from Letitia Bodine's hands.

A small frown crossed the old woman's face. "Where's Peggy?"

Emily Spencer gave me a look of exasperation. "See?" She bellowed at the old gal. "Your sister is dead! Remember? That's why we're here! Those are Peggy's ashes in that box! That's your sister!"

Letitia Bodine looked across the desk at me. "Do you know Peggy?"

I nodded. "I knew her somewhat."

"You've got to speak up," Emily Spencer said. "She's deaf as a post."

"I knew your sister somewhat!" I said, leaning forward on my desk. "I was very fond of her!"

The woman blinked at me. "Peggy is my younger sister. Do you know her?"

"I *knew* her!"

Emily Spencer ducked forward to shout into the old lady's ear. "Peggy is *dead!* Haven't you been listening to me? We're in Baltimore to pick up her ashes! Like you wanted!"

"Is Peggy in Baltimore?"

Emily Spencer's patience had drained. I can't really say how much she had started out with in the first place. She held up the urn of ashes and shook it in the old woman's face.

"*She's dead!* This is Peggy! She's in here! This is your sister!" She set the urn back down on the edge of the desk and started to unscrew the lid.

"Don't do that," I said. But she did. She unscrewed the lid and brought the urn to Letitia Bodine's chin. I started out of my chair. "Don't."

"Letitia, that's your —"

You wouldn't have thought there was enough strength in the frail woman, but there was. She let out a small cry and batted at the jar. It flew from Emily Spencer's hand. I was already lunging across the desk. Every undertaker's nightmare. A fine gray mist obscured my view of Letitia Bodine. Emily Spencer let out a scream. Just that instant, Billie came through the door.

"What in the world is —"

The urn hit the floor on its side and rolled in the shape of the letter C, trailing what remained of the ashes in its wake. It stopped at Aunt Billie's foot.

No one spoke for several seconds. I remained sprawled partway over my desk, Letitia Bodine blinking silently a few inches from my face. At Billie's feet, the aluminum jar rocked gently back and forth, emitting a faint grinding sound.

A half hour later Billie and I stood at the

front door watching Emily Spencer's car disappear around the corner bearing away Letitia Bodine and an aluminum urn containing not quite half of Mrs. McNamara's ashes. Billie had escorted the addled woman into the chapel and run through her four-song repertoire on the organ several times while Emily Spencer and I busied ourselves scooping up what we could of poor Mrs. McNamara. Emily Spencer had managed to blame someone who was several hundred miles away.

"This is all Buddy's fault. He shoulda taken that stupid request and blown his big ugly nose with it. Just bury the poor old thing, I say. Load her on the Greyhound and send her on home."

Billie and I watched as the blue exhaust from Emily Spencer's car turned into vapor. Then Billie turned to go back inside. She brushed her fingers along my collar.

"You have some Mrs. McNamara on you. You might want to go change."

I did. I ran home and threw on a clean shirt. I was starving. The twisty things only take a person so far. My refrigerator had a good old laugh at my expense, as did my cupboards. I eyed Alcatraz's bag of dry food, but I knew no good could come of it, so I hopped into my car and drove over to Lombard Street and Jack's Deli, where I suffered gladly under a half pound of pastrami and a mountain of Tiger Sauce. Afterward I continued down Lombard to Calvert, driving a few blocks past the courthouse to the *Sun* building, where I waited two minutes while a bulky SUV wormed its way out of a parking spot. Dinosaurs once roamed our planet and sometimes I think it's slowly happening again. The obese vehicle lumbered forward and backward so many times I nearly fell asleep waiting. Finally it cleared the spot and I shot up to the curb in two simple moves. And yes, I'm bragging.

I passed through security without setting off any bells and took the elevator to the third floor. A low buzz hovered above the cubicles in the newsroom. Phones chirped. The soft clatter of keyboards mingled with the fluorescent hum. I always think of the movie *All the President's Men* when I come here. Woodward and Bernstein racing around in their shirtsleeves loading up their slingshots. The *Sun* newsroom was awfully subdued compared to the frenzy in the movie. I got no sense of giants about to fall. And no Menckens were on view either. The place could have been a telemarketing center for all the pale quiet of the place.

I found Jay Adams in his cubicle, at his desk, on the phone, finishing off a Krispy Kreme. He tossed me the box as I dropped into the folding chair he keeps for visitors. The box was warm. I picked a doughnut out of the box and it began to melt into my fingers.

Jay gave me the "I'm wrapping it up" signal. I gave him a "don't worry." Jay's tie was loose and his sleeves were folded back into perfect squares on his thin forearms. His jet black hair was comb-grooved straight back and looked freshly cut. Jay's suspenders sported little red crabs, the same red as the pencil that was tucked behind his ear. I wouldn't swear that the choice of pencil was unintentional.

Jay's end of the conversation was slightly combative. "So you're not going to tell me . . . What you're saying is, you don't recall . . . Let me make sure I've got this. What I'm supposed to believe is . . ."

Jay wrapped up his call simultaneous to my wrapping up my doughnut. Choreography you couldn't buy if you wanted.

"City councilman," he said, hanging up the phone. "He swears it was not what it seems. Imagine that."

I asked, "How does it seem?"

"It seems he was arrested last night in that alley next to the Belvedere with his pants to his knees and a young lady also around his knees. A young lady with a rap sheet."

"And how did it seem to the councilman?"

"I'm the first one to get to him. I think he's still working it out."

"Maybe the young lady was trying to tie

327

his shoes for him," I suggested.

"I could run that by him when he calls me back. How about the pants?"

"Ah, the devil is in the details, isn't he?"

Jay tilted forward and took up a doughnut from the box. "So I see where your friend has gotten himself out of jail."

"Hark," I said. "What are you saying?"

"The Sisco Kid. He made bail last night. Don't you read the papers?"

"Not unless my name is being bandied about. I don't know how I missed that. How did Sisco manage bail?"

"It was reduced to fifty thousand," Jay said.

"Still, Sisco doesn't have that kind of money. He's on the make-it-and-spend-it plan. He told me so himself."

"Well, he's out. The judge bought his lawyer's argument that the police don't really have enough on him. Plenty to make them suspicious, but no smoking gun."

"Smoking knife."

"Whatever."

Jay's phone rang and he took it. I picked up a copy of the *Sun* that was on his desk and paged through it. The article was buried in the local section. It didn't reveal much more than Jay had just told me. It recapped the circumstances of Jake Weisheit's murder and mentioned Sisco's being on the scene when the police showed up. Thankfully, this time the article skipped the factoid of my being there as well. Bail had been reduced to fifty thousand dollars. No mention of who coughed up the pennies.

Jay hung up the phone. "So what brings you here anyway, Hitch? You smell the doughnuts all the way from the street?"

"I do seem to be on a sugar kick today." I returned the paper to his desk. "But that's not it. I was hoping I could get you to do that voodoo you do."

"Right. Whatever that means."

"Briarcliff Manor. It's a nursing home in Lutherville. Owned and operated by one Marilyn Tuck."

"One Marilyn Tuck? Listen to the boy speak." Jay swung around and starting tapping his keyboard. "What am I looking for specifically?"

"Maybe nothing. You're fishing," I said. "Someone I knew just passed away there. I can't swear to it, but I'm beginning to think she didn't exactly receive the platinum treatment. Plus a neighbor of mine had a mother there who just died recently."

"Death in a nursing home. Now there's a hot story."

"My neighbor's mother was able to wander off the premises unnoticed before she died. Plus I was told about people being dropped there. I'm just curious about the place. I was talking to one of the residents yesterday and he mentioned something about one of your reporters being out there earlier this year."

"Tuck. Briarcliff." Jay stirred his mouse around. "Okay, Houston, we have liftoff."

"What've you got?"

Jay ran his finger along the screen. "I'll print this up for you."

"Anything interesting?"

"Allegations."

"We like allegations."

Jay worked the keys some more. The printer on the desk silently fed forward several sheets of paper. Jay was reading off the screen. "Blah, blah, blah . . . possible civil action. Financial improprieties." He turned from the screen. "Gosh, Hitch, it sounds sexy."

He pulled the papers from the printer, glanced at them and handed them to me. The printout was from the *Sun*'s archives, an article that had appeared in the paper earlier in the year. I scanned it quickly to pick up the gist.

"Is that it?" I asked. "Nothing else?"

Jay's fingers ran over the keys. "Nope. Goes cold."

I checked the byline. "Janet Becket. She still work here?"

Jay shook his head. "Quit this past summer. She left to go write the Great American Novel."

"I'm glad to hear it. Isn't that thing long overdue?"

"She says it's Dorothy Parker meets Dickens."

"Poor Dickens doesn't stand a chance."

Jay placed his hands behind his head and leaned back in his chair. "Janet was a good reporter. A good writer. But management dumped on her one time too many and Janet finally shot them the moon."

"Some people might enjoy that sort of thing."

Jay made one of those clicking sounds. "If you knew Janet, you're right. She's heavy into health clubs. Power yoga. Runs a thousand miles a day. All of it. Cut like a rock, but I don't mean freaky. One of those tall Texas girls."

"You Napoleons go nuts for the tall ones, don't you?"

"That works both ways, buckaroo. You'd be surprised."

"So where is she now? Is she still in Baltimore?"

"Oh, sure. Janet landed a teaching gig at Hopkins. Journalism. Giving away all trade secrets to the CNN generation."

I held up the pages Jay had printed out for me. "You tell me. Will she even remember this? You guys must do a thousand stories a year."

Jay shrugged. "Janet was a good reporter. She was a sponge. And she was the most organized person you've ever met. She might or might not remember this particular thing right off the top of her head. I mean, the details. But a girl like Janet would keep all her notes. I'm sure of it. It's what she was always saying. Everything is material."

"You're not supposed to call them girls," I said. "That's sexist."

"I know. It's okay. I'm sexist."

"Right. I forgot. So, do you think it's worth my running it past her?"

"Why not? Couldn't hurt. Hold on, and I can get you a number."

He turned back to his keyboard and tapped a few more keys. He swirled his mouse, blocked off a portion of the screen and clicked the Print button.

"Here. Home and office. I am too damn good." He handed me the paper from the printer. "Give Janet my best. Tell her we still miss her here on the slave ship."

"Will do."

"And, Hitch."

"What?"

"She's married."

"Good for her."

"About three months ago."

"Wonderful. I'll bring her a gift."

"I'm just saying. Just in case."

"Just in case what?" I asked.

"I know how you tall guys are when you encounter one of your own."

I stood up. "Thanks for the warning, Jay. I'll make sure to hold off on the flying tackle."

Chapter Twenty-four

I put in a call to Janet Becket from a pay phone on the street. I dialed her home number, and when her machine picked up, I hung up. That's how the dance is done. It was virtual Janet at the work number as well.

"You've reached the voice mail of Janet Becket. I am away from my . . ."

I was given an option to be transferred to a human and I took it. I was told that Miss Becket doesn't work on Wednesdays, but that she had several classes the following day.

"Would you like to leave a message?"

I said that I would not and that's exactly what I did not do. I hung up and tried Angela's number. By now she probably knew about Sisco's being released on bail. Guess what? I got her machine. I got back into my car and found a foul-tempered man staring back at me in the rearview mirror. These things come on us sometimes. I decided to take my foul mood over to Julia's gallery. Chinese Sue was behind the counter, reading a book about the last days of Pompeii.

"Hey, Sue, is my favorite eye candy around?"

Chinese Sue flicked a finger skyward. She

did not look up from her book. I headed up the spiral stairs and found Julia in her studio. She was at her workbench with a welding mask over her pretty little face, encased in a jittery blue glow. I'm a sucker for a woman wearing a welding mask — as all my friends know — and I stood at the top of the stairs and watched for a few minutes, apparently unnoticed. Julia was welding pieces of flat gold metal together. It took me a moment to recognize what they were. They were crushed trumpets.

"Hello, handsome." Julia snuffed out her torch and slid the helmet back off her face. "How long have you been standing there?"

"Long enough to admire your style."

"I hope that didn't take too long."

"Not to worry. So what's this you're working on?" I asked.

"Crushed trumpets."

"That's what I see. Do we have a rhyme or a reason?"

"Both. The Peabody has finally gotten around to commissioning a painting from me. It's for the lobby outside the auditorium. I thought I would frame it in crushed trumpets."

"Novel idea. Where'd you get the trumpets?"

"A few from Peabody. They had some pretty beat-up ones they donated to the cause. I scoured the pawnshops for the rest of them."

"How did you crush them?" I asked.

"With a car."

"You don't drive."

"Hans. He rented a car for his day off. We drove down to the Skyline Drive. Hans wanted to see the mountains and the fall foliage."

"That's where you crushed your trumpets? On the Skyline Drive?"

"Yes."

"You're a fun girl."

"Don't you know it."

Julia was piecing together one of the corners of the frame and she wanted to finish up. She slipped the helmet back over her face and fired up the torch. I wandered around the studio as she worked and took in the latest demonstrations of my ex-wife's inspired dementia. Julia's well of creativity is deep and silly and it makes her money hand over fist. She could long ago have afforded to move out of her converted firehouse, but she's perfectly happy there. There's a kitchenette in the rear of the place, a claw foot tub I helped her hoist up here one long Sunday afternoon, and behind several wooden screens, Julia's big bouncy bed. "I can bathe, I can nibble, I can entertain. What more do I need?" So as to bring in more natural light, Julia had arranged when she was renovating the place for a large skylight to be cut into the roof, and in order to facilitate the egress of her larger canvases she also had some bricks knocked clear from the street-facing wall and a pair of French doors installed there. Julia is often up painting late at night, as barefoot and buff as the day she was born. Informed tourists know which bench to stand on in the square for the best binocular view.

Julia finished up her welding and set her crushed trumpets aside. "So you know what I'm in the mood for?"

"I'm sorry," I said. "But I've just started seeing someone."

"You think I have a one-track mind, don't you, Mr. Smarty?"

I nodded. "Yes, I do."

"I'm in the mood for a glass of champagne."

"I could stand for a mood-altering liquid myself," I said. "You haven't even noticed that I'm in a crabby mood."

"I hadn't. You seem your perfectly delightful self to me."

"You see only what you want to see."

Julia stepped over and kissed me on the cheek. "And you have just discovered the secret to being me. Hold on. Let me change."

She ducked behind her screens and emerged a minute later in black leather pants and a black turtleneck.

"Simple," I said. "Yet bold."

Julia grinned. "I'm an Avenger."

She slid down the fireman's pole and I followed. We crossed the square to the Oyster. Sally was off doing errands, leaving Frank in charge. Julia pitched up onto the bar and gave her father a big smackeroo on the cheek. He remained as stony as the boys on Mount Rushmore. Julia turned to me.

"You know the joke? Horse walks into a bar, the bartender asks why the long face?" She reached out and put a pinch on Frank's cheek. "With Daddy you can just drop the horse part."

Frank looked past his daughter to me. "Drink?"

I had Frank pump me a Guinness. Julia got her champagne.

"Mine's a happy drink," she said, climbing onto a bar stool. She clinked her flute against my mug. "So now tell me about *your* long handsome face."

I did. I gave her the rundown on Mrs. McNamara. I told her about Mrs. McNamara's fairly rapid decline and of the growing sense I was getting that for all the outward professionalism of the place, Briarcliff was far from flawless.

"Maybe I'm overreacting," I said. "It was such a nice surprise to run across Mrs. McNamara last week. I can't really explain, but it was good to see her. Practically the next thing I knew she was dead. I had her cremated this morning . . . and that's it. She's gone." I said it again. "Maybe I'm overreacting."

Julia was watching me closely as I spoke. "And maybe you're not. You've got good radar, sweetie. It's obvious something's troubling you.

"Teresa. Teresa is troubling me. Phyllis Fitch came right out and told me that Teresa did not work the overnight shift."

"But you said the old man saw her in the morning."

"Yes. And I guess he could be mistaken, but I really don't think so. I think he saw her."

"Then you need to have a talk with this Teresa."

"I don't know, Jules. People die. It's what happens every second of every day. Somebody dies."

Julia squeezed her eyes shut. "Mmmm, I love when you talk like that."

"You know what I'm saying."

"Listen, lovey, you're a curious cat. You itch easily. You were born under the sign of skeptic. You're bothered about what happened to your friend? I say get nosy."

"I'm sure not going to get any more from the nursing home than what I've gotten."

"That's right. So track down your Teresa. See what she has to say for herself. Rough her up if you have to. You're such a brute anyway."

"I'm glad you think so."

Her eyes sparkled. "I've got the inside

dope. I know so."

"You *are* the inside dope."

"You say that only because you love me."

"You're a woman of great confidence," I said.

Julia hitched her heels onto the crossbar of her stool and leaned forward and planted a kiss on my cheek. Her lips slid toward my ear. "You'll always love me," she whispered.

I had a message from Angela waiting for me when I got back to the office. Sisco and the Kids were playing at Penny's that night. She hoped I could make it. Billie had a surprise for me as well.

"You're not going to believe this." She took me down to the basement. She was right. I didn't believe it.

"How did you do that?" I asked. "Are you using mirrors?"

They were identical twins.

"This one is Russell and this one is Randall. Or . . . wait. I had this sorted out. That one is . . . Now you've gotten me confused."

"Me?"

Billie was looking back and forth between the two cadavers. "Russell . . . Randall . . . I was going to put a little sticker on one of them, but I thought I had it straight. Shoot."

"This one has a bullet hole in his chest," I said. "Does that help?"

Billie was nibbling on a hangnail. "Randall shot Russell. Or Russell shot Randall. I had it a moment ago. Lord, Hitchcock, I'm becoming so daft."

I lifted the left hand of the other corpse. "And this one slit his wrist."

"Yes. That's Randall. I think."

I dropped the man's hand. "Billie, what we do for a living? I think we need to admit it. It's weird."

I arrived at Penny's later than I'd planned. The room was well over half full already. The owner was in his usual spot, his elevated stool next to the sound booth. His throne. Penny was running a small comb through his gray mustache and leaning sideways to bark into the ear of the soundman. He was wearing a pair of yellow-tinted sunglasses and his ubiquitous tie-dye T-shirt — this one a nausea of blue and green — pulled tightly over his bear-like torso. His gray ponytail was braided and tied off with a rawhide string. I gave it a gentle tug as I passed by. Penny turned just enough to see who was tugging on his tail and continued on with his sound man.

Penny's two bartenders were popping bottles as fast as they could. I eased my way forward and got a beer, then made my way to the far end of the bar. On the low stage against the far wall, Sisco and the Kids were operating on an adrenaline rush. Even Sisco's normally laconic pedal steel player was with the program, throwing out a rare howl after one of his slithery solos. Angela and her two fellow backup singers were pumping out a choo-choo rhythm with such force I was ready to see steam blasting from their ears. Angela spotted me and threw me a large wink. There were maybe a dozen people jammed in front of the stage, managing to dance without too seriously hurting anybody. Or themselves.

Sisco was a man possessed. No trace of the nervous, forlorn person Angela and I had visited in prison. His every move was an explosion. He was raking at his guitar strings like he wanted nothing else but to break them as quickly as possible. He practically slammed his jaw against the microphone every time he came forward to sing. The renegade smile on his face was a mile wide and it was being picked up by the crowd. They were, I suspected, Sisco's regulars. For the most part anyway. They knew of their hero's travails and they were here in force for Sisco's coming-out party. Spontaneous howls erupted around the room with the suddenness and force of exploding manhole covers. Sisco responded to each one with a return howl of his own, or a head bob, a finger pistol, or a shake of his guitar.

The two words I am looking for are *kick* and *ass*.

Somewhere in the middle of my third beer I fell into a reverie of sorts. Transcendence can strike at any moment. I was watching Angela. She and her fellow singers were in white skirts, jean vests, cowboy boots and white cowboy hats. They were riddled with rhinestones. Angela aimed her smile at me now and again. With the lights in her eyes I doubted she could make out my expression, so I simply became one more fool at the bar raising his beer bottle to the band.

My reverie snapped when Sisco called Angela over to his microphone and I heard him exhorting the crowd to "give it up for the little lady who set me free!" The crowd responded with hoots and catcalls, which Angela took with a little curtsy. *The little lady who set me free?* Sisco and Angela launched into a pair of Hank Williams's tunes, "My Bucket's Got a Hole in It" and "Jambalaya," the second of which took the crowd to a fresh new frenzy. Joint jumping. After the song, Sisco gave Angela a peck on the cheek and she went back to join her fellow Kids. Sisco closed the set with a hard-rocking version of "Folsom Prison Blues." The little showman. I guess he just couldn't resist.

Sisco was swamped when he came down from the stage. Angela waved at me and put her hand up to her throat in a choking motion. Thirst. She made straightaway for me, pulling off her cowboy hat as she approached, taking long strides in her fancy tooled boots. I had her beer waiting and handed it to her along with a little Hank Williams of my own. "Hey, good-lookin'."

She smiled and set her cowboy hat on my head. "Sisco rides again. So you got my message."

"I did. But what was that about you setting him free? What did you do, mortgage your father's service station?"

"I'll explain later." She took a hearty swig of beer.

"I like your Jambalaya," I said as she moved in next to me.

She slapped at my hand. "That's not my Jambalaya."

"Sorry. Man gets confused."

"Sisco's going to try out my song in the next set."

I was just about to respond when a woman's scream sounded from the direction of the stage. A scuffle had broken out. There was more screaming. I dashed forward, grabbing Angela by the hand and towing her with me. A group of patrons were pulling a man back from the lip of the stage.

"Move!"

I turned to see Penny wading into the crowd. Angela suddenly throttled my fingers.

"Sisco!" She released me and ran toward the stage.

Sisco was on the floor. On his knees. His

face was frozen in a rictus of pain and confusion. He was as white as paper. The bar's sound system kicked in and the Eagles' "Lyin' Eyes" saturated the air. Sisco was gripping his right wrist, holding the hand aloft as if offering to allow someone to take it from him. Angela gasped.

Three of the fingers were aiming in directions that fingers simply don't aim. They looked as if with a simple shake of the hand they might fall right off.

Chapter Twenty-five

It was Penny who pulled Toby Schultz from the heap. He knocked a few heads as he untangled the scrum of patrons who were keeping Schultz pinned to the floor.

"Move back. Come on. Show's over."

Penny got ahold of the front of Schultz's shirt and yanked him to his feet, then half walked, half dragged him back to the sound booth. The soundman scrambled out and Penny shoved Toby Schultz in behind the soundboard. His own little pen. Penny jabbed his finger into Schultz's chest.

"You. Don't. Move."

The police were called. I didn't stick around for their arrival. Sisco needed to get to the hospital to have his hand looked at. I took him. I swapped a look with Schultz as I made my way to the door. He looked ready to pounce again. Angela came with us. She sat in the backseat with Sisco trying to soothe him. His head was in her lap. By the time we hit Loch Raven Boulevard, he had worked himself down to long, low whimpers.

"I think shock is setting in," Angela said. I turned to see her caressing Sisco's damp cheeks. She crooned to him that he "was going to be fine, everything is going to be okay."

Sisco moaned. "My fingers. My fucking fingers." At one point he muttered, "Who the fuck *was* that guy?" I caught Angela's eyes in the rearview mirror. I shook my head and mouthed a silent *Later.*

"You're going to be fine, Sisco," Angela cooed. "Shhhh . . . Everything's going to be fine."

Three broken fingers and a severely sprained thumb. The emergency room doctor emphasized how lucky Sisco was that his thumb had not been broken. Sisco growled at the notion that any of this could qualify as lucky.

Angela had stayed with Sisco while he was being examined, leaving me to sit in the waiting area watching a television show that pitted a gaggle of beautiful single women against each other for the attentions of an affable-seeming bachelor from the Midwest. I watched as the bachelor took each of the beautiful women up in a hot air balloon one at a time and made out with them. It was my understanding that the bachelor was going to marry one of these women at the conclusion of the final episode. I counted seven women he made out with in the balloon. That's six smooching sessions — broadcast on national television — that the guy would have hanging over his head down the line. I see this as a definite downside.

I got into a conversation with a man whose wife's face had blown up to nearly twice its normal size, he told me, after eating a kiwi at a party. She had never eaten a kiwi before and apparently she was wildly allergic to them. He gave me his card. He was a sports equipment wholesaler. I wasn't likely to be in the market any time soon for wholesale sports equipment, but I thanked him and went ahead and gave him my card as well. A frown fell over his face as he looked at it.

"You don't, you know, like hang out here and wait for . . ." He didn't finish the question. I explained that I was here with a friend. He seemed relieved. He tucked my card in his shirt pocket. "Here's hoping I don't have to call you any time soon."

Up on the television the bachelor was at a street fair, accepting caramel apples from all the beautiful women. The sports equipment wholesaler let out a sigh. "What a life, huh?"

When they discharged him, Sisco's right hand looked more like a volleyball. There must have been a quarter of a mile of bandaging. His color was back, but his movements were shaky. "I'm doped," he said to me thickly.

"Thanks for the heads-up. I won't expect any advanced calculus from you."

Sisco worked his eyes toward my nose. "Huh?"

"The doctor suggested someone stay with Sisco overnight," Angela said. "When the sedative wears off he's going to be in a lot of pain all over again. The doctor gave me a prescription to get filled."

We got Sisco out to my car and into the backseat, where he instantly lay down. This time Angela joined me up front. Sisco attempted to make conversation, but with sentences like "I can't swim in this nude elevator," he was relegated to background nonsense.

We decided we would bring Sisco to my place. My couch is large and comfortable. "He's going to need some TLC when he wakes up tomorrow," I said to Angela. "I'm not real good at that."

"What you're saying is that I should stay over."

"It's a therapeutic consideration. I'm only thinking of Sisco."

"You're only lying."

We stopped off at a drugstore on Charles Street to fill Sisco's prescription. I left Sisco and Angela in the car, but the pharmacist insisted that "the patient has to sign for the prescription." I explained that the patient was passed out in the backseat of my car and in any case could no more hold a pen in his writing hand than a blue crab could pick up a fiddle and deliver a flawless "Orange Blossom Special." I'm not sure why I made such an elaborate comparison, but it didn't make a difference. The pharmacist insisted.

I went out to the car and half carried, half dragged Sisco into the drugstore. We went down the candy aisle looking like a couple of grunts after an ambush. "Here he is. Are you happy?"

The pharmacist put the pen in Sisco's left hand and asked me to help him sign his name in the prescription book. We scribbled a level six on the Richter scale and that seemed to satisfy the pharmacist. I paid for the drugs out of my own pocket.

Sisco sat in my ugly armchair and watched as Angela and I made up the couch for him. "It's no Ritz," I said to him. "But it's got to beat the hell out of your prison cot."

We got Sisco out of his rhinestone-studded shirt and into a T-shirt. His boots proved a challenge, but we eventually worked them free of his feet. I told Alcatraz to stand guard and flipped out the lights. I took Angela with me into the bedroom. The door clicked shut.

"You bailed him out?" I asked.

Angela took off her cowboy hat and frisbeed it onto the bed. She sighed. "Can we talk about this in the morning?"

I considered it. Why the hell not? It would keep. "Sure."

"Good." She reached around behind her to

unfasten the clasp on her skirt. She tossed her hair and gave me . . . well, a simply wonderful look. "I'll meet you under the hat."

Chapter Twenty-six

I like to show off with waffles. Sisco was too dopey to take note, but it was the honey blond I was looking to impress anyway.

"They're perfect," Angela remarked, her fork poised near her dimples. "So moist. So golden brown."

Sisco was too spastic trying to eat with his left hand, so Angela cut his waffles into bite-size pieces and fed them to him. It was as if Angela and I were the proud parents of a great big helpless child. I wanted to take a picture.

Angela and Sisco explained the bail situation to me. Polly had finally contacted Sisco in jail and agreed to post his bail. She didn't want to be listed as the person of record, so Sisco had first suggested she contact me, then decided it would be better to keep me clear of the picture. He gave her Angela's number. Polly contacted Angela two days ago — when I was out boating with Father Ted — and the two of them agreed to meet so that Polly could hand over the fifty thousand.

"Cash?" I asked.

Angela nodded. "She had it in a little red

purse. She told me to keep the purse."

"So generous."

"Hey," Sisco said groggily. "Don't knock her, she got me out."

Polly and Angela met at Ivy Books, a small bookstore in a little shopping area just several miles from Polly's house. Angela had been about to head to Ivy's to pick up a book for her father. It was a convenient rendezvous spot. She said she was picking up a book called *Scaramouche* by Rafael Sabatini.

"Never heard of it," I said.

"He also wrote *Captain Blood*."

"The Basil Rathbone movie?"

"The book."

"Good movie."

"Great book, according to my father. He couldn't stop talking about it. Don't you love that name? Rafael Sabatini."

"I do."

Sisco was watching us as if he were at a Ping-Pong match. "Jesus, enough with the Sabatini already."

Angela folded a pair of towels and stacked them on the table for Sisco's bandaged hand. He was still in my T-shirt, which was way too large for him. I brought a fresh batch of waffles to the table.

"So have you seen Polly since you got out?" I asked Sisco.

Sisco repositioned his hand. "I talked to her on the phone. She was supposed to come to Penny's last night. Maybe she did. I wasn't expecting her until late." He lifted his bandaged hand from the towels and considered it "Then this shit happens. What the hell is this all about?"

My phone rang and I answered it. I got into a staring contest with Alcatraz as I spoke to the person on the other end. The contest was short. As was the call.

"That was the police," I said, hanging up. "They got my name from Penny."

"What do they want?" Sisco asked darkly.

"They want you."

"Fuck 'em. They can't have me. I'm a free man."

"Assault charges are pending on Toby Schultz. They need a statement from you."

"Who the hell is Toby Schultz? Is he the freak who did this to me?"

"He's one of your girlfriend's boyfriends," I said.

"Polly's *boyfriend?*"

"I hate to burst your bubble, cowboy, but it doesn't look like you're the only lover boy in town."

Angela asked, "So what do you think happened?"

"I think Schultz got wind of Polly springing Sisco from jail and that she was going to meet him at Penny's."

"Break *her* goddamn fingers," Sisco whined. "Don't break mine."

"For some reason Polly must have told Schultz she was meeting up with Sisco. I can't say. Maybe she was just throwing it in the guy's face. The one time I saw them together, there looked like a lot of bad blood."

"But you just said they were lovers," Angela said.

"They've been an off-and-on item for years. Who knows? Maybe the hostility I saw at Jake's funeral was just an act, but I don't think so. Why draw attention that way? The friction between them seemed pretty real to me."

Sisco was having a hard time keeping up. "Who *is* this guy?"

"I told you. Polly had another lover. A long time back they were engaged to be married. He was Jake's alleged best friend. He's Martin Weisheit's godfather."

"Whoever he is, he's insane. I make my living with my damn fingers. Are these people nuts?"

We got Sisco back into his boots and shirt and the three of us went to police headquarters. We found out that Toby Schultz had been brought in the night before on the assault charges, then released on his own recognizance. I remembered that Betty Schultz was a judge of some sort. If a judge doesn't have pull, what's this world coming to?

While Sisco was giving his statement I was collared by Lieutenant Kruk. He brought me into his office. Angela remained behind on a bench in the hallway, jiggling her cowboy boots, to the doubtless delight of many.

"Do you want me to sit at the desk this time?" I asked Kruk. "Mix things up a little?"

He didn't.

"I want straight answers from you, Mr. Sewell," Kruk said. "That's what I want. Trust me, I'll find a judge willing to jail you for twenty-four hours for flippancy if I have to. Now I want you out of my office in five minutes and I want to have some facts to think about after you're gone."

"Fire away. I'll bet we can do it in under four."

"Why were you at Penny's bar last night?"

"The backup singer I was telling you about before? With the giraffe tattoo? That's the lovely creature out in the hall. She left me a message that she was performing at Penny's last night. I do love my rockabilly."

"This is the individual who posted Jonathan Fontaine's bail."

"She is."

"Fifty thousand dollars. That's a lot of money for a backup singer."

"It is."

"Is there any chance you helped her pull together that kind of cash?"

"Me? No, sir. I didn't post Sisco's bail. But I'll tell you who did. Polly Weisheit. At

Sisco's suggestion she called Angela and arranged to give her the fifty thousand so that she could get Sisco freed. Mrs. Weisheit didn't want it known that she was the one getting Sisco out of prison. You did hear that, didn't you? *Mrs. Weisheit?* They met at a bookstore and she gave Angela the money."

"You took Mr. Fontaine to the hospital last night."

"That's right."

"He stayed over at your place."

"Full disclosure. Angela too."

"So you're telling me that the widow of the murder victim in this case secretly posted bail to get the prime suspect out of jail, and she routed the money through an individual with whom you happen to be intimately related."

"Intimately related. It's the quaintness, Lieutenant. I think that's what I find so —"

"And that you then attended the suspect's show at Penny's last night —"

"During which the murder victim's so-called best friend muscled his way to the stage and broke three of the prime suspect's fingers."

"You're still in the middle of all this, Mr. Sewell," Kruk said sadly. "Every time I turn around, there you are."

"I have the same problem. Look, forget about me, Lieutenant. Toby Schultz. *He's* in the middle of all this. And here's a little bonus for you. Free of charge. The murder victim's so-called best friend, the aforementioned Mr. Schultz? He has also been having an on-and-off affair with the murder victim's wife. For years."

"Is that so?"

"You heard it here first."

"And may I ask where you got this information? Was it from Mr. Schultz himself?"

"No."

"From Mrs. Weisheit?"

"It was an old friend of Mrs. Weisheit's."

"Secondhand. So your information may or may not be true," Kruk said.

"As with all information, yes." I tapped my watch. "How are we doing on time?"

Kruk ignored me. "I'm going to ask you another question, Mr. Sewell. I would appreciate an honest answer. Trust me, we can find this out on our own. I'm hoping you'll save us the time."

"Ask."

"I want to know if you have ever had a sexual relationship with Polly Weisheit."

"Don't you think that's a personal question, Lieutenant?"

"That's not an answer."

"The answer is no."

"Thank you."

"I have a question," I said. "Has Toby Schultz given an explanation to you for why he snapped Sisco's fingers?"

"Mr. Schultz's statement is that he was outraged to learn of Mr. Fontaine's being released on bail. He considers Fontaine to have murdered Jake Weisheit and he states that he was livid and that he acted on pure rage. He admits to having been drinking earlier in the evening. He readily concedes that he exercised poor judgment."

"Do you buy that crock?"

"Be civil, Mr. Sewell. It's Lieutenant Kruk."

"Crock. Not Kruk. Do you buy that story? Poor judgment? How about killing Jake Weisheit. Maybe that was poor judgment."

"On Mr. Schultz's part?"

"Have you considered Toby Schultz as a suspect in Weisheit's murder?"

Kruk let the question hang in the air a full ten seconds. "Mr. Sewell, the only person I don't consider a suspect is me."

"You've really got to do something about that open mind of yours, Lieutenant. You'll never narrow things down if you keep that up."

Kruk placed his hands on his desk. "That'll be all, Mr. Sewell. Thank you for your time."

I tapped my watch again. "Look. We came in at under five."

Kruk almost smiled.

Sisco and Angela and I piled back into my car. Sisco was all for heading directly to Toby Schultz's workplace and confronting

358

him with a two-by-four. I pointed out to Sisco the difficulties of his wielding a two-by-four with any modicum of success or even worthy threat given the condition of his right hand. Sisco sat in the backseat, chewing on more painkillers.

"You do it, Hitch. The son of a bitch killed Polly's husband. I know it. I just spent a week in prison because of that asshole. Not to mention my fucking fingers."

"Or your potty mouth," Angela remarked.

"We don't know that Schultz killed anyone," I said. "We just know that he was sleeping with Polly Weisheit. So were you. Maybe you both did it."

"Right. Sure. I held him and this guy shoved the knife in."

"If Schultz killed Jake, the police will handle it," I said. "Kruk's no idiot. If they weren't looking into Schultz before, they —"

Sisco cut me off. "They weren't looking into jackshit. They had *me* rotting in jail."

I shared a look with Angela. We were on the same wavelength. *Rotting* in jail? Seven days? I looked at Sisco in the rearview mirror. "I'm sorry about your fingers, Sisco. Honestly. But if Schultz really did have anything to do with Jake Weisheit's murder, he just did you a great big favor by putting himself on Kruk's radar."

Sisco coddled his wounded hand. "Some favor."

Angela was frowning. "But . . . if Schultz murdered Jake Weisheit, wouldn't it be the stupidest thing he could possibly do, attacking Sisco? Like you said, it only draws attention to him."

"True. Though he does have plenty of cover. He has the billing as Weisheit's best friend, after all. Going after Jake's killer would —"

"I'm not fucking Jake Weisheit's fucking *killer*," Sisco snapped. "I didn't kill Polly's damn husband and she knows it. How about bailing me out seven days ago? What the hell took her so long? You have no idea what kind of crap goes on in prison."

"It'll add to your legend," I said. "Where would Johnny Cash be today without a little prison time?"

Sisco took the remark with another grumble. But the notion didn't seem to displease him. He stared out the back window with a faraway look.

I dropped Sisco off at his place. He was halfway dopey by the time we reached his apartment. I couldn't find a nearby parking spot, so Angela waited in the car while I helped Sisco into his lair. His work with the front-door keys was like an Abbott and Costello routine. Sisco's place was decorated in early needs-a-maid. I cleared a path to the bedroom and Sisco shuffled forward and dropped onto the bed. I took hold of his

360

boots. "I'm doing this just one more time. Get yourself a pair of moccasins after this."

I left him murmuring in tongues. A *Sun* papers truck drove by as I was getting back into the car. Angela and I drove to her apartment in Charles Village and I asked her if I could come in and use her phone. She made me twist her arm, but not to the point where it hurt.

"Will you be able to persevere without my sunny visage?" I asked her as I hung up the phone.

Angela posed with her hands on her hips. "Translation?"

"I've got to go talk to somebody."

"You could try simple old English, you know."

"I've got to split," I said.

She kissed the air. "Ciao."

Janet Becket rose from her desk like a graceful tiger uncoiling after its nap. She was wearing jeans over a black leotard and her short blond hair was pushed casually back off her face with a white plastic hair band. I felt like I was intruding on the off-duty time of a superhero.

Her grip was firm. Her face was open and relaxed. "I'm so sorry," she said. "When you called me I was in the middle of something and I completely spaced on what time it was. I have a lecture to give in five minutes. I'm really very sorry. If you have time to stick around we could talk afterward."

She slipped on a sheer white shirt, two times too big for her. It was practically a lab coat except that it lifted and danced with the slightest provocation. None of my professors at Frostburg ever even came close to a look like this.

I matched her stride for stride as we made our way to the lecture hall. "Would it be awkward if I sat in?" I asked.

"Not at all. Just promise not to snore too loudly."

Not an issue. Janet Becket had the chops. The auditorium was maybe half full, a good hundred or so students, and not a one of them carved their names into their chair or worked up a fleet of paper airplanes. They focused. They took notes. Their heads swiveled as if on newly greased ball bearings as Janet Becket prowled about behind the lectern pouring out what she knew into the receptive vessels. The *Sun* had clearly made a mistake in letting her slip away. Her lecture was particularly harsh on the state of journalism itself. Had I been taking notes I'd have been scribbling down words like *government mouthpiece, lazy, lacking context, sloppy,* and my favorite, *pretty fucking gutless.* A number of the students flocked around her at the end of class. Earnest faces bobbed and nodded as their professor took their individual concerns and opinions.

"What do you think?" Janet asked me as we headed across the quad. "Did I sound bitter?"

"Not at all. Passionate and pissed off."

"It's daunting. Everything today is celebrity. These kids are seeing parachute journalists. They're seeing reporters yukking it up in *Vanity Fair*. For God's sake, it's called *Vanity Fair*. Has anyone stopped to notice that? It's one big party out there. Everyone is kissy-kissy with some of the same people who are plundering" — she ticked them off on her fingers — "our privacy, the environment, our health and the education of our children. Those four. You lose those you've lost the whole game. You might as well just fold up the board and throw it in the fire. Journalists are the ones who are supposed to be calling out, 'Hey! Take a look! We're slipping into the shit.' "

We had reached a set of steps that led up to an arched walkway. "Shut me up," Janet said as we ascended the steps. "The lecture ended ten minutes ago."

"On the contrary. I'm all ears. It's inspiring to hear you rant."

"Well, thanks. Not all of my colleagues feel the same."

I followed her across another quad to a small dining hall, where we had some of the best institutional food I think I've ever eaten.

You've no idea what they're doing with salmon these days. Janet urged me to have a glass of chocolate milk. "Cafeteria milk. It's perfection."

She remembered the Briarcliff story.

"The scandal that wasn't. I received a phone call. This man says that his mother is being jerked around at the nursing home where she's been living. It doesn't say so in my article, but the guy was insanely belligerent. He said that the administrators of the nursing home were controlling his mother's finances."

"Controlling?"

"He claimed they were writing checks under her name, that they were telling her where to invest and then taking fees for setting things up for her. He even wondered if they were trying to get her to alter her will. As it turned out on that one, he had just seen a movie on TV where something like that happened. Where a rich old person has cut her children out of the will and they arrange for her lawyer to direct the money to them anyway. The lawyer gets a cut. This is the kind of guy I was dealing with. Mr. Fantasy. Still, I thought maybe there was something worth looking into."

"According to your article, there was some of this stuff going on."

"But not quite how it was being put to me. I contacted the woman who owns and operates the nursing home —"

"Marilyn Tuck?"

"Right. She told me point-blank that yes, she had been asked by the . . . God, the name is escaping me. I'll think of it in a second. The woman had wanted Tuck's help in moving some of her money around. Marilyn Tuck agreed that it maybe wasn't the most kosher thing for her to do, but she swears she didn't take any fees or anything like that, and as best I could tell, that was the case. She said she did nothing to take advantage of the situation. Certainly there was never anything to do with the woman's will. You can see what she says in the article. "We're family here. We help each other out."

"People love that *family* thing, don't they."

Janet laughed. "They do. Most families are at each other's throats."

"So the real family in this case wasn't thrilled."

"I've got to tell you, the real family are the ones *I'd* be concerned about. Turns out this guy had no relationship with his mother whatsoever. He had never once even been out to see his mother at the nursing home. Totally estranged. It seems he received a phone call from one of the financial institutions that was double-checking a large transfer of cash. The call shouldn't have even come to him. That's what got the bug in his tail. Marilyn Tuck's name came up, and when he realized that she was running the nursing home where his mother was living, he started the gears turning. That's when he called me. He wanted to raise a stink. He was talking about suing the place. Marilyn Tuck told me she wondered if the guy wasn't out to fleece his mother himself. Anything to get a little cash. This was not a man with a lot of means, as far as I could judge. You really did have to see him. There were definitely dollar signs in his eyes. Lawsuit fever. So maybe she was right. Damn, I've usually got a photographic memory, but I just can't pull up the name. I didn't use it in the article out of deference to his mother's privacy. It was all such he said/she said at this point.

"I have to admit, though, even though I thought this man was a fruit I wasn't completely convinced by the Tuck woman either. By nature I'm a skeptical person. I'm sure that's why I got into journalism in the first place. But you learn to remain as neutral as possible or you might miss the story. I remember Tuck was a little too smooth for my tastes. She brought me in to see the old lady, but she practically did all the talking for her. There's a whole dependency thing that happens in institutions like that. Of course the old woman was more trusting of Briarcliff than of her own son. But was she being coerced? I can't say."

"This is the only article Jay came up with

about any of this," I said. "What came of it?"

"Nothing. There was this flurry of nastiness between Briarcliff and our friendly nutcase and then suddenly the guy dropped it. No lawsuit, nothing. I had the impression that maybe they came to some sort of settlement. I could be wrong about that."

"Wouldn't that suggest that Briarcliff was doing something wrong after all? Why would they bother to settle?"

"It's a fair question. To tell you the truth, I sort of dropped the ball on this one. I lost interest. I was having a few personal issues of my own around that time. Things were getting bad for me at the paper. Plus I had a bad relationship I was trying to extract myself from. We do so many stories. I simply saw this one as a dud."

We were finished with our lunches. We took our trays to the standing racks and slid them in.

Janet grabbed an apple from a metal bowl of fruit at the cash register as we left. "I'm running in the New York marathon next month," she said, biting into the apple.

"Big Apple," I said.

She considered the fruit in her hand. "Not really."

"New York. The Big Apple."

"Oh. *That* Apple."

As we crossed the quad I asked her what

were her overall impressions of Briarcliff Manor.

"Based on what I saw? Inconclusive. Though like I said, I was born a skeptic. Frankly I didn't really come away feeling completely wonderful about either party in this one."

She walked me back to my car. The thin blouse blew about her like a set of wings.

"Jay tells me you're working on a novel."

"Scratch a journalist and you've scratched a novelist."

"Can I ask what it's about?"

"Boy meets girl."

"Catchy."

She laughed. "But wait'll you see the girl."

Janet was impressed with my car. "You probably don't want me to say it's cute, do you?"

"I'd hope someone with your vast vocabulary . . ."

"It's bold and timeless."

"Better."

"I'm sorry I couldn't help you more," she said. "The name of the damn family. It's on the tip of my tongue. I know I can find it in my files when I get home. I'm a pack rat. I keep everything. I can call you with it if you'd like."

"Sure. Call. That'd be fine." I gave her my card.

We said good-bye. I got into my bold and

timeless car and pulled out of the lot. I was passing by the university library when I spotted a superhero in my side mirror. She was gaining on me. I pulled over.

Janet Becket was gulping for air. "I . . . I remembered . . . I've got the name for you. It just came to me."

I grabbed a pen and found a clear spot on the folded map from my glove compartment. "Shoot."

Chapter Twenty-seven

The woman cocked her head. Her heavy earrings swayed like a chandelier on the *Poseidon*. She handed me back my card. "You're an undertaker."

"Yes, ma'am."

"I thought you said you were investigating . . . how did you put it?"

"Improprieties."

"When you called, I thought you were some kind of detective. Or policeman."

"No, ma'am. I'm here on behalf of the Maryland State Funeral Directors Association. You see, it's one of the mandates of MSFDA to encourage a broader degree of engagement in the community on the part of its members. By that I mean people like myself."

"Undertakers?"

"Exactly. We would like our members to do more than simply sit around waiting for the phone to ring. Morticians are not vultures. There are many pre-death issues that the layperson — that would be someone like yourself, ma'am — wouldn't necessarily be expected to be equipped to handle. People have their own lives to live. They have their families. They have their business to attend to. Who thinks about pre-death issues? You shouldn't be expected to, ma'am. We should. This is our bailiwick. It's our area of expertise."

My hands were clasped behind my back, the nails of one digging mercilessly into the skin of the other as I loaded on the hooey. I rocked back on my heels. Either the absurd bird would fly or the woman at the door would bring it down with the simple shot it deserved.

She scraped at her cheek with one of her impressive fingernails. "Pre-death issues?"

"As in what appears to have maybe taken place with your mother-in-law at Briarcliff Manor. That's a pre-death issue. Someone who is entering the final stages of her life. Especially the hospitalized or the institutionalized. Like your mother-in-law. The MSFDA feels a responsibility to play a role at this stage. Where appropriate, of course. A person in pre-death is, in a manner of speaking, a pre-customer."

"Pre-customer?"

"In a manner of speaking. End of life is our area of expertise." I took a deep breath. My fingers dug harder. Blood was near. "You see?"

The woman gave me a skeptical look, although in truth it was a little difficult to tell for certain what sort of expression she was sending out. Her features appeared to be locked into position. Her face was an amalgam of cosmetics, practically a sampler, obliterating any chance of knowing what she really looked like underneath it all. The mask was vaguely Zsa Zsa except for the lips, which brought to mind a pair of pink earthworms. The eyebrows were plucked to the width of fishing line and the nose had the appearance of something chosen from a photograph. It was unnaturally pinched at the bridge, flowering out in the shape of a tiny bell. Likewise, the breasts were clearly the work of a craftsman. Nature does not do what they were doing. They looked like they were trying to join the conversation. Dominate it, even. Certainly they were testing the limits of the woman's powder blue tank top. Perhaps the pink Corvette parked outside — the one with the PURR license plates — should have braced me for the exotic tastes of the woman of the house. Like the woman herself, the car was equally anomalous to the setting, a small clapboard shack of a house in a one-corner community in Baltimore County called Texas, home of Campbell's Cement Quarry and as far as I could tell, little else. The entrance to the quarry was directly across from where we were standing.

"Why don't you come in?" the woman in the tiny tank top said. "I don't understand what in the world you're talking about."

I crossed into Graceland. Actually, I've never been to Graceland, but the stories I've heard suggest an excess of shag carpeting and a violent tribute to a lava lamp way of life. I paused.

My hostess beamed. "It's something, isn't it? Ross let me pick everything myself."

We settled into the living room, the centerpiece of which was a swivel chair that was a large white plastic molded hand. Cupped. The ersatz Zsa Zsa settled snugly into the palm of the hand, placing her hands on thumb and pinkie in a Queen of Sheba pose.

I took the beanbag couch. Very low to the ground. Very crunchy. I sighted the woman through my knees.

"Yes, it's quite a place," I remarked. The carpet was a green and yellow combination and could stand a mowing. I recognized the lamps and the glass coffee table from episodes of *The Jetsons*. There was a large gold frame on the wall. What precisely was being represented within it, I couldn't say with full certainty. Naked torsos? Some sort of goblin underworld? The way the sunlight was catching the velvet, I just couldn't get a handle on it.

"It's my dream come true," the woman said, her eyes dancing about her domain. There wasn't a trace of shame in her voice. "Sometimes I just sit here and stare."

373

Sure. Move too fast and you might get nauseated. I adjusted myself on the beanbag.

"Are you okay there?" she asked. "We can switch." She patted the hand on the thumb.

"I'm fine." My elbow had just disappeared within a Naugahyde fold, but otherwise I thought I could manage. "Mrs. Greenwood, what I was hoping I could —"

"Amanda." She smiled a toothy grin and looked at my card again. "That's quite a name you've got there, if you don't mind my saying. I never met anyone called Hitchcock before. Are you named after that director?"

"It's a long story," I said. "My mother lobbied for Giovanni. I am indebted to my dad."

"Giovanni." She rolled the name around with her surgically swollen lips. "Giovanni. I kind of like that. It's cute. That's Italian, isn't it? I like it. I could call you that." She batted her eyes. "Giovanni."

"Hitchcock would be fine."

She chirped, "Whatever swings your boat."

I adjusted myself on the beans. "I appreciate your taking the time to talk with me."

"Well, I hope you're going to make more sense than you just did at the door. Pre-death, pre-customer." She laughed. "I don't pre-understand what you're talking about. You want a drink or something? Pink pussycat? Beer? Coke?"

How tempting was that first one? I declined. Amanda Greenwood brought one leg up and tucked it under her tush. "Okay. So tell me again what it is you want."

"Your husband's mother has been a resident at Briarcliff for how many years?"

"Claudia? Gosh, I couldn't really tell you. It was, like, at least three or four years, I guess. You'd have to check with Ross."

"Ross is your husband?" I knew this, of course. It was the name Janet Becket had given to me.

"Yes. I'm expecting him back any minute. He's at the club. Ross is a slave to his body." Her false eyelashes made a series of moves. I felt it best not to attempt to interpret them. "Ross has always been in good shape and everything. He used to work at the quarry. But he does love his club. He goes all the time now."

"I understand your husband no longer works at Campbell's. Is that right?"

"He quit that. Life's too short, you know what I mean?"

"So . . . Amanda. Concerning Mrs. Greenwood's stay at Briarcliff, I'm interested in the sort of treatment she has been receiving."

The woman frowned at me . . . at least as much as her frozen features would allow. "Has been? You've got to check your records, Giovanni. Claudia is dead."

"Mrs. Greenwood died?"

"She certainly did."

"I wasn't aware of that. I'm sorry."

"Don't be sorry to me. I never really knew the woman. Ross and his mother didn't get along much. You know what they say sometimes about families. Can't live with 'em, can't leave 'em on the highway. Ross's daddy died about ten years ago and Claudia married rich and Ross says his mother turned into a snob. She turned her back on him. She didn't even come to our wedding. She sent us a gift, but Ross took it out back and smashed it."

"I'm curious. When did Mrs. Greenwood die?"

The woman sat back in the molded hand and counted off on the chair's fingers. "One, two . . . something like six months ago? Five or six? I'm bad with numbers. She was real sick." She laughed, "You know . . . pre-death?"

I was about to ask another question when a chirping sound came from the direction of the kitchen. Amanda Greenwood slid out of the hand. "Excuse me."

She disappeared into the kitchen. Her earrings jangled as she strode back in a moment later. She settled back into her chair.

"That was Ross. He was calling from the car. He'll be home in a minute. He doesn't want me to say anything else to you."

"Why not?"

"Don't know. He just said."

Given the furnishings of the house and the

furnishings of the woman in the plastic hand across from me, to say I had a bad feeling about Ross Greenwood seems a waste of effort. Amanda was looking apologetic for her husband's having gagged our little chat.

"I have only a couple of quickie questions," I said.

She darkened. "I don't know. Ross said."

I pressed. "There was a matter earlier this year concerning your mother-in-law's finances."

"I can't talk about it. Ross'll kill me."

"I'm just curious how everything resolved, that's all. Your husband was considering a lawsuit, if I understand it correctly. Was there some sort of settlement with Briarcliff?"

"You're going to have to ask Ross about all that. I really don't pay attention to anything like that. Now I've got to shut my mouth."

She ran an invisible zipper along the fleshy mountain range and we fell silent and sat staring across the room at each other. I probably should have averted my gaze, but I was memorizing all the details so that I could tell Julia later. Our gazes finally snapped a few minutes later with the sound of a car pulling into the driveway. Amanda Greenwood announced darkly, "That's Ross." She rose from the chair. "Ross can be very jealous. You just stay where you are."

As she started for the front door I twisted my head to look out the window. A yellow Corvette was parked next to the pink one.

The license plate read ROAR.

"Honey," I heard Amanda Greenwood say, and then a man in a raspberry jogging suit was in the living room. He was short and stocky, with a leathery tan and a hostile attitude. "What's this about?"

I noticed he was not offering me a pink pussycat.

"I was just speaking with your wife about your mother," I said. I didn't like the sound of the sentence the moment the words left my mouth. Neither did Ross Greenwood.

"What about my mother? My mother's dead."

Amanda piped up. "He's an —"

"Shut up. I asked *him*." He aimed a finger at me. Had it been closer, my instinct would have been to bite it. "Who the hell are you? How's any of this your business?"

I suspected that my Maryland State Funeral Directors Association rap would likely get a pretty poor reception from Ross Greenwood. He was speaking pure testosterone. I felt at a disadvantage folded into the stupid beanbag couch.

"I'll leave," I said. I tried to get up from the couch. It wasn't easy. Less so when Ross Greenwood took a step forward and shoved me back down onto it. He fell into a karate stance, legs spread, arms cocked.

His wife started. "Ross —"

"Shut up, Mandy!"

"I'm not going to fight you," I said. "I'll just go."

"My ass! I come home, you're sitting here with my wife."

He adjusted his stance, rabbit-hopping a step closer to me. It was impossible to tell if he actually knew what he was doing or if he had simply ingested a sufficient diet of kung fu films to have the moves down pat. I made another attempt to get up out of the couch. The man hopped forward and shoved me down again. He bounced his hands around.

"You don't fuck with me, buster. You hear that? You don't fuck with my wife either."

"You're right on both counts," I said wearily. For a third time I tried to extract myself from the beans. For a third time he caught me on the way up and shoved me back down. My ancestral warriors were beginning to stir. This could take all day. I glanced down at my shoes and saw that the laces on one of them were slightly loose. One of the ends was hanging just above the carpet.

"Look, I only came out here to ask you some questions concerning your mother's treatment at Briarcliff Manor. I explained all this to your wife. Obviously this isn't the best time."

Greenwood snarled. "Bullshit. What's going on here?" He bounced closer. The hands were up and ready. Just my luck. The Karate Kid.

"Damn," I muttered. "Shoelace."

I leaned forward to reach for my shoe. As my tail left the beanbag I lunged forward. I caught Ross Greenwood dead center on the jogging suit and grabbed on. He grunted as his breath left him. Amanda Greenwood let out a scream. I plunged forward, driving the man backward. The only thing between Ross Greenwood and the far wall was the swivel chair. I landed him cleanly in the palm of the hand. It was nowhere near as sturdy as it looked. The chair, Ross Greenwood and I tumbled over and landed on the carpet. Soft landing, you have to give it that. Greenwood had a grip on the back of my windbreaker. He smelled of Aqua Velva and sweat. He was growling like a mad dog.

I went Zen. I released my hold on Greenwood and shimmied backward, like a snake moving in reverse, allowing my arms to rise over my head. The snarling man still had a hold of my windbreaker, but writhing as swiftly as I could, I pulled myself down along the carpet and right out of the jacket. Hitchcock Houdini. Before Greenwood knew what was happening, I was up on my feet and he was still on the floor, clutching an empty windbreaker.

He started up. I grabbed his shrieking wife by the shoulders and, using her as a battering ram, shoved her against him. He went down. His head hit the shag hard. The move took the air out of Amanda Greenwood. Which was nice. Quieted things down. As Ross Greenwood again attempted to get to his knees, I gave his wife a gentle push of the shoulders and she tumbled down onto him.

In five strides I was out the door.

Chapter Twenty-eight

The wake for Russell and Randall was scheduled to begin at six. I showered and shaved
and slipped into my somber suit. I brought
Alcatraz with me to the funeral home and
left him with Billie while I went down to the
basement and brought the twins upstairs.
Billie joined me and helped arrange the
flowers. I still didn't know which was Randall
and which was Russell. I'd have to sort that
out before the burial.

We went back upstairs to Billie's apartment. Billie brewed up a pot of heady tea
and laid out a tray of crackers and a particularly stinky cheese called the Bishop's Nose.
Billie said it was the only kind of cheese she
could taste right now. Alcatraz begged for
some cheese, and when I gave him some on
a cracker, the flavor didn't register until the
cheese was halfway to his stomach. He appeared confused by the flavor, and not all
that pleased with his master. Frankly, I
agreed with him about the flavor, but after a
few crackers full, it began to grow on me.
Scary thing to say about something that is
essentially mold.

I gave Billie an abridged version of my visit

to the Greenwoods. I spared her the image of her nephew rolling around on the shag carpet with Ross Greenwood. The salient point of my story was not lost on Billie. The matching Corvettes, Amanda Greenwood's apparent cosmetic surgical extravaganza, the little shack's furnishings makeover.

"This is a man who works at Campbell's quarry?"

"This is a man who quit his job at Campbell's quarry."

Billie smeared a slab of Bishop's Nose onto a cracker. "So he robbed a bank?"

"His mother died five or six months ago," I said.

"Did *she* rob a bank?"

"Amanda Greenwood said that she married rich. Second marriage."

"Why didn't I ever think of that?"

"Claudia Greenwood seemed to have left a decent little pot when she died," I said.

"And she passed it on to her son?" Billie passed her cracker on to Alcatraz, who looked offended that she would even think of it. He followed his tail into a spiral that ended at Billie's feet.

"The problem there is that all reports are that Ross Greenwood and his mother were completely estranged. He never visited her once in the nursing home. She didn't attend his wedding. Does that sound like the kind of person who is going to turn around and bequeath her little fortune to her son?"

Billie agreed that it did not seem automatically likely. "But there he is," she said. "Fancy cars and all the rest of it."

"Exactly. The Greenwoods are living like they've just won the lottery. I don't think you save up that kind of cash working in a cement quarry."

"So there must have been a reconciliation with the mother."

"That's one thought," I said.

Billie eyed me suspiciously. "I gather you have a few others."

"Briarcliff. Ross Greenwood's big beef with Briarcliff just suddenly vanished. He was all hot to make a stink of things and then . . . nothing."

"A settlement."

"Or something. Look at it. Here you have an elderly woman who is apparently loaded. Or at least plenty well off. If we believe the story that Janet Becket picked up, Claudia Greenwood is asking Marilyn Tuck to assist her with her finances. She's putting her trust in Marilyn. Either that or she is already far enough along that Marilyn sees an opportunity."

"I see where you're going, Hitchcock. But I don't see the logic, dear. You're suggesting that Miss Tuck could have persuaded Mrs. Greenwood to alter the terms of her will to reward her son? What does Miss Tuck get out of this?"

"A settlement. Ross was ready to blow the whistle on Briarcliff for messing around with Mama's money. If he happens to be correct, Marilyn Tuck was facing a disastrous situation. Fines. Lawyer's costs. Very likely jail time. Briarcliff would go down the tubes. So how nice if she could offer Ross Greenwood a big chunk of change to simply drop the whole thing. And I mean a *big* chunk of change. Mama's money."

Billie was shaking her head slowly. "Nephew, your grasp of the criminal mind is beginning to disturb me."

"It's just a theory, Billie. But somehow Ross Greenwood got hold of a whole lot of feel-good money. And if it was from the estate of the mother who had nothing to do with him . . . I find that curious."

"If," Billie said. She checked her watch. "Dear, we need to get downstairs."

I took the steps two at a time and popped into my office. I flipped through my Rolodex and found the number for Constance Bell, a lawyer friend of mine. It was after hours, so I left a message. "Constance, Hitchcock Sewell. Look, I have a small favor to ask of you . . ."

Not five seconds after I hung up the phone, it rang. Constance is good, but she's not that good. I picked up the phone.

It was Jenny Weisheit. She sounded upset. "Good. I caught you. I just tried you at your place."

"I've got evening hours tonight. What's up?"

She sounded upset. "I'm just really spooked. It's . . . I just had a talk with Martin. I don't know what to do. I need to talk to someone. You're the first person that popped into my head."

I glanced up and saw the first of the mourners drifting in the front door. "Listen. This isn't a great time. I'm sorry. Are you free in a couple of hours?"

"Yes. Absolutely."

"Good. Let me tell you where to meet me. Any time after about eight-thirty. If I'm a little late, just hang tight."

"Thank you."

I told her where, then I hung up.

Billie had just appeared at my door. "Hitchcock?"

A pair of men were standing with her. They were somewhere in their late fifties. Tall. Thin. Wearing identical blue suits and red ties. Their faces looked familiar. Actually, it's just as accurate to say that their *face* looked familiar.

"Hitchcock, I'd like you to meet Randall and Russell's father, Raymond. And their uncle —" She turned to the men. They answered in unison.

"Richard."

"Right. Richard and Raymond."

A pair of hands came forward. Along with

an identical pair of smiles.

I damn near backed away.

Sally was winking at me as I stepped up to the bar. I asked, "What's with the winking?"

"I'm not winking. I've got something in my eye."

"Oh. I thought maybe our relationship was moving to a new level."

Sally fitted me out with a couple of cubes and a Maker's and shared some local gossip with me. Nothing to catch your pants on fire, but it's always good to keep up. Jenny Weisheit hadn't shown yet. Scotty and Nance were holding down a table near the dartboard, so I joined them for a while. The two were in the process of renovating a little brick place just around the corner on Bond Street and they regaled me with some of their horror stories. Plumbing. Electricity. Cracks in the ceiling. Buckling dry wall. Home Sweet Money Pit.

"But really, it's okay," Scotty said.

Nance snorted. "Okay. You know Sisyphus?"

"The guy with the rock," I said.

"Exactly. Uphill all the way. The Rock. That's our new name for the house." Nance told me she was ready to murder the electrician. "He doesn't know his ass from a sixty-watt bulb. And he's got these damn nun jokes he keeps telling. Every time you turn around, it's another one. 'What did the nun say to the pig?' 'Did you hear about the nun and the Chinese diplomat?' 'What would you get if you crossed a nun with a bowling ball?' Do I look like I care about this guy and his goddamn nuns? Screw the nuns, just hook up the juice and get the hell out. Jesus H. Christ."

Scotty tried to sneak a giggle my way, but Nance caught her. "And *you're* too damn polite, missy. That's your problem. If you wouldn't *laugh* at the idiot's jokes maybe he'd lay off 'em."

"I think they're funny. I'm sorry."

Nance jerked a thumb at her partner. "Mr. Nun Joke thinks this one's cute."

"Scotty is cute," I said.

"Fine. Go be cute somewhere else. If we want Bob Hope we can rent a video. How about just running the wires and getting the hell out?"

Several minutes later the door opened and Jenny Weisheit stepped into the bar. She paused, as if she wasn't quite sure she really wanted to enter. The Oyster's entrance is two steps above the actual floor; the effect of Jenny's pausing was that for several seconds she was on display. Not a few heads swiveled to have a look at the pretty young woman standing at the door.

I rose from my chair. "You'll have to excuse me, ladies."

Nance gave a low whistle. "Go get 'em."

I headed Jenny off before she reached our table. She was carrying a small Stieff's shopping bag, the loop handles pushed up to her elbow. Instinctively I took hold of both of her hands. It's an occupational hazard. Work at a funeral home long enough and you'll find yourself grabbing people's hands in your sleep. I released her hands.

"Is this place going to be all right?" I asked. "If it's too noisy here or too crowded for you, we can go somewhere else."

She glanced around the bar again. "No, it's fine."

I steered her toward a table by the far wall. As she was taking a seat she started. "Oh my God, is that you?"

She was referring to a painting on the wall just above the table. Several dozen of Julia's paintings adorned the walls of the bar. Old pieces of hers, for the most part. The particular one that gave Jenny the start was a goof Julia had done some five or six years ago. It was a decently faithful mock-up of the Mona Lisa, except that the face was a decently faithful mock-up of me. Julia had given me a little Clark Gable mustache, which along with the original painting's infamous smirk gave me something of the look of a riverboat gambler.

"You remember the ex-wife I mentioned to you? She painted that. It was her very brief

Leonardo da Vinci phase."

Jenny took a seat and looked up at the painting again. "It kind of creeps me out."

"We can move somewhere else. I wasn't choosing this table specifically. I don't even see these paintings anymore. Shall we move?"

"No. This is fine."

"How about a drink?"

"Yes." She fell back in her chair and twisted a finger into her hair. "Definitely a drink."

She wanted a vodka on ice. A tall one. I went over to the bar and asked Sally for a vodka and a refill on my Maker's.

"Have you got ID, bub?"

"Look at this weathered face," I said.

Sally grabbed up two glasses and plunged them into her ice bin. "I'm not talking about you, sweetheart. I'm talking about the child over there."

"I'll vouch for her, Sally."

"She's pretty. Of course you'll vouch for her. Who is she?"

"Her daddy is the guy who was murdered last week."

"Oh, in that case." She poured out a healthy measure of vodka. "Compliments of the house."

Jenny winced a smile to me as I returned to the table. I set her drink down. The Stieff's bag was up on the table.

"Is that for me?" I asked.

"It's Gran's birthday tomorrow. Martin and I are taking her out to dinner. This is a silver picture frame we're getting her from Stieff's. They were engraving it for us. I didn't want to leave it in the car."

"So," I said, settling into my chair, "what's the problem?"

"I'm scared. It's about Daddy."

"About his murder?"

She nodded her head once and stared down at the table. I didn't prod her. Jenny had made the phone call. She had asked to meet me. If she wanted to sit silently under my patient gaze — and underneath the patient gaze of me as a mustachioed Mona Lisa — and then get up from the table and go on back home, that would be her privilege. I doubted this was her wish, so I waited. I stirred my drink with my finger, fiddled with my ice, looked around the room. A faux wrestling match was playing on the TV set above the bar. The volume was off. A barrel-chested guy with a Mohawk was being chased around the ring by a swarthy figure wearing a velvet cape. Somebody had punched up a Bobby Darin song on the jukebox, and behind the bar Sally was clutching her heart and warbling along with the song. I looked over at Scotty and Nance. Nance was holding her hands up at the back of her head like they were rabbit ears and was making funny faces at Scotty, who was lost in the giggles.

"It's Martin," Jenny said at last, looking up from the table.

"What about him?"

"He is totally wigged out, that's what. And now I'm totally freaked."

"Why don't you tell me what's happened?"

She looked over her shoulder, as if afraid she would be overheard. "Do you know about Toby Schultz? Did you hear what happened last night?"

"You're talking about what happened at Penny's?"

"You heard."

"I was there."

"You were *there?* You saw Mr. Schultz break Sisco Fontaine's fingers? That's so horrible."

"It wasn't a pretty sight. Schultz did a real number on him, no question about it. I took Sisco to the hospital."

"Betty Schultz called my mom this morning and the two of them ended up in a screaming match over the phone. Mr. Schultz could be in real trouble. That's assault. It was a stupid thing to do. Really stupid."

"You do know that it was your mother who posted Sisco's bail?" I asked.

She hadn't known. It was clear from her expression. "You're kidding."

"Sisco's bail was reduced to fifty thousand dollars the other day and your mother posted it. Actually, she had it posted anonymously.

What the police think is that Toby Schultz wasn't too happy with any of this. Schultz told them that he was outraged at the idea that the murderer of his best friend had been let out of jail and that that's why he went storming over to Penny's."

"God, it's such a mess."

"What's your take on Toby Schultz?" I asked. "What's your opinion of him?"

She didn't respond immediately. She averted her eyes and stared nowhere for several seconds. Her mouth drew into a grim line.

"They've always creeped me out a little. Both of them. The Schultzes. He's not as bad as her. I mean . . . he can joke around and stuff like that. Her, I just can't get my head around her. I can't see why he married her, but that's not my business."

"I assume you saw a fair amount of the Schultzes?"

"Yes. Mr. Schultz and Daddy played tennis together once a week. They were good friends. Sure, I saw them a lot."

She looked off into space again. I leaned forward on the table. "You're not saying something."

"I know." She heaved a large sigh and her eyes locked onto mine. "Okay. It's this. This past spring I was home from college. Spring break. I was out in the pool. It was still a little cold to be swimming, but it felt good.

I'm an otter, I love to swim. I always have. I was doing laps. I didn't even see him at first. It was like he just suddenly appeared."

"Toby Schultz?"

"Uh-huh. No one else was home but me. I had finished my laps and had pulled myself out of the pool and suddenly he was standing there. It scared me. I get in a real zone when I'm doing laps. I have no idea how long he'd been standing there watching me. He said he was just dropping by to see if my father was in. Mr. Schultz is one of the trustees of Grandpa's foundation. He said he had some foundation stuff to go over. I had . . . it was just one of those feelings. I wasn't comfortable.

"He was standing between me and my towel. He saw it there on the stone wall and he fetched it and handed it to me. But when I grabbed it he didn't let go. He acted like it was a little game, but I didn't like it. He finally let go and then he . . . he told me how pretty I was and how much I'd grown into a woman in the last year. I don't know, maybe he was just trying to be nice. It's so easy to misinterpret. All I know is that he said that and then he took a step toward me and I ran into the house. I dropped the towel. I ran up to my room and closed the door and stood there sopping wet, shivering.

"I heard him come into the house and up the stairs. I panicked. We don't have locks on our bedroom doors. I was scared. I just stood there frozen. I had goose bumps. I was literally holding my breath. He came upstairs, then I heard him in Daddy's office. I quickly got dressed, but I stayed in my room. I wouldn't go out there. Finally he left. He didn't try to find me or call out good-bye or anything. He just took off. It sounds silly, now that I'm saying it, but I waited at least five minutes before I left my room."

"Did you mention this to anyone? To your father?"

"No. Like I said, maybe I had it all wrong. He's a friend of the family. He's Martin's godfather. I might have been overreacting."

"And the next time you saw him?"

"He was pleasant to me as he always is. He was with his wife. He acted like nothing had happened. Of course, nothing *had* happened. I felt uncomfortable. Running away like that, it's an accusation. I'm sure this is all in my head, but the look Mrs. Schultz was giving me was like she knew something wasn't quite right, but that whatever it was, I was the one to blame."

I wanted to ask her if she was aware of the relationship between Schultz and her mother. My guess was that she wasn't. I wondered if Betty Schultz knew about it, or at least had her suspicions. Maybe Betty Schultz was seeing the mother in the daughter. The physical resemblance was certainly there. Jenny lifted up her glass and took a sip. Her eyes peeked at me over the lip of the glass.

"So why are you telling me this?" I asked.

Jenny set the glass down with deliberate precision. "Martin. I told you how Martin has been so bottled up ever since Daddy was killed? How he has been this walking volcano all week?"

"Yes."

"I know why now. He told me today." She paused. Her voice lowered. "Martin thinks Mr. Schultz killed Daddy. He's been holding it in all week."

"Why does he think that?"

"Martin overheard the two of them, Daddy and Mr. Schultz. They were in Daddy's office at home. Mom wasn't home and Martin had just gotten in from football practice. He says they didn't know he was there. He must not have made any noise coming in. Martin said the door to Daddy's office was cracked open and he could hear this arguing going on. So he listened. Daddy was furious. Martin says he'd never heard him like that before. For our father to blow up like that is a big deal. It just wasn't his style."

"Could Martin tell what your father was angry about?"

"It was about the foundation. Martin couldn't sort it all out, but the gist of it was that Mr. Schultz has been ripping off the foundation. From what Martin could tell, there was some organization that was getting money from the foundation. As a trustee, Mr. Schultz had recommended the grant. It sounded like Mr. Schultz was involved with them somehow. He runs a consulting firm — corporate research, public relations, stuff like that. It sounded to Martin like Mr. Schultz was getting this money paid out from the foundation and then getting himself hired by the organization and funneling a portion of the money right back into his own pocket. What Martin heard was Daddy demanding that Mr. Schultz return the money. He said this was foundation money that had been illegally allocated and that the integrity of the foundation was at risk if the truth came out. That's classic Daddy. 'Integrity of the foundation.' "

"So what was Schultz's reaction? What did Martin say?"

"He says Mr. Schultz was really angry too. He was denying everything and he was yelling at Daddy and telling him he was crazy and all wrong. When he really went nuts was when Daddy told him he was giving him five days to return the money to the foundation. That's what's had Martin spooked. Daddy said he wanted everything straight by the coming Monday. He gave him a time. Noon Monday. If not, he was blowing the whistle himself."

"On his so-called friend?"

"It's pure Daddy. He could get so righteous sometimes. I can totally see it. Like I said, especially about the foundation. If Mr. Schultz was ripping off Grandpa's foundation, you can bet Daddy would not put up with it."

"When did all this take place?" I asked.

Jenny sat back and picked up her drink. She stirred it with the plastic straw but she didn't take a sip.

"That's what's got Martin spooked. It was the Wednesday before Daddy was killed. Daddy told Mr. Schultz that he had until Monday at noon or else all hell was going to break loose."

"And your father was murdered in the wee hours of Sunday morning."

Tears welled in Jenny's eyes. She choked out a hoarse whisper. "And my daddy was killed on Sunday morning."

Chapter Twenty-nine

The sun rose at six-ten the next morning, took a brief look around, then slipped into the pocket of the nearest cloud and wasn't to be seen for the rest of the day. In my perfect life I would have missed its brief appearance. But then in my perfect life I would not have been jolted awake at five-thirty by a dream of Mrs. McNamara lying facedown on a kitchen floor in a pool of Guinness lager. Had this been the sum total of the dream it might not have spooked me. Possibly not even the large knife sticking in Mrs. McNamara's back would have spooked me. In the dream, Mrs. McNamara was still alive and was talking to me, asking me to please remove the knife from her back. I tried. Kneeling on the floor next to her, I tried. But every time I took the knife out, another appeared in its place. Instantly. I'd pull out the new knife and another would appear. The faster I pulled the knives out, the faster the next one appeared, until finally the action became so blurred it was almost as if I were plunging the knives into her myself. Throughout, Mrs. McNamara remained calm and sweet. *"Please, Hitchcock . . . I don't want . . . to be here."*

That's what spooked me.

I sat on the end of the pier and looked out over the harbor. The surface of the water was unnaturally smooth, a flat black sheet of glass. One could be tempted to consider that the water had somehow congealed overnight into a solid form and that you could step out onto it and make your way around the harbor on foot. One would hope that one would not be so idiotic as to actually give in to such a temptation. Leave walking on water to the experts, I always say. I sat on the pier and waited for my mind to go as clear and smooth as the surface of the water or for Stoney's to open at seven — whichever came first. Stoney's came first. No huge surprise there. Clarity of mind was a no-go. *Way* too many ripples. Way too much sloshing about. I dragged my unenlightened carcass to its feet and made my way over to the bakery. I ordered a walnut brioche and a cup of Stoney's mighty brew and sat at a table by the window, watching the steam bead its way up the glass.

Before loading up Randall and Russell for their trip to church and then the cemetery, I put in a call to a fellow named Jeff Falkenstein. Jeff used to live in Baltimore, where he worked primarily as a fund-raiser for local charities and nonprofits. He was brought in by one of the board members of the Gypsy

Players, our local amateur theater troupe, to help us goose things up a little in the begging-for-bucks department, which was when I met him. He'd since moved to Chevy Chase, a Maryland suburb on the outskirts of D.C., to take a job in Washington with an organization called the Foundation Center, which as Jeff explained it to me is a sort of central clearinghouse for grant-making foundations from all over the country. The center collects information from foundations, tracks giving patterns, runs seminars on how best to apply for grants, this sort of thing. I got hold of Jeff at work, shot the breeze for a minute or so, then asked him if it would be possible for him to get me some information on the James E. Weisheit Foundation.

"Are you kidding? Of course I can. That's what this place is all about. What specifically do you need?"

I told him that I wasn't exactly sure. "What about a list of who they give money to?" I said. "Can you get your hands on something like that?"

"Grants lists? No problem. Let me just check something in the system here while you're on the phone." I heard what I guessed was Jeff's tapping on his keyboard. "Right, okay. They report their grants quarterly. A lot of foundations do. That's good. How far back do you need?"

"I don't know, Jeff. How about the most

recent lists and then . . . say, back an entire year?"

"Can do. Why don't you give me a fax number? I can get to this later today and send it right out to you."

"That'd be peachy." I gave him the number.

When I hung up, Sam was standing in the doorway. "A twofer," he said.

"Excuse me?"

He held up two fingers. "A twofer."

"Oh, right. A twofer. You mean the twins."

"Mrs. Sewell called me yesterday to let me know."

"Yes, she told me she was going to. So you're all set with the second hearse?"

"Should be here any minute."

Sam and I rolled Randall outside (or maybe it was Russell), and as we were loading him into the hearse, a second hearse rounded the corner and pulled in behind us. The driver turned out to be Ellis, a.k.a. Dr. Puppy, the fellow who Mrs. McNamara had hired to bring her to Anna Papadaki's funeral. Sam and Ellis greeted each other with an elaborate set of gestures. I held up my hand. "How." Ellis high-fived it. We went inside and fetched Russell (or maybe it was Randall). As we were closing the rear door of the hearse a car came tearing up the street and skidded to a stop in front of St. Teresa's, across the street. I recognized the car and I

402

recognized the driver. We met in the middle of the street, the car door hanging open.

"It's bullshit! Total bullshit!" Polly Weisheit's face was dangerously red. "It's totally ridiculous."

"Good morning, Mrs. Weisheit," I said.

"Martin doesn't know what he's talking about! Neither does Jenny! Toby did *not* murder Jake. It's the most ludicrous thing I've ever heard."

"You should close your door," I said.

"Screw my door! Are you listening to me? Jenny came downstairs this morning and told me what you two talked about last night. She told me the whole ridiculous story! Do you know what she wants to do? She wants to call the police and tell them to arrest Toby for Jake's murder."

I scratched at a spot over my ear. "Funny thing, Polly. I sort of had the same idea."

"He didn't do it. Jenny just wants to punish me. She wants to humiliate me." I stepped past her and closed her car door. "Leave my car alone!"

"You've got to settle down."

"You've put this whole stupid thing in her head!"

"You're wrong. Martin's the one who has been holding on to this for over two weeks now. He's the one who overheard your husband and Toby Schultz. I don't know why you're coming after me."

"Martin doesn't know what he heard. Some sort of disagreement between Jake and Toby. Big deal. He's letting his imagination run away with him. He knows full well Toby would never hurt Jake. He's just confused. For God's sake, someone murdered his father in his own house. How do you think you'd feel?"

"I'm sorry, Polly, but he heard what he heard. There's surely no reason for him to be lying about it, is there? Jake was putting the squeeze on Toby Schultz. And I know from Chip Cooperman that Jake knew about the two of you. Cooperman told him."

"Chip? When the hell did you talk to Chip?"

"We went swimming together the other day," I said.

"What are you talking about?"

"Never mind. The point is, Jake had plenty to be angry about with Toby Schultz. When an old friend is ripping off the family foundation and having a little fun on the side with the family wife, I —"

"You bastard!"

Aunt Billie had just appeared in the doorway. "Hitchcock? You should be leaving soon." She spotted Polly. "Hello, dear. How are you doing today?"

Polly ignored her. She moved closer to me. She was seething. "You don't know what you're talking about."

"I think I do. I'm talking about a woman who didn't call the police the instant she saw her husband lying on the kitchen floor with a knife in his back."

"I told you, I was half doped on —"

"People can punch 911 in their *sleep.* You waited. For hours. Of course you had the flexibility, didn't you? How are the police going to know what time you actually found Jake's body? That's entirely a matter of what you decide to tell them. You've got time to play with. Time to let the killer get far the hell away from the house. Time to put a story together. Time to think."

Polly stomped her foot. "God! How do I convince you you're wrong?"

Billie called out again. "Hitchcock? The guests will be arriving."

"I'm coming!" I turned back to Polly. "I'll tell you how. You take Martin in to see the police and have him tell them what he told Jenny yesterday. Like he should have done in the first place. Better yet, get your boyfriend to fess up to his fight with Jake. If he's innocent, why doesn't he just tell them?"

"Because it's not relevant. Because he didn't do it."

"The foundation. Whatever finagling Schultz was doing with the foundation, he has gotten away with, hasn't he? Assuming Jake is the only person who knew. And Jake is dead. Regardless of who killed him, your boyfriend is nearly in the clear."

A minute later I had rejoined Sam and Ellis and Billie. Ellis and Sam were snickering. Billie took hold of my chin. "Let me see." She turned my face to get a look at my cheek. "Not so bad. It was certainly very loud from over here."

"I didn't think she had the reach."

"I've told you, dear, sometimes you slouch."

I rode with Sam over to St. Agnes. Ellis followed. We got the caskets set up just a few minutes before the mourners began arriving. The service ran a little longer than usual — you can expect that with a twofer. Then we moved on to the cemetery. We had enough pallbearers for a pickup basketball game, and for a moment I was afraid we had mixed up our Randall and our Russell again. But I think we kept it straight. As the graveside service commenced, I returned to the hearses, where Ellis and Sam were standing around chewing toothpicks together.

"Ellis, you're actually the man I'm looking for," I said.

Ellis nodded. "I'm the man you got."

"I want to get hold of Teresa."

"Teresa." For some reason the name made him chuckle.

"You remember Teresa," I said.

"I sure do. Skinny and stupid. That the Teresa you mean?"

"I don't like to pass judgment," I said.

"Yeah, that's fine. I don't either. These are the facts."

"I want to get hold of her," I said again.

Ellis shrugged. "Sure." He pulled a cell phone from his pocket and flipped it open. He punched in some numbers, put the phone to his ear, then handed it to me.

"Have a sparkling conversation."

Chapter Thirty

The waiter brought me back my change. I left a fat tip. Unless the soup ends up on my head or the special of the day makes its home on my lap, I leave a fat tip. It makes me feel good, it makes the waiter/waitress feel good. Feel Good 101. What could be simpler?

The only wrinkle here was that I wasn't feeling good. But it wasn't the food or the service; they were both fine. And thus the fat tip.

It was Teresa. More specifically, it was what Teresa had just told me. My phone call had reached her at a nursing home in Pikesville and she had agreed to meet me for lunch. She hadn't agreed with anything approximating enthusiasm — I could practically hear her shrugging over the phone — but I told her to pick a spot and damn the cost. For a beanpole she had proven to have a healthy appetite. We ate at the Steak and Ale on Reisterstown Road, about a half mile from the nursing home. A low lighting, fake wood beams, ye-olde-tavern kind of a place. Teresa ordered the large rib eye steak, the baked potato — which she doused with sour cream and bacon bits — and the open-ended salad bar. She also guzzled about a gallon of Coke and at the end of the meal had no trouble with a fudge brownie à la mode ("I want the fudge brownie à la mode with ice cream") and on the way out the door, a fistful of candy-covered mints that she popped into her mouth with metronomic steadiness as I drove her back to work.

"I'm sure you've been asked about your metabolism," I said as we pulled up in front of the nursing home.

"Uh-huh. I have. I got one."

She slipped her headset back on over her ears as she shoved the door open. I watched her move like a walking rubber band in through the front door.

According to the sign a few feet from my bumper I was in a no standing zone. I'm such a rebel sometimes, I remained where I was. A pair of nurses emerged from the building and stood smoking cigarettes just outside the front door. To me that's a peculiar sight, nurses smoking. It made more sense for me to think of them as actresses who were portraying nurses and who were taking a break between scenes. One nurse was tall and blond, with a jaw like a man's and a lot on her mind. The hand holding the cigarette moved about like she was conducting a symphony orchestra. The other was square and completely devoid of neck. She punctuated her end of the conversation with a pounding foot, like one of those trained horses running the math tables. From where I was sitting, I couldn't make out what they were saying, but I enjoyed the choreography.

A few minutes later a car pulled in behind me. I watched in the side view mirror as the door opened. There was a logo painted on the door, a single word in orange trapped within a green heart. Because it was in the mirror, the word was backwards. A woman got out of the car and headed for the front door. She stopped and addressed the nurses, then continued on into the building. As soon as the door had closed, the blond started wagging her finger in her colleague's face in apparent mockery of the woman. They then threw their half-finished cigarettes onto the pavement and crushed them out. My brain had unreversed the backward word by then and presented it to me. The nurses were heading back into the building as I shoved my door open and stepped over for a look at the logo on the side of the car behind me. ElderHeart. In smaller print below the green heart, *Quality Through the Ages,* followed by a phone number. I returned to my car and fetched a pen.

The ElderHeart offices were located in a two-story office building along the hellish York Road strip mall north of the Padonia

Road exit off of I-83, just past the fairgrounds. Despite my best piloting, I overshot and turned into a muffler place. Had I undershot I could have ogled wedding gowns, ordered a pizza, baked an hour inside a tanning booth or gotten my taxes taken care of.

The ElderHeart offices were on the second floor, around in back, facing away from York Road. The reception area was carpeted in soft gray. On the walls were a set of blowups of senior citizens playing softball, enjoying picnics on the beach, dancing cheek to cheek, blowing out birthday candles on a cake. There was even one photo of a gray-haired fellow standing in a parachute harness beaming into the camera, the deployed parachute a white blur behind him.

At a desk behind a sliding glass window sat a woman who reminded me a bit of Aunt Billie, if Billie had been somewhat heavier, wore half-glasses and could let down her defenses against the blue hair rinse. "Good afternoon. Welcome to ElderHeart. May I help you?"

"I'm here to see Scott Monroe," I said. "I called."

"Certainly. Your name?"

"Hitchcock Sewell."

"Well there's a name you don't hear every day."

I corrected her. "I hear it every day."

She gave me a frighteningly flirtatious look.

411

"Why don't you have a seat, Mr. Sewell? I'll let Scott know you're here."

I took a seat across from the photograph of the elderly man with the parachute. He reminded me of Philip Berrigan, who was a Catonsville priest who got himself in all sorts of hot water protesting the Vietnam War in the late sixties. A play was written about Berrigan and his brother Daniel, who was also a priest, and the shenanigans they and several of their cohorts pulled. The play is called *The Trial of the Catonsville Nine*. Catchy title, is it not? Catonsville is located just outside of Baltimore; you get productions of the play mounted in town all the time. The Gypsies mounted one a number of years ago and I played Philip Berrigan, which is how I knew what he looked like. He wasn't an elderly man at the time of his war protests, but he lived into his late sixties and my research for the part brought his picture my way. May I say I was a big hit in the role of Philip Berrigan? Although you wouldn't know it from the review we received in the *Sun*. The review included a photograph of me as Philip Berrigan, my lower lip jutting and my fist raised in anger. *He doth protest too much* read the caption. Good for an easy laugh, sure, but completely dismissive of the nuanced pathos that I wove into my portrayal of the radical priest. I was cited in the review, negatively, for my volume as well as for a particular set of physical choices I had made that the critic chose to regard as "petulant." They weren't petulant, they were impassioned. I specifically worked against petulance, I really did. The reviewer didn't care for the play itself. I think that was part of the problem. Hating the whole, he picked apart the pieces. Churlish. I think anyone who read the review several times could see how churlish it actually was. I could see it. Just look at that caption. *He doth protest too much.* It's so ridiculous.

I picked up a magazine from the table next to me. John Raitt was on the cover, with his arm around his daughter, Bonnie. I leafed through the magazine, wondering how hard Billie would hit me if I told her I'd signed her up for a gift subscription. I glanced at the article on the Raitts. John Raitt was quoted as saying about his daughter, "I don't know how she does it," right behind a quote from Bonnie wondering the same thing about her dad. Maybe the two ought to sit down together over a nice supper and explain to each other how they both do it.

I was debating the merits of dipping into an article called "Sex in the Seventies" when I was rescued by Scott Monroe.

"Mr. Sewell." I rose to greet him, dropping the magazine back onto the table. Monroe pumped my arm. "Sorry to keep you waiting."

"That's okay." I indicated the magazine. "I was just catching up on those pesky Raitts. I appreciate your taking the time to see me."

"Not a problem. You found me with a small window. Why don't you come into my office."

I followed him through a door and past the receptionist's desk. She gave me a pert smile over the top of her half glasses.

Monroe's office was a tad larger than mine. Not that size matters. He had more books on his shelves, more certificates on his walls and a squishy carpet underfoot. The furniture was Danish modern, tasteful teaks, a pair of matching chairs, a fuss-free couch and a slender egg-shaped desk, impressively unclut-tered. A pair of sleek file cabinets stood like sentries on either side of the desk. I can't say what exactly I had expected, but I suppose something a bit more bland and Spartan would have seemed more appropriate.

Monroe directed me to one of the chairs as he settled in behind his desk. He offered a big loud clap of his hands as he came for-ward and rested his arms on the table. "So. How can I help you? I hope you're not here to sell me a casket."

"Not today. What I'd like is your opinion of Briarcliff Manor. Your professional opinion."

"Briarcliff Manor." He brought his fingers together in a ball and took a moment to mull over the question. "Briarcliff is a highly regarded institution. It's a good facility overall. I'd say they run a fairly tight ship there. Not without a little leak here or there. Nobody's perfect of course. And the institutional care of the elderly, I think it goes without saying, presents its share of challenges. It's demanding work. There is room for improvement, sure. There is always room for improvement. Nobody's perfect. But I'd say I run across far fewer problems at Briarcliff than in many of the other facilities I monitor. Marilyn Tuck does a fine job."

"I see."

"Does this concern Anna Papadaki? I'm just curious. I am aware that her son is a neighbor of yours. Marilyn had a discussion with me concerning that entire situation. I should say, I had a discussion with her. You can believe she's looking into it. You can't have residents just wandering off like that."

"It's not about Mrs. Papadaki specifically," I said. "Although I suppose her being allowed to wander off the way she did does speak to the situation."

Monroe cocked his head. "The situation?"

"What do you know about a Claudia Greenwood?" I asked.

Monroe unballed his hands and sat back in his chair. "I'm sorry, I haven't asked you if you'd like anything to drink. Would you care for some coffee? Tea?"

"I'm fine, thanks."

"If you don't mind." He picked up the phone and pushed a button. "Sarah? Could you bring me a cup of tea . . . No, nothing for Mr. Sewell. Thank you, dear." He set the receiver back down and drummed his fingers against it. "Claudia Greenwood. Yes, I know what you're referring to. That was in the spring of this year. A misunderstanding between Briarcliff and Mrs. Greenwood's family."

"A misunderstanding."

"Yes."

"Her son accused Briarcliff of interfering with his mother's finances."

"That's correct."

"Was ElderHeart by any chance involved with that?"

Monroe frowned. "Involved? What do you mean?"

"I mean as an advocate. I was just wondering if this is the sort of situation where your organization might have gotten involved. What you told me the other day when we met, that ElderHeart exists to protect the elderly from abuse and from being taken advantage of. I got the sense that Claudia Greenwood was caught in something of a tug-of-war."

"As I understood the situation, Mrs. Greenwood was not being taken advantage of. There was a misunderstanding. If I recall, it ended up having been much ado about nothing."

"So you didn't get involved in the dispute?"

"We didn't."

The door to the office opened and Monroe's tea was brought in. I took a cheeky smile before the door closed.

"Your receptionist is flirting with me," I said.

Monroe laughed. "I'll sneak you out the back door when we're through if you'd like."

"No need. I can handle the likes of her."

Monroe took up his tea and cupped it in both hands. "So may I ask why you're interested in Briarcliff? Or in the Greenwood situation? Are you considering Briarcliff for someone you know?"

"It's not that. I'm just getting the impression that something is seriously wrong out there."

"I don't understand."

"Marilyn Tuck."

"Marilyn? What about her?"

"I think she intervened in the case of Peggy McNamara. Mrs. McNamara died two days ago. You're aware of that, aren't you?"

He ignored the question. "What do you mean, intervened?"

"I can't prove any of this of course, but it seems to me that Mrs. McNamara suffered an awfully swift decline. From the time I first saw her last Sunday to the night before she died, it was quite a skid."

"I can't disagree with you. But I have to say, it's not uncommon. This is a nursing home, after all. It shouldn't really surprise you. Decline is inevitable."

"I know that. But Mrs. McNamara was complaining about her treatment. She questioned some of the medications she was being given."

"With all due respect to Peggy McNamara, she was not a doctor."

"Of course not."

"What precisely does any of this have to do with Marilyn?"

"Maybe it will surprise you though to hear that the night before Mrs. McNamara died, Marilyn Tuck personally requested a Princeton temp named Teresa to stay on for an extra shift, to look after Mrs. McNamara."

Monroe set his cup back on the desk, unsipped. "I don't understand."

"Marilyn Tuck told Teresa that one of the nurse's aides who was supposed to work that night, a girl named Louise, was sick and not able to come in to work. Marilyn asked Teresa to stay on to cover for her."

"That's not as unusual as maybe it sounds. Staffing is always an issue. Trust me."

"I'm sure it is. But Teresa is about as attentive as a dust mote. She's horrible. Marilyn Tuck had to know that. The girl just plugs into her Walkman and drifts away. Phyllis Fitch told me that she explicitly asked Princeton not to send Teresa to Briarcliff again, but that they sent her anyway. It wasn't until after Phyllis Fitch was off duty that Teresa was asked to stay on. I had lunch with Teresa just an hour ago. She told me that Marilyn Tuck came to her in the parking lot and offered to pay her in cash to work the night shift. She said they were in a bind because of Louise's getting sick. She told her that if they bypassed Princeton they could keep it all off the books, make it all very simple and straightforward."

Monroe frowned. "That's not good."

"No, I didn't think so either. She told Teresa that because Princeton was out of the loop she could even offer to pay her a little extra beyond the time and a half overtime pay. Something to do with the fee that Briarcliff has to pay the temp agency. I don't really know how it all works. I don't really think Teresa knows either. All she knew was that Marilyn Tuck was waving a handful of cash in front of her face to stay on overnight and be responsible for Mrs. McNamara."

"I see your concern. This was not terribly professional behavior."

"Anything but. And another thing. Louise. If Louise was too ill to work her shift, she had an awfully swift recovery. She was there the next afternoon when I came in to pick up Mrs. McNamara's body. I spoke with Phyllis Fitch on the phone later on that day and she insisted that Louise had worked the overnight shift and that Teresa hadn't."

"So someone is lying."

"And I don't see what Teresa stands to gain by lying."

Monroe made a temple of his fingers and brought it to his lips. "It's a peculiar scenario you're giving me, I admit."

"Mrs. McNamara died some time around three in the morning under the care of a known incompetent that Marilyn Tuck arranged for. She paid the woman in cash, then hustled her off first thing in the morning. You'd better bet it's a peculiar scenario."

Monroe lowered his hands. "But you're not suggesting Marilyn purposefully attempted to harm Peggy McNamara. I'm sorry, I can't accept that. Why in the world would she do something like that? And how?"

"Two good questions. I was hoping maybe you could help me with the first one. I'm thinking about this Greenwood situation back in the spring. Is there a chance that Marilyn Tuck really was somehow finagling with Mrs. McNamara's finances?"

"How do you mean?"

"I don't know. I'm just trying to think of why she might want Mrs. McNamara dead. I'm just trying to make some sense out of this."

"Don't you think you're jumping to some pretty rash conclusions?"

"Unfortunately, it's going to be hard to determine how she might have done it. Mrs. McNamara was cremated as soon as legally possible. I'm afraid I helped with that one. Supposedly there was a written request from Mrs. McNamara to the point that she wanted to be cremated and have her ashes scattered over her husband's grave. Her sister in Cumberland presented it to a local mortuary. They prepared the cremation request form and sent it to us. Maybe Marilyn Tuck had something to do with that as well. I should call the mortician in Cumberland."

"If you don't mind my saying, this is all sounding a little farfetched. Why in the world would Marilyn go to all these lengths? It just doesn't make any sense."

"I don't have that answer, but it's usually one of the big three. Money, sex or power." I tapped my finger against the tip of my nose. "Smells like money."

"I don't like this." Monroe swiveled his chair and pulled open one of the file drawers and ran his finger along a line of folders. He pulled one out and dropped it onto his desk. "I'm going to look into this. I'm not going to be an apologist for Briarcliff, but I have to imagine there is a logical explanation."

"People take all sorts of advantage of the elderly," I said. "You know that more than I do."

421

"I certainly do. And it sickens me. That's why I'm in this business." He stood up and reached his hand across the desk. "Thank you, Mr. Sewell. You can be certain I'll look into this. I'd like to keep you posted. What's the best way to get hold of you?"

I pulled a card from my wallet and handed it to him.

"How about a home phone?" Monroe asked. "Or is that intrusive?"

"Not at all." I gave him the number. He jotted it down and put the card in his pocket."

"We'll get to the bottom of this."

Chapter Thirty-one

I headed back into the city under a cloud. It was a low-hanging cloud. Very low-hanging — inches below the roof of my car, inches above my head. I flipped around in the low end of the radio dial and came up with a selection by Mahler. The cloud darkened, as clouds generally will when fed with the German composers. Kettledrums exploded against an angry and urgent brass section. Equally urgent strings shrieked under a swirl of frenetic slashing. Windows rolled up, I took the volume up just shy of distortion, pressed down on the gas and for the next ten minutes was a white-knuckling menace to society. Not a few drivers threw their horns into the cacophony, and rightfully so. Why no police siren joined in with the mix as I careened south on the Jones Falls was a simple matter of luck, fluke or miracle, whichever faith suits you.

As I passed by Television Hill, where my parents used to work, I finally let off on the gas and began making my way back into civilized society. I allowed my grip on the wheel to loosen; by the time I zipped by the old London Fog factory, cars were passing *me*.

The Mahler was over and I lowered the volume on a piano piece I couldn't identify. More cars moved by me. I crested the long curve just before the Druid Hill cloverleaf and another car honked at me, though now because I was puttering along at a granny-on-Sunday pace. I pulled onto the shoulder and drifted to a stop. I sat motionless for nearly a minute, then finally lifted my hands from the steering wheel and turned the cupped palms toward me.

There. Right there between those two hands. That's where I wanted Marilyn Tuck's neck.

I'm not proud of it. But that was the thought.

Ten minutes later my wannabe homicidal paws were being gently squeezed by Constance Bell as she greeted me at her office door. Constance kisses European style and soaked me up pretty good on both cheeks. A striking black woman with several miles of hair cleverly arranged on a single head, Constance was made partner several years ago, her name tacked to the end of the long list of names of the other partners. Constance has been included in *Baltimore Magazine*'s Top Eligible Singles for five issues running. She has her page from each issue framed on her office wall.

"It was sort of fun the first couple of years," Constance said as I stepped over to have a look. "Now I'm starting to feel like one of Baltimore's top ten losers."

"You could snap your fingers and get a dozen proposals just like that," I said. "Isn't that right?"

"Trust me, when these issues come out, the roses come in. Total strangers. You wouldn't believe what some of the cards say. I've told the magazine, leave me out this year. I can find all the wrong men I need without their help, thank you."

We settled in and Constance asked after Billie and Julia. I told her they were both still enjoying their time on the planet.

"That crazy girl settled down yet?"

"You mean Billie?"

"You know who I mean. Miss Fire Pants."

"The day Julia Finney settles down is the day the earth drops off its axis and rolls into a corner."

"Every time I run into that girl she's got the damn catbird smile on her face," Constance said.

"Count on it. A mouthful of feathers."

Constance flipped through some papers in a wire mesh basket on her desk. She found what she was looking for, several pages held together with a butterfly clip.

"I made some calls. I've got the information you were looking for. Except I don't think it's the information you were looking for. I think you're going to be disappointed."

"Claudia Greenwood's will?"

"Her money didn't go to her son," Constance said.

"It didn't?"

"Uh-uh. The woman had a soft spot for animals."

"Ross Greenwood is an animal."

"The soft and furry kind. ASPCA. PETA. The Humane Society. She left it all to animal rights groups. There's some to the Guide Dogs for the Blind. That's about as close to a human being as it gets."

"Nothing for Ross?"

"Not a penny. You said something on the phone to me about those two being estranged. You don't get much more estranged than this."

She removed the butterfly clip, setting it on the edge of the desk, and handed me the pages.

I skimmed through them and then set them back on the desk. "I guess it was a long shot," I said. "It felt right, though."

"Why don't you explain to me what you were expecting?"

"Money to Ross." I explained the situation. Or at least what I thought had been the situation. Constance nodded her head several times as I laid it out for her. "So then Ross Greenwood gets wind of Marilyn Tuck's 'helping out' with his mother's finances and he makes a stink. And suddenly the stink goes away. A few months later Mrs. Greenwood dies, and the next thing you know, Ross Greenwood is quitting his job at Campbell's quarry and buying all sorts of toys for himself and his wife. He's behaving like a man who has just got a windfall. I just figured it had to be the will."

"But you said he and his mother were practically strangers."

"Exactly. So how does Ross end up in the will? My guess was that he got to Marilyn Tuck. If Marilyn is pulling the strings on Claudia Greenwood's finances . . . well, it doesn't matter. It didn't happen."

"It's not so easy to falsify a will," Constance said. "Though it's not impossible, of course."

Constance's phone rang. She picked it up and spoke for less than a minute. Pure legalese. Not a single solitary word of what she was saying made any sense to me whatsoever. She hung up. "Sorry. Where were we?"

"Ross. I don't get it. Ross Greenwood didn't win the lottery and he wasn't in his mother's will, but somehow he came up with a big raft of cash. And it seems to be soon after his mother died."

"Life insurance."

"Life insurance. You mean his mother's life insurance?"

"Uh-huh."

"With Ross as the beneficiary? Somehow I doubt that."

"Why not? If this Tuck woman had access to Claudia Greenwood's accounts, it would be a lot easier for her to manipulate life insurance policies than to fool around with the woman's will. Plus it would be a nifty way for the nursing home to essentially pay Greenwood off. Think of it. It's almost what you had in mind. It's still buying his silence with his own mother's money. It's nothing out of their own pockets."

I thought about it. It made sense.

"I'm assuming Claudia Greenwood was frail," Constance said.

"That's what I gather."

"So then it's simply a matter of being patient and waiting for her to die. A huge scam like this took place a few years ago. I think it was out in Chicago. It was on a much larger scale."

"How do you mean?"

"It wasn't a nursing home. It was one of those retirement communities. You know the type I mean? Where everything is provided? Shopping, recreation, housing, all under one roof, so to speak. Very upscale. This was a very elaborate scam. In this case the managers of the community were siphoning off funds from the monthly payments of some of their residents and the money was going into payments on life insurance policies that the residents had no idea they even had. It was a huge scandal. I'm surprised you didn't hear about it. It included mail fraud, because the managers were systematically extracting any of the statements that were supposed to go to the people they were ripping off. They had all the access they needed to information about these people. Social security numbers, all of it. In this case, the beneficiaries of the policies were friends and relatives of the people running the scam. If I remember correctly they chose judiciously. That is, they ran this number on the most infirm of the residents. The ones most likely to die soonest. It went on for years before they got caught. It's frightfully simple if you think about it."

I picked up the copy of the will and stared at it. But my gaze was going right through the paper.

"A scam like that would be even simpler in a nursing home," I said.

"How so?"

"The population. The sick and dying. You're going to get a quicker turnaround."

Constance agreed. "You're right. It's like having a whole bunch of cash cows at your fingertips and simply having to wait until one of them falls off the cliff."

My eyes rested on the butterfly clip on the desk. I reached out and nudged it to the edge of the desk. "Or maybe you don't have to wait."

"What do you mean?"

I flicked the clip off the desk. It landed next to my shoe. "You don't wait," I said again. "You give a little nudge."

Constance's eyes narrowed. "Hitchcock. Is *that* what you think happened to Claudia Greenwood?"

I rolled the papers in my hand into a cylinder and rapped them against the side of the desk.

"Claudia Greenwood? Sure." I stood up. "For starters."

I had it. At least I was fairly certain I did. The reason why Marilyn Tuck could want to murder Mrs. McNamara. I tried to sort out the details as I drove back to the funeral home. I played around with possible scenarios and with timelines. Of course there were numerous gaps of information that I couldn't readily fill in, but regardless, the more I ran through the possibilities, the simpler and more logical it all became. My only real question was, were there more? Were Claudia Greenwood and Mrs. McNamara the only victims to the scheme?

A new body had come in while I was out, and Billie was down in the basement in her rubber smock and gloves, singing "Oklahoma" under her breath as she went about the business of prepping the corpse.

"We're running low on formaldehyde, dear," she said to me. "Would you be sure to put that on the list?"

Billie sprayed the body with a disinfectant, then proceeded to sponge it down. I scrubbed it down and helped her massage the arms and legs. Then Billie stuffed cotton wads up the cadaver's nose.

"I need to talk to you about something," I said to her. "I want to run something by you."

"Certainly, dear." Billie made a small incision on the superior border of the sterno-clavicular notch — she's so damn good at this. Then with a pair of what we call aneurysm hooks, she exposed the cadaver's carotid artery and placed a pair of ligatures around the artery with forceps. A thing of beauty.

"It concerns Mrs. McNamara," I said, and as Billie continued with her embalming, I gave her the rough outline of my theory. She interrupted me once to swear gently at our Porta-Boy pump — neither of us much cared for the grinding sound we had recently been noticing — but otherwise listened in near silence, save the low humming of her Rodgers and Hart.

As the outline of my theory took shape, Billie paused in her work, pulling off her rubber gloves. "I'm afraid there might be something to what you're saying, Hitchcock," she said.

"Sounds sound, does it?"

"No, it's not only that. I took a phone call about an hour before you came in. It was a Mrs. Matthews."

"Dorie Matthews?"

"That's right Mrs. Matthews said she has been out of town for several days. She had a message from Briarcliff Manor to give us a call concerning Mrs. McNamara. Apparently it was left with her the morning Mrs. Mc-Namara passed away."

"I remember Phyllis Fitch mentioning that she had called her."

"Mrs. Matthews sounded perturbed over the disquisition of Mrs. McNamara's ashes. I told her you would give her a call. I left the number on your desk. Now help me get our guest here on his side, will you?"

I did, then I ran upstairs to my office. The phone picked up after three rings. A woman answered. "Hello?"

"Is this Dorie Matthews?" I asked.

"Yes, it is."

"This is Hitchcock Sewell. You called here?"

"Yes. I did. What is this I hear from your aunt that Margaret McNamara's remains have been sent to Cumberland? On whose authority?"

"It was my understanding that this was Mrs. McNamara's wish."

"It was not her wish at all. May I ask where it was you got that idea?"

"We were contacted by a Spencer's Funeral Home in Cumberland. They'd been in touch with Letitia Bodine. That's Mrs. McNamara's sister."

"Those were not her wishes," the woman said. "I have a document right here in front of me stating Margaret McNamara's wishes."

"What were they?"

"It's . . . it's a private matter. I'm not at liberty to say exactly."

"It's my understanding that Letitia Bodine was in possession of Mrs. McNamara's wishes."

"I'm looking at the document as we speak," she said.

"What was your connection with Mrs. McNamara? If I might ask."

"I am trustee to an account of hers at First National Bank of Maryland. Margaret's day-to-day expenses as well as expenses covering her stay at Briarcliff Manor came through this account."

"So you're a friend? A financial adviser?"

There was a pause on the other end. "It's complicated."

"I'm a decently intelligent man, Mrs. Matthews. Why don't you try to explain it to me."

"I'm not sure that I care for your tone."

"I apologize for my tone." I switched the phone to the other ear. "Mrs. Matthews, something is not right here. I've got some questions about Mrs. McNamara. Maybe you can help me out with them. You're in Baltimore?"

"I am."

"Is there any chance we could meet?"

"Well . . . yes, I suppose so."

"Is there any chance we could meet soon? Now, for instance?"

She hemmed and hawed a little, but apparently she couldn't find a good argument. We agreed to meet at Marconi's. The woman said that she normally dines on her own at Marconi's on Fridays . . . "but I'm certain they can locate an extra chair."

We agreed to meet in an hour and a half.

"I'll be seated at the table alongside the stairs."

I popped back downstairs to see if Billie was all squared away. She was up to her wrists in shampoo, cradling the corpse's head in the basin.

"The clippers are on the counter, dear. Could you do the nails for me?"

Before I left for Marconi's I noticed several sheets of paper hanging from the fax machine. They were from Jeff Falkenstein at the Foundation Center. I folded them up and stuck them in my pocket as I headed out the door.

Marconi's restaurant is located on the ground floor of a townhouse on Mulberry

Street. Everybody raves about their sweetbreads, though personally, I've never been terribly keen on the thymus gland of baby lambs; I can give no report. I told the hostess that I was here to meet Mrs. Matthews. I was escorted to the table alongside the stairs. A woman was already seated there, her back to us as we approached. I thanked the hostess and stepped over to the table.

"Mrs. Matthews?"

The woman looked up at me. Her face held a glassy translucence. Her eyes were pale and they considered me with a cold sadness. "I know you," she said.

On her head was a greenish silk scarf, wrapped turbanlike. She lifted a hand reflexively, giving the turban a poke and a little tug. Her pale eyes followed me as I slid into the chair opposite her.

"Yes," I said. "I know you too."

Chapter Thirty-two

Teddy loves Maggie.

Dorie Matthews had the photographs in her possession. It was a last-minute impulse, she told me, to bring them with her to Marconi's. They were old black-and-white photographs, the small, square type with a rippled white border. In the one, the boy is proudly displaying the bowie knife he has apparently just used to carve the words into the tree. It's an open face, somewhat gawky, under a shock of curly blond hair. He is standing to the right of the freshly carved inscription. Ear-to-ear grin. A beaming fifteen-year-old in love.

In the other photograph is the girl. She is shorter than the boy by a head. She is standing to the left of the inscription. The border on the left-hand side of the photograph has been sliced off in a clean line. The intention is clearly that the one photograph overlap the other, creating a single picture of the two kids posing with their carved declaration of love. In young love especially, three's a crowd. There would have been no one else present to take the single picture of the young lovers posing together. These are private matters.

436

The girl is a cute little pixie with a bow tie ribbon in her silky blond hair, a small pointed chin and a shy hesitant smile.

Teddy Weisheit loves Maggie Conkling.

Teddy and Maggie were sweethearts, the romance first becoming public some time during Teddy Weisheit's thirteenth year. Maggie was two years younger. She lived all of two blocks from the Weisheit residence, in a quiet neighborhood in the northern section of Cumberland, Maryland. I know the section. Modest two-story houses, decent-sized backyards nicely kept up. The romance grew all through junior high school and on into high school. Teddy and Maggie saw numerous firsts together; first kiss, first caress, first fight, first making up . . . Teddy rode Maggie on the handlebars of his Raleigh bicycle. Later in the family Chevy. Dorie Matthews encouraged me to apply a nostalgic patina to the story, for in the decades to follow this is exactly what Teddy Weisheit was to do. The lines between fact and memory and willful self-delusion are wobbly ones, I'd be the first to admit it. Mostly we exist somewhere in the mix. And as the years passed, Teddy Weisheit appeared to have pretty much wallowed in the mix. His great gamble was to come when he confronted his own memory, and with a willful self-delusion, determined that it *was* the truth.

As Dorie Matthews explained it to me, it went like this:

Teddy Weisheit left Cumberland. He graduated from high school and headed off to Boston, to MIT, to study architecture. Margaret Conkling still had two years of high school remaining. Whether or not Margaret was going to go on to college herself after graduation was uncertain at that point. Frankly, it didn't seem terribly important one way or the other. What was certain was that she and Teddy Weisheit would be reuniting and getting married and continuing with their life together. *Teddy loves Maggie.* As sure as taxes and death. This was the plan.

It didn't happen. The larger world's pull on Teddy Weisheit proved too strong. Gravity got him. So did an attractive Baltimore debutante named Evelyn Beale, who was in the Boston area attending Radcliffe. Literally, figuratively and all points in between, Teddy Weisheit did not go home again. Upon his graduation from MIT, James followed Evelyn Beale back to Baltimore, where they married and where Evelyn's family assisted Teddy in setting off on his career.

All this, Dorie Matthews told me over dinner. I had the baby lamb chops, which were pink and perfect. And served with a tureen of squash and something or other. I started with a vegetable soup, a little thin in the broth, but otherwise fine. Dorie Matthews had the vaunted Marconi's sweetbreads, and God bless her for it, I shouldn't

438

be so squeamish. She said they were delicious.

I wouldn't have been so rude as to ask, and she didn't immediately volunteer the information, but clearly she had undergone some sort of radiation treatment. Aside from the turban, I saw that her eyebrows had been drawn on by hand. She spoke in a low voice, forcing me to remain pitched slightly over my plate. She rarely looked up, but told her story to the glass salt and pepper shakers on the table between us. I mean this literally. At one point I picked up the pepper shaker to give it a few passes over my squash thingy and she fell silent, waiting until I had returned the shaker to the table before resuming with her story.

"He left Cumberland as Teddy and arrived in Baltimore as James. James Edward Weisheit. That was Evelyn's doing. A small thing, perhaps, but emblematic." She raised her pale eyes from the shakers. "Evelyn Weisheit is a very controlling person."

Margaret Conkling was gone. Cumberland was gone. James Weisheit launched into the successful career that Evelyn Weisheit had described for me during her visit to Sewell and Sons. He built his office buildings, his libraries, his impressive homes. He made his mark. Just past midway through his career he took on an assistant, an earnest and competent woman who had recently married. Dorie

Matthews. Within a year, tragedy struck. Dorie and her husband were hit by a drunken driver while out walking their dog. Dorie's husband died — as did the dog — and Dorie embarked on a painful year of rehabilitation and recovery from a broken back and a crushed hip.

"James either came to see me or he spoke to me on the phone every single day. Without fail. I had never known anyone to have such a large heart. He was astonishing."

Dorie recovered. She remained on with James Weisheit. She became his confidante.

"We were not lovers," she said softly. "That . . . didn't happen. But regardless, Evelyn grew to despise me. James and I were close, and that threatened her. That threatened her very much. I know for a fact that she tried to have James fire me more than once. She was always on the lookout for any excuse. They had . . . the two of them had a complicated relationship. I could never explain it to you. It was nowhere near what they projected to the rest of the world."

"I know," I said. "I've seen the letters."

"You've seen James's letters?"

"Polly Weisheit showed them to me."

"And you know who they were written to?"

"I do now," I said. "Margaret Conkling."

"That was her maiden name, of course."

"Of course," I said. "I knew her only by

her married name. And the nickname version of Margaret."

"Peggy."

"Yes. Peggy McNamara."

Dorie Matthews called the waiter over and asked if our plates could be cleared. "Would you care for a drink?" she asked me. "I allow myself one." She ordered an old-fashioned. I beamed at her across the table.

"You're a girl after my own heart." I turned to the waiter. "Make that two."

"I'm not well," Dorie said to me as we waited for our drinks. "I've got Hodgkin's. I was diagnosed a year ago."

"I'm sorry."

"I'm under good care. James saw that all of my medical expenses and needs were to be taken care of."

Our drinks arrived a minute later.

"I love this place," Dorie said, looking around the room. "It never changes. There aren't too many things you can say that about anymore." She took a sip of her drink and closed her eyes briefly to savor the taste.

"Margaret Conkling married," she continued. "She went on with her life. Her husband owned a diner in town."

"I know," I said, and I explained how it was I knew Mrs. McNamara.

"Well, when her husband died — this would have been maybe fifteen years ago — I can't even recall how it was that James came to hear about it, but he did. He had not been in contact with Margaret for close to forty years. It still astonishes me. He sent her a card. A sympathy card. He sent it to her from the office, not from his home. I think that fact held more significance than even he realized at the time."

"She wrote back," I said.

"Yes. She wrote back. 'Thank you for your kind note.' James says it was nothing more than that. He wrote her again."

"Again from work."

"Precisely. And . . . it started. Like that. They struck up a correspondence. As simple as that. I was right there. I sorted the mail each morning. I watched her letters come in. I watched the frequency build and build. It was a peculiar time for James. I suppose you could say it was his midlife crisis, though somehow to me that demeans it all. James's parents were both dead and his brother had moved to Baltimore years ago. James had no connection with Cumberland anymore. If I recall, it was a little over a year after this correspondence struck up that James took his first trip back to Cumberland. It was just a day trip, out and back. All he said to me was that if Evelyn called, I was to tell her that he was involved all day in meetings. He went to Cumberland and he came back a changed man. James could always be extremely charming and extremely confident. Now he seemed positively to glow. At times he was almost giddy. The letters kept going back and forth. Of course there was the telephone, but James confided in me later that there was something special he got out of writing to Margaret and in receiving her letters. It was strictly for the romanticism of it all. Teddy loves Maggie."

"And this went on for years?"

"Years, yes. To be precise, twelve. He fell in love. Or he fell back in love. And the same with her. James's visits to Cumberland became more and more frequent, and then finally one day he called me into his office and told me to shut the door. He was exploding, he had to tell someone. He told me he was bringing Margaret to Baltimore. He had purchased a small cottage in Stevenson and Margaret was going to move there. He was beside himself. "Here, Dorie. She's going to be right *here*, where I can see her whenever I want!"

"And this whole time, Evelyn was clueless?"

"Evelyn was clueless. Like I said, she had her suspicions about James and me. Of course a lot of wives go that route, don't they? And James didn't exactly do his utmost to dissuade her from thinking it. I think he saw Evelyn's suspicions of me as a convenient distraction from what he was really up to. In a way, it played nicely into his hand."

"So he moved Peggy to Baltimore."

"He did."

"Why didn't he leave his wife?"

"He didn't, that's all I can tell you. He told me that he would never divorce Evelyn. Don't ask me to explain it. Was it guilt? A sense of obligation? Her family had helped him get started in his career. I really don't know what it was, but he wasn't going to do it. Instead, he tried to have his cake and eat it too."

"It sounds to me like he succeeded."

"For many years, he did. James was extremely fortunate, I suppose. Frankly, I think he became intoxicated with the whole affair. He even continued writing Margaret letters after she had moved here. It was either true love or a deep fantasy of love. But Margaret surprised him. I think James had come to take for granted that she was willing to put up with their arrangement indefinitely. She wasn't. Think of it. Sitting out there in her cottage in Stevenson waiting for James to visit. She didn't uproot herself from her home only to sit patiently in the shadows. Not forever, anyway. But she put up with it for nearly three years. Ultimately, she wanted James to make his choice. She certainly didn't rush him, but in the end she needed to know that he was going to acknowledge her to the world and allow the two of them to live openly. This was last fall. He wouldn't do it. He just couldn't. She sent back the letters he had written to her over all those years. She had kept them all. She told him it was time to end the fantasy, which I suppose was exactly what it had been for James. A fantasy come true. Teddy loves Maggie, carved onto a tree. James suffered a horrible heart attack not a month after this. It very nearly killed him. He was scared. That's when he opened up a bank account for Margaret and named me as trustee. He was desperate to see that Margaret be taken care of if anything were to happen to him."

"Which it did."

She nodded and took a sip of her drink. "James saw her again. Christmas of last year. He made some sort of excuse late in the day and slipped away and went out to Stevenson to see her. I don't know what they said to each other. Margaret certainly never told me."

"Nor did James?"

"James died." She said it simply and seemingly without emotion. But I was coming to see that this was one of her talents. "He suffered another heart attack right there in Stevenson. Margaret called the ambulance and James was taken to the Valley Medical Center. She went with him and she called Evelyn from the hospital and told her that she needed to get out there right away. She did not identify herself. And she was gone by the time Evelyn arrived. James never regained consciousness. I received a call from Evelyn that night. She accused *me* of being the woman who had phoned her. That was ridiculous, of course. Evelyn would know my voice over the phone. When I finally convinced her of that, she demanded to know who 'that woman' was. I told her I didn't know, but she knew I was lying. She gave me twenty-four hours to remove any of my personal belongings from the office and she declared that she wanted me to never have any business whatsoever with any members of the family again. Essentially, I was exiled. I worked for her husband for nearly fifteen years. I had been diagnosed with Hodgkin's at this point. None of it mattered to Evelyn. That's who she is. She is an absolute harridan."

"The letters," I said.

Dorie shook her head slowly. "It never occurred to me until it was too late. I should have removed them from James's office, but I just didn't think of it."

"She found them."

"I disobeyed Evelyn's directive about not remaining in contact with the family. Who does she think she is that she can tell me what to do and who I can talk to? I heard through Jake that the letters had been discovered when James's office was being cleaned out. Of course I was not surprised to hear of

Evelyn's fury. The truth is, I was overjoyed to hear of it."

"Why didn't she destroy them?"

Jake took them. They were a side of his father he had never known. He told me that he needed to spend time rethinking what his father was all about."

"And you never revealed Mrs. McNamara's identity to anyone?"

"No."

"Not to Jake?"

"He asked, of course. But he respected my refusal to betray his father's confidence. If Margaret Conkling wanted to reveal herself to Jake, that would be her business. I didn't feel it was my place to interfere. Jake told me that Evelyn had become an unholy terror about the whole thing. She had hired a private investigator to determine who the woman was. I think Jake was just as glad not to have to keep the secret from her himself."

"Don't know, can't tell," I said.

"Exactly."

We fell silent. Dorie Matthews sat ramrod straight, but not rigid. She looked as if she might have once been a dancer. Maybe yoga. There was an elegant stillness about her, and when she did move — when, for example, she picked up her glass and sipped her drink — the movement was fluid, a minimum displacement of the surrounding molecules.

I attempted to emulate her movements,

reaching forward and gliding the pepper shaker over to my right, next to my spoon. Then I slid the salt shaker over to my left, directly opposite.

"Jake," I said, tapping the salt shaker lightly with my finger.

She saw what I was about. She tilted her chin in the direction of the other shaker. "Margaret McNamara."

"Yes. Both dead. About a week apart."

"But Margaret's death was natural, wasn't it?"

I told her I didn't think so and briefly ran through my suspicions. As I concluded, Dorie's eyes closed. Her voice was barely above a whisper.

"Dear God."

"What?"

"Evelyn." She opened her eyes. "The private investigator. Evelyn's private investigator. He must have found her."

"At Briarcliff."

"Yes. In the nursing home."

"Minding her own business," I said.

Dorie nodded. "She was a sitting duck."

Chapter Thirty-three

It was Mrs. McNamara's wish that at the time of her death she be cremated and that her ashes be scattered over the grave of James Weisheit. No memorial service. No public ceremony. Certainly no member of the Weisheit family was to be informed, nor their permission requested. Dorie Matthews was in possession of the document. It had been her intention to be the one to carry out Mrs. McNamara's final wish.

Dorie Mathews excused herself to go use the restroom. I stood up as she left the table.

"Manners," she said and she drifted past me.

I sat back down. The waiter came by and asked me if we would care for anything else. I asked for the check. He went off and I found myself staring at the salt and pepper shakers that I had set up opposite each other. Frankly, I didn't know what to make of them. Could Evelyn Weisheit really be so vindictive as to want to see her late husband's lover murdered? Dorie Matthews felt that there was no question. Absolutely. But then, how much trust should I be putting in Dorie

Matthews's version of events? It was obvious to me that she had been in love with James Weisheit. She and Evelyn had been crossing swords over James for years and years. Couldn't Evelyn Weisheit be sitting at this table making many of the same arguments for Dorie Matthews's simmering hatred of Peggy McNamara?

And what of Jake? What if I was as wrong about his murder as I might possibly be about Mrs. McNamara's? I picked up my fork and pinged it a few times against the salt shaker.

Toby Schultz? Polly? I set the fork down and tilted the shaker with my finger, closer and closer to the point of tipping. Closer . . .

Evelyn?

"Here you are, sir. Thank you very much."

The waiter left the check on the edge of the table. I released the salt shaker, letting it tip over. I reached into my jacket pocket for my wallet and my fingers found the rolled-up sheets of Jeff Falkenstein's fax. I took the papers out and looked them over. Jeff had sent me, as promised, the list of grants paid out by the James E. Weisheit Foundation over the past year and a half. Most of the awards were for amounts ranging from five hundred to five thousand dollars, with a few exceptions. The Baltimore Symphony received a ten-thousand-dollar grant, as did the Literacy Council. I didn't really know what I was looking for. If Toby Schultz had ripped off the foundation in some fashion, I realized I wasn't really likely to pick up much of a suggestion from these lists of organizations receiving grant money. Barring an entry reading "Toby Schultz Money Siphoning, Inc.," the lists wouldn't do me much good.

I pulled some bills from my wallet and set them on the check. I was still scanning the grants list as Dorie Matthews returned to the table. I stood again. Another of the waiters was passing behind me and we bumped slightly. Several of the papers in my hands fell to the floor. As I bent to fetch them, my eye snagged on a figure. It was a large figure. Much larger than the other figures I'd been seeing. Hundreds of thousands of dollars higher. The entry was dated for earlier in the spring. I looked to see what organization had received such a sizable sum. I guess my reaction showed on my face.

"What is it?" Dorie asked.

"I'm not sure."

She stepped to my side and looked at the paper in my hand. I tapped my finger against the entry. She started. "Gracious."

"It's too much money," I said. I rolled the papers back up and rapped them against my palm. "It's too much," I said again, sticking the papers into my pocket. "And I don't like it."

On the sidewalk in front of Marconi's I asked Dorie for directions to Evelyn Weisheit's house.

"I can show you," she said. I put up an argument and so did she. "Evelyn can't hurt me. She's a bully, but she doesn't hold any power over me. She holds power only if I allow her to, and I don't." She laced her arms and fixed me with a look. "I'm going with you," she said simply. "That's all there is to it."

I followed Dorie's directions north on the expressway to the point where it merges with Falls Road and then a half mile further on, took a left and headed up into what is known as Greenspring Valley. A few sub-developments had managed to find their way into the valley, but for the most part the area still consisted of large rural estates, many of the houses set so far back they were not even visible from the main road. Evelyn Weisheit lived in one of these.

"Left here," Dorie said, and I turned the wheel, passing through a stone gate onto a tree-lined gravel driveway that curved gently to the right before dipping down a mild slope. The house rose into view as we started into the curve, a rambling stone mansion set in a copse of towering oak trees. Our approach was on the rear side of the house; the driveway opened to an elliptical parking area.

A black Lexus was parked in front of the garage, which was attached to the house, off to the left.

We parked the car and got out. A walkway of flat stones arched around the side of the house. Dorie tilted her chin at the stones. "The front door's that way."

We followed the stone path around the side of the house to the front, which looked out onto a vast, perfectly green yard, bordered some three or four hundred feet away by a low stone wall, beyond which nature had been allowed to remain wild. A generous porch fronted the house, looking out over the property. As we came up onto it I was reminded of the atrium at Briarcliff, fashioned out of a similar if smaller porch during the renovation of Mathers Tuck's home. The front door stood partway open.

I rapped my knuckles against the door. "Hello? Mrs. Weisheit?"

I took a step inside the house. As I did, I heard a popping sound from inside and a chip of wood flew off the door inches from my head and caught me on the cheek. I grabbed Dorie Matthews by the shoulders and jerked her off her feet, dropping to the floor as a second popping noise sounded. She landed partly on top of me.

I looked up as a figure darted from the room to my right into a shadowed hallway off toward the rear of the house. In front of me, a set of stairs ran up. I squirmed from under Dorie. "Get to the car!" I heard the tromping of footsteps somewhere in the house. I pointed to the stairs. "No. Go upstairs!"

She looked puzzled. Jumping to my feet, I grabbed hold of her by the hips. She lifted almost too easily. Her feet skittering on the wooden floor, I crab-walked her swiftly forward and landed her on the stairs.

"Go! They might go out a back door. Get upstairs! Hide!"

"But —"

"Go!"

She did. Half walking, half crawling she made her way up to the landing, turned and disappeared. I remained in a crouch and hurried into the room that the shooter had just vacated. It was a large open room with windows running all along the front and the far side, paralleling the porch. I was on a slate stone floor, poised on all fours behind a wide wooden chair. Poking my head around the side of the chair I saw a thin carpet in the middle of the floor, and on the carpet an overturned lamp. I scooted around to the side of the chair facing away from the hallway, should whoever it was with the gun decide to come back the same way they had just left. I peeked out from the side of the chair at the fallen lamp and saw something that I've seen often in my life. But rarely in this context.

Legs. Still as death.

I became aware of a pulsating sound and I dropped flat onto the floor, thinking as I did what a big easy target I was making of myself. I would like to have rolled myself up into the size of a ball bearing and pitched myself into a corner, but that's a skill I've not come even close to mastering. Maybe with practice. I heard another sound, this one from overhead. Dorie. At least . . . I hoped. A large old house like this, I suddenly realized that chances were pretty good there was more than the one set of stairs leading upstairs. My instinct had been to send Dorie upstairs as the safest possible option. Now I wasn't at all sure of the wisdom of that instinct. As I crawled back onto my knees I recognized the pulsating sound. It was the electronic bleating phones make when they have been left off the hook. On the far side of the room, on the other side of the carpet, was a white couch. I was a sitting duck — a crouching duck — where I was. The couch could give me some cover. Just as I got to my feet I again heard noises from overhead. I ran, crossing the room in five swift steps, and with what might be considered an unhealthy viewing of too damn many television and movie stuntmen, vaulted wildly over the couch, landing ungracefully on the floor behind it. During the brief sprint, I had seen whose body it was sprawled on the floor next to the overturned lamp, next to the telephone. I had even spotted the circle of blood just below the collarbone, below the necklace of large gray pearls.

It was the lady of the house, Evelyn Weisheit.

I waited a good minute, then came around the side of the couch and crawled over to the still body. Evelyn Weisheit's head was twisted at a violent angle. I put my fingers on her bloody neck. Nothing at first; then I seemed to detect a terrifically faint thrumming. I pressed and held, watching the blood beneath my fingers for any movement. It was there. A small pulsing; she was still alive. I released her neck and took hold of her left hand. Caressing the cold fingers, I bent down close to her ear. "Mrs. Weisheit. You're going to be fine. We'll get you all taken care of, okay? Just hang in there."

She didn't make a sound. Not a peep, not a gurgle. I reached for the telephone receiver. As I did, I became aware of a shadow passing on the floor in front of me and I turned just in time to see Martin Weisheit in midair. His arms were outstretched and he let out an ugly snarl. I tried to roll out of the way, but he came down hard on my shoulder and we skidded together against the couch.

"You bastard!"

The boy was on top of me, his thighs jamming into my ribs, pressing the air out my lungs. Fire ripped through my chest. I opened my mouth to cry out, but nothing sounded. I tried to twist my torso free, but Martin was too heavy. His legs had my arms pinned at my sides. His knees were pressing against my jaw. Martin shifted his weight and grabbed me by the neck, digging his fingers into my throat. He was wearing a tie and it danced across my face as he bore down on me.

"You prick! You son of a fucking bitch!"

I had no air whatsoever. My legs kicked, but I was unable to dislodge the large boy. Whiteness was creeping into my vision as Martin continued pressing down on my throat. A tremendous hissing sound was filling my head, along with the continued bleating of the telephone, much louder sounding now, almost mocking in its redundant urgency. There was another sound, and I realized it had come from me. A garbled gasp. The absolute end of any oxygen at my disposal. The boy was killing me. My vision was going splotchy.

A desperate fury surged through me and I tried to reach for Martin's face, but my arms were blocked off by the boy's legs. The knuckles of my right hand banged against something hard and round. I twisted my hand and was able to wrap my fingers around it. Kicking as hard as I could, I lurched my head forward and sank my teeth into Martin's left knee as hard as I possibly could. He cried out, shifting his leg to pull the knee clear from my chompers. It was what I needed. I managed to free my right arm and to bring it up in a wide swinging arc. The hard round thing turned out to be the telephone receiver. It came down hard on the side of Martin's head, just behind his ear. I heard a cracking sound. Whether it was the phone or Martin Weisheit's skull, I couldn't tell. It was an ugly sound. Martin's fingers loosened, and as he fell forward, I gave a mighty heave and was able to propel him off me. He landed on the floor next to his grandmother, lying on his side, his head nuzzled up against her hip.

I expected a rush of air to plunge into my lungs, but it didn't. Instead I gasped — a thin whimper — and watched as the ceiling above me rolled into blackness.

Chapter Thirty-four

One.

Two.

Five.

Four . . .

I became aware of a small pinpoint of red, expanding into a jagged sunburst. For a moment, there was a chorus of what sounded like laughing. Or Munchkins chattering. Or crickets. But it was only the buzzing in my ears. My eyes opened. I was breathing. I was gazing up toward a window, outside which a bare branch was dancing up, down, up, down, scraping against the glass. I had no idea how long I had been out. My ribs remained on fire. As I rolled slowly to my side, I heard a cry. From upstairs.

Dorie.

I scrambled to my feet and slipped on the edge of the rug as I ran from the room, tumbling forward, arms spinning like one of the original Keystone Kops. That's pretty much how I took the stairs as well, lurching forward with a reckless momentum. I reached the second floor literally on my hands and knees, where once again I skidded on a rug, this one a long runner that traveled the length of the hallway. I felt partway dead, which a minute or so ago had not been far from the truth. I looked up. Midway down the hallway stood Dorie Matthews. For someone with an arm around her neck and a pistol held to her head, she looked, I thought, outrageously composed. I started to get to my feet, but the pistol waved in my direction, then returned to Dorie's temple.

"Don't move. Stay right there. Stay down."

I did as I was told. I'm not even certain I could have stood. My legs were rubber. My throat was ravaged from Martin's choking. I wasn't sure that I would even be able to speak. I tried. It was raspy and it hurt like hell. I tried to swallow but couldn't.

"Nice to . . . see you again."

"Shut up." Scott Monroe's cheeks were puffed out. His face was beet red. There was no trace of the composure he had shown just several hours ago when I visited with him in his office. No well-oiled manners. No aplomb.

"You can't . . . just kill us," I said. "That's insane."

Monroe pulled Dorie tighter to him. "You see a goddamn choice?"

I nodded once. Deeply. "You put the gun down," I said. I was gaining a little strength in my voice. "Just put it down, Scott, and you cut your losses. That's your choice."

"Bullshit."

"Evelyn Weisheit is still alive. If we get her to a hospital in time . . . that's one less murder charge you're going to have to face."

Monroe barked a laugh. It was short and ugly. "I don't think so. I'm not going to jail. Not for anything. I'll be damned."

"But you are," I said. "You're going to jail for killing Peggy McNamara."

"Bullshit. I had nothing to do with that."

"I think you did."

"It was her." He waved the pistol in the direction of the stairs.

"I know. Evelyn Weisheit wanted Peggy McNamara dead. I know that. She tracked her down at Briarcliff after she discovered the box with her husband's letters. And sometime after that, ElderHeart received all that money from the Weisheit Foundation. Very big bucks, Scott. What exactly did it buy?"

I reached for my pocket. Monroe jerked his grip on Dorie. "Don't."

The calmness in Dorie Matthews's pale eyes was nearly as unnerving as Monroe and his pistol. My hand froze in midair.

"I've got a copy of the foundation's grant list right here in my pocket. Five hundred thousand dollars, they gave to you. That's not the kind of loot the foundation normally gives away. What did you do, come flying out here after I left your office? You let Evelyn know I was getting close to what really happened?"

"Just shut up!" Monroe jerked his arm even tighter around Dorie Matthews's throat.

"Think," I said. "You're not thinking. Let her go. You don't want to do this. We've got to get Mrs. Weisheit to the hospital. You don't want her to die."

"She deserves to die. She started this whole fucking mess. None of this should have happened."

"Why did you shoot her, Scott?" I shifted my weight slightly. I wanted to get myself ready to lunge forward if at all possible. "She's an old lady. I thought you were dedicated to looking after old ladies."

"Shut up."

"You didn't do such a good job of looking after Mrs. McNamara either, did you? Now, come on. Put the gun down. Are you really ready to start piling up the bodies in the living room?"

Monroe removed the muzzle of the pistol from Dorie Matthews's head. He aimed the gun at me. It was a little gun. A derringer-style pistol. Even so, I didn't much care for staring at its quivering muzzle.

"I'm not going to jail."

"You shoot me, that's exactly where you're going." The words echoed in my head as if they were being spoken in a small hollow room. These are not words a person wants to hear himself saying. I wanted to melt into the runner. Dorie Matthews looked at me with an expression of extraordinary sadness. Monroe straightened his arm.

"Don't," I croaked.

There was a sound from the far end of the hall. Monroe spun around just as Martin Weisheit lumbered around the corner. I cried out.

"Martin! He has a —"

Monroe's gun went off. Simultaneously my fingers dug into the runner and I pulled with all my strength. There was a sound of glass shattering. Monroe and Dorie Matthews tumbled to the floor as the runner jerked beneath them. I scrambled forward, though not nearly as swiftly as Martin Weisheit. Blood had soaked his collar from where I had smacked him with the telephone receiver. Martin reached Scott Monroe in three quick strides and on the third he landed a tremendous crushing kick to Monroe's ribs. I grabbed hold of Dorie Matthews and dragged her free as Martin kicked Monroe a second time and then a third. The pistol was still in Monroe's hand. He started to raise it, but Martin brought his foot down on Monroe's wrist with a sickening crunch. Monroe let out a scream. His fingers uncurled and Martin kicked the gun clear with his foot. It slid across the wood floor to where Dorie Matthews and I sat in a heap. I picked it up and fell back heavily against the wall as

Martin drew back for another kick.

"Stop!"

Martin's leg froze in midair. I waved the gun lazily in his direction.

"Come on, Martin. It's over now. Just stop."

He did. He lowered his leg. Scott Monroe was doubled up on the floor, groaning. On the floor next to me, Dorie Matthews folded into my side.

Martin glared at me. "Who killed Gran? Which one of you bastards shot her?"

I shook my head. "She's not dead, Martin. But we have to call an ambulance immediately."

Martin looked down at Scott Monroe. "Did he shoot her?"

"Yes," I said.

"I thought it was you. I came to pick up Gran for her birthday and I saw you in there and I thought —"

"It's okay. It doesn't matter. Just go call an ambulance. Pronto. We need to get her to a hospital."

He hesitated just a second. "Are you all right, Mrs. Matthews?"

Dorie nodded her head. "I'm fine, Martin. Thank you very much."

The boy turned and retreated back down the hallway and disappeared into one of the rooms. I turned to Dorie. She was reaching up to give a small tug to her head scarf.

"Back stairs?"

She nodded. "Yes. He came up from the kitchen."

"I'm sorry. I was afraid maybe he'd go outside. I wasn't sure. I thought it was safest up here."

"I'm fine," she said. "What's happened to Evelyn?"

"She's been shot in the chest. She's alive. Barely."

As if lifted by an invisible string, Dorie came to her feet. She adjusted her scarf again and ran a smoothing hand along the front of her skirt.

"I'll go to her." She moved soundlessly down the stairs.

Several minutes later I had Martin help me roll Scott Monroe up in the hallway runner. Monroe was conscious and he put up a feeble protest, but his vote didn't count for much. Martin rummaged around in the kitchen and returned with a roll of duct tape. God bless the makers of duct tape. I should send them a letter. One more use for their fine product. Martin and I supported Monroe on either side and the three of us made our way awkwardly downstairs. We left Monroe in the front hallway and Martin and I went into the front room, where Dorie was kneeling next to Evelyn Weisheit. She stood up as we entered.

"Martin," she said softly, "I'm sorry."

Chapter Thirty-five

Evelyn Weisheit was buried three days later. Sewell and Sons did not handle the burial. Sewell and Sons did not want to handle the burial. Sewell and Sons would manage to survive just fine without the business. A fact of life is that there is never any shortage of corpses to be had in this world. We're bumping into them all the time. On the day of Evelyn Weisheit's funeral, Billie and I were happily occupied burying a barber from Carney. He had left behind a widow and five grown children, all of whom wept openly and without shame. Before the casket was lowered into the ground the family gathered in a circle around it, linking hands, and sang "You Are My Sunshine." The gesture rated extremely high on the schmaltz meter, but it was touching nonetheless. Sometimes in life, things can't be corny enough. My guess was that just over the hill from us, there wasn't a whole hell of a lot of singing going on.

The police picked up Marilyn Tuck for questioning. They questioned Phyllis Fitch and they questioned Louise. Ross and Amanda Greenwood were brought in for a little chat, as was Teresa. Dorie Matthews too. Toby Schultz. Polly, Jenny, Martin and Gregory Weisheit. And me. Lieutenant Kruk closed his office door and filled my head with all sorts of sage advice. At the top of his lungs. Billie told me she felt a little left out, but she promised not to lose sleep over it.

I was completely off base with my thinking that Marilyn Tuck had been working some sort of life insurance scam on some of her residents at Briarcliff. However, it did turn out that the degree of her assistance to Claudia Greenwood with her finances had indeed ventured well into the improper and illegal range. Deposits were found to have been made from Mrs. Greenwood's accounts into those of Marilyn Tuck and Scott Monroe as well. Rather than pursue the legal and public course of retribution for the crimes — a course that could certainly have landed Tuck and Monroe in prison — Ross Greenwood had easily been persuaded to drop the matter in exchange for a nifty little payoff of three hundred thousand dollars.

Neither Marilyn Tuck nor Scott Monroe happened to have that kind of money lying around. However, Monroe had an idea as to where he might be able to get it. When he was first getting ElderHeart off the ground, some six years before, Monroe had received start-up support from the James E. Weisheit Foundation. He had been a charming and passionate and enterprising beggar, not at all beyond launching a considerable schmooze offensive in Evelyn Weisheit's direction in order to convince her to allocate a nice chunk of change from the foundation to allow ElderHeart to get up on its feet. The two had struck up a friendship of sorts, a harmless flirtation in fact, the sort of harmless game that can develop between an elderly woman of means and a younger man of need and want. ElderHeart had since been an annual recipient of the customary five-thousand-dollar award from the Weisheit Foundation. In negotiation at the time of the Greenwood situation with the foundation for their annual grant, Monroe told the police that he had begun pressing for a considerably larger sum. Monroe's attempts to cajole Evelyn Weisheit into substantially increasing foundation support of his organization would ultimately lead to his outright begging for the cash. He confided in Evelyn that he was backed into a serious financial corner and didn't know what to do to get out of it. As luck would have it — temporarily good for some, fatally bad for others — Evelyn Weisheit had only recently received word from her private investigator that Margaret McNamara was residing in Briarcliff Manor in Lutherville. She met with Scott Monroe and placed a check on the table in the amount of five hundred thousand dollars.

She did not lift her hand from the check until it was understood exactly what was expected of Monroe in exchange for the money.

He understood. And in due course he was to make Marilyn Tuck understand. The ball was rolling.

Chapter Thirty-six

I met up with Jenny Weisheit the day she was leaving to return to Ohio. She had an evening flight. I drove out to Ruxton and Jenny met me at her front door with a canvas tote bag. I followed her through the trees at the edge of the backyard, along a narrow path and then down an embankment to a small clearing on the edge of Lake Roland. Jenny pulled a blanket from the tote bag, along with some sandwiches and a plastic jug of fresh apple cider. She told me that she had gotten into her father's car the day before and headed north, with no destination in mind. She simply wanted to be moving, to be going anywhere. She had driven as far as Gettysburg, which is about an hour north of Baltimore, where she remembered a day trip her family had taken years and years ago, to wander the battlefields, go up into the observation tower and look out over the farms.

"It was the same time of year," Jenny said. "Autumn. Most of the leaves were already gone. The kind of cold where the air is real fresh smelling. I don't even remember why we went there. Martin and I couldn't have been much more than four and six. What did we know about the Civil War? I remember Mom with a scarf over her head that she had to keep holding on to or it would blow away. It was very windy, I remember that. Daddy read every plaque out loud. At least that's what I picture. I remember Martin tripping and falling on one of those rocks that are everywhere and getting a cut on his head. It wasn't that bad, but they bleed a lot. Head wounds." She laughed. "Wounded at Gettysburg. A hundred and something years after the fact. That sounds about right for this family. He cried like crazy. I remember Mom hugging him and trying to get Daddy to take care of him. Finally she took the scarf off her head and wrapped it around Martin's head like a bandage. He loved it. It shut him right up. Daddy got me and Mom and Martin together to take a picture of us. I had completely forgotten all that until I was up there yesterday just walking around. It all came rushing back to me. It's like a whole different family, that memory. We drove out to this old Civil War battlefield and laughed and played and got along. Like . . . like everything would always be all right."

She looked out over the lake. A single duck was chugging along in the water, its faint pie-slice wake growing wider and wider behind it. Fainter and fainter.

"We stopped off at an apple orchard on the way back," Jenny continued. "Martin and I

471

took a basket and filled it up, mainly with apples that were already on the ground. We got some cider. I remember Daddy taking up the cider jug onto his arm, you know, at the crook of his elbow, and chugging from the jug. He was like a kid. I stopped off at an orchard yesterday on my way back. I'm sure it wasn't the same one, there are hundreds of them up there. I got a gallon of cider. I took it back to Daddy's car and set it on the seat beside me and the next thing I knew I burst into tears. I sat there in the driver's seat and I felt like a six-year-old. I probably cried enough tears to fill the jug."

She poured me a cup of cider and one for herself. She held up her cup and tapped it against mine. The smile was wistful, sad and brave.

"Cheers."

Sometimes in life, things can't be corny enough.

I offered to take Jenny out to the airport, but she declined. A friend of hers in town was going to run her out.

Before I left, we discussed the state of irony these days. As healthy as ever, it seems. Jake Weisheit had canceled the family trip to Ohio for Parents' Weekend only two days before he and Polly and Martin were scheduled to leave. It was the day after Jake's reading the riot act to Toby Schultz for his foundation shenanigans. This was also, I learned, the same day that Chip Cooperman had informed Jake of the long-running affair between Toby Schultz and Polly. It seems likely that Jake already knew about Sisco, but that he simply had not yet confronted his wife about the affair. This same night, however, was the one in which he drove out to Penny's and locked horns with Sisco. Jake canceled the trip to Ohio. Likely he couldn't bear the thought of eight hours in the same car with his wife.

Evidently he didn't mention this change of plans to his mother. Why would he?

Scott Monroe's story to the police was that Evelyn Weisheit had an additional request of him. It was this request that would cost her own son's life. Monroe went to see Evelyn Weisheit that Saturday night. He told the police that he was attempting to get Evelyn Weisheit to drop her demand concerning Margaret McNamara. Evelyn Weisheit would not hear it. She promised to use all her influence to see to it that Monroe and Marilyn Tuck ended up behind bars unless they followed through with the arrangement. Then she added the additional request. She wanted James Weisheit's letters to Margaret McNamara back in her custody. Jake had taken them and was refusing to give them up to his mother. They were a fifteen year record of a very private side of James Weisheit, but for all that they so understandably incensed his mother, Jake was not about to agree to their being destroyed. It was a battle royal between mother and son. Two hardheads. Evelyn prevailed upon Scott Monroe to fetch the letters for her. She provided him with a key to Jake and Polly's home. She also provided him with the information that the Weisheit family would be gone the entire weekend. She suggested he head over there immediately. Monroe took the keys. He took the keys to a bar, along with the weight of the dilemma he had gotten himself into. When the bar closed, he headed off to Ruxton.

Thus it was that Scott Monroe was taken by surprise when he let himself into the Weisheit home around three on a Sunday morning and was confronted only a few minutes later by Jake Weisheit, entering the kitchen in the dark with a pistol in his hand. According to Scott Monroe's statement to the police, he leaped onto Jake Weisheit's back in an attempt to catch him in a bear hug and to wrest the pistol from his hand. The gun went off as Jake rammed backward into the counter. Monroe panicked. Jake jerked his arm free, and when he did, Monroe's arm slapped against the top of the kitchen counter and his fingers folded around a knife that was sitting there. Monroe swore to the police that Jake's pistol came waving into his face and that without even thinking he shoved against Jake as hard as he could. The knife ran into Jake's back all the way to the handle and Jake slumped forward onto the floor. Monroe left Jake there and he left the house, swearing to himself the whole ride home that he would call 911 just as soon as . . .

He never did. He drove home, took a long hot shower and crawled into bed. Monroe figures he hit the pillow around five o'clock. That would be nearly the time my phone began to ring.

I left the Weisheit home without seeing either Polly or Martin. I was fully at peace with this development. I stopped off at Sisco's on my way home and brought him a cheese-steak sub and a six-pack of beer. I treat 'em right, don't I? Sisco said he had heard from Polly. She had called just to talk, he said. He was able to get the truth from her about why she hadn't called the police immediately upon seeing her husband lying in a pool of blood on the kitchen floor. Toby Schultz. She thought Schultz had killed Jake. Schultz was in an uproar over Jake having called him to account concerning the foundation money. And Jake now knew about Toby and Polly. Polly told Sisco that she had panicked. She needed time to think. She thought she was giving Toby Schultz time to think. Time to get far away and to put his story together.

"She wasn't trying to set me up," Sisco

said, laying into his sub like it was the first thing he'd eaten all day. "She really did want to see me."

He followed his bite with a swig of beer. He came out of it with a humorless grin. "Whoopee."

Angela and I drove out to Valley View Farms on Halloween for all the pumpkins we could carry. She told me she was counting on me, counting on my long arms and my male pride.

"It's girlie to drop a pumpkin?"

Angela grinned. "If I say it is."

I performed a couple of deep knee bends, stretched my arms to the sky, then went into a half crouch, cupping my arms.

"Load me up."

She did. A few medium-sized pumpkins as a base and then a bunch of smaller ones piled on top. I braced myself as she stacked the pumpkins in my arms, fitting them on like pieces of a puzzle.

"Hang on, Hercules, you can do this."

Her stack of pumpkins came up past my eyes. My forehead was responsible for holding the pivotal pumpkin in place. Angela guided me gently by the elbow toward the parking area. I was so severely bowlegged and close to the ground I was convinced I was going to crumble, but somehow I held on long enough to reach the car and dump my excessive armload into the trunk.

"You are such a sexy hunk," Angela declared. "I just love a man who can carry his pumpkins."

We took the pumpkins back to my place, where we carved faces into the three largest ones and set them in my windows. We took the others down the street to Billie's. Angela and Billie worked on a pumpkin together while I set about scooping out the others and carving them into slices. Billie had promised a half dozen pies for the harvest festival at St. Teresa's the following day, and Angela had been gung ho to help. The two of them brought out one of the ugliest faces I think I've ever seen on a pumpkin, but they seemed happy enough with it. We greased a few pans and stacked on the pumpkin slices. The idea was to heat them up a little so as to make it easier to strip the skin from the meat. Don't ask me, I just work here.

I was keeping my eye on the time. Angela knew I wanted to be ready to go by eight o'clock. I was scheduled to meet up with Jay Adams at the Oyster at eight. If need be, Angela would catch up with me. Angela and I did most of the pumpkin stripping and mashing while Billie rolled out pastry and flour for the crusts. We were interrupted several times by the doorbell. Billie had a plastic skull filled with candy by the front door. Also a witch's hat, which she insisted on putting on as she opened the door to the various little neighborhood goblins and Cinderellas that came to the door. I answered the door one time, jamming the pointy hat on my head. Darryl Sandusky was standing there holding a red plastic pitchfork.

"You really go all out, don't you?" I said.

Darryl had his little brother with him. Brian Sandusky was covered with black and white feathers from his shoulders to his feet, on which he was wearing a pair of swim fins. The boy was wearing a flesh-colored skullcap on his head and clutching a dime store American flag.

"What did you do to this boy?" I asked Darryl.

Darryl sneered. "He's a bald eagle. Can't you see?"

Darryl produced a shopping bag and held it out. He nudged his brother, who held up a somewhat smaller bag.

"You're thinking big here, Darryl," I said.

He shook the bag. Impatiently. I dug into the plastic skull and forked over some candy.

"Nice hat," Darryl sneered as I shut the door.

By a quarter to eight we had our half dozen pies lined up for their turns in the oven. Billie shooed us off and we headed down to the Oyster. Jay was already there. So was Julia. The two were sitting together at the bar. I knew that must make Jay very happy. Two burly guys in tutus were seated next to them, pounding back their beers. Sally had affixed a tinfoil halo over her head, but this was the bar's only real concession to the holiday.

"Hey there, sugar beet," I said to Julia. "You've met Angela before, right? Angela, this is Julia."

"Hitch won't stop talking about you," Julia said, grinning mischievously.

Angela nodded her head thoughtfully. "He won't stop talking about you, either."

I turned to Jay. "See that? That's the secret to my success. Communication. Women lap that up."

"Big of you to share your secret," Jay said.

I asked Julia about her Dane and she told me that the Hamlet had closed and that Hans was on his way back to wonderful, wonderful Copenhagen.

"Are we sad?" I asked.

"We are philosophic."

"I suppose we could use some rest anyway?"

Julia shrugged and repeated herself. "We are philosophic."

Sally threw a few extra beers at us and we retired to a table. Jay had spent the afternoon nosing around with his sources at police headquarters as well as over at the district attorney's office. He had the dirt.

"Marilyn Tuck is being charged tomorrow

with murder in the second degree. It's a compromise, but it stands the best chance for sticking. They got this girl Louise to flip."

Angela asked, "And who is Louise?"

"Louise was the nurse scheduled to work the night Mrs. McNamara died," I said.

Jay picked up his drink. "Exactly. What seems to have happened is that Marilyn Tuck waved her off that night. She called her at home and told her there was a schedule change and that she wasn't to come in until the morning."

"She wanted Teresa to work that evening," I said.

"Oh, they love that one down at the station," Jay said. "That Teresa. They say she's completely out to lunch."

"I took her out to lunch," I said.

Angela turned to Julia. "Is he always like this?"

Julia rolled her lovelies. "You have no idea."

Jay continued. "The setup seems to be that Marilyn Tuck had been messing with Margaret McNamara's medications. Strictly off the books. You saw it, right, Hitch? The old woman was getting weaker and weaker?"

"I did. She even complained about it to me."

"Louise had her suspicions too. Not about Marilyn Tuck specifically. But she didn't feel

480

good about Margaret McNamara's condition. But she didn't say anything to anyone. She kept it to herself. Margaret McNamara died, as we know. Louise showed up in the morning, and the first thing Marilyn Tuck had her do was falsify a nurse's report. Louise says she feared for her job if she didn't obey. This Teresa girl had been on duty overnight, as we also know, and what it seems took place was that she hooked Margaret McNamara up to the wrong kind of feeding bag. The woman was on a pump. It's actually the bags for those pumps that regulate the flow of the feeding supplement. It's supposed to feed out over something like a ten-hour period. But Teresa used an enema bag instead. They're similar enough looking. And they fit. But the enema bags don't regulate. They empty everything out at once. The whole enchilada. Which is what happened to Margaret McNamara. The entire feeding supplement was delivered in probably less than an hour. She starts in with the violent vomiting and the diarrhea. Intensely severe stuff. A system already weakened like hers? Too much strain. And you've got this Teresa nobody standing around with her thumb in her ear. Middle of the night. The poor old thing didn't stand a chance."

"How did Teresa end up using the wrong kind of feeding bag?" Angela wanted to know.

481

"According to Louise, things had been moved around in the supply closet. When she came in in the morning she was instructed to put things back where they belonged."

"Marilyn Tuck counted on Teresa not bothering to notice that she was using the wrong bags," I said.

Jay nodded. "Looks that way. When Louise showed up for work in the morning, Marilyn got her to fill in the false nursing report claiming that she had worked the night shift and that all the procedures with Margaret McNamara had been legit. Teresa was paid off in cash. No record there."

Jay went on to explain that it was Marilyn Tuck who had falsified a document claiming to be from Mrs. McNamara requesting that her body be cremated.

"She wanted there to be no chance of an afterthought autopsy, in case someone started getting suspicious. The part about scattering the ashes on her husband's grave was just to make it look good."

"Verisimilitude," I said.

"What do you do?" Jay asked. "Carry a dictionary around in your pocket?"

"What about Phyllis Fitch in all this?" I asked.

"Loyalty. Louise says Fitch didn't really care much for Marilyn Tuck. There was some real animosity there. But she was loyal to the name. Fitch used to work for old man

Tuck. He specifically tapped her to run Briarcliff and he made her promise to help his daughter out in any way she could. Begrudgingly, Phyllis Fitch carried her loyalty over to the daughter. To Marilyn Tuck. She knew something wasn't right about the McNamara situation. She saw that the enema bags had been moved to the area where the regular feeding bags should have been. Marilyn Tuck tried to convince her that an honest mistake had been made and that for the sake of the nursing home they had to cover their fannies. Louise is convinced that Fitch knew better. Phyllis Fitch fell on her sword."

We fell on our drinks. I thought back to the morning of Mrs. McNamara's death. I had sensed an edginess in Phyllis Fitch when I came to pick up Mrs. McNamara. And in Louise. Both of the women knew too much and neither was happy about it. The long arm of Evelyn Weisheit had found its way into Briarcliff Manor and manipulated Marilyn Tuck into ending Mrs. McNamara's life. Arrogance and intimidation. And pride. Those were the forces that had killed Peggy McNamara. Along the way — collateral damage, I suppose you could say — they snuffed out Jake Weisheit as well. Evelyn Weisheit's efforts to erase the past became something of a brushfire that neither she nor her son managed to outrun. It was tempting to wonder how things might have turned out had James Weisheit possessed the courage to declare himself publicly years ago and to bring his love for Peggy McNamara out of the shadows. Tempting, but fruitless. The message coming in from the wiser portion of my brain tells me that the notion of transforming ifs into something they're not is only so much wishful thinking. Folly. Life is an extremely leaky boat. That's its nature. We don't have enough capacity to plug all the holes. More will always appear anyway. Of course we do try to plug them, we can't help it. That's *our* nature. But the boat is going to go down. That's the only guarantee. And I guess we might as well just get used to the idea.

I thought about Mrs. McNamara. Not as I had seen her the several times over the past week. I thought of her as I had run across her in the greeting cards section of the drugstore in Cumberland, fifteen or so years ago. The look on her face in that brief instant when she knew I had seen her husband clip her on the chin. It was such a sad look, mixed with shame and embarrassment. We had swapped the briefest of glances before she went her way and I went mine. There was something in her expression that also seemed to be saying that she was okay with my not coming down the aisle and confronting her husband. The look said that she didn't expect it and that she thought no less of me for not doing it. It was the look of a lonely person. And in my view, I was wrong in simply accepting it. It's a look in general that the world could do much better without. Fat chance, I realize. But still . . .

Somebody's foot had fallen on mine. I eyeballed Angela seated next to me and Julia across the table. Poker faces, the both of them. Jay and Julia excused themselves from the table to go play some darts. The same foot still rested on mine after they had left. I pulled my baseball cap from my rear pocket and jammed it onto my head.

"Shall we go?"

Angela's arm looped through my elbow and we made our way up Thames, past the various ghosts and devils. Rounding the corner onto my street, the temperature dropped noticeably, as if at the end of the block someone had pulled open the door of a gigantic refrigerator. We passed a tall gaunt figure with a gray plastic scythe, half hidden in the shadows. The figure nodded sagely at us, and I took hold of the brim of my cap and gave it a little tug.

"Top of the evening."

"What's that for?" Angela asked as we continued up the street. A strong gust of wind caught us head-on. I glanced back at the corner. The shadows had shifted as we passed. There was only a drainpipe, pulled partway free from its braces, hanging freely along the brick wall. Shifting slightly in the wind.

Funny what the mind can do.

About the Author

Tim Cockey is the award-winning author of four previous Hitchcock Sewell novels, including *Hearse of a Different Color* and *The Hearse Case Scenario*. Born and raised in Baltimore, Maryland, he now hangs his hat in New York City.